WITHDRAWN FROM STOCK

KEEPING IT IN THE FAMILY

KEEPING IT IN THE FAMILY

Sinéad Moriarty

WINDSOR
PARAGON

First published 2008
by Penguin
This Large Print edition published 2009
by BBC Audiobooks Ltd
by arrangement with
Penguin Books Ltd

Hardcover ISBN: 978 1 408 42927 3
Softcover ISBN: 978 1 408 42928 0

British Library Cataloguing in Publication Data available

Printed and bound in Great Britain by
CPI Antony Rowe, Chippenham and Eastbourne

For Sue

'Niamh, you're going to get whiplash,' said Pierre, reaching over to hold my hand as I turned back from the door.

'I don't want to miss him when he comes in,' I said, tensely.

'Well, then, maybe you should stand beside it,' said Pierre, sighing. I'd been snapping at him all morning and he'd clearly had enough.

I was about to apologize when I saw Finn pushing open the door of the brasserie. I leapt up and ran over.

'Hi,' I said, hugging my younger brother.

'Hey there. So, come on, where's this boyfriend you've been so coy about?' he said, looking around the bar. 'No, don't tell me, let me guess.' He scanned the faces in the room and a smile spread over his face. 'Oh, yes, very you—blue shirt, sandy hair, big smile,' he said, pointing to a jolly-looking, round-faced guy in the corner.

I shook my head. I was afraid to speak. I felt sick with nerves.

'I was sure it was him,' said Finn. 'OK, I give up.'

'Over there,' I said, pointing at Pierre.

Finn squinted. 'In the red jumper?' he said, sounding surprised, as he stared at a middle-aged man with glasses in a scarlet sweater.

'No,' I whispered. 'There, in the green jumper.'

Finn's jaw dropped.

'Oh, Jesus, you've really done it this time!'

1

Dublin, September 1998

I heard laughing behind me. Then a voice said, 'This is priceless, Tom. Listen. "The difference between men and women: I was out for lunch with two male colleagues yesterday. The conversation went as follows. Male 1: 'I can't believe you ordered the burger. You're a fat fuck.' Male 2: 'Yeah, well, I'd rather be fat than an ugly fucker who hasn't had sex in a year.' Male 1: 'I had sex last week.' Male 2: 'Dogs don't count.' Male 1: 'She wasn't that bad.' Male 2: 'She looked like Danny De Vito.' Male 1: 'Only smaller.'

' "They both roared and began to talk about the Manchester United v. Chelsea game.

' "I was gobsmacked. If one of my female colleagues called me a fat bitch for ordering a burger, not only would I never speak to her again but I'd stop eating, become anorexic and die of food deprivation.

' "If she told me I was ugly, I'd enter the witness-protection programme where I'd undergo an extreme makeover: eyebrow lift, cheek implants, Botox, lip-plumping and veneers (yes, I have thought about it before). A year—and a lot of pain—later I'd come back and confront her as a stunning supermodel type with pearly white teeth." '

'Niamh, that's your column he's reading,' said Emily, a fellow journalist I was having coffee with. 'Go over to him.'

'No way,' I said, shrinking back in my chair.

Emily peered over the top of the couch and gasped. 'He's gorgeous—you have to go over.'

I shook my head. I was far too embarrassed to stroll over to some complete stranger and say, 'Hi, I'm the journalist who wrote that.' But before I could stop her, Emily stood up.

'Sorry to interrupt. I couldn't help overhearing you laughing at that column and I wondered if you'd like to meet the woman who wrote it. She's right here beside me.'

'I'd love to,' said the voice. He had an English accent.

I blushed and thumped Emily's leg. 'Stop it,' I hissed.

'Come and join us,' said my ex-friend.

I heard movement, then two men came over and sat down. I stared into my cup, mortified.

'This is Niamh O'Flaherty, columnist *extraordinaire*,' said Emily.

'Very pleased to meet you,' said my fan, proffering a hand. I looked up—and froze. In front of me was one of the handsomest men I'd ever seen.

'I'm Pierre and this is Tom,' he said, introducing his not-so-attractive older friend.

'Pierre?' said Emily. 'You don't sound French.'

'I moved to England when I was ten, so my accent is long gone.' He smiled. Then, turning to me, he asked, 'So, what's in store for next week's column?'

'Oh, I'm not sure,' I mumbled, trying not to stare at him.

'Maybe you guys can give her some ideas,' said Emily. 'Let's order some coffee and brainstorm.'

'I'd love to,' said Tom, 'but I have to go. I've a lecture in ten minutes. I'm sure Pierre will give you plenty of material. Nice to meet you,' he said, and hurried out of the door.

'Are you a journalist too?' Pierre asked Emily.

She sighed. 'Kind of. I write the obituaries. I'm still waiting for my big break.'

'I'm sure it'll come soon,' he told her.

'What about you?' Emily asked him.

'Nothing as glamorous as Fleet Street, I'm afraid. I'm a boring old professor.'

'That's not boring at all, it sounds fascinating,' Emily gushed.

'One of my students fell asleep in a lecture today.'

'She must be short-sighted,' laughed Emily.

'Is your friend OK?' Pierre asked her, pointing to me. I was staring at the floor, trying to stop my legs shaking. I'd never felt such an instant attraction to someone. I was afraid to look up in case it was written all over my face.

'Normally you can't shut her up. I think she's annoyed with me because I dragged you over,' Emily admitted.

'I'm not annoyed,' I said, finding my voice, 'but I am incredibly embarrassed. I don't normally go around accosting people who read my column.'

'Well, I'm glad you did. I'm a big fan. It never fails to make me laugh.'

'Thanks, it's really nice of you to say so,' I said, smiling at him.

'Where do you get the ideas from?'

'To be honest, I spend a lot of time in coffee shops like this one, listening to other people's conversations.'

'Were you listening to mine?'

'No—should I have been?' I asked.

'Tom and I were talking about phonetics. I don't think even you could make that funny.'

'It's not actually the subject matter that counts, it's the way it's being discussed that can be humorous,' I said, batting my eyelids, just a little.

'Even a conversation about auditory phonetics and speech perception?' he asked, leaning closer.

'You might have me there,' I said, giving him a flirty raised eyebrow.

'Will you look at the time!' said Emily. 'I have to run. I'll talk to you later, Niamh. Nice to meet you, Pierre.' She winked at me as she left.

'I've never met a real-life columnist before,' said Pierre.

'I hope you're not going to stalk me.'

'Do you have many stalkers?'

'Tons.'

'Men?'

'Yep.'

'Young?'

'And handsome.'

'So I've a lot of competition?'

' 'Fraid so.'

'How do I get to the front of the queue?'

'Flattery, diamonds and furs.'

'Can I start with flattery?'

'Sure.'

'*Tu es très amusante*.'

'What happened to *belle*?'

'Isn't funny better than beautiful?'

'Not even close.'

'Men like witty women.'

'As friends.'

'Not necessarily.'

'When was the last time you went out with a woman who looked like a horse but made you laugh?'

'I'm about to.'

'Excuse me!'

'A beautiful, witty colt.'

'You need to work on your technique.'

'I'm out of practice.'

'Are you married?'

'No.'

'In a meaningful relationship?'

'No.'

'Seeing someone casually?'

'No.'

'Gay?'

'No.'

'Pervert?'

'No.'

'Police record?'

'No.'

'So what's the catch?'

'There is none. Are you always this suspicious?'

'No.'

'So why are you giving me the third degree?'

'Because you're a thirty-something professor who's very easy on the eye. How come you're single?'

'How come you are?'

'How do you know I'm not in an incredible relationship?'

'You wrote about being single last week.'

'Me and my big mouth.'

'It's serendipity.'

'What is?'

'This. The fact that I happened to be reading your column while you were sitting at the next table and you heard me laugh and we met.'

'It could just be a coincidence.'

'Cynic.'

'Realist.'

'*Tu es la plus belle femme du monde*.'

'Much better.'

'Thank you.'

'Still room for improvement, though.'

'Is there?'

'You could say, "*Tu es* the twin of Claudia Schiffer."'

'I prefer Gisèle.'

'She'll do.'

'Can I ask you a personal question?'

'Depends how personal.'

'I think you'll find it acceptable.'

'I'll be the judge of that.'

'As a phonetician I'm fascinated by accents and yours is fantastic. You speak English with an English-Irish accent peppered with Irish sayings.'

'That's because I'm a mongrel.'

'That makes two of us. What's your excuse?'

'Born and bred in Finchley, North London, of Irish parents. I spent my youth constantly surrounded by Irish relatives and family friends. I came to Dublin to study and never went back. You?'

'Born and raised in Paris until I was ten when we moved to Oxford. Parents are from Martinique. That's where the tan comes from.'

'I was wondering about that.'

'But too polite to ask.'

'Didn't want to be politically incorrect.'

'Very thoughtful.'
'I try to be.'
'Dinner?'
'Love to.'
'Eight o'clock in Gatsby's?'
'Perfect.'
'Excellent.'
'Pierre?'
'Yes?'
'Do I call you African-French?'
'Martinique's in the Caribbean.'
'Caribbean-French?'
'No. Just plain black.'

2

I don't remember going home. I was floating. No one had ever had such a strong impact on me. As I caught my reflection in a shop window I smiled. Thankfully I had to interview a cute up-and-coming actor that morning so I'd got dressed up and put on makeup. If Pierre had met me on a normal day—tracksuit bottoms and T-shirt—he'd have run a mile. Maybe it *was* serendipity. I'd never been to that coffee shop before. And what were the chances of him sitting beside me reading my column? It was all a bit freaky.

Normally I met guys in pubs or nightclubs and they never seemed to have real jobs. My last boyfriend, Sean, had been an apprentice jockey. The fact that he was a foot shorter than me hadn't bothered me too much. The fact that he weighed a stone less than I did bothered me a lot. I could never bring myself to sit on his knee because I'd have crushed his legs—which wouldn't have been great for his career.

Whenever Sean and I went out for dinner—which was rare—he'd comment on everything I ate and inform me how many calories each forkful contained. He was permanently dieting to try to meet his target weight. Eventually we stopped eating out. Sitting across the table from someone who's eating a plate of lettuce is no fun. Food—or lack thereof—affected every aspect of our relationship. When we went to the cinema, I couldn't have popcorn, when we went for coffee, we had to have skinny-milk lattes, which tasted rotten.

Sean also had an unhealthy obsession with his horse. He talked about Prancing Queen as if she was another woman. He was always going on about how beautiful she was, how elegant and sophisticated, fit and feisty. I actually found myself becoming jealous of an animal!

Things came to a head one day when I walked into my apartment to find him wrapped in clingfilm doing star jumps in the living room, sweating all over my new rug. I was going out with an anorexic midget who preferred his horse to me. It was time to call it a day. But before I could get the words out, the cellophane man said, 'I'm sorry, Niamh, but it just isn't working. Prancing Queen has to come first and she needs my full attention. I just called over to tell you that and to borrow some clingfilm. I'll see you round. I'm off for a ten-mile run. I need to lose five pounds before my weigh-in on Saturday.'

And with that, he jogged out of the door and

down the road, leaving a trail of sweat in his wake. How dare he dump me for his horse? It doesn't get more humiliating than that. I cried for weeks afterwards. My already fragile self-esteem was completely shattered. I couldn't even bring myself to write about it in my column, I was so ashamed.

* * *

So here I was, having just met a normal man who drank coffee with full-fat milk, had a proper job and was incredibly attractive. Where was the catch?

My phone rang. It was Emily.

'Hi.'

'So, what happened after I very discreetly left you?'

'Thanks for that.'

'To be honest, the sparks between you were so hot I was afraid I'd get burnt.'

I giggled. 'Was it that obvious?'

'Serious sexual tension.'

'He's gorgeous, isn't he?'

'I think he's one of the best-looking men I've ever seen.'

'I know, so why's he interested in me?'

'Come on. You look great at the moment, thanks to the jockey. Going out with him did wonders for your figure.'

'At least something good came out of it. Pierre asked me out to dinner tonight.'

'Lucky you.'

'It's too good to be true. There must be something wrong with him.'

'Oh, for goodness' sake, don't jinx it. Just enjoy

it.'

'I'm really nervous.'

'I'm not surprised. I've never seen you so smitten. You were dumbstruck.'

'That's what's freaking me out.'

'It's serendipity.'

'That's what he said.'

'Niamh, just get dressed up, go out and have a great time. Otherwise, I'm going instead of you.'

I spent ages getting ready. I wanted to look as good as I possibly could, so that he wouldn't take one look at me and run off in the opposite direction screaming, 'Sorry, mistake.'

When I arrived at the restaurant he was sitting at the table drinking a glass of wine. He stood up and kissed my cheek. My stomach flipped. He was gorgeous.

'You look great,' he said, smiling at me.

'Ditto.'

'Wine?'

'Large glass, please.'

'Thirsty?'

'Nervous.'

He filled a glass to the brim and I slugged it back.

'Better?'

'Much, thanks.'

'So . . .'

'So . . .'

The waiter came over and we ordered our food. When he'd left, Pierre leant over. 'I have a confession to make.'

'I knew it, you *are* married.'

'I'm forty-two.'

'Botox?'

'Good genes. You?'
'Twenty-eight.'
'Young!'
'Do I look older?'
'No, you act it.'
'Is that a good thing?'
'For an old codger like me, yes.'
'Makes you feel less like a paedophile.'
'You could say that.' He laughed.
'OK, my turn to confess. This is my first date with a man who is black, over thirty-five and has a proper job.'
'That's a lot of firsts.'
'Tell me about it.'
'What did your previous boyfriends do?'
'Confession number two. There haven't been very many previous boyfriends. There was an apprentice jockey, an out-of-work actor and a photographer.'
'Photography's a proper job.'
'You didn't see his photos. You?'
'Boring, really. Went out with the same girl for nine years. We broke up six months ago.'
'Reason?'
'It just fizzled out and I moved to Dublin.'
'Define "fizzled".'
'We realized it wasn't meant to be.'
'Who realized first?'
'I suppose I did.'
'Was she English?'
'French.'
'Ugly?'
'Good-looking.'
'Obese?'
'Slim.'

'Thick?'

'Doctor.'

'Selfish?'

'She works for the Red Cross.'

'I'm just going to pop outside and shoot myself.'

Pierre laughed. 'She wasn't funny.'

'Funny's all very well, but it has to come as part of a package. I'm not beautiful, French or intellectual. I hate flies and creepy-crawlies so I could never go and save people in Africa even if I was a doctor. Besides, my hair goes fuzzy in the humidity and I look worse than normal. So maybe you should save yourself a few quid on the dinner and we'll call it a day now.'

'I think you missed the part about Brigitte and me breaking up.'

'And I think you need your head examined. She sounds amazing.'

'She was in lots of ways, but she wasn't right for me. I'm sure she'll make someone else very happy.'

'Pierre, you need to understand something here. I'm not a clown. I'm not funny in the morning or, truth be told, for most of the afternoon. I can occasionally be amusing in the evening—alcohol units depending—and in my column. But that doesn't mean I'm a barrel of laughs to be with. In fact, I can be a right grumpy old cow.'

'I happen to think you're gorgeous, sexy, very clever and witty. Maybe you won't save the world, but I can live with that.'

'What did your family think when you broke up with your girlfriend of nine years?'

'My parents were fond of Brigitte and I think they hoped we'd settle down, but it was my decision and they respect that.'

'What about your brothers and sisters?'

'I'm an only child.'

'Oh.'

'That's bad?'

'Very.'

'Why?'

'Only children are used to undivided attention, not having to share their toys and are bossy.'

'And this is based on?'

'Observation.'

'I'm forty-two. I've learnt to share my toys.'

'That remains to be seen.'

'How many siblings do you have?'

'If my father had had his way I'd have ten. But my mother put the skids on after three children. I've one older sister, Siobhan, and a younger brother, Finn.'

'Middle child!'

'Yes.'

'Don't they tend to be chippy and resentful because they have an undefined place in the family?'

'Not necessarily.'

'How did your family feel about your break-ups?'

'The only one I bothered to tell them about was the jockey because my dad's mad into horse-racing. He had high hopes we'd be going to Cheltenham celebrating Gold Cup winners. He was a bit put out when I told him I'd got dumped for a horse. Needless to say, the rest of them thought it was hilarious.'

Pierre roared laughing.

'I was quite upset at the time.'

'Sorry.'

'It's OK, I'm over it now.'

'What was the horse called?'

'Prancing Queen,' I said, and we both giggled.

Our food arrived and we ate in silence for a while.

'How did you get into journalism?' Pierre asked.

'My auntie Nuala suggested it and I liked the idea. English was the only subject I was good at in school. So I came to Dublin to study.'

'Why Dublin?'

'I wanted to get away from my family. It was a bit crowded in my house before I left and I needed some space. My sister, her husband and their two kids were living with us, not to mention the steady stream of relatives that come through the kitchen door every day. We're a very close family, which is great, but when you're a teenager it can be a little claustrophobic. I knew my parents would be supportive of me coming to Ireland so it kept everyone happy. Then I got a job on the paper, writing about anything that needed to be covered—literally from obituaries to shaggy-dog stories. You name it, I wrote about it. It was good training and it eventually led to me getting my own column. So I stayed.'

'Do you miss London?'

'I miss my family but I go home regularly. What about you?'

'Studied phonetics at Cambridge followed by a PhD. Then I decided I'd like to lecture so I went to teach in Berlin for a while, moved to Paris and now I'm here.'

'Do you like it here?'

'I like it more and more by the minute.'

'I was just thinking the same thing.'

'Dessert?'
'Not hungry.'
'Coffee?'
'Not thirsty.'
'My place?'
'I thought you'd never ask.'

3

As I walked into Pierre's apartment I realized that this was another first. I had never gone back to a man's place on a first date. If I liked them enough, I always brought them back to my apartment. It was safer that way. If they turned out to be a psychopath and attacked me with an ice pick, kitchen knife or some other culinary utensil, I could scream and my neighbours would hear me through the paper-thin walls and call the police.

Yet here I was, strolling into Pierre's apartment without a care in the world. Everything about this day had been surreal. I looked around me. The place was gorgeous. Unlike the jumped-up broom cupboard I lived in, this was a proper, grown-up apartment with floor-to-ceiling glass windows that looked out on to the river Liffey. The walls were painted a creamy-beige, the furniture was chocolate brown, and beautiful rugs were strewn on the wooden floors. The walls were covered with incredible paintings and tall, striking sculptures filled the corners of the room.

The bookshelf beside me groaned under the weight of French literary greats—Flaubert, Balzac, Hugo, Maupassant, Baudelaire—plus a copy of

Joyce's *Ulysses*. I had had *Ulysses* beside my bed now for six months. But somehow, every time I went to read it, it got replaced after the first page by Dan Brown on a good day and *Hello!* on a bad one.

'Welcome to my bachelor pad,' said Pierre, coming out of the kitchen with a bottle of wine and two matching, unchipped wine glasses.

'So this is how real grown-ups live.' I smiled.

'I'm sure your place is lovely.'

'It's a dump and you're never going to see it. This is incredible. I feel as if I've stepped into another world.'

'I'd like to take all the credit but my mother came over and helped kit it out. It's her thing.'

'Is she an interior designer?'

He nodded. 'Yes, she's been running a business for years. Very successful.'

'I'm not surprised. She's got amazing taste. Is this her?' I asked, picking up a photo from the mantelpiece.

'Yes. It was taken a couple of years ago in Paris at her sixtieth birthday party.'

'She looks about thirty!' I said, peering at the photo. The woman smiling back at me was beautiful, stylish and youthful. Pierre was sitting beside her. He had one arm round his mother and the other round a woman of about thirty, who looked like Jennifer Aniston, only better.

'Is that your ex-girlfriend?' I asked, praying he'd say it was his cousin.

'Yes, that's Brigitte.'

Bollox.

'Have you read all of these?' I asked, gesturing at the bookshelf in an attempt to divert from the stunning supermodel ex-girlfriend beaming down at me from the mantelpiece.

'Yes. My father was a professor of French at Oxford, so French literature has always been a high priority for him. I didn't get footballs for my birthday, I got books.'

'Did you mind?'

'They wouldn't have been my first choice. But we only children don't have anyone to kick a ball with so reading was something I did a lot of.'

'To be so well read is such an achievement. Your dad did a good job.'

'What did you get on your birthdays?'

'I never got what I wanted either. When I asked for Barbie Ballet, I got Barbie with a home-made Irish dancing costume sewn on to her. When I asked for luminous pink leg-warmers, I got scratchy woolly socks that my great-auntie Josie knitted. And on my fourteenth birthday I asked for a Duran Duran T-shirt and ended up with one that said, "Éirinn go Brách" instead.'

'What does that mean?'

'I hadn't a clue because I never paid attention in Irish class, but my father proudly announced that it meant "Ireland for ever". Needless to say, it never saw the light of day.'

'Poor Niamh, you sound more deprived than I was.'

'I was very nearly a social outcast.'

'What saved you?'

'My sense of humour. You?'

'I was good at sports. When you're a guy and you're good at sports, you automatically have kudos.'

'I wouldn't say you were too shabby

academically either, Professor.'

'I got by.' He grinned.

'Confession.'

'Uh-oh.'

'I've read precisely none of the books on your bookshelf. I still haven't even got round to reading *Ulysses* although I bought it two years ago.'

'Don't bother.'

'Really?'

'In my opinion it's overrated.'

'Fantastic. Now I don't have to feel guilty every time I see it staring accusingly at me from under the bed.'

'Confession.'

'Go on.'

'I didn't invite you back here to discuss literature.'

'And there I was thinking it was my intellect that had attracted you.'

Pierre moved in closer and kissed me. Usually I would play hard to get on a first night, but this was a whole new universe. I was consumed with lust. It took me precisely ten seconds to rip off my clothes, ten seconds to rip off his and then, thankfully, it took a little longer to have the most passionate sex of my life.

* * *

I woke up early the next morning, my eyes stuck together with mascara. Thankfully, Pierre was still asleep, so I slipped out of bed and into the bathroom to do some damage control. What I saw in the mirror was not pretty. I had smudged, panda eyes and bed hair. But not the tousled look of a woman who has just been ravished by her lover—I had the bird's nest of someone who has over-bleached it. I rubbed my eyes and tried to find a brush but all I could see was a nailbrush, so I used that. Bad idea. Now I looked like I'd had an electric shock. I scrubbed my teeth so he'd think I woke up with fragrant breath and I patched up my makeup, so I looked less scary and 'natural'.

I walked out to find Pierre in the kitchen, cooking breakfast. Gorgeous, clever *and* a cook. Was this really happening? He grinned at me. 'Morning.'

'Smells good.'

'Scrambled eggs and bacon OK for you?'

'Fantastic.'

'Grab a seat.'

'Do all your conquests get this treatment?'

'Only the good ones.'

I smiled.

'Did you enjoy last night?'

'Average.'

'You're a good actress.'

'Meaning?'

'When you shouted, "This is the best sex I've ever had," I believed you.'

I blushed. 'Me and my big mouth.'

'I like your big mouth very much,' he said, kissing me. 'Now, eat up before it goes cold.'

'Great eggs.'

'Thanks. So, what plans for today? I'm free until eleven. Do you fancy grabbing the papers and chilling out here?'

'Oh, God, I'd love to but I have a twelve o'clock deadline for my column.'

'Have you started it?'

'I've sketched out a few ideas.'

'Can I hear them?'

'Not yet. I need to work on it first.'

'Why don't you do it from here? Use my computer.'

'Are you sure?'

'Of course. I promise not to bother you until you've finished and then I may have to take you back to bed.'

'For an old guy, you've a lot of energy.'

'It's the younger woman I'm seeing. She's making me very frisky.'

'Is she good in bed?'

'Best sex I've ever had.'

'Copy-cat! Come up with your own line.'

'OK, the most passionate sex I've ever had.'

'Really?'

'Yes.'

'Wow.'

'My thoughts exactly. Now get on with your work. The sooner you finish, the sooner we can pick up where we left off last night.'

I wrote my column in record time.

4

A month later we were having a drink in the local pub and Pierre asked me to move in with him.

'As in live in your apartment?' I asked.

'Well, yes. I don't think we'd both fit into yours.'

'I've never lived with a man before. I might not be very good at it.'

'You'll be a natural.'

'I have some bad habits.'
'Everyone does.'
'What if I drive you mad?'
'You won't.'
'I can be very annoying and I'm not very chatty in the mornings.'
'I can live with that.'
'I like watching really cheesy TV.'
'How bad?'
'*Melrose Place*.'
'Sounds great. What time is it on?'
'I'm not very tidy.'
'Nor am I.'
'I work irregular hours.'
'Ditto.'
'Sometimes I wake up at three in the morning and make myself toasted sandwiches.'
'What type?'
'Cheese and onion.'
'My favourite.'
'It's one of the only things I can cook. I'm hopeless in the kitchen.'
'Not a problem, I like cooking.'
'My favourite film isn't *The Mission*, it's *Steel Magnolias*.'
'I knew you were lying.'
'I find classical music boring. I prefer Kylie, it's more uplifting.'
'Kylie's fine with me.'
'I only ever read the magazines in the *Sunday Times*.'
'Perfect. I never read them, so we won't fight over the paper.'
'Sometimes I eat chocolate for breakfast.'
'Niamh, do you want to move in or not?'

'I'd absolutely love to.'

'Well, then, stop gabbing and get packing.'

*   *   *

So there I was, Niamh O'Flaherty, twenty-eight-year-old columnist, moving in with my forty-two-year-old professor boyfriend. And it felt so right. I was in seventh heaven. I was finally in a proper, grown-up relationship with a man who had a real job and who made me feel ten feet tall. I had never been so happy.

I unpacked my things and got a real buzz from seeing my clothes hanging beside Pierre's in the wardrobe. One night while he was making dinner in the kitchen, I rearranged the pictures on the mantelpiece, so that a photo of Pierre and me sat in front of the one of Brigitte and his mother. No offence to his mother, but I didn't want to have his supermodel ex beaming down at me every day.

The weird thing was that it didn't feel strange. Living together was the most natural thing in the world. We slotted into each other's lives like old pros. I loved living with him and he seemed to like it too.

We did everything together. We lived in each other's pockets, it never felt claustrophobic and we never ran out of things to say. It was perfect and I was terrified. I'd never felt like this about anyone before and I was petrified that Pierre would come home one day and say, 'It's over.' I was completely in love with him and totally open to having my heart broken.

I knew he liked me a lot. He had, after all, asked me to move in with him. But I wasn't sure if he was in love with me. I began to obsess about it and then one night, after a few glasses of wine, I started to probe.

'So, you know the way you were with Brigitte for nine years,' I said.

'Yes.'

'Well, you must have really loved her.'

'I suppose I did in the beginning. But it faded.'

'Yes, I know, but why exactly did it fizzle out? What did she do to make you want to break up with her?'

He shrugged. 'I don't know. The spark went out of it. We didn't seem to have anything to say to each other and we were getting on each other's nerves.'

'What bugged you about her?'

'I can't remember.'

'Try.'

'She was very jealous.'

Was he pulling my leg? Who could she possibly have been jealous of? She was one of the best-looking girls I'd ever seen.

'Of who?'

'Anyone I paid attention to.'

'Were you flirting?'

'No! That's the whole point. I'd be having a normal conversation with another woman, it could be about the weather, and Brigitte would go mad.'

'What would she do?'

'Oh, you know, sulk and go off in a strop. She threw a drink over me once.'

'Wow.'

'We broke up soon after.'

'Were you ever jealous of her?'

'No. Jealousy's a waste of time. If you're that

insecure the relationship isn't working.'

'So you're not a fan of drink-throwing.'

'Definitely not. I hate couples who argue when they're out. It makes everyone else uncomfortable. Brigitte thrived on drama. Come to think of it, we really weren't very suited at all.'

'How did you last so long?'

'We lived in different countries for a lot of it. I suppose that helped.'

'So you fell out of love.'

'Why are asking me about a relationship that's dead and gone?'

'I'm just curious.'

'Are you satisfied?'

'Have you ever been in love with anyone else?'

He looked at me and nodded. My heart skipped a beat. 'Sandra White. She lived across the road and was two years older than me. We snogged on my thirteenth birthday, but then she told me she'd only done it as a dare to see if black boys kissed the same as white boys.'

I laughed. 'Poor you.'

'It took me a long time to get over it.'

'Anyone else, apart from Sandra?'

'A couple of girls in university, a girl I met in Greece, an American colleague—'

I put my hands up. 'OK, I get it. You've been in love a lot.' I sighed.

Pierre leant over and took my hand. 'I'm winding you up. The minute I met you I realized I'd never really been in love before. This is the relationship I've been looking for. This is what it's supposed to be like. I want to spend the rest of my life with you, so can you please stop dredging up the past and getting yourself worked up about nothing?'

'Do you really?'

'What?'

'Love me?'

'Yes, darling, I do.'

'Me toooooo,' I sobbed, as he pulled me into his chest.

'Come here, you fool.'

'I promise I won't go all boil-the-bunnies if you talk to other women.'

'I'm very glad to hear it.'

'As long as they're under thirteen or over sixty,' I mumbled.

* * *

Pierre loved me! I had never felt so wonderful. I no longer walked, I glided. I had a permanent grin on my face, to the point at which people in the office kept asking me if I was all right. For the first time in my life I felt beautiful. I didn't look in the mirror and groan. I made more of an effort with my appearance. I wore matching underwear and expensive scented body lotions. I painted my toenails and shaved my legs regularly, instead of seasonally. I felt like a woman and no longer a girl. And it was fantastic.

* * *

We continued to live in our blissful domestic cocoon. Everything was perfect . . . until my mother rang and said she was coming to Dublin to see me.

'When?' I asked, beginning to panic.

I had pushed the fact that Pierre was black to the back of my mind. It didn't matter to me, it didn't matter to him, so who cared? My mother would. My mother would care very much. In fact, I knew fine well that she'd blow a fuse when she found out.

'Next weekend. It's your granddad's birthday and I haven't seen you in two months so I've booked my flights and I'll be arriving at ten past five on Friday.'

'OK.'

'Well, you don't sound very pleased,' she said.

'Sorry, Mum, I'm just really busy in work.'

'I hope you can find the time for your poor mother.'

'Of course I can. It'll be great to see you.'

'That's a bit more like it. Shall I bring anything over for you?'

'No, thanks. I have everything I need.'

'Well, I bought a few bits for your flat, so I'll bring them with me.'

'What did you buy?'

'A nice lampshade, a shower mat, and your auntie Pauline's taken up crochet so I've six crochet place mats and a tea cosy for you as well.'

'Oh, God!'

'You have to support your relations in their endeavours,' Mum huffed. 'She hasn't quite got the hang of it yet and they're a bit lopsided, but it's the effort that counts.'

'Wonderful.'

'There's no need to be sarcastic, young lady. Besides, you need to brighten up that flat of yours. It's so small and poky. I'm going to give it a good shake-up when I come over.'

'No!' I said. Damn. How was I going to explain my new living arrangements?

'What do you mean?'

'I don't want you wasting your time cleaning my apartment. You're coming over for a break—and I'm twenty-eight. I can do my own cleaning.'

'Well, miracles do happen.'

'Yes, Mum, they do,' I said, thinking of Pierre.

'How's work?'

'Good, thanks.'

'Are you still writing those racy columns?'

'Yes, and they're not racy, they're a humorous look at real-life situations.'

'Why don't you write book reviews or nice articles about gardening?'

'Because I like what I do and I'm good at it. Can we just leave it at that?'

'There's no pleasing you today, very contrary altogether. Well, I'll go. Your father and brother are due home any minute and I've to put the tea on.'

'How are they?'

'They're both in good form. Sure I'll fill you in next week when I see you—I don't want to run up a big phone bill.'

'OK, 'bye, Mum.'

I hung up and sighed. How was I going to explain Pierre to Mum? She'd flip. We'd only been together for three months and I really didn't want to rock the boat or put the relationship under any pressure. This was the best thing that had ever happened to me and I was determined to protect it at all costs. I decided that it was best for Mum not to find out about Pierre yet. I'd tell her about him in a few months' time.

My other problem was explaining to Pierre why I didn't want him to meet my mother. I knew he'd think it was strange, so I did exactly what I shouldn't have done and stuck my head in the sand.

That Friday, as Pierre was leaving for work, he said, 'Let's go to the movies tonight. I want to see that new Scorsese film.'

'I'm not around.'

'You never said.'

'Yeah, I forgot.'

'What's on?'

'Oh, it's nothing really. My mum's over and I'm meeting her in my grandparents' house for dinner.'

'Hold on a minute. Do you mean to say your grandparents live here and you never mentioned it before? And now your mother's coming over and you forgot to tell me that too?'

'It's no big deal,' I mumbled.

'Yes, it is. What's going on?'

'It's all very last minute. Mum only rang me last night to say she was coming,' I lied.

'If my grandparents lived here you'd have met them weeks ago, and if my mother was coming to see me, you'd be the first person I'd want her to meet. So why am I only finding out now?'

'You don't understand, my family's not very . . .' How was I going to explain tactfully that my family were going to go absolutely ballistic when they found out that my boyfriend was black?

'You mean they won't be too thrilled when they find out your new squeeze is black.'

'They may need a little time to adjust to that fact.'

'Introducing me to them is the best thing to do.

Once they see how much I love you, they'll come round.'

'The thing is, Pierre, they're kind of old-fashioned. My dad would freak if I went out with a Protestant, so a black agnostic is going to be tough for him to accept. We need to tread very softly. Trust me.'

'That's why we need to work on your mother first. I'm great with mothers. They love me. Once we have her on-side, your dad will follow.'

He just wasn't getting it. 'To be honest, my mother isn't going to like it either. She has high hopes that I'm going to end up with a nice Irish Catholic doctor. You have to let me break it to them very slowly.'

'How slowly?'

'Very.'

'Hours.'

'I said slowly.'

'Days?'

'Months.'

'Joking?'

'Deadly serious.'

'That's ridiculous.'

'Believe me, it'll be easier in the long run. Let me do it at my own pace. I know my parents and I know how to deal with them. This is going to be a big shock for them.'

'You were born and bred in England. How realistic was the chance of you ending up with an Irish Catholic?'

'I'm the only person in my family—and I have nine married cousins—to live with someone not of Irish descent and Catholic.'

'You mean to tell me that none of your cousins

have gone out with non-Irish Catholics?'

'No. One cousin, Dermot, went out with a Swedish girl for a while but it didn't last. My uncle refused to speak to his son or the Swede until they broke up. He eventually married an Irish Catholic.'

'That's insane.'

'That's my family, Pierre. My father and his brothers are obsessed with keeping things traditional. So far, they've succeeded.'

'Why move to London? Why not stay in Ireland?'

'There were few opportunities here in the sixties. They emigrated to make a better life. If they could have stayed at home in Ireland they would have.'

'My parents emigrated for a better life too, but they integrated into French and then English society. They didn't try to create a Martinique ghetto and force their offspring to intermarry.'

'It's different.'

'Why?'

'From what you've told me, your parents couldn't wait to get out of Martinique and never wanted to go back. My father still gets tears in his eyes when he talks of his childhood. He plans to move back to Ireland when he retires. And the other difference is that your parents are both only children.'

'What's that got to do with it?' asked the only child.

'My father and his four brothers all emigrated and work together. Their wives became friends and we went everywhere with our cousins. It was a ready-made social life. Everyone we knew growing up was Irish, our doctor, dentist, accountant, milkman, butcher. You name it, they were Irish.'

'That defeats the whole purpose of emigrating. You're not making the most of your new life. You're not integrating.'

'They don't see it that way. They think their values, morals and principles are better than anyone else's and they're trying to protect their children.'

'But you can't protect a child from outside influences.'

'You can try very hard.'

'Isn't it stifling to live that way?'

'Yes and no. On the one hand it's lovely to have such a big network of people who love you. Whenever anything happens to one person in the family, everyone comes together to help them. You can't buy that kind of love and loyalty. On the other hand you never get a minute to yourself and it can be claustrophobic and overbearing at times, which is why I left. I needed to breathe by myself.'

'Wouldn't Australia have been better—further, more adventurous?'

'Yes, but then I wouldn't have met you.'

'No, but you might have met a nice Australian-Irish Catholic boy, which would have been an easier sell.'

'I've never taken the easy road.'

'How difficult is it going to be for them to accept me?'

'Scale of one to ten?'

'Yes.'

'Eleven. But you're worth it.'

'Can I do anything to help?'

'Be patient and trust me. I love you and I will tell them all about you. But you have to let me do it my way.'

'OK. But don't wait too long. I'd like to meet them before I'm old and grey.'

'You are old.'

'OK, grey, then.'

Irish Daily News

‘The Blind Date Set Up’

Niamh O’Flaherty

Jane, Fred and Paul are discussing Paul’s upcoming blind date with Fiona. Jane and Fred know Fiona. Paul doesn’t.

PAUL: ‘What’s she look like?’
JANE: ‘Oh, she’s lovely. She has the most amazing skin. She tans so easily.’
PAUL: ‘Skin?’
FRED: ‘Skin?’
PAUL: ‘Who gives a toss about skin? Is she a minger?’
JANE: ‘No! She’s really attractive. And good skin is a huge deal.’
FRED: ‘No, it isn’t.’
JANE: ‘Really?’
PAUL: ‘Trust me, I don’t care about how good a tan she gets.’
JANE: ‘All that money I’ve wasted on fake tan.’
PAUL: ‘Is she good in bed?’
JANE: ‘I don’t know!’
FRED: ‘She looks a bit gamey. She’s not exactly Angelina Jolie, I’d say she’d be grateful for a shag.’
PAUL: ‘So she’s a minger who gets a tan in the summer.’

FRED: 'No, she's not a minger, she scrubs up well. Sticky-out ears. Looks a bit like your one in *Spiderman*.'

JANE: 'Kirsten Dunst? No, she doesn't.'

FRED: 'She looks like her uglier sister.'

PAUL: 'Uglier sister, your one's no supermodel.'

FRED: 'Nice rack, though.'

PAUL: 'I like big tits.'

JANE: 'She has the most amazing wrists—they're tiny.'

FRED: 'Wrists?'

PAUL: 'Wrists?'

JANE: 'It's incredible, they're so delicate. She can never find a bracelet small enough to fit her.'

Fred and Paul look at each other and sigh.

PAUL: 'Good legs?'

FRED: 'Hockey legs.'

PAUL: 'Chunky?'

FRED: ' 'Fraid so.'

JANE: 'She does not have chunky legs. They're half the size of mine.'

Silence.

JANE: 'Jesus, do I have big fat legs?'

Silence.

5

London, June 1985

Growing up is difficult enough when you're not blessed with beauty or brains, but it certainly didn't help with a father who insisted on re-creating rural Ireland in the middle of London. Trying to fit in and make friends is not easy when your house is a shrine to Ireland. My father thought that if he only allowed his three children to live, breathe and think things Irish, we would somehow be saved from the perils of becoming English.

We had a tricolour hanging from a flagpole in our garden, the hedge was cut in the shape of a shamrock, we had leprechaun gnomes with fishing-rods sitting round the pond and the doorbell was set to the tune of 'Danny Boy'.

We were known as the 'mad Paddies'. My father spoke Gaelic to us when we were out in public, even though none of us could understand a word he said. Well, my saintly sister Siobhan pretended she understood him, while I begged him to keep his voice down in case anyone heard him.

'You should be proud of your heritage,' he'd say. 'You come from the land of saints and scholars. Hold your head high and proclaim your Irishness.'

It was all very well for him, but I was a fourteen-year-old trying to blend in. Besides, I didn't feel Irish. I was born and bred in London. England was the only home I had ever known and I liked it. What was the use of learning Gaelic? No one else spoke it. I hated everything Irish. It made us stand out and I was desperate to fit in.

The problem was that my older sister Siobhan loved all things Irish. She also happened to be good at Irish dancing. In fact, she was brilliant. She'd come second in the Great Britain Irish-dancing Championship the year before and my father had almost burst with pride. He'd kept saying it was the best day of his life, until he felt the weight of my mother's glare, and added that, of course, his wedding day had been the best day, this was the second best.

I hated Irish dancing with a passion. It was about as cool as train-spotting. You had to wear ridiculous dresses that looked suspiciously like they had been made out of curtains—even Fräulein Maria in *The Sound of Music* would have had a hard time making dresses as hideous as those.

Then there was the hair-curling. You had to have ringlets, no matter what. You were forced to sleep with damp hair in curlers with the big pins drilling holes through your skull. No sweet little rags tied in bows like Nellie Olsen in *The Little House on the Prairie* for us—it was Roller City. When you woke up the next day, in my case with fuzzy clumps of knotted hair from thrashing about in the bed trying to find a comfortable position to sleep in, the torture really began. The rollers had to be extracted from the knots, and my mother was not blessed with the patience of a saint or, say, Caroline Ingalls (neighbour of the Olsen family, wife of Charles and mother of Laura, Mary, Albert and Carrie). The rollers were ripped out of my head, pins and lumps of hair in tow, while she huffed and puffed about unruly hair and bloody ringlets.

You see, secretly my mother hated doing the ringlets and found Irish-dancing competitions very dull, but she knew how much they meant to my father so she played along. I heard her telling my auntie Nuala one day that her idea of a perfect Saturday afternoon was to curl up on the couch with a good book. Instead of which, she spent all her weekends sitting in cold town halls watching curly dancing curtains jump about the stage with their hands pinned to their sides.

Anyway, while my sister's hair bounced out of the rollers in perfectly formed ringlets that Shirley Temple would have coveted, mine always hung in limp clumps. So I'd end up having them tied back in an enormous bow (made of the same bright green curtain material as the dress) and then we'd go to the competition. Siobhan, looking angelic, would leap gracefully about the stage, twisting and clicking her legs like Michael Flatley on speed, while I would try to do the same but end up like someone with a bad case of St Vitus's Dance. I just couldn't—no matter how hard I tried—keep my hands still. It wasn't natural and they always flew up as I danced. I also wasn't blessed with a huge amount of co-ordination, and dancing in general was clearly not my forte. I wasn't sure what my forte was—if, indeed, I had one—but I was damn sure it wasn't Irish dancing, and at fourteen years of age, time was running out and I wanted to explore other possibilities.

I decided I'd have to tell my father so I ran my speech by Siobhan and Finn.

'Dad, I'm sorry but I don't want to do any more Irish-dancing lessons. I'm not good at it and I hate it,' I said, frowning into the mirror.

'You must be mad,' said Siobhan, admiring her legs. 'He'll do his nut if you stop. You know what he's like.'

'Niamh,' my younger brother, Finn, said, 'you're going to have to come up with something better than that. Otherwise he'll hit the roof. Think of a good reason why you can't do it any more—like a new hobby. Tell him you want to take tin-whistle lessons to learn the old Irish songs, or concentrate on camogie or something like that.'

My brother Finn had got out of having to do Irish dancing by excelling at hurley. He said Irish dancing was for fags and there was no way he was going to prance around on a stage in a velvet suit. He was sympathetic to my plight.

'But I don't want to play a made-up Irish game where you run after a little ball with a stupid stick,' I wailed. 'I want to do tap-dancing classes with Sarah. She said it's brilliant.'

'You're a sucker for punishment,' said Finn, in alarm. 'Look, bring it up at dinner tonight and I'll do what I can to help you out. But he's going to go mad.'

Later that day, I waited until my mother had served everyone their apple crumble, then pounced.

'Dad,' I said, my voice shaking, 'you know the way I'm not very good at Irish dancing and Siobhan is brilliant and wins all the competitions? Well, there's something I think I could be really good at and Sarah's started lessons already and says it's great fun. So I was wondering if maybe I could stop Irish dancing and take up tap instead. If that's OK with you.'

Silence from my father. My mother shook her head to warn me to stop before I made it worse and Siobhan was running her knife across her throat, mouthing, 'You're dead.' Finn sank back into his chair.

My father turned a deep shade of red, put his spoon down, leant over to me and roared, 'No daughter of mine will be prancing around in her underwear to that racy black music. You will continue with your Irish dancing and you will take extra lessons so that you can improve like your sister Siobhan who never gives me a day of trouble. I did not move to this country twenty years ago, with nothing but the shirt on my back, to raise children with no respect for their heritage and culture. I have worked myself to the bone . . .'

That was when he launched into his usual litany: 'I had no money . . . I came over to London at sixteen years of age and worked on a building site . . . I saved my money, I started up my own company and now employ my four brothers and sixty other Irishmen . . . I didn't want to leave my beautiful country, but I had no choice.' Normally at this point tears welled in his eyes. 'I had to make my way and help out the family . . . I was lucky enough to meet a lovely Irish girl and settle down. You are Irish through and through and don't you ever forget it.

'Niamh,' he said sternly, 'I will have no more of this nonsense. I don't want you seeing that young Sarah Cooke any more. She's a bad influence on you.'

'You can't stop me seeing her—she's my only real friend. I promise I won't bring up tap again,' I squealed, feeling sick at the prospect of not seeing

Sarah. I'd die without her. She kept me sane. Although her parents were atheists, they had sent their daughter to an all-girls' Catholic convent school because it had excellent exam results. They were very cool: she was allowed to watch *Top of the Pops* and *Dallas*. I was only allowed watch *Top of the Pops* when Foster and Allen were on it in their leprechaun suits with my father howling along to 'A Bunch of Thyme'. And *Dallas* was considered almost pornographic in our house, although I had caught my mother watching it once or twice when Dad was out.

Sarah went on holidays to Brighton and Cornwall, snogged handsome English boys and had adventures. Her parents let her live the life of a normal teenager. For our summer holidays, we were always shipped over to my aunt Nora's farm in Ballyban to help milk the cows and fetch the eggs. It was really boring. Her house stank of cow dung and there were flies everywhere. Getting up at six to milk cows was supposed to be a treat for us city slickers, but we hated it. The local kids teased us about our English accents, threw stones at us and told us we had no place in their country. This was not conducive to snogging, so while Sarah racked up experience during her summer months, I got pelted with stones in Ireland. To top it all my auntie Nora was a bitter old witch.

When Finn said he didn't like black pudding—hardly surprising as it's made up of boiled pig's blood and pork fat—she ate the face off him. 'Well, I'm sorry it's not good enough for you. What do you get in London, then? Caviar and smoked salmon, is it?'

'No, just cornflakes,' mumbled Finn, squirming

in his seat.

'Oh, well, little Lord Fauntleroy, you'll just have to do without breakfast. Coming over here refusing to eat good food, who do you think you are?'

Auntie Nora could be really mean sometimes, but there was no point in telling my father because he wouldn't have believed us. He thought she was wonderful because she had moved in with Granny O'Flaherty when she was sick and looked after her until she died.

In the meantime, she had inherited Granny's house and land, all of which my father had bought for his mother when he started doing well in London. And Granny had had the decency to die within three months of becoming ill—come to think of it, she'd probably died of black-puddingitis—so it wasn't as if she had ruined her daughter's life by taking ten years to die, thus thwarting her chances of getting married—not that Auntie Nora had had a hope in hell of getting married: all men were terrified of her.

To my father and his brothers, Auntie Nora would always be the saintly one who had stayed behind to care for Granny while they had moved to London to work together, and that was all that mattered. The fact that she was a bitter, jealous old woman, who made our summers hell, was irrelevant. She was a martyr and my father had the utmost respect for martyrs. In fact, the only reason she had us to stay was money. He paid her a princely sum to immerse us in Irishness for three weeks every year.

After the three weeks with Auntie Nora, my parents would come over on the ferry and take us on a two-week tour of the country. My father would bore us to death with the history of Ireland—always remembering to note the four hundred years of oppression by the English—and we would try to look interested and ask relevant questions. Well, Siobhan asked relevant questions. Finn and I played hangman.

On our tour we would visit every dead relation's grave, followed by every living relation's house. The pre-arrival routine was always the same: before we got out of the car, my mother would try in vain to glue my hair down with her spit, sometimes aided and abetted by Finn gobbing on to my scalp. He thought it was hilarious. I didn't. The spit never worked, but she never stopped trying. Eventually she would sigh, rustle in her bag and fish out an elastic band. The big brown ones that are supposed to be used to hold paper together, not human hair. No matter how hard I prayed, she always found one. Those elastic bands actually create knots and cause much suffering the world over when misused as hair ties. But on it would go, despite my squeals of pain—my mother was a determined woman when she wanted to be. Then a hankie would be produced, also spat on and our faces rubbed raw.

Despite the mind-numbingly boring afternoon ahead of us, it was a relief to get out of the car and away from our saliva-frenzied mother. As my father rang the doorbell he would remind us to behave ourselves, accept only one biscuit and never, ever take the chocolate one, always the plain. This was Ireland, where chocolate biscuits didn't grow on trees.

The door would be flung open and in we'd troop to the kitchen, smiling politely and playing down our English accents. The uncle/aunt/second-cousin-twice-removed would proceed to tell my father how badly they were doing, despite the new extension they had just built, doubling the size of their house. My father would nod and sigh and say it was hard all right, he remembered the bad times, and could he help at all? 'No, no, Mick, not at all. Jaysus, you don't think we're looking for money off you? Go away out of that, not at all. Sure it's just lovely to see you and hear you're doing so well over there,' they would say.

'Well, I'd like to help. After all, family is family,' my poor, generous fool of a father would say.

'Not at all, Mick. Sure it's a bit of a struggle all right but we're managing to keep our heads above water. We couldn't take anything from you. I see things are going well for you, though, with the big new car you've outside. Well, sure isn't it great that one of us is doing so well anyway?'

'Things are good all right and sure isn't that why I want to help? How much would tide you over?' my father would say, opening his wallet, while my mother sat rigid with a fake smile plastered on her face.

Ten minutes later, after many 'No, no, Mick, not at all's and 'Oh, go on, now, let me help's the relation would mention a large figure and my father would dutifully fork out the money. Whereupon another ten minutes of 'Oh, now, aren't you very good to us, Mick? When we get sorted out we'll pay you back' and 'Not at all don't mention it again' would ensue.

Then my mother would nudge me, I'd yawn (as previously arranged) and she'd say we had to go because the children were tired and we'd pile into the car with the relations thumping the roof and sticking their heads in the windows, blessing us, wishing us a safe journey and thanking my father again as they planned how to spend their winnings.

Afterwards in the car my mother would give out yards to my father for being so generous to his sponging relations. 'They'll bleed you dry, Mick.'

'Ah, come on, now. If you can't help your family when things are going well what type of a person are you?'

'Are you blind? Did you not see the extension they've had done? You're a fool, Mick, they know you're a soft touch. We needed that money to put towards getting a new cooker,' my mother fumed.

'They'd do the same for me if I was stuck.'

My mother rolled her eyes. 'They'd do no such thing. You're too kind.'

'Better than being mean,' said my father, smiling at her. 'Sure isn't that one of the things you love about me.'

She sighed and smiled.

*   *   *

The best part of the holiday was going to visit Granny and Granddad Byrne in Dublin. My mother's parents were great. They were the type of grandparents you wished for, like Charlie's sweet old granddad in *Charlie and the Chocolate Factory*. They didn't have much but what they had they were happy to share.

My mother was an only child—unheard of in Ireland in the 1950s when a pill was something you took to cure a disease, not prevent childbirth—and was doted on by her parents. They also thought their grandchildren were wonderful. We could do no wrong. But the best thing was that they seemed to like me best!

It's not that I ever thought my parents didn't love me, it's just that I was third in line when the love was being dished out. Siobhan, as the eldest and most perfect child—Irish-dancing champion, fluent in Gaelic (or so they thought), going out with a boy from an Irish family (both sets of grandparents had emigrated to London, no half-measures there)—was my father's pet. My brother Finn, being the youngest and a boy, had my mother's love pretty much sewn up. That left me with slim pickings.

I knew I was a disappointment to my father because I was a terrible Irish dancer, spoke no Gaelic and, truth be told, I wasn't the most attractive child you ever saw. I had wiry brown hair while Siobhan had sleek auburn locks (except when they weren't sleek because they were soft bouncy ringlets in honour of some championship event). She also had cat green eyes and I had big round brown ones, like a cow's. Finn, in fairness to him, was no looker. He had dark brown hair, brown eyes and big brown freckles all over his body. But he had a cheeky grin and lots of confidence because he was good at hurley, so somehow he got away with it.

I think my grandparents felt sorry for me. Granny was always telling me I had great potential. She never specified in what area, but it still made me feel better. I didn't feel like a complete loser when I was with them. They lived in a small house on the outskirts of Dublin and when we arrived we were made feel like the most important guests in the world. They always had our favourite food waiting for us. Siobhan liked potato cakes (she would, wouldn't she?), Finn liked roast chicken and I liked bacon butties with HP brown sauce, much to my father's disgust.

Granny Byrne always had HP brown sauce especially for me and I loved her for it. She was also the first person I confided in about my hatred of Irish dancing.

So it was Granny Byrne I called after my row with my father.

'I know it's hard, Niamh, darling, I never liked it much myself. Maybe you could say you were going to Irish dancing on Saturdays and do tap instead. Didn't you say they were in the same building?'

'You mean lie to Dad?' I said, shocked. Grannies didn't encourage their grandchildren to lie to their parents.

'No, not lie to him,' Granny Byrne said, back-pedalling furiously. 'But maybe you could do a tap class after the Irish-dancing class. You wouldn't have to tell your dad you were doing it. Just keep it to yourself.'

Granny Byrne was a genius.

6

For the next three months, using money I was given on my confirmation, I tapped my way enthusiastically through Saturday mornings. Fred Astaire wasn't exactly shaking in his boots, but I was a lot better at tap than at reels and jigs. I told my parents I was staying late to practise my Irish dancing and everyone was happy . . . except Father Hogan who said lying to my parents was a sin when I confessed my porky-pies. But I knew he was bound by the sacred gagging order of the confessional so my secret was safe.

For my fifteenth birthday my parents decided to throw me a party at home. I know it may sound ungrateful, but I was dreading it. I knew the format. I'd seen it enough times at my cousins' parties.

My three uncles, Donal, Neil, Tadhg, plus their wives and children, all came over. I actually had another uncle—'poor Pat'—but he was on holidays again. Uncle Pat was a roaring alcoholic who went to dry out at least once a year. The brothers chipped in for his treatments, although they were getting fed up because this was his fifth time. The adults tried to protect us from Uncle Pat's condition by telling us he was on holidays, but we all knew he was in rehab.

There were sixteen cousins altogether and we ranged in age from seventeen (my sister Siobhan being the eldest) to two. They descended upon the house bearing gifts. Some brought the type of presents a fifteen-year-old girl would want, like luminous pink leg-warmers, Duran Duran's latest album and some fingerless lace gloves. The rest gave crossword-puzzle books and Irish-dancing socks.

My mother forced me to wear a dress. I wanted to wear my jeans with the rip in the knee. I was fifteen, for God's sake. But no amount of pleading and sulking worked.

'Niamh,' my mother said, grabbing my arm and frogmarching me back up the stairs, 'only tinkers wear trousers with rips in them. Now, put on your blue dress and stop whingeing. Why can't you be more like your sister?'

Bloody Siobhan and her bloody perfectness! I was sick of her.

'I'm not Siobhan,' I roared, losing my temper. 'Stop telling me to be like her. I'm a different person. Sister Patricia says you should accept people the way they are and not try to change them like the English did when they came to Ireland and tried to make everyone speak English and stop speaking Irish and all the people had to go to makeshift schools hidden in the hedges.'

Brilliant. A stroke of genius. I was delighted with myself.

My mother, despite herself, began to laugh. 'You are some chancer, Niamh O'Flaherty. Nice try but you're still not wearing your jeans. Now, come here to me with that hair.'

'*Noooooo*, Mum—please let me do my own hair. You're too rough with the brush.'

'OK, but I want you downstairs in ten minutes with your dress on and your hair neat.'

'OK,' I grumbled.

'Oh, and by the way, Niamh,' she said, turning towards me as she closed the door, 'I wouldn't change a fuzzy hair on your head.'

That was the problem with my mother: she always made you love her, even when you wanted to hate her.

* * *

When I came downstairs half an hour later with a hundred and fifty clips keeping my fuzzy hair in check, Finn was standing in the hall looking grumpy in a shirt and dickie-bow. I felt much better. I might look bad but he looked ridiculous.

'Oh, Danny boy . . .' The doorbell tinkled. The relations had arrived.

I answered the door and my cheeks were then squeezed by my aunties, my head patted by my uncles, and I was told for the zillionth time that I was the spitting image, head cut off, twin separated at birth from Granny O'Flaherty. I had only ever seen one picture of my father's mother and she was a boot, so I was none too pleased to be constantly reminded that I looked like her.

After the squeezing and patting, the grown-ups went into the kitchen to gossip and have a few drinks. Us youngsters were expected to entertain ourselves while making sure our younger cousins didn't choke on their food, drink too much Coke, eat too many sweets, go into the garden unaccompanied, go upstairs unaccompanied, go to the loo unaccompanied, burn themselves, cut themselves, bump their heads or interrupt their parents while they were getting sloshed.

I had only one cousin I liked. Maura was a year older than me and was also rubbish at Irish dancing. But she had got out of having to do it by feigning weak ankles. Her mother, my auntie Nuala—by far the most progressive of the bunch—had helped her out. She'd lied to my uncle Tadhg and told him that the doctor said poor old Maura's ankles just wouldn't hold up to the clicking and jigging.

Ever since Maura had told me that story I had had the utmost respect for Auntie Nuala. She was a legend in my eyes. I wished my mother could have been a bit more sympathetic to my plight. But she very rarely disagreed with my father. The only time I could remember her shouting at him was a year ago when my father suggested that boarding-school in Ireland would be good for me. They had just come back from a parent-teacher meeting at school at which Sister Patricia told them I had said Ireland was a backward place full of thick people with red hair.

My father was furious and mortally embarrassed that a child of his would be so ignorant. He said England was corrupting me, and it was time for me to go back to my roots and see Ireland for what it really was: a beautiful country full of wonderful, warm people with deep souls and big hearts. I sat under the stairs listening to their conversation and sobbed. My life was over. But then my mother saved me. For once, she turned on him and said, in a scary voice, that over her dead body would a child of hers be sent away to boarding-school. She said I was a great girl who was just trying to find her way. I didn't mean to insult anyone, she said, I was only rebelling as all teenagers do.

'It's hard for the children, Mick. Their whole lives have been spent in England. It's confusing for them to be living in one country and expected to behave as if they live in another. Kids don't want to be different, they don't like standing out. I know you want them to appreciate where they've come from, but you have to let them breathe. You're suffocating them with Irishness. I love Ireland, too, and I miss it, but we left for a reason. We left because there were no opportunities and the country was in a deep recession. We came here to England and made a success of things. This country has been very good to us.'

'I know it has, but I came over here out of necessity, not choice. I want my children to grow up in an unspoilt land, raised with the morals I was raised with. I don't want them running wild. I'm trying to protect them, Annie.'

'Children need to make mistakes, Mick. It's part of growing up. If you over-protect them, they'll rebel. Ease up on Niamh. She's a good girl, just different from Siobhan—she's more strong-willed and stubborn. And she didn't lick those traits off a stone. The two of you are very alike. That's why you clash.'

'I'm not stubborn,' my father said, sounding genuinely shocked.

'You're the most stubborn man I ever met,' my mother laughed, 'but tonight, you've met your match. I'm digging my heels in. There'll be no more talk of boarding-school.'

I breathed a huge sigh of relief. I was safe. But I'd have to be careful from now on and try to be more positive about my Irishness in front of my father.

* * *

As my birthday party progressed, us elder cousins sat around the TV room playing records and giving out about our parents, taking it in turns to lunge after the sprinting toddlers and trying to stop them crying when we blocked their exit routes. After much experimenting, we discovered that stuffing marshmallows into their mouths was a far more effective way of stifling their tears than putting our hands over their gobs and watching them turn blue.

After a few hours the parents trooped in, some reeking of booze, and told us we were marvellous kids. They hugged us and planted slobbery kisses on our cheeks while congratulating each other on being great parents.

Then the sing-song began, as always led by my father, singing 'Danny Boy'. All the uncles and aunts cheered when he howled out the last line: 'Oh, Danny boy, I looooooooove you so.' Then Uncle Tadhg sang 'The Fields of Athenry' and everyone tut-tutted about the heartbreak of emigration.

Siobhan was called upon to dance. She pretended she didn't want to, and made everyone beg, even though she already had her shoes on. It'd make you sick. Maura rolled her eyes to heaven and we giggled. My uncle Donal took out his fiddle and accompanied Siobhan as she leapt and whirled around the room to the clapping and whooping that accompanied her.

All the parents then got up, some a little more unsteady on their feet than others, and twirled each other round with great gusto, then dragged us up to join in. Although I pretended to Maura that I found it embarrassing to see my parents dancing together, I actually loved it. They were wonderful. They never missed a beat and my mother looked so young and carefree as my father twirled her this way and that as they relived their courting days in the dance halls of London.

After an hour or two of dancing, singing and poetry-reciting, the whiskey came out and things began to deteriorate. My uncle Donal said what a saint my grandmother O'Flaherty had been, and my father and his brothers nodded and sniffled into their hankies while my mother and aunts sighed.

From what I could gather during my years of covert eavesdropping under the stairs while my mother and Auntie Nuala bitched about Granny O'Flaherty in the kitchen, she'd been a right old witch. Not only was she ugly (and me the image of her!) but apparently she was scabby and rude to her daughters-in-law.

'She was an oul bitch, so she was,' said Auntie Nuala, cutting to the chase. 'Sure the first time I met her she said to me, "I think you forgot to put on your skirt." Imagine the cheek of her! Tadhg, of course, then went from thinking I was fabulous to thinking I looked like a cheap tart. And she wouldn't give you the leftovers on her plate. She was always milking the boys dry. You must have really felt it, Annie. She was always asking Mick for money.'

'Ah, well, Mick liked to spoil her when the business got up and going. I think he felt it was almost his responsibility as the eldest to look after her,' said the champion fence-sitter.

'Don't give me that holy-Joe talk,' said Auntie Nuala. 'It's me you're talking to and I know you hated the old bitch.'

I could hear my mother laughing. 'OK, I admit I wasn't her biggest fan. But with her living in Ireland and us over here she didn't really have a chance to get up my nose.'

'Mmm. Well, she got right up mine. When Tadhg said Mick wanted us to move over here and work in the business I practically sprinted on to the boat. Like the Road Runner I was,' said Auntie

Nuala, and they giggled.

* * *

After bemoaning their mother's early demise, my father and uncles proceeded to have a huge argument about who had shot Michael Collins. They shouted at each other, glasses were slammed down, fingers were poked into chests (their own when they were making a point, the other person's when they were accusing them of being wrong).

Uncle Tadhg stormed dramatically out of the house, nearly taking the door with him, after my father called him an ignorant fool. He was chased down the road by Uncle Donal and coaxed back into the house, but said he'd only stay if my father apologized. Dad said he wasn't apologizing for anything, so Uncle Tadhg stomped out and said he'd never darken our door again. My father ran after him and shouted that that was the best news he'd ever heard. Uncle Tadhg yelled that he could shove his job up his uptight arse. My father bellowed that he'd rather be uptight than thick. Mr Green from next door stuck his head out the window and told them both to stop causing such a racket and take their argument indoors.

'Mind your own business,' said Uncle Tadhg.

'Don't you curse at me, you drunken Irish fool,' shouted Mr Green.

'How dare you call my brother a fool?' roared my father. This from the same man who, minutes earlier, had chased his brother out of the house for being thick. 'My brother here is the most intelligent man you'll ever meet, and the best friend a man could wish for,' he said, staggering towards Uncle Tadhg and swinging his arm over his brother's shoulders.

'If you don't pipe down I'll call the police, O'Flaherty. I'm warning you,' said Mr Green, and slammed his window shut.

'Am I your best friend, Mick?' said Uncle Tadhg, beaming at my father.

'The best, Tadhg.' My father beamed back, and they stumbled into the house arm in arm, the best of friends and not a stupid man between them.

7

Now that I had turned fifteen and left my early teens behind, the pressure was on for me to snog someone. Sarah had snogged four boys already and I was still a virgin kisser. There was a party on for the fifteen to eighteen-year-olds in the local Irish club on Saturday night, and I was determined to get some experience. Even if I had to kiss the biggest leper there, I wasn't coming home without a snog.

I decided to ask Siobhan for some tips. She had been going out with Liam O'Loughlin, champion Irish dancer in Great Britain for two years. They were the Torvill and Dean of Irish dancing. It'd make you sick. Anyway, I was always catching them kissing in her room and recently had found him with his hand up her skirt. She had screamed at me to get out and given me a dead arm later on when I teased her about it. The perfect Siobhan was not so perfect, after all. I was thrilled.

I knocked on her door instead of barging in. I

wanted to get her in a good mood.

'Get lost,' she shouted.

'Come on, I need to talk to you. It's really important.'

'Sod off.'

'I'll tell Mum I saw Liam's hand up your skirt.'

'Bitch.'

The door opened. Sometimes you had to use tough measures to get what you wanted and I was desperate.

'Well? What do you want?'

'Look, Siobh, I need your help. I'm going to the disco on Saturday and I want to get off with someone. I've never snogged anyone before and I just wanted you to tell me what to do.'

'Who are you planning to snog?'

'Anyone who'll have me at this stage. I'm the only one of the girls who hasn't got off with anyone yet,' I said, sorry for myself. 'If I don't snog someone soon, I'm going to end up having to be friends with Noreen O'Reilly and you know what a nerd she is.'

'Oh, for God's sake, stop being so dramatic. Here, sit down and watch me closely.'

I sat on the edge of her bed and watched her with the concentration I normally reserved for my prayers to God that Simon Le Bon from Duran Duran would see me in the audience at one of their concerts, lift me out of the crowd and whisk me off to a life of glamour and luxury.

After slobbering over her hand for a few minutes Siobhan told me to have a go. I licked my lips and set to it. Round and round my tongue went.

'Stop,' she said sharply. 'You haven't been

watching properly. There's far too much saliva—you'll drown him.'

'Well, tell me what to do,' I wailed. 'You've enough practice—you're always sucking the face off Liam.'

'I told you, less saliva. Look, just stick your tongue out and twirl.'

'Clockwise or anti-clockwise?'

'Oh, for God's sake.'

'What?' I thought it was a perfectly valid question. The last thing I wanted to do was announce my inexperience by heading in the wrong direction.

'Get out. You're annoying me now.'

'OK, but just one more question. Should I let him go to second base?'

'No,' she snapped, frowning. 'If you give them an inch, they'll take a mile.'

'Thanks, Siobh.'

'Hey, Niamh, don't worry, you'll be grand.'

Sometimes Siobhan could be almost human.

* * *

Sarah called over and we spent hours in my room getting ready. Well, she actually arrived ready. She was wearing stretch denims that clung to her stick-thin legs and a long white T-shirt that said 'RELAX' in black on the front. She had tied it up on one side in a little knot and her hair was all messy and sexy like Madonna's. She also had black fingerless lace gloves on. She looked amazing—cool and gorgeous.

She helped me French-plait my hair, which was brilliant because I couldn't do it on my own, and when my mother tried, I ended up looking like Pippi Longstocking, which wasn't cool. Once my hair was done, and the stray frizzy bits had been controlled with a large can of hairspray, I tried on my entire wardrobe.

This wasn't as dramatic or time-consuming as it sounds—after all, I wore a school uniform five days a week. Brown skirt, brown jumper, white shirt, brown and black striped tie, white socks and brown shoes. You were only allowed to wear small stud earrings, no hoops: they were considered highly dangerous. Someone could apparently easily stick a large tennis racket through the three-centimetre size hoop in your ear and rip the lobe off. One finger ring was allowed—a claddagh ring worn upside down by losers like me who had no boyfriend or the right way up by the lucky few who had. Mind you, you could tell a girl who had a boyfriend a mile away—you didn't need the ring. Girls with boyfriends strutted; girls without shuffled. Siobhan strutted; I shuffled.

So, Sarah watched patiently as I tried on my long pink fishtail skirt with my long white shirt with the Elvis collar and a pink belt hanging over the shirt at the hips. Then I tried on my long black fishtail skirt with a long black and white striped shirt and a black belt. My red cords with the white shirt and a red satin waistcoat. My black leggings with my black miniskirt over them, and the white shirt with the black belt.

'Yes,' said Sarah. 'That's what you should wear.'

We then put on our makeup. Egypt Wonder—lots of it—black eyeliner, and pink lipstick. I put on my chandelier diamanté earrings and brooch to match, then got undressed. I put on my jeans and packed my leggings and mini in Sarah's bag. My father did not view leggings as trousers. He said they were nothing more than tights, and he was not a fan of the miniskirt: only cheap girls wore minis . . .

When we finally came out Finn was hovering by the door. He sniggered when he saw us.

'What's so funny?'

'Your faces are bright orange.'

'It's called makeup, you nerd, and at least we don't have buck teeth.'

I know it was mean, but I was really nervous. I'd be nice to him tomorrow after I'd snogged someone.

We went downstairs and my mother told us we looked lovely. My father glanced up from the paper and muttered something about girls in trousers giving the wrong impression to young lads. My mother winked and told us we'd knock all the boys dead, then gave me two pounds for a Coca-Cola.

* * *

Did I get off with someone? Yes. Was it nice? No. For the first half-hour we stood around trying to look cool, sipping our vodka and Coke. Sarah had nicked some vodka from her parents' drinks cabinet, which we had mixed with the Coke in the loo while I was getting changed.

When we'd finished our drinks we went to dance with the rest of our group, Suzanne, Saoirse and Deirdre. We danced in a circle, shuffling from side to side, trying to blend in. Then the DJ played a slow song, so we sprinted to one side of the room, as did the lads. We stood praying that someone would ask us to dance. One by one the others got asked up and just as I was wishing the floor would open up and swallow me, I heard a voice asking me to dance.

He had greasy hair and a bad case of acne. But he was a boy and he wanted to dance. Besides, when we snogged I'd have my eyes closed so I wouldn't see the spots. We shuffled around to 'Careless Whisper', 'True' and 'Stairway to Heaven'. It was during 'True' that Frank shoved his tongue into my mouth and for the whole of 'Stairway to Heaven' I twirled mine—anti-clockwise, by the way—and tried desperately to breathe through my nose. There was saliva everywhere and it was gross, but at least I could say I'd done it.

When Frank finally came up for air, he wiped the saliva off his chin with his jumper and asked if I wanted to go outside. Now, I knew that going outside meant more snogging and maybe second base. I decided I might as well get some more experience and was also secretly hoping that the kissing would get better. As we walked outside, squeezing between the other couples lined up against the wall, I tried to suck all the saliva I could out of my mouth so it was bone dry. Off we went again, anti-clockwise, cold wet saliva being recycled in our mouths. Then Frank asked if he could go down.

Go down? What the hell was that? No one had ever mentioned going down. I had no idea what he meant. Maybe it meant give me a love bite. Aha! That would be cool. Going to school on Monday with a love bite! Yes, I wanted one of those. 'Sure,'

I said, smiling.

So Frank shoved his hand down my leggings and into my knickers. I screamed like a banshee. He nearly died, and so did I when I saw everyone staring at us. I pushed him away and ran home.

Siobhan was up when I got back. When she saw the state I was in, she brought me into the kitchen and tried to calm me down. 'What happened to you?'

'You stupid cow.' I blubbed. 'You never said anything about going down. I didn't know what it meant and then when he did it I nearly died. So I screamed and everyone saw and it was awful.' I was sobbing into a tea-towel—my life was over. My friends would desert me. No guy would ever go near me again. I'd be known as tight. I'd be lucky if Noreen O'Reilly gave me the time of day.

'Who was he? What did he do?' Siobhan sounded genuinely concerned.

'Some rapist called Frank. He stuck his hand down my pants.'

'Oh, my God, that's awful. Why on earth did you let him?'

'Because I didn't know what it meant and I didn't think you jumped from first base to third without going to second! What am I going to do? Everyone heard me screaming. I can never go back to school. I'll have to pretend I have a vocation and join the nuns.'

'Stop being so dramatic. It's not that bad. He was obviously a creep and you were right to scream. Forget about it, and if anyone slags you just ignore them.'

Siobhan didn't understand. How could she? She was surrounded by girls who embraced their

Irishness and thought she was a goddess because of the dancing and Liam. She was full of confidence. I, on the other hand, hung out with girls who shunned their Irishness and I had no confidence because I was the loser of my group.

I knew Deirdre would be vicious on Monday and make a fool of me. I was dreading it. The others always laughed at her slags because they were a bit afraid of her. Deirdre was the only girl in school who answered back to the nuns. She was always in detention. The only reason she hadn't been expelled was because Sister Patricia, the headmistress, had a soft spot for her: Deirdre's father had run off to Scotland with Mrs Hogart from our road and her mother now suffered from depression. Sister Patricia was determined to save Deirdre's soul. It was a lost cause as far as I could see, but she wasn't one to give up easily.

I would be a laughing-stock at school. 'I'm going to bed. My life is over,' I said, getting up to make a dramatic exit.

'You're not the only one with problems,' said Siobhan, beginning to cry.

'Let me guess. You only got an A minus in your latest exam,' I said, and stormed out.

8

The next morning, I dragged myself out of bed and went to Irish dancing, then tap to meet Sarah and dissect the awfulness of what had happened. She was very sweet, as always, and assured me I'd been right to scream. I made her tell me what the others had said after I left, and eventually she admitted that they hadn't been very nice.

I was devastated. My life at school would be hell now. Sarah said she'd stick by me, but I knew how difficult it would be for her: if she did, she'd be an outcast of the cool group too. It wasn't fair on her. I told her it was OK, she could hang around with the others. I'd have to ask Noreen O'Reilly if I could hang out with her group. It was the worst day of my life—and then my mother walked into the class as we were mid-tap. She was bawling.

I nearly died. I actually think my heart stopped. My mother very rarely cried. I had broken her heart by lying to her about tap dancing. As she walked towards me I began to cry too. I felt awful. 'I'm sorry, Mum, I didn't mean to upset you. Please forgive me. Don't cry, please, Mum.'

She looked utterly devastated. She took me by the hand and walked me out of the class.

She didn't speak to me until we were sitting in the car. When she closed her door, she began to howl. I didn't know what to do. I'd never seen her like this. My God, she must really hate tap dancing—Granny Byrne should have warned me. This was awful. The weekend was turning out to be a complete nightmare. I wouldn't have to worry about snogging boys any more. By the looks of things I'd be grounded until I was forty. Then it hit me. If my mother was this upset, imagine what my father would be like.

I panicked. 'Mum, does Dad know?'

She didn't answer me, she just kept sobbing. Oh, my God, this was awful! He must have found out, gone mad and sent her down to collect me. He was waiting at home to torture me for lying. Oh God oh God oh God! Stupid bloody tap dancing.

My mother's crying was really distressing me now. She was almost hysterical. 'Mum,' I said, 'Mum, listen to me. I'm so sorry, I am so very, very sorry. I swear it will never happen again. I'll never lie again.'

Suddenly she stopped crying and looked at me. Then she hugged me and started bawling again. My mother wasn't normally a hugger. This was all most irregular. I had clearly pushed her over the edge this time. She'd end up going on 'holidays' like Uncle Pat. Oh, God, what had I done?

Eventually she was able to speak. 'Niamh, I want you to listen to me very carefully,' she said. She was speaking slowly, as if she was talking to a foreign person. 'Your sister has done a terrible thing and has brought shame on our family. Our lives will never be the same again. It's going to be very hard for you and Finn, but especially for you because you're a girl. Your father is devastated, as am I, but we're going to have to put our best foot forward. I'll need you to be very strong. People are going to talk about us and spread nasty rumours. I want you to hold your head up high and ignore them. Remember, Siobhan is your sister, and although she has done a terrible thing, it's going to be harder for her than anyone else.'

I had no idea what she was talking about. Siobhan bringing shame on the family? What on earth did she mean? Had she come last in the Irish-dancing competition? 'Mum,' I said gently—she had started crying again—'Mum, I don't know what you mean. What has Siobhan done?'

My mother stared out of the window. Her mouth was set in a tight hard line. 'Your fool of a sister has gone and got herself pregnant.'

OH MY GOD. I was gobsmacked. Siobhan! Pregnant! I just couldn't believe it. No wonder my mother was so upset. This was the worst thing that could happen to an unwed Irish girl. Wow, I thought. So Siobhan was having sex with Liam. I saw her in a whole new light. But to have got caught by getting pregnant! My father would go insane. He'd never get over it.

Then it occurred to me, in my self-obsessed fifteen-year-old way, that this might work in my favour. Clearly my mother hadn't noticed I was doing tap so my secret was safe. Plus, I'd be in the cool gang again because they'd all want to know about my wild sister. Siobhan a rebel—who would have thought it? And I would no longer be the one who always messed up. I know it's awful, but that was what I was thinking when my mother interrupted me.

'Now, you listen here, missy. That disco you went to last night is the first and last one you will ever go to. You are not even so much as to look at a boy. Siobhan has ruined her life and I'll be damned if you'll go the same way. You'll put your head down and start working really hard in school. You're going to college like Siobhan was supposed to and make the most of the opportunities your dad and I could only dream of. There will be no more messing and no more bad reports. I'm warning you.'

Oh, God, my life *was* over. My mother had one main obsession and it was that we all go to university. My father saw no need for women to study after school. He thought we should focus on getting married and having children—as opposed to having babies unwed at seventeen. But this was one area in which my mother put her foot firmly down. She drilled it into us that we were to go to college, get a proper education, have a career, and then meet someone nice and settle down. But college came first.

That was OK for Siobhan, who was planning to go to university in Ireland and study Gaelic. This was the only option my father would agree to. It was the compromise he and my mother had reached, regarding higher education. You could go to college but only in Ireland.

Well, that had been Siobhan's Plan A. I was sure Plan B would be a lot different. I, on the other hand, wanted to be an air-stewardess. I wanted to wear a glamorous uniform, bright red lipstick and three-inch heels. It seemed so easy—get dressed up, look beautiful and smile a lot. And you got to travel for free.

Also, I wasn't very good in school and I didn't like homework. Apparently at college you had loads of work to do, with massive essays called theses, and I had no interest in that. Besides, I didn't want to go and live in Ireland. I loved London—it was vibrant and cutting-edge. Rock stars lived in London, for goodness' sake.

I decided to remain silent for the rest of the journey home. My mother was driving like a lunatic, swerving all over the road as she thumped the steering-wheel and repeated over and over, 'Stupid girl, stupid girl.' I actually began to feel sorry for Siobhan. My father must be giving her an awful roasting.

When we got home, he and Siobhan were sitting in the front room. Siobhan's face was puffy and blotched from crying and she looked shattered. I went over and gave her a hug. It was awkward and I felt a bit embarrassed, but she clung to me like a terrified child, so I was glad I'd made the effort. Eventually I prised her hands off my back and sat down. Finn had gone to Leeds to play in some hurley league, so he was spared the drama.

It was only when I glanced at my father that the magnitude of what was happening hit me. He had aged ten years in one morning. He was utterly deflated, like a man who has lost everything. He sat in his favourite chair, shoulders hunched, head down, sobbing into his big white hankie. I knew then that I might as well pack it all in and join a nunnery. My social life, which hadn't even begun, was never going to happen now. As I tried to picture myself in a nun's habit the doorbell rang out 'Danny Boy'.

It was Uncle Tadhg and Auntie Nuala. They were brilliant. Auntie Nuala hugged my mother, then my father, Siobhan and even me. She said loudly, and a little too cheerfully, 'It's like a bloody morgue in here. Come on, now, no one's dead. We'll sort this out,' and squeezed my mother's hand. Mum smiled gratefully. She needed Auntie Nuala. She was too shell-shocked to think straight.

Uncle Tadhg went over and thumped my father awkwardly on the back—displays of brotherly affection were strictly post a tumbler or two of whiskey. 'Come on now, Mick, don't be getting yourself into a state. It'll be OK. We're all here for you.'

'It's a bloody mess,' said my father. 'A disgrace. I've broken my back working to give my children a better life, a good education, food on the table and a roof over their heads, and what do they do? Bring shame on me.'

I wanted to interrupt and point out that it was only Siobhan who was pregnant, not me, but decided to keep quiet.

'Thank God my poor mother didn't live to see this. My eldest and finest pregnant at seventeen out of wedlock. We should never have left Ireland. I've sweated and toiled for this family and sent my daughters to convent schools to be educated by the nuns and what do they do? Behave like wanton women.'

'Ah, now, Mick,' said my mother.

'Hussies, I tell you,' shouted my father. 'Well, I won't stand for it. You're going to marry that young fella and that's the end of it. You can forget your fancy notions about going to college because you're spoilt now. You'll have to leave school without even doing your exams. My God, I'll be the laughing-stock of the community. How could you be so stupid?'

'Stop it now, Mick,' said Auntie Nuala, coming over to comfort Siobhan, who was shaking and sobbing. 'Siobhan's life is not ruined and it's not over. I'm not saying this is an ideal situation and she has been silly, but these things can be fixed.'

As she said 'fixed', she raised her eyebrows at my mother, who shook her head. Auntie Nuala stood up and said she could murder a cup of tea, and the two women went into the kitchen, leaving my father to rant about this country having no morals and how it had rubbed off on his daughters. I was sick of being tarred with Siobhan's brush so I followed my mother and Auntie Nuala and took up my position under the stairs where I could hear everything.

'Annie, listen to me,' said Auntie Nuala, firmly. 'She doesn't have to have this baby. How far gone is she?'

'Two months. Nuala, you know as well as I do that Mick would never agree to it. And I don't think I would either. It's wrong. It's murder.'

'Oh, come on, Annie. It's the twentieth century. The poor girl's life doesn't have to be ruined. If she has this baby and marries that spotty youngster she'll never go to college and have the life you want for her. Getting married at seventeen is what people did in the old days. We've moved on from that. Think about it.'

'It's murder, Nuala. It goes against everything we've been brought up to believe. The Church is very clear on abortion.'

ABORTION! I fell back on to the coats. I couldn't believe Auntie Nuala was suggesting that Siobhan get an abortion. She couldn't! She'd be struck down by God! Everyone knew that abortion was killing. Only prostitutes had abortions. Even women who were raped had to have the baby: it was a gift from God. Sister Patricia had told us so. I was shocked at Auntie Nuala. Siobhan would go to hell and the baby would too.

'Annie,' said Auntie Nuala, sharply, cutting across my mother, 'Mick wouldn't have to know. We could just say she lost it naturally. It's perfectly feasible. Women have miscarriages every day.'

My mother was silent. I couldn't believe how devious Auntie Nuala was. I wondered did Uncle Tadhg know she thought this way. She must be watching too much *Dallas*. Sister Patricia said programmes like *Dallas* were the scourge of modern society.

'Think of Siobhan. She's been brought up to believe that abortion is murder. She'd never get over it,' whispered Mum.

'Yes, she would. We could organize for her to get some counselling afterwards. Then she could go off to college in Dublin and have all the wonderful opportunities you want her to have.'

'But where would we go?'

'I have a friend who had one and she knows a good clinic. At least give her the option. Will you do that? Just ask Siobhan what she wants instead of railroading her into a wedding at seventeen.'

My mother came out and called Siobhan. Then Auntie Nuala explained calmly to my sister that she had options and laid them out for her. My mother said nothing. I held my breath. What would Siobhan say? I could hear her crying softly and then she said, in a very steady voice, which sounded like someone much older was speaking, 'I'm very grateful to you for offering me a way out, but I could never forgive myself if I had an abortion. I love Liam and I'm happy to marry him. I'm sorry not to be going to college and for letting everyone down, but I know I'd be more unhappy if I murdered this child.'

Sister Patricia had done a good job on Siobhan. She didn't even take a few minutes to think it over.

'Are you sure, pet?' said Auntie Nuala. 'You're such a bright girl, you've your whole life ahead of you.'

'I'm sure.'

My mother finally spoke. 'I think you've made the right decision, love. We'll all help you. Don't take your father's outburst to heart. He's just very upset. He doesn't even know what he's saying. He thinks the world of you and he's disappointed, that's all, but he'll get over it. We all will. Don't worry, pet,' she said, hugging Siobhan, and stroking her hair. 'Now, Nuala, in God's name will you open that bottle of wine? I'm in need of a drink.'

9

I couldn't sleep that night. My head was spinning. I felt as if I'd aged at least three years. Having tossed and turned for hours, I finally got up and went downstairs for some hot chocolate. As I was walking past the lounge, I could hear my father crying softly. My first instinct was to bolt back to bed—I'd had quite enough emotion for one day. But I knew that would be mean and selfish. Sister Patricia always said that compassion and kindness would lead you to heaven. You only had to look at Mother Teresa, she said, to see a living example of what miracles compassion and kindness could perform. I decided on a compromise. I'd go and make my hot chocolate, and if I could still hear him crying on my way back to bed, I'd go in and be saintly.

After a nice hot cup of Nesquik I felt decidedly better and very sleepy. I tiptoed past the lounge, praying to anyone who'd listen for the crying to have stopped. But it hadn't. It had got worse. Shit, I was knackered and a fifteen-year-old needs her sleep, I thought. But then I looked up and saw one of the fifteen pictures of the Pope staring down at me and knew I had to go in.

My father was sitting in his big green velvet chair (all our furniture was green, our national colour) and crying into his hankie. He looked old and distraught. I took a deep breath and went over to him. 'Dad? Are you OK?'

I realized it wasn't the most intelligent or comforting thing to say, but I was new at this.

He tried to talk and I made out, '. . . ruined . . . work . . . for nothing . . . shame . . . eldest . . . beautiful . . .'

'It's OK, Dad. It'll be all right. They'll get married and everything will be OK.'

'It'll be a sham of a marriage,' he wailed. 'I've always dreamt of having a big wedding. The best of everything, all the relations over from Ireland . . . Me walking her up the aisle, as proud as Punch. I've been saving for it for years. Now it'll be a fiasco. My beautiful Siobhan, how did it all go so wrong? I blame myself. I should never have moved to this country with its wayward morals. But what could I do? I had to get out of Ireland and make a life for myself, and sure haven't I helped out my brothers? What a mess. I'll never have a lovely wedding now . . .'

As my father debated with himself on the pros and cons of moving to England, I fumed. How dare he say he'd never have a lovely wedding? What about me? What about dreaming of walking me up the aisle? Where was I in his matrimonial savings plan? He'd obviously taken one look at me when I was born and said, 'Stuff that for a game of soldiers. No point putting my hard-earned cash away for that one. She'll never get a guy to marry her.'

Mind you, I thought, suddenly remembering my fiasco on Friday night, he was right. I never would get married. I couldn't even snog a guy without causing mayhem. I began to cry as the image of my life of loneliness rolled out before me. Even my own father didn't think I had a hope in hell.

He handed me his hankie and smiled at me. 'Poor old Niamh. It's been a shock for you too,' he said, patting my head. 'Come on, it's way past your bedtime and you've school tomorrow.'

'School? I can't go to school tomorrow, Dad. Everyone will be looking at me. Besides, I'm suffering from traumatic shock. I want to stay at home tomorrow with Siobhan and Mum. I'll go in on Tuesday.'

'You'll go to school tomorrow and act as if nothing has happened. Nobody knows anything yet, and until we speak to Liam's parents no decision will be made. I've one daughter with her future ruined, I won't have another. You'll go to school and concentrate on your books. I want no nonsense out of you, Niamh. I'm going to ask Sister Patricia to keep an extra eye on you. I'll be damned if this happens again. In fact, I've a good mind to send you to boarding-school in Ireland.'

'*Nooooo*, Dad, don't do that. I promise I'll be good. I swear I will!'

'Go on now, off to bed with you. I'm too tired to argue. I'll see you in the morning.' And with that he shuffled upstairs in his slippers, shoulders slumped.

Could this day get any worse? Now I was to be banished to boarding-school in Bally-go-sideways because Siobhan was an old slapper. The injustice of it!

First I was always in the wrong because the perfect Siobhan was always in the right, and now that she'd gone and got herself up the duff, I was being punished too. I couldn't win. No matter what she did, I suffered. My sympathy for her was fading rapidly.

When I got back to my room the fallen woman was waiting for me, weeping into my pillow, making it wet and soggy and snotty—yuck. I was all out of compassion so I grunted at her to move over and climbed in, grabbing my pillow and turning it snotty side down.

'What were you talking to Dad about? Was he giving out about me? What did he say? Do you think he'll forgive me?'

'No, I don't think he will,' I said grumpily.

She started so howl at this news and I felt a bit guilty. 'Of course he'll forgive you. You know what Dad's like. He always blows his top and rants and raves and then he calms down. He'll be fine tomorrow. I'm really tired, I need to sleep now.'

Siobhan sighed and blew her nose. 'It wouldn't be so bad for him if it was you. He expects you to mess up. He always had me on a pedestal. I'm his favourite, that's what makes it so bad. I don't think he'll ever get over it.'

'Well, maybe you should have thought about that when you were having sex with Liam.' I was fed up with Siobhan's moaning, and her insensitive remarks about being Dad's favourite child.

'Liam said he knew what he was doing. He said we didn't need condoms because he'd pull out early.'

Oh, God, not this—not details. The last thing I wanted to hear was what Liam did and said during sex. Gross! The thought of the two of them at it was making me feel ill. She rambled on about Liam's early-exit plans and I had to shut her up. 'Do you love him, Siobh? Do you want to marry him?'

'Of course I love him. What type of a person do you think I am? I would never have had sex with him if I didn't love him. That's why I thought it was OK, because we were always going to get married. Liam said so. As soon as we finished college we were going to get married.'

'So you don't mind if you have to marry him now?'

'No. I love Liam and I want to have his baby. It's a mortal sin to think of any other options. I never really wanted to go to college. I only said I did to please Mum.'

I knew she was lying because her voice was shaking—and, anyway, I knew how badly she wanted to go to college. She wanted to be the first O'Flaherty to go to university. She had told me so a million times. I was the one who wasn't interested in going, but not because I wanted to shack up with an Irish dancer who lied about sperm control. Still, if Siobhan was going to play pretend, I would too. 'Sure college is crap. Who wants to waste three years studying when you could be married and have a family instead?' I said, mustering as much enthusiasm as I could at three a.m.

'Yes, but, Niamh, not everyone is lucky enough to meet the man of their dreams at my age. Some girls find it hard to meet boys. But don't worry, I'm sure you'll find someone eventually.'

Condescending cow, after I had been so nice to

her.

'Yeah, well, I wouldn't worry about me, Siobhan, because thanks to you behaving like a cheap tart, I'm being sent to boarding-school in Ireland. Get out now. I'm tired and I want to go to sleep. It may be my last night under this roof.'

I pushed her off the bed and shoved her out of the door before she could think of a bitchy retort. I climbed under the covers and was asleep before my head touched the pillow.

* * *

What seemed like a mere thirty seconds later, my mother came to wake me for school. I was exhausted. I begged and pleaded with her to let me stay at home. I told her I'd only had five minutes' sleep and I felt awful. She looked pretty rough herself. Her face was puffy and her eyes were like two tiny raisins in the back of her head. She felt my forehead and sighed. 'Well, you do feel a bit hot and you do look tired, pet. Maybe just this once.'

I couldn't believe my luck. I was never allowed to stay at home from school. Even if my leg had been ripped off in a car crash, I'd have been given two Anadin with a glass of boiled red lemonade and sent off on my merry—or not so merry—way. Nobody stayed home from school in our house. Ever.

'Thanks, Mum. I really do feel bad. I'm not pretending, I swear.'

I was always prone to dramatics and she normally reprimanded me for it, but that day she just ruffled my hair. 'Niamh, I want you to listen to me for a minute. Really listen.'

I hoped she wasn't going to launch into the birds-and-bees chat. I was fifteen, for goodness' sake.

'What has happened to Siobhan is awful. It has ruined her chances of going to college, getting a proper education, having a career and the freedom to choose what she wants to do with her life. Women my age would kill for those opportunities. Your generation are so much freer. Don't waste it, Niamh—make something of your life. Every decision you make affects your future. Siobhan made a mistake and she's going to pay for it for a long time to come. So be very careful when you make your choices. Think them through first. Weigh up the pros and cons and then decide. The world is your oyster. Study hard, then go out and travel the world, experience different cultures and countries. Live your life to the full. Now, try to sleep and I'll come in later to check on you.'

'OK. Thanks, Mum.'

'You'll be the first O'Flaherty to go to university if I have to sit the exams for you myself. I want you to have those opportunities I could only dream of. So after today you're to focus on your school work. All right?'

'Yes, Mum, I will. I promise.'

She patted my hand and as she opened the door she said, over her shoulder, 'Oh, and, Niamh, there will be no more tap dancing.'

Irish Daily News

'What women mean when . . .'

Niamh O'Flaherty

Beware when we say, 'Fine,' accompanied by a raised hand: this is a very dangerous area. When a woman says, 'Fine,' with a raised hand it means she's furious with you but doesn't want to argue with you any more.

When a man says, 'Fine,' he means 'Fine' (as in OK—no hidden meaning).

When a woman says she'll be ready in 'five minutes' she doesn't mean five minutes. She means she'll be ready when she's ready. If all is going well and she fits into the outfit she wants to wear and her hair turns out OK, you should be looking at twenty minutes. However, if she doesn't fit into the outfit she wants to wear or her hair frizzes up, you could be looking at a good hour during which there will definitely be tears and vows never to eat again.

When a man says he'll be ready in five minutes, he's actually ready but wants to catch five minutes of the football without being nagged.

When a woman is asked what she wants to do for her birthday and she says, 'Nothing', beware. 'Nothing' is code for 'I want something really special, but I don't want to have to tell you. I want you to surprise me with your thoughtful present and romantic gestures.' It does not mean that she wants nothing. Should you do nothing for her on her birthday, believe me, she will throw all of the toys out of the pram.

A man will never say he wants 'Nothing'. He'll ask for sex.

When a woman prefaces a sentence with 'Oh, by the way'—run for cover. We only use 'Oh, by the way' when we've heard something negative about you. 'Oh, by the way' means you're in big trouble.

A man would never say, 'Oh, by the way,' unless maybe he was gay.

A loud sigh is often misinterpreted by men as a sign of tiredness in their partner. What it actually means is that she is feeling unloved, unappreciated and undervalued. When you hear the big sigh, pay attention. A storm is brewing.

A loud sigh in a man means he's just had great sex.

On the other hand if a woman lets out a gentle, soft sigh, it means that she's happy. Don't ruin the moment by saying or doing anything. If we're soft-sighing, we're content. Don't think it's a good time to tell us you've booked a five-day rugby trip with the lads.

A gentle sigh in a man means he's just had good sex.

When a woman says, 'Thanks a lot,' it really doesn't have anything to do with gratitude. A woman will say, 'Thanks a lot,' when she's annoyed. It can often be followed by a 'loud sigh', never a soft one. She is not content, she is angry, and you have done something to annoy her. Rack your brains, figure out what it was and apologize before she implodes.

When a man says, 'Thanks a lot,' he is grateful for something—usually food, being left in peace to watch sport, or sex.

10

Dublin, December 1998

I was hugely relieved that I had managed to persuade Pierre it was too early to introduce him to my mother. He had no idea how conservative my parents were. I knew they were going to react badly when I told them my boyfriend was black. To get my mind off it all, I went to work to finish my column.

While I was typing, Emily came to read it over my shoulder.

'So, is the love affair still going well?'

'Amazingly.'

'Oh, God, you're literally glowing with happiness. It's sickening.'

'Sorry, I can't help it.' I grinned.

'Is it really that great?'

'Brace yourself—it's incredible.'

'Doesn't he ever do anything that annoys you?'

'Nope.'

'Don't you get sick of looking at each other?'

'I can't get enough of him.'

'OK, now I'm depressed.'

'Look, if it can happen to me, it can happen to anyone. This should be giving you hope.'

'If only he had a brother.' She groaned. 'Have you told your family yet?'

'No, and my mum's flying in tonight for the weekend.'

'So she'll meet Pierre?'

'Not exactly. I've decided to wait a bit. I want to have another few months of this cocooned bliss before I tell my parents.'

'How do you think they'll react to him being black?'

'How would yours react?' I asked.

'Not well. My mother still clutches her bag when she sees a black fella walking towards her,' she said, giggling. 'Ireland's only recently come out of the dark ages. But I'm sure your parents will be more enlightened, having lived in England for so long.'

'I wouldn't bet on it.' I sighed. 'I'd better go, I don't want to be late for dinner.'

'Good luck!' my friend called after me.

* * *

I arrived at my grandparents' house to find Granny Byrne on her own, preparing the meal. Granddad had gone to collect Mum from the airport. Granny was worried about him. 'He shouldn't really be driving. His eyesight's got very bad, but he wanted to pick up his little girl, so I let him at it.'

I smiled at the idea of my mother still being referred to as a little girl. It was sweet. You never stopped being a parent and you never stopped being a child.

'Sorry I haven't called in for a while. Work's been hectic. How have you been?' I asked, taking my coat off.

'Not too bad, thanks. We're keeping busy going to our friends' funerals. They're dropping like flies.'

'Oh, Granny, that's awful.'

'That's life.' She shrugged. 'We give them marks out of ten for turnout, quality of coffin and post-funeral refreshments. The best so far has been May Mespil's. They had a sit-down lunch at the Four Seasons. Can you imagine? It was very swanky altogether. I said to your granddad, we'll have to remortgage the house to pay for our send-offs. It's got very competitive and we don't want to be letting the side down.' She winked.

'Isn't it a bit morbid?'

'You have to laugh, pet. Your granddad's eighty-three and I'm eighty-one. We're not getting any younger.'

I shuddered. I couldn't bear the thought of anything happening to either of my grandparents. They were the loveliest people I knew and for some reason had always had that soft spot for me, possibly because I was the underdog in the family. It had been wonderful to grow up basking in their support.

'And for the record,' Granny added, 'if I get Alzheimer's, put a pillow over my face.'

'Your request is noted. Now, can we please change the subject? What shall I do to help?'

'You can chop these carrots,' said Granny, handing me a knife. 'How are things with you?'

'Brilliant.'

'Brilliant?' she repeated. 'You've never said that in your life. What's going on?'

'Nothing,' I said, turning a deep shade of red. Damn. I should have been more careful.

'Niamh O'Flaherty, are you in love?'

'No!' I protested.

'You are too. It's written all over your face.'

'I'm not. Seriously, Granny, I'm just hot,' I said, beginning to sweat under the scrutiny.

'Don't lie to me, young lady,' she said, waving a carrot at me. 'I know you far too well. Who is he?'

'No one . . . I . . . It's just someone I met a few weeks ago,' I said, shaving a few months off the relationship. 'It's very early days, nothing to make a fuss about. I don't want to talk about it. There's nothing to say. Honestly.'

Granny put her arm round my shoulders. 'Oh dear, it's worse than I thought, you're completely smitten. It's all right, I won't ask you any more questions. I just hope he's a nice boy and worthy of you.'

'He is, believe me. He really is.'

'I'm so pleased for you, pet, you deserve it.'

I wanted desperately to spill my heart out to her about Pierre, but for once in my life I took the sensible option, clamped my mouth shut and kept busy helping with dinner. By the time Granddad and Mum had arrived in from the airport, I'd managed to steer Granny away from talk of my romance.

'Hello, sweetheart,' Granny said, giving Mum a kiss.

'Hello, pet,' Mum said, giving me a kiss.

'Happy birthday,' I said, giving Granddad a kiss.

'Haven't seen you in a while,' he said. 'That

newspaper must be keeping you very busy. That, or you've a new lad who's taking up your time.' He grinned.

I turned round quickly and went to get some wine so they wouldn't see me going red again. My God, what was wrong with me? I hadn't blushed so much since Siobhan was breastfeeding and had made me go down and ask the cute chemist for nipple cream.

We sat down and, after an off-tune rendition of 'Happy Birthday', had dinner. Granny Byrne did a great roast chicken. It was comfort food at its best, lashings of stuffing and roast potatoes lathered in butter.

'How's everyone at home?' Granny asked Mum.

'Not too bad, thanks. Apparently Finn is making a big difference to the business. Mick says he can't believe how good he is with numbers. He's come up with all these new ways to cut costs and improve efficiency. Mick says he'll be able to retire soon and hand it over to him.'

'That's great news,' said Granddad.

'I don't know about that. What would I do with my husband under my feet all day? I prefer him out at work,' said Mum.

'Men need to be out and about,' Granny said. 'When your dad retired, it was a total nightmare. He followed me round all day asking what I was doing and complaining about the house being a mess. I was driven demented.'

'I did not,' Granddad objected.

'Yes, you did, I remember it all too well. You were very grumpy for the first few months until you took up golf,' said Mum.

'Slanderous accusations to be making on my

birthday,' muttered Granddad.

'Maybe that's what Dad needs to do,' I suggested.

'You need patience to play golf,' Mum said, 'and that's one virtue your father is not blessed with.'

'True,' we all agreed.

'How's Siobhan getting on?' Granny asked.

'You know Siobhan. She wants to get pregnant again. I told her five children is enough. She's worn out chasing after them and Muireann can be a handful at times. She's very stubborn.'

'She just knows what she wants. I don't think she's stubborn,' I said, defending my niece.

'Of course you don't because she takes after you,' laughed Mum.

'I'm not stubborn!' I said, shocked at the accusation.

'Niamh,' said Mum, 'remember the tap-dancing lessons? You're the most stubborn person I know, apart from your father.'

'Being stubborn isn't necessarily a bad thing,' said Granddad. 'As long as you channel it correctly.'

'Like how?' I asked.

'Standing by your convictions when other people disagree with you. Not being swayed by the crowd . . . that kind of thing.'

Little did he know how much my stubbornness was going to be tested when word of my black boyfriend got out. It was a good thing I'd inherited this gene. I'd need to lean on it very soon.

'Anyway, Miss Stubborn, what have you been up to? Any news?' Mum asked.

'She's in love,' Granny burst out.

'Granny!' I couldn't believe she'd blabbed. Shit!

Now I was going to get the bloody Spanish Inquisition.

'Sorry, pet, I'm just excited for you and I know your mum'll be delighted to hear you've met a nice man.'

'Niamh?' Mum turned to me.

'It's nothing. It's only just started, and we're still getting to know each other.'

'What's his name? Where did you meet him? What does he do?' Mum demanded.

'We met in a coffee shop, he's an academic and his name is . . . uhm . . . Pierre.'

'Pierre?' said Mum.

'French,' said Granddad.

'How romantic!' said Granny.

'Your father won't like that,' said Mum. 'He thinks the French are a slippery lot.'

'Why?' I asked, beginning to panic. His Frenchness was the least of my worries.

'Because they surrendered to the Germans in the Second World War.'

The Second World War? Was she kidding me? 'Well, he's more English than French because he was brought up in Oxford,' I said, trying to distance Pierre and his family from the Vichy government of 1940. Give a girl a break!

'Lovely,' said Granny.

'Nice part of the world, Oxford,' said Granddad.

'Hmmm,' said Mum, decidedly unimpressed.

'More wine?' I asked, pouring myself a large glass.

*   *   *

I spent the rest of the weekend fudging Mum's

probing questions about my relationship and trying to keep her as busy as possible so that she wouldn't break me. My mother was a total pro when it came to getting information out of people, and I knew that, given enough time, she'd wear me down with her questioning. The KGB could have used her. She was relentless.

I took her shopping, to the theatre, art galleries, exhibitions. She didn't have time to grill me until we sat down to dinner after a dreadful play that I'd booked at the last minute to stop her quizzing me.

'As you know, I'm getting the first flight home tomorrow morning,' she said.

I nodded.

'In case you think I hadn't noticed that you've avoided me coming to see your flat, you're wrong. Now, I want you to be honest with me. Is that man living there with you?'

'No, Mum, he isn't,' I said, relieved at not having to lie.

'I'm very glad to hear it. Now, why haven't you introduced me to him? Who are you ashamed of? Me or him?'

'Come on, Mum, don't be silly. I'm not ashamed of anyone. It's just that it's very early in the relationship and I want to get to know Pierre better myself before I introduce him to anyone else. We could break up in the morning. But if we're still going out the next time you come over, I'll introduce you to him. I promise.'

She sniffed. 'Well, if you do get serious about this boy, you'd better let me know. I'll need to work on your father. He won't like it that he's French or English or whatever mixture he is. He wants you to meet a nice Irish boy and settle down here in Ireland. He plans to move back when he retires.'

'What about you?'

'I'd like you to meet a nice boy, come back to London and live near us. I want all my children close to me. I miss you.'

'I miss you too, Mum,' I said, squeezing her hand. 'Do you want to move back to Ballyduff when Dad retires?'

'Not at all. Sure what would I do all day? My life is in London. Our family and friends live there. We talk about moving back, but none of us has and none of us will. It's a very different Ireland from the one we left behind. Once Granny and Granddad are gone I doubt I'll come back at all. Your father has romantic notions of us buying a little cottage in the middle of nowhere. What in God's name would we do? We'd kill each other. We're used to having the family around us, coming and going day and night. I like being able to go to the pictures or the theatre or to a new restaurant. I know we don't do it often, but I like the fact that it's there if we want it.'

'How are you going to get round Dad? He's been talking about retiring to Ireland since he stepped off the boat in Liverpool thirty-five years ago.'

'You leave your father to me. I know exactly how to deal with him.'

'How?' I asked, desperate for some tips on how to get Dad to change his mind.

'It takes a lot of patience. You plant the ideas drop by drop, give him time to mull them over, and he ends up thinking they were his ideas in the first place so everyone's happy. Men are all the same,

Niamh. They need to think they're in control but, really, the women are the ones steering from behind.'

'So if I did get serious about Pierre, you'd help me with Dad?' I asked.

'Once I've met him and approved of him, I'll help to bring your father round to the idea of a foreign boyfriend. But it won't be easy.'

'Thanks, Mum,' I said, relieved.

'Is he handsome?'

'Very.'

'Debonair like all the French men?'

'Extremely.'

'Charming?'

'Incredibly.'

'Are you happy, pet?'

'Yes, Mum,' I said, forcing myself not to get emotional and tell her how in love I was and how happy Pierre made me and how I knew he was The One.

'Well, I hope it works out for you. Keep me posted on how it goes. I can pop over any time to meet him.'

'I will, Mum, I promise. And thanks for agreeing to help with Dad, if I need it.'

She smiled at me. 'Don't you worry. I could persuade your father that black was white.'

11

'So, how's your mum?' asked Pierre, when I got back from dropping Mum to my grandparents' house where she was spending the night.

'Good, thanks,' I said.

'Did she ask you if you had a nice boyfriend?' he asked, grinning at me.

'No.'

'Really? The first thing my mother asks when she sees me is if I have a nice girlfriend.'

'My granny did, though, and when I told her I was seeing someone she went and blurted it out to Mum.'

'What did your mum say?'

'She asked if you were good-looking, debonair, charming and if I was happy.'

'And?'

'Ugly, dresses like a homeless person, manners of a caveman but, yes, blissfully happy.'

'Did you tell her we were living together?'

'No.'

'Did you tell her I was older?'

'No.'

'Black?'

'It didn't come up.'

'So what exactly did you tell her?'

'That your name was Pierre and you were an academic.'

'What did she say to that?'

'She said it was a pity you were French because Dad thinks the French are a slippery lot.'

'I'm not exactly French.'

'It's a technicality.'

'A big one.'

'One that can wait a while to be exposed.'

'Why does your father think the French are slippery?'

'Because they gave in to the Germans.'

Pierre laughed. 'Are you serious?'

'Deadly.'

'That's a lot to be tarnished with.'

'I know. Hopefully when he finds out you're from an overseas department of France that'll work in your favour.'

'Overseas department of France! Niamh, I'm impressed.'

'I looked it up on the Internet.'

'Not just a pretty face.'

'And don't you forget it.'

'Did you tell your mother anything else about me, or was that it?'

'I just told her I'd met someone I liked but it was still early in the relationship and I wanted to get to know you better before introducing you to the family.'

'Oh,' he said, a bit crestfallen.

'What I didn't tell her was that I'd met the person I want to spend the rest of my life with. That I'm so happy I want to shout it out loud when I'm walking down the street. That I can't believe you love me. That I keep thinking I'm going to wake up and realize it was just a lovely dream. That I love you so much it scares me. That I'm willing to face the wrath of my father because I know you're my soulmate.'

'Oh,' he said.

'Speechless?'

'No, I just had a flashback to my time in the trenches before we surrendered.'

'Hilarious.'

'You're not the only funny one around here.'

'At least I get paid for it.'

'*Touché*,' said Pierre.

'Are you OK about not meeting my mother?'

'For now. But you're going to have to tell them about me some time.'

'I know, but not now. Let's not open the floodgates yet. I'd like to have some more time to ourselves first.'

'To get to know me better,' said Pierre.

'Exactly.'

'I think you know me pretty well.'

'There's always more to learn.'

'What's my favourite colour?'

'Red.'

'Oh,' he said, surprised I'd got it right.

'What's mine?' I asked.

'Green.'

'I hate green.'

'No, you don't.'

'Yes, I do. When have you ever seen me wear green?'

'That jumper you always wear is green.'

'It's blue! Turquoise blue.'

'Well, it looks green.'

'No, it doesn't,' I huffed.

'Let's move on,' he said wisely. 'What's my favourite movie?'

'You claim it's *12 Angry Men*, but it's really *City Slickers*.'

'Slander.'

'Sue me. What's mine?'

'You say it's *The Mission* but it's actually *Steel Magnolias*.'

'How did you know that?' I said, impressed.

'You told me.'

'Oh.'

'OK, what's my favourite book?' he asked, warming to the game.

'Norman Mailer's *The Naked and the Dead*. What's mine?'

'*Pride and Prejudice*.'

'No, it isn't. Where did you get that from?'

'I thought all women loved it.'

'Well, I don't,' I snapped.

'What is your favourite book then?'

'*The Prince of Tides*.'

'Seriously?'

'Yes.'

'The one with Barbra Streisand?'

'That's the film. The book's much better.'

'OK. Music. Favourite song.'

' "Mack The Knife".'

'You're good at this,' he said, smiling at me.

'Well, you're not. Mine?'

'The one Whitney Houston sang—"I Love You" or whatever it's called.'

' "I Will Always Love You". I hate that song! You don't know me at all. You just guessed that cheesy one because you think all women like it. For your information my favourite song ever is "She's Always A Woman to Me".'

'I like that one too,' he said, beginning to sing it.

'Don't try to placate me. I'm furious. I know everything you like and you haven't a clue about me. Do you ever listen? Do you care? I'm putting myself on the line for this relationship,' I said, upset. Didn't he get it? My father might well disown me for this and Pierre couldn't even get my favourite song right.

'Do I care?' he said quietly. 'I think you know that I care very much. And as for not knowing you, I might not know what your favourite song is, but I do know this. You like your scrambled eggs milky.

You rinse your teeth three times after brushing. You hate the rain because it makes your hair fuzzy. You like dogs and hate cats—you think they're sly. You have a love-hate relationship with Creme Eggs. You love eating them but you always feel sick and guilty afterwards. You don't understand raisins—they're a pointless addition to any dish. You love your family, mini Milky Way bars, *Hello!* magazine, hot chocolate with marshmallows and Oprah, but only when she's interviewing famous guests and not when she's doing the self-help shows.'

I smiled. 'I actually prefer *OK!* to *Hello!* but you're forgiven.'

'Completely?'

'And utterly. There's one area I think still needs work, though,' I said.

'What?' he asked, nervous.

'Bedroom.'

'Fantastic,' he said, picking me up and rushing towards the bed.

12

After my mother's visit, our lives continued as before. We spent all our spare time together, falling more and more in love, until the day Pierre announced that his parents were coming for a visit in a few weeks' time and he wanted me to meet them.

'Now? Already?' I asked, terrified at the prospect.

'It's been five months, darling, I want to show

you off.'

'But what if they don't like me? What if they take one look at me and say, "Are you mad? Get rid of her"?' I groaned.

'Don't be silly, you'll be a big hit.'

I loved it that Pierre was so keen for me to meet his parents, but they were used to sitting across the table from a supermodel type who spoke their language and saved the world in her spare time. How were they going to react to a five-foot-four Irish columnist?

'When exactly are they coming?'

'Three weeks' time. The fifteenth,' he said.

That gave me twenty-one days to become fluent in French, starve myself down a size, and read up on current affairs so I could have stimulating political discussions with them.

But instead of doing all of the above, I did what I always do when I'm nervous—I ate. And I mean everything. I ate everything I could get my hands on and then I ate some more. In the space of two weeks I had put on half a stone and it was not needed. Pierre's cooking had already made me pile on the pounds.

I stepped off the scales. This was ridiculous, I had to calm down. What was I so worried about? Simple. I was worried that they wouldn't like me and Pierre would dump me. And that was something I couldn't bear. I knew if Pierre left me I'd shrivel up and die. I had to make a good impression on his parents. They had to like me.

With a week to go, I swore off food. Having gone five whole hours without eating anything, and feeling thinner already, I wasn't too happy when Pierre arrived home and announced that he was taking me out for a slap-up meal.

'Sorry, I can't.'

'Why not?'

'I'm trying not to eat for the next week. I need to shift a few pounds before the big visit.'

He laughed. 'Niamh, you look great. Now come on, get dressed up, I'm taking you out for a nice meal.'

'Why?'

'Because I need to talk to you about a job offer I've just been made.'

* * *

I squeezed myself into my favourite black dress and swore I'd never eat again after tonight. Pierre had booked L'Assiette, one of the most expensive restaurants in Dublin. We were placed at a cosy table for two in the window and once our food arrived—I had consommé to start: how anyone can justify charging for hot water with an Oxo cube in it is beyond me—Pierre told me his news.

'I've been offered a professorship at the University of British Columbia in Vancouver.'

My spoon froze in mid-air. 'Did you just say Vancouver?'

'Yes.'

'As in Canada?'

'The very one.'

I began to cry. 'I knew it! I knew it was too good to be true! You're going to bugger off to Canada and leave me. You'll pretend to try a long-distance relationship for a month or two, then dump me via email,' I sobbed.

'Niamh, listen to me, you lunatic. I'm not going

anywhere without you. I've been offered the job and I wanted to talk to you about it. It's an amazing opportunity and I want you to come with me.'

'To Canada?'

'Yes. I want us to go together. It'll be fantastic. Vancouver's supposed to be amazing.'

'So you're not trying to get rid of me?'

'No, you idiot. I love you. I wouldn't move down the road without you. So, what do you think?'

'Hang on,' I said, and had a swig of wine. 'I need to settle my nerves. You want me to go with you.'

'Yes.'

'But I like it here. Everything's perfect. If we change things something might go wrong.'

'What's going to go wrong?'

'I dunno. You might not like me in Canada.'

'Why not?'

'Because it's freezing and I look stupid in Puffa jackets and I won't know anyone and I won't have a job and I'll be clingy and dependent, and if we break up, I'll be stuck on my own in bloody Vancouver in minus forty degrees looking like an Oompa Loompa in my snow jacket.'

'We're not going to break up.'

'You don't know that for sure.'

'Yes, I do.'

'No, you don't.'

'Will you shut up and listen to me?'

'Excuse me!'

'We're not going to break up because we're going to get married.'

I stared at him, open-mouthed. 'Was that a proposal?'

'Yes.' He winced.

'But you didn't ask me. You told me.'

'I know. It came out wrong, I'm sorry. I had this big speech prepared but I got nervous. You threw me off guard with the crying and ranting.'

'So it's my fault?'

'Kind of. I just didn't expect you to react like that about Vancouver. I thought you'd be pleased. I thought you liked adventure.'

'I only like adventure when it's been organized by me. You might want to remember that for the future. I'm having a heart-attack here, in case you hadn't noticed.'

'I'm sorry, darling. Will you please marry me?'

'I'll have to think about it.'

'OK.'

Silence.

'Have you made up your mind?'

'Not yet.'

Silence.

'Now?'

'Are you asking because you don't want to go to Canada on your own?'

'No! This is supposed to be a romantic moment, not a debate about Canada.'

'I'm sorry, but it's all a bit out of the blue. When would we have to go to Vancouver?'

'I need to be there by June to spend the summer getting set up, so we've got over three months.'

'Do you want to get married before we go?'

'That's the general idea, yes.'

'But it takes ages to organize a wedding.'

'You said your sister's was organized in days.'

'That's because she was pregnant.'

'We've got three months. I'm sure we can manage.'

'But my family haven't even met you yet.'

'So introduce me to them.'

'But I need to prepare them first.'

'Get on with it, then.'

'You've just pounced this on me.'

'I only got the offer yesterday.'

'I knew there was something up with you last night. You were behaving very strangely.'

'I was trying to work up the courage to propose.'

'Were you nervous?'

'Terrified.'

'Really?'

'Yes.'

'Why?'

'In case you said no.'

'Why would I do that?'

'I don't know. Women are weird. I wasn't sure you'd want to move to Canada.'

'If I say no to Canada, is the proposal withdrawn?'

'Of course not. I've wanted to marry you since the day we met. I'd like to take this job in Vancouver, but if you don't want to move there, we'll come up with a Plan B.'

'Do the Canadians have a good sense of humour?'

'I'm sure they do.'

'Where will we live?'

'The university will provide us with a house.'

'Is it nice?'

'I don't know, I haven't accepted the job yet. So, will you?'

'What?'

'Marry me, come to Vancouver and spend the rest of your life with me.'

'Yes, yes, and most definitely yes.' I laughed and leant in to kiss my husband-to-be.

13

Once the shock of Vancouver and the marriage proposal had worn off, my mind began to de-fog.

'We really don't have much time. Your parents are over next week and then I'll have to go home and do some bomb-dropping. Actually, it could work out well. I'll go home for St Patrick's weekend and tell them then.'

'We'll go together,' said Pierre.

'No. Let me pave the way first, then you fly over and meet everyone.'

'All right.'

'I just need to ask you one more time. Are you absolutely sure you want to marry me? You'll be taking on my family and it's not going to be easy.'

'Yes, I am. Besides, I'm marrying you, not your family.'

'Technically, yes, but in my family's case they tend to get very involved.'

'Niamh, we're getting married and moving to Vancouver, which is a long way away so your family won't really be a problem.'

'They'll come and visit, believe me,' I said, remembering the time my cousin had moved to New York and a steady stream of relatives, friends of relatives, colleagues of relatives, neighbours of relatives and pretty much anyone his relatives had ever spoken to arrived on his doorstep every week. He'd gone to New York to get away for a while and ended up running an Irish B-and-B.

'Great. I hope they do,' said Pierre.

'Do you know anything about Vancouver?' I asked.

'I looked it up last night. It has a population of almost two million people, you can ski and sail in the same day. It has great restaurants, shops and galleries. The population is extremely diverse, so we'll fit right in.'

'Does it get to minus forty in the winter? Will we have to live underground for months at a time wearing Puffa jackets to bed?'

Pierre grinned. 'As attractive as that sounds, no, we won't. Apparently it rarely goes below zero because it's on the coast. But it's close to Whistler, which is supposed to be incredible for skiing.'

'I don't know how to ski.'

'I'll teach you.'

'I have really bad co-ordination.'

'You'll be fine. I'll help you.'

'Pierre.'

'Yes.'

'I'm scared.'

'Of what?'

'Everything.'

'Don't worry, it's all going to be fine.'

'What if I can't get a job and I end up sitting in the house all day waiting for you to come home and being resentful of you because my career is down the toilet and I've no friends and no one to talk to, while you're out teaching ski-toned, leggy Canadian young ones about linguistics?'

'I've already asked the dean of the university to put out feelers for you with local editors. Once they read your columns, they'll snap you up.'

'I hope so. I'll go mad with nothing to do.'

'Actually, darling, I was hoping we could start a family sooner rather than later,' Pierre admitted.

'Already?'

'I'm forty-two. I don't want to be too old to kick a ball around with my kids. I'll be sixty-three when they turn twenty-one. That's old.'

'So that's why you're taking me to Canada. To get me barefoot and pregnant.'

'It'd be nice to have children.'

'Yes, but I'm still trying to get my head round marriage and emigration to another continent. I don't have the head space for kids.'

'But you wouldn't be against having them quickly?'

'No. But you're not that old and I'm young, so we don't need to panic yet. Can I enjoy my honeymoon first?'

'All right. You can have those two weeks off, but after that it's down to making babies.'

'Two weeks? Where are we off to?'

'It's a surprise.'

'Have you booked it yet?'

'I was waiting to propose first.'

'Wise move.'

'Thanks.'

'A few pointers for you. I don't like humidity, creepy-crawlies, any kind of trekking, climbing or mountaineering. I don't like really intense heat because I get heat rash. I'm not a fan of camping. I think spas are overrated. How many massages can a person get? I like a bit of culture but not too much, because then you feel guilty if you haven't gone to see all the museums and galleries. I prefer pools to beaches—I find sand high maintenance. I prefer small, family-type hotels to big flashy ones. A fishing village an hour's drive from a cool city would be great.' I grinned.

'Could you be more specific?' said Pierre.

'Seeing as this is probably my last holiday before I get pregnant and my life is over, I think I'm entitled to be fussy.'

'No donkey-trekking in the Himalayas?'

'Not unless you want to go to Vancouver alone.'

'So, you're OK about having children soon?'

'How many were you planning on having?'

'Six.'

'Well, you need to propose to someone else.'

'Four?'

'Let's start with one and see how we go.'

'I don't want an only child. I'd like them to have siblings.'

'You turned out OK.'

'I was lonely.'

'OK, two kids.'

'Let's keep an open mind.'

'Three is my final offer. Take it or leave it.'

'I prefer even numbers but I'll take it.'

'How magnanimous of you.'

'I try to be.'

'Hey.'

'What?'

'Thanks for asking.'

'Isn't it fairly normal practice for a man to ask his wife-to-be if she wants to have children?'

'I mean the marriage proposal.'

'Even though I botched it up?'

'Yes.'

'You're very welcome. And thank you.'

'For what?'

'For saying yes.'

*   *   *

The next day we went to several jewellers and picked out a beautiful solitaire. I couldn't stop staring at it. The ring made the whole thing so real. I was Pierre's fiancée! His wife-to-be! I was in seventh heaven and dying to tell my family the good news, but I couldn't. It would have to wait until St Patrick's weekend when I went home.

In the meantime I had to starve myself for my in-laws' imminent visit, keep up with current affairs . . . and write a column.

Irish Daily News

'The new girlfriend'

Niamh O'Flaherty

When a man's best friend turns up in the pub with a new young girlfriend, who is drop-dead gorgeous, his friend whoops. He high-fives him, says how the hell did a dog like you manage to pick up a babe like that, and then he goes home that night dying to tell his wife all about her.

HUSBAND: 'I just met Tim's new girlfriend. She's a young one.'
WIFE: 'How young?'
HUSBAND: 'I dunno, about twenty-four, twenty-five. A total fox, fair play to him.'
WIFE, *buttoning up her fleecy pyjamas*: 'What do you mean "fox"?'
HUSBAND: 'A cracking-looking girl.'
WIFE, *getting grumpy*: 'In what way? What's so amazing about her?'
HUSBAND: 'She's a six-foot blonde with legs up to her neck. She looks like your one, Cameron Diaz.'
WIFE: 'What? There is no way. Tim's going out with someone who looks like Cameron Diaz? You've had too much to drink. You've got your beer goggles on.'
HUSBAND: 'No, I don't, I said it to Tim and

he said people come up to her and say it all the time. She's the image of her.'

WIFE, *feeling irrationally threatened by a girl she's never even met*: 'I bet she's only using him for his money.'

HUSBAND: 'Apparently she's loaded. She runs her own recruitment agency.'

WIFE: 'I bet you she's one of those high-class hookers. They always have good cover stories. I bet you Tim met her on the Internet.'

HUSBAND: 'That's a terrible accusation. He met her in the gym. They have the same personal trainer.'

WIFE, *furious with herself for being such a jealous wench, but even more annoyed with Tim for going out with a young stick-insect*: 'So, she has to work at keeping the weight off?'

HUSBAND: 'No, she's training for a triathlon.'

Wife now feels violent hatred for this super-fit, super-rich supermodel.

HUSBAND: 'Tim wants us to meet up for a meal on Friday.'

WIFE: 'Tell him we're busy.'

HUSBAND: 'I've already told him we're free.'

WIFE: 'I've nothing to wear, I hate all my clothes.'

HUSBAND: 'Wear your red dress, you always look nice in that.'

WIFE: 'I can't bloody well fit into it. I'm not going out with some rich, successful beanpole, who'll make me look like an old, fat, unsuccessful hag.'

HUSBAND: 'Don't be ridiculous. You're not old or fat and you're not unsuccessful.'

WIFE: 'I'm at least ten years older than this new girl and I'd say a good two stone heavier.'

HUSBAND: 'You look much younger than you are. Besides, she's not that thin.'

WIFE, *raising an eyebrow*: 'I thought she had an incredible figure.'

HUSBAND: 'Actually I think her legs are a bit chunky from all the training.'

WIFE: 'Really?'

HUSBAND: 'Yes, and she doesn't look like Cameron Diaz close up, only from a distance.'

WIFE: 'Do you know who I look like from a distance?'

HUSBAND: 'Who?'

WIFE: 'Humpty bloody Dumpty. And do you know who I look like from close up?'

HUSBAND: 'Who?'

WIFE: 'Humpty Dumpty with boobs.'

HUSBAND: 'You're being silly now.'

WIFE: 'No, I'm being honest. Tell Tim we'll go out with them next month. It'll give me time to lose a stone.'

HUSBAND: 'Do you want me to get the name of their personal trainer?'

Wife glares at husband in manic, serial-killer type way. Husband makes himself scarce.

The new boyfriend

When a woman's best friend turns up in the

pub with a new young boyfriend, who is drop-dead gorgeous, she whoops. She high-fives her friend, says, where did you meet him, he's amazing, and goes home that night dying to tell her husband all about him.

WIFE: 'You're not going to believe this. Tara has a new boyfriend and he's six years younger than her!'
HUSBAND, *glancing up from watching* Match of the Day: 'Cool.'
WIFE: 'He looks like Brad Pitt. I swear he's the image of him.'
HUSBAND: 'Bit like myself then.' *He laughs, patting his beer belly.*
WIFE: 'They want us to go for dinner with them on Friday.'
HUSBAND: 'No can do. I'll be shagging Angelina now she's a free woman.'

14

London, September 1985

When Liam's parents found out that Siobhan was pregnant, they went ballistic. Mr O'Loughlin called my father late that night and an emergency meeting was arranged in our house the following morning to discuss the sorry state of affairs.

The O'Loughlins lived in a big, detached house on Brewer Avenue. Mr O'Loughlin was a very successful lawyer and Mrs O'Loughlin was a lady who lunched. They both had fake English accents. They sounded like they were doing really bad imitations of the Queen. They spent their time trying desperately to socialize with other English professionals, but could never shake their Irishness enough to fit in. They had to make do with being king and queen of the Irish professional set.

They were members of the Irish-owned Westbrook Golf Club (having tried unsuccessfully for ten years to gain admission to Greenlawn Golf Club, where all the public-schoolboys hung out smoking cigars and talking about the fun old days at Eton, being buggered in the showers by the upper sixth). The O'Loughlins only deigned to speak to other successful professionals and sneered at those who had not cast off their Irishness. They drank Earl Grey, shopped in Harrods, ate from Wedgwood plates.

Liam was the youngest of four. His love of and natural talent for Irish dancing were a great source of embarrassment for the O'Loughlins, who abhorred Irish dancing and everyone involved in it. Liam's three older sisters were clones of their mother and the eldest had married a posh English boy, much to her parents' delight—despite the fact that he had no job, and that although his family claimed to be landed gentry they appeared to have no money at all. He was *bona fide* English and the O'Loughlins were beside themselves. He even had a double-barrelled name! They paid for a lavish wedding, paid for the groom's suit, paid for his family to be put up at the Savoy, paid for Mr and Mrs Thompson-Black's wedding outfits, the honeymoon and a house for the happy couple to live in.

The O'Loughlins had done everything in their power to persuade Liam to stop dancing, but he loved it. He was a real natural. His parents never attended any of his performances so mine had felt sorry for him and taken him under their wing. Then he had fallen for Siobhan and the rest is history. My parents were very fond of Liam, but were not fans of his parents. His parents thought Siobhan was a peasant. This was going to be some show-down.

My mother disliked Mrs O'Loughlin intensely. She hated snobs, but she was also a little intimidated by her and her Harrods clothes. She changed ten times and made my father put on his best suit, then change his shirt and tie twice. Finally he exploded. 'What difference does it bloody well make what I'm wearing? Their son has got my daughter pregnant and he's going to marry her or I'll skin him alive.'

'Is it too much to ask that you look respectable when they arrive, and not answer the door in your dusty workboots? Do we have to look like tinkers?'

'I'm not dressing up for those snobs. I am what I am and I'm proud of it.'

'Will you shut up and change that shirt? I won't have them looking down their noses at us, saying Siobhan isn't good enough for them.'

'She's worth twenty of them and you're worth fifty of that stupid woman,' said my father. 'We're a respectable, honest family doing its best to get on. We've never pretended to be anything we're not and I'm not going to start now. We're good people, Annie.'

'I know, sweetheart, I know. You're right, we are what we are. To hell with the O'Loughlins.'

My mother never called my father 'sweetheart', and he only called her mushy names when he was drunk. It was nice, though. It was comforting.

'Oh Danny Boy . . .' The doorbell tinkled. My father stood on the stairs for a few minutes until my mother hissed at him to stop being so childish and let them in.

They stood in the hall, Mr O'Loughlin looking furious, Liam looking terrified and Mrs O'Loughlin looking around with her nose turned up like she'd smelt something nasty.

'Come in and sit down,' my mother urged, in a stilted voice.

They went into the good room. Siobhan came downstairs in her best green dress, her hair tied back in a green bow. She looked really young and really scared. I wished her luck as she went in to face the scary O'Loughlins.

I snuck round the back through the dining room and glued my eye to the crack in the folding doors. I could see Mrs O'Loughlin perched on the edge of the good chair in her expensive suit, reeking of perfume and plastered with makeup.

My father was pouring drinks into the good glasses we only ever used on Christmas Day. Liam and Siobhan were sitting on the couch holding hands, and my mother was beside them, very stiff and awkward. Mr O'Loughlin was standing by the fire. My father handed him a drink.

'Well, Mr O'Flaherty, what's to be done about this terrible situation?' said Mr O'Loughlin, in his finest English accent.

My father took a sip of his drink and said firmly, 'There is only one solution, as I see it. Your son marries my daughter and makes an honest woman of her.'

'Over my dead body,' said Mrs O'Loughlin. 'I have a friend who knows of a place in France where Siobhan can go and have the baby. They'll find a nice home for the child, she can come back here and no one will ever find out what happened. It'll be expensive, they don't take just any girls, but you needn't worry about money. We'll look after it.'

I could see my mother's face slowly turning scarlet.

'Yes, well, we think it's for the best,' said Mr O'Loughlin. 'It will cause the least fuss and disruption and Liam can get on with his studies. As my wife said, we'll be happy to cover the expenses.'

'I don't want Siobhan to be sent to France,' Liam blurted out, coming to life at last.

'Liam.' Mr O'Loughlin scowled at his son. 'We discussed this last night. It's the best solution all round. It will save us a lot of embarrassment.'

'It seems to me that your solution is a little

subjective,' my mother said, a little too loudly. I could see she was struggling to keep calm. 'You are suggesting that we send our seventeen-year-old daughter away to some strange place in France to give birth to a child, then hand it over for adoption, come back and pretend nothing has happened. Why don't we ask Siobhan what she thinks of this wonderful idea?'

Siobhan was glaring at Liam. 'How could you? You promised you wouldn't leave me. I don't want to go to France on my own and give up our baby. You promised we'd get married, Liam. You promised.' She started to cry. 'Don't send me away, Dad, please.'

My father stood up. His hands were shaking, but his voice was steady. 'Now, listen very carefully because I'm only going to say this once. We have no intention of abandoning our daughter in her time of need to a bunch of strangers in France and forcing her to give up her child. Your son will clear up this mess, marry my daughter and make an honest woman of her. If he refuses to marry her, I will cause a scene the like of which has never been witnessed. Every man in my employment will go to your golf club, home and office, and patrol up and down with banners shaming you. The choice is yours. If you want the whole country to know that your son made my daughter pregnant and abandoned her, I'm happy to oblige. Otherwise we have a wedding to organize.'

I have never been more proud of my father. He was wonderful, majestic. I wanted to clap and cheer and jump up and down.

There was a deathly silence in the room. Eventually Mr O'Loughlin spoke: 'Would you mind leaving us alone for a few minutes, Mr O'Flaherty? We're not used to being threatened, and I'd like to talk this over with my wife and son in private.'

My parents and Siobhan left the room. I stayed to hear what happened.

'You stupid boy!' Mr O'Loughlin spat at Liam, his accent raw Irish, not a trace of posh English left. 'You couldn't use condoms like normal boys. You had to get that hussy pregnant and cause this bloody mess. We have no choice now. You'll have to marry her. I won't have our name dragged through the mud by that tinker O'Flaherty. Well, it's your mess, you deal with it. Congratulations. You've ruined your life, and thrown all the opportunities I gave you in my face.'

Liam shrank back in the couch.

Then Mrs O'Loughlin had her say: 'How could you do this to us, Liam? How could you? To get that girl pregnant is the worst thing you could have done. We'll never get over this, never.'

'I'm sorry I've let you down,' Liam mumbled.

'Go and get them back in here. Let's have this sorry mess over with,' Mr O'Loughlin said, ignoring his son.

My family came back in and Mr O'Loughlin said that Liam had agreed to marry Siobhan but he himself wouldn't be putting a penny towards the wedding or his son's future. As far as Mr O'Loughlin was concerned, Liam was on his own. And with that they stormed out of our house and our lives.

Liam stayed behind and apologized. 'I'm very sorry, Mr and Mrs O'Flaherty, for causing all this trouble. I love Siobhan and I do want to marry her.

I'll leave school and get a job so I can support her and the baby. I promise to look after her. I'm sorry for getting Siobhan into this mess and I'll do my best to make her happy.'

My father shook his head. 'It's all right, Liam. I don't want you dropping out of school. You'll be more use to Siobhan with a decent career instead of rushing out and getting a dead-end job. You're a bright lad and you should go on to university. So here's what we're going to do. You'll marry Siobhan and move into the garage. I'll get the lads in to convert it into a little apartment for the two of you. We'll help you out with the baby so you can continue your studies. In a couple of years, when you get a decent job, you can get your own place. Until then, to pay your way, you'll be working for me every weekend on the sites. Treat my daughter well and you'll not hear a cross word from me. We all make mistakes. The important thing is to learn from them and move on. Now, go home and tell your parents the wedding will take place next Saturday in the Church of Our Lady and we'll have a small reception here afterwards.'

And with that my father walked out of the room, head held high, followed by my smiling mother.

15

By the time I got to school on Tuesday, everyone knew about Siobhan. It was the worst-kept secret in the world. Siobhan had called her best friend Jackie the night before to ask her to be bridesmaid so the secret was out.

I was surrounded when I arrived and the gory details were demanded. When did it happen? Where? Why didn't she have an abortion? Was Liam the only boy she'd had sex with? What did she say it was like? Was there loads of blood? What did your parents say? Would the baby go to hell? Would Siobhan?

I was queen of the moment—not a mention of my fiasco on Saturday night with Frank the octopus. They only wanted to know about Siobhan and the sex. I hadn't asked Siobhan about it. I really didn't want to know. But sometimes ignorance is bliss, and I made up for my lack of hard facts with Mills-and-Boonesque descriptions of thrusting manhood, pools of virginal blood and multiple orgasms.

'I can't believe she didn't have an abortion,' said Deirdre, that afternoon, as we were walking home. 'I mean having a baby at seventeen is pathetic. She'll be tied to the kitchen sink for the rest of her life now. It's so backward.'

'I think she's right to have the baby,' said Sarah, defending Siobhan on my behalf. 'They love each other and they're getting married, so why on earth would she have an abortion?'

'Because, Sarah, you fool, she'll never get out of this community now. She'll be stuck married to a stupid Irish guy for the rest of her life.'

'Actually,' I piped up, 'Siobhan loves the Irish community and everything that goes with it. She'll be happy to stay here. She's not like me. She embraces her Irishness.'

'What an idiot,' said Deirdre. 'Who the hell could like it here? She must be simple. Mind you, at least she's not tight like her sister,' she said, sneering at me.

I was gutted. I'd really thought that Siobhan's pregnancy had taken everyone's mind off Saturday night—and that I'd got away with it. I should have known Deirdre wouldn't forget. I was beginning to wonder why I wanted to be friendly with her. She was always putting me down and making me feel small. Still, she was the coolest girl in the year and being in her gang gave me status I wouldn't otherwise have had.

I tried to talk to Sarah about it but she was totally distracted because she had snogged Declan Andrews on Saturday night. He was half English—English father, Irish mother—and had been there with his cousin Malachy Doherty. Declan went to a public school where he was captain of the rugby team. He was also really good-looking and Sarah was in love, big-time. He'd said he'd meet her after school so she was lashing on the Egypt Wonder as I droned on about hating Deirdre.

'I'm sorry, Niamh, but can we talk about this later? I'll call you after my date. How do I look? Too much makeup?'

'No, not at all. You look lovely,' I lied. She had actually brushed a large amount of Egypt Wonder on her shirt, tie and jumper and it was a bit blotchy round the forehead, but it was too late to take it off, so I rubbed it in a bit and told her she was gorgeous. She bounced off to her date and I slumped home, feeling jealous of her and sorry for myself.

Finn was in the kitchen, drinking a glass of milk and looking a bit shell-shocked when I came in.

'So you've heard, then,' I said.

'Yep. Not only that, but I was subjected to the

birds-and-bees chat from Dad.'

'No! You poor thing.'

'I'm fourteen, for God's sake! Where does he think I've been—in a monastery? Even the priests in school told us when we were twelve.'

'Did he give you the whole ambassador-for-your-country speech?'

'Oh, yes, I got the lot. How I'm responsible for my actions, how we're all representatives of Ireland here in England—even though I'm a British citizen and have never lived in Ireland. I was told it's more important for me to behave well than anyone else because I'm an ambassador for my country, blah blah blah. Then he told me how babies are made, which was the worst part. He got hot and bothered and couldn't look me in the eye—it was painful. Then he said I was to focus on football and not look at girls, especially fast English girls. And all this before I'd even taken my coat off.'

We went into fits of giggles. I couldn't stop. The thought of my father waiting in the hall to ambush Finn as he walked in the door to tell him the facts of life was too much. Siobhan came in and demanded to know what was so funny. But she didn't laugh when we told her. She started crying again and said that our father obviously considered her a fast girl now too.

We distracted her by asking how the wedding plans were coming along. She cheered up no end as she described the dresses that she, Mum and Auntie Nuala had seen that day. She told us how the woman in the shop had said she had a fabulous figure, and she had said she was a dancer, and the woman had said she'd known it the minute she saw her because she had such good posture. How all the dresses in the shop fitted her perfectly and how the woman had said she was a real clothes-horse. We heard about veils, silks, duchesse satin, crushed velvet, covered buttons, built-in bras, her tiny waist, her long legs, her elegant neck, until Finn could take no more and asked, 'So did you get one?'

'Well, yes, I did. But I'm not sure—'

'Good for you. I'd say you'll be gorgeous. I've got to go—see you later.' He bolted out of the room, leaving me alone with the bride of the year.

'Well,' she said, turning on me, 'what did everyone say in school?'

'Nothing, really. Just that they heard you were getting married and that you were a good couple 'cos of the dancing and all that.'

'What did they say about me being pregnant?'

'Not much. I think people were surprised because you don't look like a slapper.'

'What?'

I hadn't meant to say that. I really hadn't.

'I mean because you look so prim and proper and are never in trouble, so people wouldn't have thought that you'd be, you know, doing it with Liam.'

'They're jealous because I'm the first to get married and because Liam's so good-looking.'

'Yeah. By the way, how was it?'

'What?'

'You know—*it*.'

'Are you referring to making love?'

'Yes.'

'It was beautiful, very romantic, just like in the movies.'

'Really?'

'Well, it was a bit sore, but it felt very natural. When you love someone it's a beautiful experience.'

'Was there much blood?'

'Don't be disgusting.'

'I'm not. Was there?'

'Not really, no.'

'Where did you do it?'

Siobhan giggled. 'Actually, we did it in the back of Dad's car in the garage.'

'Siobhan! That's disgusting.'

'No, it's not. Besides, I brought a towel.'

'What for?'

'Forget it.'

'No—what was the towel for? Tell me!'

'No.'

'Come on.'

'For wiping up the sperm.'

'Urgggg—gross! I'm never sitting in the back again.'

We giggled. Two sisters who hadn't laughed at the same thing at the same time in about ten years giggled about wiping sperm off the back seat of their father's car.

* * *

I spent the rest of the week running around like a headless chicken doing messages for my mother. The minute I came home from school I was given a list of things to collect, clean, buy, mix, chop, whip, whisk or iron. My mother was like a lunatic trying to organize a wedding in six days. All the aunties pitched in. Our house was full of frantic women, sewing, cooking, cleaning, telling my mother she was a saint and bossing the rest of us about. They were so generous and kind. That week, I began to understand the true meaning of community.

Within six days, those formidable women had convinced my mother that this wedding was a blessing in disguise, made dresses for two bridesmaids and my mother, cooked enough food for sixty guests, transformed our house into a wedding shrine and, best of all, made my mother laugh.

The day before the wedding, Granny and Granddad Byrne arrived over from Dublin. They were, as always, wonderful. They bounced into the house and said all the right things. How wonderful we looked, how stunning the house was with the wedding decorations up, what a great day this was going to be for them, their first grandchild getting married . . . When they hugged my mother she started crying so Granny took her into the kitchen for a heart-to-heart. When they emerged an hour later, my mother looked as if a weight had been lifted off her shoulders and I loved Granny Byrne just a little bit more.

Meanwhile Granddad Byrne was meeting Liam and telling him how he had heard what a great lad he was and how delighted he was that his wonderful granddaughter Siobhan had made such a good choice. It was as if the wedding wasn't rushed, as if Siobhan wasn't pregnant. Everything seemed nice and normal once they'd arrived, and so much better.

Later that night when I went in to say goodnight to my grandparents, they hugged me and told me I was a great girl and a wonderful help to my mother.

'I'm so glad you're both here,' I said, suddenly tearful. 'Everything's so much nicer now and even Mum's happy.' I kissed them both and they told me I wasn't to worry about Siobhan. Everything would be fine.

16

Liam's parents boycotted the wedding. They were taking the line that Siobhan had trapped their son into marriage by getting pregnant. Granddad Byrne and Tadhg had to pin my father to the floor when he found out, to stop him going to kill Mr O'Loughlin. They calmed him down and talked some sense into him. He was not to ruin the wedding day by involving himself in a brawl.

I was woken up at the crack of dawn by an excited Siobhan to run her a bath with the special little Body Shop balls to make her skin smell gorgeous for Liam. I was going to ask her what her last slave had died of when I remembered that it was the last time she'd boss me around—she'd have Liam to boss around from now on in their apartment in the garage—so I climbed out of bed and turned on the taps. As I was getting back into bed, Finn came in and told me we had to put tricolour bows on our father's car and on the trees in the front garden.

He and I tied bows until my mother called for me to come in and have my hair done. Mrs Keane, who ran the hairdresser's, had arrived to do our hair. My auntie Sheila was doing the makeup. She had volunteered and my mother didn't have the heart to say no.

Auntie Sheila was 'poor Pat's' wife so we had to be especially nice to her. The only problem was that she looked like a drag queen most of the time. She was a great believer in pillar-box-red lipstick, blue eye-shadow and bright orange blusher. She was actually pretty scary-looking. Siobhan had gone mad when she'd found out Auntie Sheila was doing her makeup. But my mother had made us both promise to say nothing, smile and then, when Auntie Sheila had left, she'd tone it down for us.

Mrs Keane was not blessed with the gentlest hands. She yanked my hair into curlers, then shoved me under the hairdryer—which was a shower cap with a bendy tube coming out the side of it blowing scalding air at one side of my head. By the time she had finished Siobhan and my mother's hair, we knew every tragic story in our neighbourhood. Nothing was too gruesome or private for Mrs Keane. We heard about young Tony Ryan being struck down by leukaemia, Mrs Wall having a hysterectomy, Jessica Tunney being arrested for stabbing her father, though apparently that was because he had been interfering with her, so he'd had it coming. My mother interrupted at this point and said maybe Mrs Keane would like to go downstairs and have a cup of tea while our hair dried.

'What does she mean, interfering?' I asked.

'Nothing, love. Don't pay any heed. She's an awful woman for telling sad stories.'

'Yeah, but what did she mean? Interfering how?'

'Niamh, don't wind me up today. Drop it,' my mother said sharply.

What did she mean, 'interfering'? Checking her homework every night? My mother did that and I wasn't planning on stabbing her, although I was annoyed at her for snapping at me. Maybe she meant that Mr Tunney was always asking her questions about school and stuff. But she'd said he'd it coming to him. He must have been a real pain if he'd had a stabbing coming to him, or maybe Mrs Keane just had a very short fuse and could relate to attacking someone who was annoying her. I'd better be enthusiastic about my hair. I didn't want to give her any excuse to knife me.

Once our hair was done—that being a flattering way to describe the bird's nest I ended up with—Auntie Sheila set to work. She plastered me in thick wet makeup, then drew two large blue lines across my brown eyes. My mother said I was too young for lipstick, so at least I was spared a big red mouth like Siobhan's. When she was finished, my mother thanked her profusely for making us look like models (how did she manage to keep a straight face?) and ushered her out of the door.

Within five minutes we were scrubbed clean and my mother redid our makeup, with her fancy French foundation and mascara that she only used on very special occasions. I have to admit that even I looked quite nice. But she had to put some blue eye-shadow back on so Auntie Sheila wouldn't notice. I hated it, but then again, Auntie Sheila wasn't the most stable because 'poor Pat' had her driven round the bend and so, for once, I didn't moan.

After hair and makeup, Auntie Katie came in with my bridesmaid's dress. It was a baby blue meringue—at least it'd match my eye-shadow. She had spent day and night making it so I smiled enthusiastically and told her I loved it.

We gathered in the hall and waited for Siobhan to come down the stairs. Only my mother and Auntie Nuala had seen her dress. There was more secrecy over it than there had been over Princess Diana's. We were left waiting in the hall for fifteen minutes, and just as my father was about to explode, she appeared at the top of the stairs. And I have to say she looked lovely. It helps to be tall, slim and gorgeous, but the dress was perfect on her and she was beaming. We oohed and aahed, and my father's eyes filled with tears as he went up to kiss her and escort her to the car.

'You're magnificent,' he said, smiling at her, his big, open face full of love and pride.

I was green with envy. I knew that he'd never look at me that way. He worshipped Siobhan, and even though she was an old slapper who was pregnant, he was still besotted with her.

Granny Byrne whispered in my ear that I looked lovely too. It was nice of her, but I knew she was only being charitable. Feeling miserable, I climbed into Uncle Declan's car with my mother and Finn. I cheered up when I saw Jackie in her equally hideous bridesmaid's dress at the church.

Liam was standing at the altar with his best friend Fergal, looking sweaty and nervous. I felt sorry for him. Apart from Fergal he had only six people on his side of the church. Still, at least Siobhan wouldn't have to worry about entertaining his family or putting up with a bossy mother-in-law. Mind you, I wonder how Liam felt about living in our garage, right next door to his in-laws. Even though Dad's builders had transformed the garage in a week—it now had a bedroom, bathroom and small living area—we'd be sharing the kitchen.

'Niamh, are you deaf?' I heard from behind.

I turned. Siobhan was glaring at me. 'What?'

'Come here and fix my veil. You're a useless bridesmaid.'

She might have looked like an angel in her white dress, but she was the furthest thing from it. She barked orders as I crouched down to do it: 'Smooth it down. No, not like that, flat. No, lower. OK, leave it now. Go on, go up.'

Bloody hell, did Liam have any idea what he was letting himself in for? I walked, or rather sprinted, up the aisle as commanded.

Father Hogan, who had been persuaded to overlook Siobhan's delicate state with a large cheque from my father for the refurbishment of the church roof, was performing the wedding ceremony. He warbled on about love and partnership and how wonderful it was when two young people found each other and committed themselves to a life together. He talked about life being a journey and everything was a stepping-stone and the wonder of soulmates, and said that when you're old and wrinkly not to forget why you fell in love . . . He went on for a good thirty minutes by which stage my bum was numb from sitting on the hard chair behind Siobhan at the altar.

They said their vows, and everyone clapped and whooped, and we trooped back to our house for the reception. My aunties had outdone themselves: a banquet worthy of Buckingham Palace awaited us when we got home.

An hour later my father cleared his throat loudly and asked for silence. After welcoming everyone, he said what a nice lad Liam was and how he knew he would be a good husband to Siobhan, and how nice it would be for Finn to have another male in a family of women. He praised Finn for his prowess at hurley and for being a credit to his family. Then he went on to say how wonderful Siobhan was and how proud he had always been of her—not just because of her Irish dancing and beauty, but because she was a good person and he was delighted with how she had turned out. This led nicely into his praise of my mother's parenting skills and how wonderful she had been as a partner to him all his life. Then he began to wrap up and I fought back tears as I knew he was going to forget to mention me.

'And now I'll ask you to raise your glasses and toast our chief bridesmaid, my younger daughter, Niamh, who has worn that big blue frock without moaning once.' He winked at me.

Although I was relieved that he had remembered me, he hadn't exactly raved about my many qualities but I supposed I should be grateful for a mention. I did feel put out that he had said such nice things about Finn and Siobhan, though. He clearly couldn't think of anything nice to say about me so he'd focused on the dress. I had to plaster a smile on my face for the rest of the day, I was so upset about the speech.

*   *   *

Later that night, when the guests had gone and I was getting ready for bed, there was a knock on my door. It was my father and he was holding a box. 'Have you got a minute?' he asked.

I shrugged. I wasn't in the mood for a chat. I was hurt and angry.

'Niamh, pet,' he said, 'I have something for you here.'

He handed me the box and I opened it. Inside was a brand new pair of tap shoes.

'But—but I thought . . .' I stuttered, too overcome to speak.

He smiled. 'Your mother told me about the tap dancing, and although I was angry at first because you lied to us, she made me realize that you can't pin a bird's wings down or it will just stretch them further.'

I wasn't sure what he meant about the bird and the wings—it must be some old Irish saying, I thought—but I was thrilled with the shoes.

'I know it's been difficult growing up with a father who tries so hard to make you Irish. I'm sorry if I've smothered you with it, but I just want you to appreciate the wonderful things about your homeland.'

'I do, Dad. I just don't want to be different all the time.'

'OK. Well, we'll just have to find a happy medium. I worry about you more than the others because you're headstrong, like your old dad,' he said, patting me affectionately on the head and walking towards the door.

'Dad?'

'Yes.'

'Sarah's asked me to go on holidays with her to Cornwall this summer instead of going to Nora's.'

'Niamh?'

'Yes?'
'Don't push your luck.'

Irish Daily News

'What men want to say to women but are afraid to'

Niamh O'Flaherty

In an attempt to better understand the male psyche, I've done a survey round the office of the things my male colleagues wished that women understood.

We wish you'd stop moaning about the bloody toilet seat being up. You'd be much more annoyed if it was covered with badly aimed urine.

Don't ask us if you look fat: if the mirror is telling you you look fat then, chances are, you do.

When a stunning waitress in a low-cut blouse serves us, please don't ask us if we think she's attractive. We're not good liars.

Men are useless at remembering dates. Let's just focus on one—your birthday or our wedding anniversary. Other anniversaries, like the day we first met, kissed, shagged, got engaged, are beyond our mental aptitude.

We don't like shopping. We want to spend Saturday flaked out in front of the TV watching sport. It's our 'downtime'. We're delighted for you to go on marathon shopping sprees on a Saturday.

We hate—please note the word 'hate'—

when you talk during important games, particularly when penalties are being taken. Please do not bring up any 'issue' you may have while the Premiership is on. Wait until it's over—or, better still, don't bring it up at all.

Most of what we said while trying to get you into bed that first time is not the truth. We don't like chick-flicks and we don't think *E.R.* is the best programme on TV (the women in it are mingers). We don't admire Celine Dion's vocal range and we definitely don't like going for walks on a Saturday afternoon.

When you ask us what we're thinking it's either about sex, sport or cars, so don't be disappointed when the answer isn't 'You.'

17

Dublin, 1 March 1999

I was dreading meeting Pierre's parents. I now knew how poor Liam must have felt all those years ago when he had to face mine. On the day of the lunch, I woke up with a pit in my stomach. What if Mr and Mrs Alcee hated me? I was a white Irish-English mongrel who wrote columns for a tabloid.

Pierre's parents sounded so sophisticated. Even in photos they oozed confidence and style. His father, Jean, had recently retired as a professor of French at Oxford and his mother, Fleur, only did interiors for special clients, so she was pretty much retired too.

They spent half the year at their house in Oxford and the other half at their apartment in Paris. Pierre had told them about me and said he was very serious about me. (He hadn't admitted we were engaged: he said his mother would be furious that he'd proposed to me before she'd even met me.)

I hadn't even met his father but he terrified me. I had picked up a fax he'd sent over once and it was about existentialism. I'd had to look the word up in the dictionary. I'd no idea what it meant. He was going to think I was a total airhead. I had been poring over the newspapers for the last few weeks in the hope of being able to hold some kind of sensible, informed conversation.

We were due to meet for lunch at one. By twelve thirty I had changed at least ten times. Sweating and panicking, I came into the lounge.

'I don't know what to wear!' I wailed. 'I want to look appropriate.'

'Just be yourself. Wear whatever you feel like wearing.'

'Have you spoken to them?'

'Yes. They're in a taxi on the way to the restaurant.'

'And they know I'm white?'

'Yes.'

'And Irish?'

'Yes.'

'And Catholic?'

'When I told them you were Irish, they presumed as much.'

'Do they mind?'

'No, darling. I told you, they're very relaxed about these things.'

'Did they really like your ex? Did you have long conversations about philosophy and existentialism?'

'No. Most of the time my mother and Brigitte talked about fashion.'

That was not what I wanted to hear. My knowledge of fashion stretched to buying *Hello!* on a weekly basis, seeing what Liz Hurley was wearing and knowing it wouldn't even fit over my big toe. I stomped back into the bedroom and dug out the corset knickers I'd bought a few months ago and never bothered to wear. I'd put back all the weight I'd lost with the anorexic jockey. I squeezed into the pants and, by not breathing, managed to do up the zip. I was now sweating profusely, but at least I looked as if I had a waist. With Pierre shouting at me to hurry up, I opted for a simple black dress, which I had to safety-pin to my bra because it gaped open in the middle. You could see the pin sticking out, but it was the best I could do.

'Come on, let's go,' Pierre said, hustling me out the door. 'My parents hate tardiness.'

'You didn't tell me I looked nice!' I said, panicking.

'You look fine, although you do seem a bit hot. Are you feeling all right?'

'Fine? Hot? Is that the best you can do? I'm having a nervous breakdown here.'

'Well, that explains the flush,' he said, smiling. 'Calm down. You look lovely and my parents will love you as much as I do. Now, can we please get a move on?'

I got into the car and winced as the corset dug into my ribs. I prayed silently that I wouldn't pass out during the meal from lack of oxygen.

* * *

Mr and Mrs Alcee were sitting at a round table in the window of the restaurant. They were even more intimidating in the flesh, both tall, good-looking and dressed from head to toe in perfectly tailored clothes. Mrs Alcee was a vision in cream Chanel, including the bag. Her tights had probably cost more than my entire outfit. I felt like a cheaply dressed heifer and shoved my Marks & Spencer *faux*-leather bag under the table. If I'd been able to take a deep breath to calm my nerves, I would have, but the corset was so tight I could only take small shallow ones so I took a lot of those.

'*Maman, Papa, je vous présente Niamh*,' said

Pierre.

'*Monsieur et Madame Alcee, je suis ravie de faire votre connaissance*,' I stuttered.

Mrs Alcee laughed. 'Oh, my dear, you don't need to try to speak French to us. Didn't Pierre tell you? We've lived in England for over thirty years now.'

I blushed. 'Yes, of course.' Her English was better than mine.

'Call us Jean and Fleur,' said Mr Alcee. 'It's very nice to meet you at last. Pierre has told us a lot about you.'

'Well, I hope it was all good,' I said, trying to be jovial.

'He told us you were very amusing,' said Jean. 'A good sense of humour is important in life.'

Of course I couldn't think of anything amusing to say, so I smiled and nodded like an imbecile.

'Darling, you look tired,' Fleur said, reaching to touch Pierre's face. 'You're working too hard.'

'I'm fine.'

'Well, then, you can't be eating properly,' she said. 'Do you cook for him every evening?' she asked.

As I was about to lie and tell them I created *cordon-bleu* meals on a nightly basis, Pierre laughed and said, 'Niamh doesn't cook. Her speciality is scrambled eggs on toast. I do the cooking.'

Fleur and Jean both looked appalled.

'Doesn't cook?' Fleur said. 'But how can that be?'

'Pierre's exaggerating,' I said, desperately trying for damage control. 'I can cook. I just need time to learn his favourite dishes.'

'I will send you copies of all his favourite recipes. He is particularly fond of *bavette au porto*. It is ridiculously easy. Anyone could manage it,' she said, waving a bejewelled hand in the air.

Bloody hell. Now I'd have to spend months learning to cook big heavy meals with half a cow simmering in a bottle of wine with goose fat.

'What is it you do exactly?' Jean asked. 'Pierre said you are a journalist. Do you write for the *Irish Times*?'

'I write a column for the *Irish Daily News*.'

Jean frowned. 'I have not heard of this newspaper. Is it a new publication?'

'It's been around for about three years now. It's not a broadsheet. It's more of a popular newspaper.'

'I think she means a tabloid,' said Fleur, who was doing a really good job of making me feel three inches tall.

'Well, some might call it that,' I admitted.

'What is your column about?' Jean asked.

'It's a kind of social commentary.'

'So, you deal with morality and ethics?' Jean probed.

Oh, God, this was torture. I felt like I was at a job interview and it was going really, really badly.

'In a way, yes. It tends to be quite light and humorous, but I do try to tackle the issues of the moment.'

'What was your last column about?' asked Fleur.

Jesus, she was like a dog with a bone—give me a break!

'Uhm, let's see,' I said, trying to think of something clever and relevant to lie about.

'That one you did a few weeks ago was

hilarious,' said Pierre, stepping in. 'It was a rant about why women always have to sleep in the wet spot after sex.'

Jean and Fleur glanced at each other in horror.

Kill me now, I prayed. Please, someone, kill me now. Maybe if I breathed deeply the corset would puncture my lungs and I'd die.

I decided to take the moment of stunned silence to excuse myself and go to the bathroom. I sat on the toilet seat, corset open, and hyperventilated. This was a total and utter disaster. How could I possibly salvage it? After dumping the corset in the bin and splashing water on my face, I went back upstairs and decided just to tell them how much I loved Pierre. If we could focus the conversation on him, I might have some chance of winning them over.

When I sat down I asked Jean what had brought him to Oxford.

'They made me an offer I couldn't really refuse.'

'They begged him to come. Jean is considered the leading expert on the French language in the world,' said Fleur.

'My wife is very kind,' he said, not denying it.

'It's a wonderful language. I'm going to have lessons to improve,' I gushed.

'You know, French is among the most widely used modern languages in the world, with more than 120 million speakers. It is an official language in such diverse places as Louisiana, Martinique—of course—and Belgium, as well as France itself, and the many different kinds of French that exist ensure that the language remains central to a thriving variety of cultures. The literature, art and cinema of France are among the richest and most influential in the world. Have you been to France?' Jean asked.

'I've been to Lourdes with my family, but the rest of our holidays were spent coming over here to Ireland to see our relatives.'

'Lourdes!' Jean and Fleur laughed loudly.

'My auntie Teresa was sick, so we hired a coach and drove over to pray for her. She went into the baths and got better.'

'*Un miracle*,' said Jean, thumping the table with glee. Even Pierre was laughing.

I didn't particularly like the fact that my family trip was causing them such amusement. Poor Teresa had had cancer and everyone was devastated, but after Lourdes she had got better. Granted, the chemotherapy probably helped, but even the doctor had said her recovery was remarkable.

Sensing my annoyance, Pierre changed the subject. 'I have some exciting news. I've been offered a post as head of linguistics at the University of British Columbia in Vancouver,' he said.

'That's wonderful,' his father said. 'It's an excellent university. *Félicitations*.'

'When do you have to move there?' his mother asked.

'I'll be leaving in June. But before I go Niamh and I are getting married.'

They turned to stare at me. The silence was deafening.

18

'But you barely know each other,' Fleur snapped.

'It seems somewhat hasty,' said Jean.

'I went out with Brigitte for nine years and we broke up because I didn't want to spend the rest of my life with her. I knew after a minute with Niamh that she was the person I wanted to marry. I'm forty-two. This is not the action of an impulsive teenager.'

'Why don't you go to Vancouver and see how things work out?' said Jean. 'Why do you have to get married?'

'Because I want Niamh to be my wife and for us to have children together.'

'Look, Mr and Mrs Alcee, I know this is a bit sudden, but I can assure you that I love your son, and I will do everything in my power to make him happy. I'll even learn to cook!' I said, trying to lighten the mood.

They looked at me, then turned back to Pierre and launched into French. Although my language skills weren't up to much, I understood enough to know that I was not their idea of the perfect daughter-in-law.

There was a lot of hand-waving and head-shaking. I heard words like '*impossible*', '*folie*', '*ridicule*' and '*imprudent*', none of which needed much translation.

Pierre was getting more and more irate and kept saying, '*Je l'aime*', and '*parfaite*' and '*heureux*', which gave me hope.

Eventually, after twenty minutes of sitting there

like a lemon, I stood up and interrupted them.

'I'm going to leave you to it. You obviously have a lot to discuss. It was very nice to meet you. I'll see you later, Pierre,' I said, kissing him, and with that, my *faux*-leather bag, badly fitting dress and I strode out of the restaurant and ran round the corner to cry. It was an unmitigated disaster. *His* parents were supposed to be the easy part—*mine* were the ones who would cause trouble. Yet it was clear to me that the Alcees considered me a completely unsuitable bride for their son.

* * *

Two hours later, when Pierre came home, he was still fuming.

'I'm so sorry, darling,' he said, hugging me. 'They can be so stubborn and superior sometimes. Anyway, I've told them the wedding is going ahead regardless, so they eventually came around. But they're keen to meet your family as soon as you tell them about our plans.'

I must confess I was relieved. With such a negative reaction from his parents, I thought Pierre might see me suddenly through their eyes, realize he was getting a raw deal and call the whole thing off.

'One family down, one to go,' he said, smiling.

I grimaced. If his parents' reaction was bad, mine were going to go loop the loop.

'Did they really hate me?' I asked, desperate for some comforting words.

'No, of course not. They would just prefer it if you were French and wrote about philosophy or history. Don't worry, darling. They'll grow to love you when they get to know you better.'

'Why did you have to tell them about the wet-patch column?'

'Because it was hilarious.'

'Did you see their faces? They thought it was about as funny as my inability to cook or speak French.'

'They're a little old-fashioned. My mother always cooked for us.'

'Even when she'd worked a ten-hour day doing up houses?'

'Yes. It's just the way it was. French women cook.'

'So do Irish women.' I bristled. 'My mother always cooked for us.'

'What happened to you?'

'I chose not to.'

'Because?'

'I find it boring.'

'Ah, but if you learnt to cook you'd enjoy it.'

'I don't need to. One cook in the house is plenty.'

'Sometimes it would be nice for me not to have to cook.'

'No problem. That's what restaurants are for.'

'*Touché!*' He grinned.

Suddenly we heard a noise behind us. It was the fax machine. Pierre went over to pick up the pages. He started to laugh. 'Well, Niamh, my mother doesn't think you're a lost cause. Here is the recipe for my very favourite dish—*bavette au porto*.'

He handed me the page and I read:

This is Pierre's preferred dish. More recipes to follow. Fleur

Ingredients

1 ½lb flank steak

for the marinade

⅓ cup port
¼ cup balsamic vinegar
1 teaspoon Worcestershire sauce (well, when in Rome . . .!)
2 garlic cloves, pressed
1 tablespoon fresh thyme, leaves only
½ teaspoon salt
¼ teaspoon pepper
2 shallots, finely chopped

2 teaspoons butter

The cooking is ridiculously simple.

Whisk the marinade in a small bowl, then pour it over the steak and place it in the fridge for a few hours.

When you are ready to cook it, remove the steak from the marinade and grill it—Pierre likes his meat bloody. I know Irish people like to burn theirs, but please do not overcook it. It destroys it. As the steak is grilling, place the marinade in a small saucepan and heat it while mixing in the butter.

Pierre likes this with a salad.

There was no 'nice to have met you', 'you seem like the perfect bride for my son', 'welcome to the family'. She hadn't even bothered to write 'hello'. And she had insulted Irish people for liking their meat well done. So what if we didn't like eating an animal that was still winking at us? Where's the crime in that?

Pierre read it over my shoulder. 'Excellent! I'm looking forward to dinner tonight.' He grinned.

The fax machine continued to churn out pages of recipes. Fleur was on a mission to turn me into a chef. What she didn't know was that the raw ingredient she was dealing with was as stubborn as she was.

As I stuffed the recipes into a drawer, the phone rang.

'*Oui, Maman*. The faxes arrived. Yes, she's here beside me.' Pierre handed me the receiver.

'Hello?'

'Hello, Neeev,' she said, making my name sound like a curse. 'I wanted to make sure the recipes arrived safely.'

'Yes, thanks, they did. All of them.'

'I would like to take you for coffee tomorrow. I think we need to have a chat, us girls alone.'

Although it was the absolutely last thing in the world I wanted to do, I couldn't refuse. She was, after all, my future mother-in-law. 'That would be lovely.'

'We will meet at La Maison des Gâteaux. I believe it's the only place in Dublin that serves palatable coffee. I will see you there at eleven.'

'I can't wait,' I said, through gritted teeth.

'Well?' Pierre asked.

'She wants to meet for coffee.'

'That's great. It's a really good sign. She obviously feels bad about her reaction to the wedding. I knew she'd come round. I'm glad that's sorted,' he said, and sat down to read the paper.

I went into the bedroom and buried my head in the pillow to stifle a scream.

* * *

The next morning, I got up early and went shopping. I was determined to look good for my head-to-head with Fleur. I went to the most expensive boutique I knew, one of those really intimidating shops where the assistants are like supermodels. I'd never had the nerve or money to go in before, but this was an emergency. I took a deep breath and opened the door.

No sooner was my foot over the threshold than a tall, rail-thin girl came over to ask me if I needed help. Instead of scurrying away to the other side of the shop with a grunt, I said, 'Yes, I do. I need all the help I can get.'

I explained my situation and she was very sympathetic. Turned out Paula had worked in Paris for a few years and knew how intimidating formidable French women could be. 'Don't worry, we'll have you looking a million dollars,' she assured me.

I fingered my credit card nervously and hoped it wouldn't burst into flames when it came to paying.

An hour later, having tried on everything in the shop, I left looking a hell of a lot better than I had going in, and feeling a whole lot poorer. I winced every time I thought of how much I had spent, but then I caught my reflection in a shop window and knew it had been worth it. Paula had persuaded me to buy a pale blue dress with ribbon detail on the sleeves and hem. I never wore pale blue and the dress was more girly than my normal taste, but it was great on. The waist was empire line, which hid my stomach and made me look slim. I bought shoes to match and she even persuaded me to get a daisy clip for my hair, which she had made to look stylish rather than stupid in the way she had placed it.

When I arrived, Fleur was chatting to the owner in French. When she saw me she did a double-take and the owner actually whistled. I was thrilled.

'You look different,' she said.

'Thanks.' I decided to take it as a compliment.

'I wouldn't have thought blue would be a good colour on such pale skin, but in fact it is quite flattering.'

She was a vision in a pale pink wrap dress and high-heeled shoes to match. Her waist was the size of my calf—forget the French lessons and cooking: I could have done with a few tips on how to be skinny. After we had ordered, a young woman sat at the table beside us. She was wearing a tracksuit—a nice one. Fleur frowned. 'I don't understand how anyone with any self-respect can go out in public in a jogging suit,' she said. 'Sportswear is for the gymnasium, not for town.'

'They're comfortable.' I shrugged.

'They are slovenly. A woman should make an effort to look nice every day. If you look good, you feel better about yourself.'

She had a point there. I felt a lot better about myself today than I had yesterday in my ill-fitting dress.

'Besides,' continued my style guru, 'a man will not be faithful to a woman who dresses like a slob.'

I was going straight home to burn my tracksuits before Pierre took off with a woman in a skirt and high heels.

'Thank you for the recipes,' I said, deciding to change the subject before she slated people who wore jeans and thus my whole wardrobe would have to be thrown out.

'You're welcome. I know Pierre joked about your failure to cook yesterday, but I think it is very important for a woman to look after her husband in every way. Men are very simple creatures. They need to be fed, encouraged in their work and satisfied in the bedroom.'

I choked on my coffee.

'Oh, Neev, there's no need to be shy about sex. Don't tell me you're one of those frigid Irish girls.'

'I can assure you I am not frigid,' I said, highly insulted that she thought I might be. Granted, we weren't at it every night, but I put up a good show in the bedroom. Pierre hadn't complained anyway. 'I'm just not that comfortable talking about sex with my boyfriend's mother.'

'*Pffff*! In France we talk about it all the time. It's a very important part of a relationship. If you keep Pierre satisfied sexually then hopefully he won't need a mistress. A clever woman knows how to keep her husband happy. You also need to stimulate him mentally. You will have to take an interest in phonetics, French culture and history. A man needs a wife he can take to a dinner party with his colleagues and know that she will be engaging, articulate and well informed. You will, of course, have to learn to speak French like a native.'

I was beginning to wonder if it was worth it. Marrying Pierre was going to require years of intense study, becoming a chef and—if I had any energy left after cooking the seven-course meals—being a tiger in the bedroom. Maybe I should pack it in now.

'It was a shock to us to discover yesterday that our only child is getting married to someone we don't know, from a different background and culture. We didn't mean to react in a rude fashion. Pierre was very angry with us. We were merely concerned that you were rushing into the wedding. But my son has assured us that it's a *fait accompli*.'

'Fleur, whatever reservations you may have about me—and I can see you have many—I love your son. I may not be what you had in mind as a daughter-in-law, but I make Pierre happy and we're a good team. I'm willing to take French lessons and try to cook, but the bottom line is that we love each other and none of the other stuff matters.'

'That, my dear, is where you are mistaken. The excitement of falling in love will fade and you must make sure that your marriage has a solid base to fall back on. You need common interests, goals, aims, desires. The "other stuff" matters very much. A good marriage is like a good figure. It requires hard work, discipline and sacrifice. You are very naïve if you don't realize that.'

So now I was naïve as well as everything else. I felt as if I'd been rapped on the knuckles for being silly. 'I know how a good marriage works,' I said testily. 'My parents have been married for thirty-five years, and although they're very different people, they have made a success of it through compromise, respect, love and laughter. I'm not entering into this marriage lightly. In fact, there are a thousand reasons why I shouldn't marry Pierre, but I love him, I want to spend the rest of my life with him and that's exactly what I intend to do.'

'And how do you think you parents will react when they meet Pierre?'

'They'll go absolutely mental, but once they get to know him and see how happy he makes me, they'll come round.'

'And if they don't?'

'We'll go to Plan B.'

'Which is?'

'Vegas,' I said, and grinned as Fleur's face dropped.

Irish Daily News

'Bathroom habits'

Niamh O'Flaherty

The difference between men and women can be summed up perfectly using the example of showering.

When a woman takes a shower she

Takes off her clothes and divides them between the laundry baskets: white with pastel and black with dark colours. Sighing, she fishes out her husband's black socks and transfers them to the correct basket.

When in the bathroom, she locks the door and examines herself in the mirror, sticking her stomach out and groaning at how fat she's getting. She vows never to eat desserts again.

She gets into the shower and washes her hair with nutmeg and red earth shampoo, handmade by the indigenous people of Peru. Then she conditions it with nettle and mint conditioner, handmade by the war-torn refugees of Nicaragua. This must be left on for ten minutes.

She exfoliates her face with a cucumber and apricot scrub and washes her body with a poisonberry and redcurrant moisturizing gel.

While waiting for the conditioner to work

she shaves her legs and underarms with her husband's razor.

Then she rinses off the conditioner and combs her hair.

She opens the shower door, reaches for a large towel and dries herself in the shower so that she doesn't wet the bathroom floor.

She plucks her eyebrows, screeching with pain.

Finally she applies exorbitantly expensive French anti-cellulite cream to her dimpled legs and prays for a miracle.

When a man takes a shower he

Peels off his clothes and dumps them on the floor.

He walks into the bathroom and admires himself in the mirror, shadow-boxing.

He gets into the shower and fishes around for his crusty soap. He uses this to wash his hair, face, armpits, arse and penis, leaving pubic hair stuck to the bar.

He throws on some shaving cream and begins to shave, cursing his wife as he cuts his chin on the blunt blade.

After peeing in the shower he throws back the curtain and steps out, dripping, on to the floor.

He dries himself with a face towel and flexes his muscles in the misty mirror.

He walks out dripping all over the bedroom carpet.

He throws his wet towel on to the bed, sniffs the clothes he dumped on the floor, and if they don't smell like stale fish, he puts them on again.

19

London, December 1985

With her baby looming, Siobhan turned into a monster. I'd like to say that marriage and impending motherhood made her calm and serene, but I'd be lying. My mother told me to bite my tongue because my sister's hormones were all over the place: she didn't mean to be a bitch, she just couldn't help herself.

I had hoped she would stay in her one-bedroom flat in the garage, but although she had her own TV and bathroom she had no kitchen. Unfortunately I had to look at her grumpy face at mealtimes. Liam, who was supposed to be taking the brunt of her moods, was never at home. He spent twelve hours a day studying to make sure he got into college.

The pressure was on, now he had a family to support. When he wasn't studying, he was on the building sites, working for my father. The result was that I was on the receiving end of my sister's temper, and I was fed up.

Apparently, being pregnant meant you could not get up off the couch at any time, for any reason, cried if you didn't get your own way, had full custody of the TV remote control, demanded that trips be made to the shops for your cravings, which ranged from Curly Wurlies to salt-and-vinegar crisps, and were excused from helping with household chores and generally for being a contrary cow.

I glared at my calendar. Three months to go. It was going to be a long three months. Still, at least it was nearly Christmas and I'd be off school for three glorious weeks. I was really looking forward to Christmas. It was my favourite day of the year and our family went all out. Dad would buy the biggest tree he could find and put it up at least two weeks beforehand. Then we'd decorate it with shiny, sparkly baubles, tinsel and a beautiful angel at the top.

All the presents, and I have to admit we were spoilt at Christmas, went under the tree and we opened them together on Christmas morning. My mother made the yummiest Christmas dinner and we'd put on paper hats, pull crackers and laugh at the crummy jokes. Then, when dinner was over, we'd sit in front of the fire and play games—Monopoly, Cluedo, Charades—and eat sweets from enormous tins of Quality Street and Roses. It was perfect.

My mother broke the news to me as we were decorating the tree. Uncle Pat, recently back from his 'holidays', and the family were coming for Christmas Day. I was devastated.

Uncle Pat had been to every clinic in the UK. The pattern was always the same: he'd go and dry out, then promise faithfully never to touch another drop. Everyone would say what a great guy he was and hope would spring anew. The longest he'd lasted was eight months. Then Auntie Sheila would call my father and ask for his help.

Uncle Pat was the youngest in the family. He

had been spoilt by his mother and everyone did everything for him. He seemed to feel as if the world owed him something and expected to be bailed out every time he messed up—and he messed up a lot.

When he had come to London, my father had set him to work in an office, ordering building supplies. It was a cushy job and things had gone pretty well until his fondness for drink affected his daily life. He was constantly arriving late, nursing a hangover. He'd swan in, hang up his jacket, then take one of the suppliers out to the pub to 'discuss business'. Things went from bad to worse and Dad began to worry about his little brother.

My father and uncles decided that Uncle Pat needed stability, so they set him up with Auntie Sheila, who was Auntie Denise's second cousin. Auntie Sheila was thirty-seven, worked as a nurse and drank only on birthdays and at Christmas. She had told Auntie Denise that she was afraid she'd never get married and she desperately wanted children. She was getting on and needed to find a man. She said she wasn't fussy what he looked like or did for a living, as long as he was a good person.

Uncle Pat's brothers decided she was perfect for him. She was older, mature and sensible. Marriage and children would keep him at home and out of the pub. They encouraged him to go out with her. Somehow Pat managed to keep it together most of the time he was courting Auntie Sheila. She'd seen him drunk all right, but not on a daily basis. She knew he was a drinker, just had no idea how bad he was. On the morning of the wedding, he was found passed out in our front garden, face down in the grass. My father and mother plied him with coffee, threw him into the shower and managed to get him coherent enough to go through with the ceremony.

Marriage, however, didn't stop him drinking. Neither did fatherhood. He got worse and worse. Once when Auntie Sheila had thrown him out of the house, he had come to stay with us for a few days and I'd had to give up my bed. On his last night, he had peed in his sleep, and when he left to go to rehab, I had refused to get into my bed until my mother had bought me a new mattress.

I dreaded Uncle Pat's visits because he had nasty breath and was always crying into my hair because I looked like Granny O'Flaherty. I tried to make myself scarce when he was around. And now he was going to ruin my favourite day.

'Why, Mum? Why do they have to come? They'll ruin Christmas. Uncle Pat'll just get drunk and cry and fall over. It'll be awful.'

'Don't be so selfish. Poor Auntie Sheila could do with a nice day out and your cousins have had a hard time with Pat not being so well. You should be generous to them, poor things. Besides, we're not ones to be taking the moral high ground, with Siobhan pregnant before marriage.'

Great! Now, because of Siobhan's lusty ways, we were the poor cousins whom everyone felt sorry for. My God, *Uncle Pat*'s family probably felt sorry for us. How weird was that? We were the loser cousins for once. I needed to talk to Finn.

I pounced on him when he came in from training.

'You'll never guess who's coming for Christmas dinner?'

'Who?'

‘Smelly Pat and his family.’

‘Oh, Jesus. We’d better hide the drink and get the plastic sheets out.’

‘Do you think we’re the sad cousins now because of Siobhan?’

‘What do you mean?’

‘Well, you know, because she got pregnant and it was shameful and hush-hush.’

‘Dunno. Do you think we are?’

I shrugged. ‘Mum said something about it.’

‘Wow. That’s embarrassing.’

‘Yeah, I know. Do you think we’ll have to share our presents?’

‘I hope not. I’m not sharing my skateboard with anyone.’

‘Yeah, me neither.’

‘Are you getting one too?’

‘No, you thick, I’m getting a stereo for my bedroom.’

‘What’s Siobhan getting?’

‘A year’s supply of Pampers.’

We had a good laugh about that.

* * *

Christmas Day arrived, and Santa was as generous as always. We were given everything we asked for. Liam spent Christmas in our house as his family had disowned him, and Santa had given him and Siobhan a second-hand car. They were thrilled. Liam was all emotional when my father handed him the keys. Siobhan said she liked it, but would have preferred a red one—my mother whispered, ‘Hormones,’ to my father to stop him getting annoyed.

I got my stereo and the new A-Ha album, so I was thrilled. Finn got his skateboard and a Rubik's cube. My father was keen for him to improve his concentration. Finn may have been a great footballer but he didn't do a tap of work, and maths was not his best subject. My father reasoned that focusing on doing the Rubik's cube would somehow make him better with figures. I knew it'd end up in the bottom of his cupboard.

While we were outside admiring the car, Uncle Pat and Co. trooped up the drive. Uncle Pat was swaying from side to side and I heard my father mutter, 'I'll kill him,' under his breath. My mother rested her arm on his.

'Leave it, Mick. He's too far gone now. Talk to him tomorrow when he's sobered up.'

'That's another thousand pounds down the drain. I'll kill him.'

Uncle Pat's 'holidays' were getting more expensive. I had heard my parents talking about them before and five hundred quid seemed to be the going rate. Obviously he had been sent to a new place. At this rate we'd be broke in no time. Shamed *and* broke—we'd really be the poor cousins then. My dislike of Uncle Pat intensified.

My cousins, Sally and Brian, looked really pissed off, while Auntie Sheila, who had outdone herself with the makeup today, bounded up the driveway full of cheer. She was talking very loudly and kept laughing hysterically at nothing.

Uncle Pat hugged us and told us we were wonderful kids, that our father was a saint and our mother an angel. My recently canonized father didn't seem very saintly as he grabbed Uncle Pat's arm and frogmarched him into the kitchen. Auntie

Sheila kissed us, leaving large red lipstick marks on our faces and Sally and Brian mumbled, 'Happy Christmas,' avoiding eye contact with any of us.

My mother took charge and ushered everyone in out of the cold. She closed the kitchen door to drown my father's raised voice telling Uncle Pat 'Drink the bloody coffee or I'll make you drink it myself.'

Auntie Sheila continued to laugh hysterically. My cousin Sally was fourteen and Brian was fifteen; they were always very quiet at family gatherings. They stuck together like glue and said little.

My mother always made a fuss of them. You could see she felt sorry for them having Uncle Pat as a father. But they seemed to be doing OK. Brian was really good at the violin, and Sally was clever in school—a fact my mother never failed to remind me of. 'If poor Sally can get good grades with that useless fecker as a father, what's your excuse?' asked Mum.

She sometimes called Uncle Pat a 'useless fecker' when my father wasn't around. I could see she thought he was a lost cause, but she never stopped my father sending him to dry out. Family was family and that was that.

'Maybe the teachers feel sorry for her and give her good marks because of him,' I suggested.

'Maybe if you spent less time giving cheek to your mother and more time to studying your grades would improve.'

'Sally's a weirdo. She hasn't got any friends. No wonder she has so much time to study. Would you prefer it if I was weird too?'

'Now, you listen here, madam. Your cousin has a

very difficult home life and you should be extra nice to her. You should be friendly to her, let her pal around with your gang and introduce her to your friends.'

Did I look like a masochist? Sally hang around with my gang? I was just about hanging around with them myself. Dragging my younger cousin along would tip the balance and I'd be an outcast. Besides, she was in the year below me. Everyone knew that you never hung around with anyone in the year below. It was a capital offence and guaranteed you a place among the goons. But I could see that my mother thought this was a great idea and I wanted to get her off the subject of my brainy cousin ruining the meagre street cred I had in school so I nodded.

We had been told on Christmas Eve that we had to give one of our presents to our cousins. Naturally we moaned and groaned and kicked up a fuss, but my father insisted this was a good lesson for us in giving. I reluctantly agreed to give Sally my *Just Seventeen* annual, even though it had a really cool pull-out poster of Duran Duran in the middle, with John Taylor looking utterly divine, his long tousled hair blowing in the wind. Finn agreed to give Brian the Rubik's cube, but my father insisted that he part with something bigger so he gave him his new dartboard.

My mother handed the presents—our presents—to Brian and Sally, who were clearly embarrassed, while Auntie Sheila oohed and aahed and said how marvellous it was and how we shouldn't spoil them and how generous we were and how good we were and how she hoped we didn't think that they had come here today expecting presents. It was enough of a gift not to have to spend Christmas alone with 'him inside' and how she had hoped and prayed that, for once, they'd have a peaceful Christmas but he'd started again two days ago and—She began to cry and my mother asked us kids to go into the playroom and play.

Children play. Teenagers shuffle around feeling awkward, which was what we did. Well, all of us except Siobhan, who lay on the couch like a beached whale. Liam sat beside her looking a bit lost. Christmas Day in his house probably didn't seem so bad after all.

Finn broke the silence by asking if they'd seen the new *Back to the Future* movie. Sally said she didn't go to the cinema and Brian said he'd been supposed to see it two days ago but his father had got drunk, started a fight and been arrested, so he'd gone with his mother to bail him out.

That was a conversation stopper, I can tell you. We shuffled around some more until Siobhan piped up that Uncle Pat had better get a grip on himself because our father wouldn't be able to pay for him to dry out any more as he had to help her and Liam buy a house once the baby was born.

'Shut up,' I hissed. I couldn't believe she'd said that. The cousins were shocked and embarrassed. 'Don't mind her. It's her hormones. She doesn't know what she's saying.' I blushed at my sister's insensitivity.

'My mum said your baby will go to hell because it's a sin to have sex before marriage,' said Sally, clearly not as meek and mild as we'd thought.

'How dare you say that? Your dad's just a sad old piss-head who bleeds everyone around him dry.

If anyone's going to hell it's him,' said the future mother.

'I hope he does,' said Brian, quietly. 'The sooner the better.'

'That's your dad you're talking about,' said Finn.

'Has your dad ever turned up to a hurley match drunk out of his head and pissed behind a tree?'

Finn looked appalled. Christmas was beginning to seem more like Hallowe'en. Thankfully, before Brian could tell us a few more horror stories about his dad, Mum popped her head round the door. 'It's very quiet in here. Everything all right?'

We nodded, but she sensed the tension and ushered us all into the lounge. Uncle Pat was having a 'rest' upstairs—I prayed not in my bed—so we sat in front of a roaring log fire and watched *It's a Wonderful Life* for the zillionth time. I sank back in the couch, flooded with relief at not having to make conversation any more. Some things were better left unsaid. Even the fact that Siobhan had eaten all the strawberry, coffee and orange Quality Streets didn't bother me. I had a father who peed in the bathroom. Life was good.

20

After Christmas, Siobhan went from big to absolutely huge. She had to wear tent-type dresses and moaned about her back being sore. Even Mum got fed up and told her that pregnancy wasn't an illness, it was a natural condition, to stop complaining and get on with it.

'But you don't understand, I'm in agony,' she

whinged as Nuala came in and put the kettle on.

'I had three children, Siobhan. I understand perfectly,' said Mum.

'Stop your groaning. You're young and healthy,' said Auntie Nuala. 'Think of those poor pregnant African women walking twenty miles for water and giving birth on the side of a road.'

Siobhan glared at her and waddled out of the room.

'She's a regular ray of sunshine,' said Auntie Nuala.

'Ah, leave the poor thing alone, she's just big and uncomfortable,' said Mum. 'Besides, she's bored here all day long. She misses her schoolfriends.'

'You should never have allowed her leave.'

'I couldn't send her in there with a big pregnant belly on her. It wouldn't have been fair. Besides, with the baby due in March she wouldn't have been able to sit the exams anyway. She can go back and finish next year, if she wants to.'

'You should make her go back or she'll end up a frustrated housewife like the two of us.' Auntie Nuala sighed.

'Are you frustrated?' I asked.

'No, we're not,' said Mum, giving Auntie Nuala a stern look.

'Well, I am,' Auntie Nuala said. 'I wish I'd studied harder, gone to university and had a career.'

'What would you like to have been?'

'A lawyer, I think,' said Auntie Nuala, smiling. 'I'd have made a very good one.'

'You're good at talking, all right,' said Mum.

'And you're very persuasive,' I added.

‘Oh, well, ’twasn’t to be. I was barefoot and pregnant at twenty. What do you want to be?’ Auntie Nuala asked me.

‘I used to want to be an air-stewardess but now I think that’s kind of crap. I’m thinking of being a beautician.’

Mum choked on her tea. ‘Over my dead body will you be painting people’s toenails. Your father’s paying a fortune for a private education and you’ll not waste it on that rubbish.’

‘Why don’t you be a doctor?’ asked Auntie Nuala.

‘I hate science and I’m crap at it.’

‘OK, an accountant, then.’

‘I’m even worse at maths.’

‘What about a lawyer? You’ve the gift of the gab,’ said Mum.

I shrugged. ‘It seems kind of boring.’

‘OK, let’s try a different tack. What are you good at?’ asked Auntie Nuala.

‘English and tennis.’

‘Well, it’s a bit late for Wimbledon so what about journalism?’

I’d never thought of being a journalist. It sounded like a great idea. I could write about pop bands and work for *Just Seventeen*. It’d be fantastic.

‘Thanks, Auntie Nuala, that’s exactly what I’ll do.’ I beamed.

‘It’s no profession for a girl.’ Mum sniffed. ‘They’re a rough lot, those journalists. You’re going to university, young lady, and while you’re there you can figure out what it is you want to be. But whatever happens, you’re not going to mess up like Siobhan. So put your head down and work on your maths and science. Do you hear me?’

'Loud and clear,' I muttered, as Auntie Nuala winked at me.

*　　*　　*

A few weeks later I was making myself a sandwich when I heard Siobhan shouting my name. Assuming she was being her usual dramatic self, I ignored her and continued to pile HP sauce on to the bread . . . until I heard a bloodcurdling howl. I dropped the knife and ran into her room.

'Are you deaf?' she roared. 'I've been calling you for the last ten minutes.'

'What's wrong?'

'My waters have broken.'

I stared at her blankly. She might as well have been talking Swahili.

'Don't just stand there! Get Mum! The baby's coming.'

'She's gone out.'

'What? Where?'

'To have her hair done.'

'Jesus Christ! Well, call an ambulance—DO SOMETHING!' she screamed, as water trickled down her leg on to the carpet.

I ran in and dialled 999. Then I boiled some water, ripped up a sheet and went back to her.

'Where the hell have you been?' she snapped. 'And why have you cut up that sheet? It's one of my favourites.'

'They do it in the movies when someone's having a baby. The doctor always says, "Get me some hot water and sheets." '

'What for?'

I shrugged. 'They never show you what happens

next—you just hear the baby crying and it's all over.'

'How long did the ambulance say it'd take?'

'Ten minutes.'

'Aaaarggh—I don't think I can wait that long. I'm going to die—the baby's going to die. I'm in agony,' she said, doubling over.

I began to panic. What if she had the baby there on the floor? What was I supposed to do with the sheets and the hot water? I got up to ring Dad's office, but Siobhan grabbed my arm. 'Don't leave me—I'm scared,' she said, beginning to cry.

'It's OK, Siobhan, you'll be fine,' I said, trying to reassure her.

'What the hell do you know—with your sheets and boiling water? I want Mum.'

'I'll ring the hairdresser.'

'*No*—the baby's coming! *Oh my God*—it's coming out. Help!'

Jesus, please don't come now, I prayed. I haven't a clue what I'm doing. Stay in there! Was I going to have to look up my sister's fanny? If I saw the head could I push it back in until the ambulance arrived?

Siobhan screeched again and began to roll around on the floor. 'I want Liam! I want Mum! I want Dad! Why the hell are you the only one in?'

'I wanted to go out, but Mum made me stay here in case anything happened,' I snapped. I'd rather be in double maths right now, I thought, fuming.

'Oh, the pain—it's excruciating. Do something!'

'Like what?'

'Wipe my brow.'

I put a corner of the sheet into the water and wiped.

'Ooow! You stupid cow, you burnt me!'

Fuck fuck fuck. Where was everyone? Before Siobhan had a chance to abuse me again I heard a siren.

I charged out to open the door for the ambulance men, who rushed in to my screaming sister. They had a midwife with them who checked Siobhan, then told her firmly to calm down. 'You've only just started labour, love. You've a long way to go. You need to stop shouting and conserve some energy for later. You're not even one centimetre dilated.'

'Give me something for the pain,' she begged.

'Too early for that. You'll have to grin and bear it for a bit longer,' said the midwife.

As they were putting her into the back of the ambulance she barked orders to me: '. . . and don't forget to pack my favourite pillow and my new pink pyjamas and bring me some magazines and . . .'

Thankfully, Mum arrived back before I killed my sister, and took over. She calmed Siobhan, packed a bag for her in the space of two minutes and went with her to the hospital.

I was told to track down Dad, Liam and Finn and tell them what was going on.

* * *

Eight hours later, at ten past one in the morning of Easter Sunday, Mum, Dad, Finn and I were still waiting for Siobhan's baby to arrive. All we could hear from the labour room was Siobhan blaming Liam for her pain and suffering. It went on and on until eventually, what seemed like days later, Liam burst out of the room and told us breathlessly, 'It's a girl.'

We were allowed in to see mother and child. Siobhan was lying in the bed looking pretty shell-shocked. For once she seemed at a loss for words. The baby was lying on her chest.

The minute Dad saw his granddaughter he welled up and proceeded to blow his nose loudly into his hankie while Mum picked up the little red bundle and rocked her like an old pro. 'Do you want to hold her?' she asked me.

I shook my head. The baby had bloody mush on her head and was roaring. I wanted to get away from her.

Mum offered the baby to Finn, who looked as if he was about to vomit. 'No way. She's covered in gunk.' He squirmed.

'I'd like to hold her,' said Dad, and once Mum had placed the baby into his arms, I knew that this child was number one in his life. The sliver of opportunity I'd had to be the number-one girl, after Siobhan's loose behaviour, was officially gone. He positively melted as he gazed down at his granddaughter.

'She's red hair like her mother, and born on Easter Sunday. Imagine that!' said Dad, smiling at Siobhan, who had now been completely forgiven. In typical Siobhan style, she had produced a kid with red hair on the day Jesus rose from the dead. I'd no hope.

'Have you decided on a name?' Mum asked.

'Muireann,' said Siobhan.

I groaned. It was just plain cruel to call a child who was going to grow up in North London Muireann. No one would ever be able to pronounce or spell it and she'd hate it.

'Gorgeous,' said Dad.

'Beautiful,' said Mum.

'Can we go now?' asked Finn.

After a further half-hour of cooing and who-does-she-look-like, we left. On our way out we ran into Liam's father. Dad bristled.

'Have you seen her?' Mr O'Loughlin asked.

'Of course, and she's the most beautiful child you ever saw. The image of her mother,' said Dad.

'How is Siobhan?'

'She's worn out, poor thing. I hope you're not going to upset her. I won't have it,' said Dad, threateningly.

'No, not at all. Liam called and, well, I just had to see the little one.'

'Is your wife with you?' asked Mum.

'No,' he said. 'Unfortunately she can't forgive Liam.'

'She's a fool,' snapped Dad. 'Liam's a lovely lad and you should be proud of him.'

'You're right, he is. I've missed him these last few months. Look, I owe you an apology for the way we handled the situation. I'm not proud of myself and I hope to make it up to you.'

'It's not us you need to apologize to, it's your son and our daughter,' said Mum.

'That's why I'm here,' said Mr O'Loughlin. 'To try to make amends.'

'You've a lot of ground to cover,' said Dad.

Mr O'Loughlin nodded. Suddenly he seemed smaller, as if he'd shrunk since the last time we saw him. He looked sad too, as if life had got the better of him. Gone was the confident swagger, and his accent was more normal.

‘They’ve called her Muireann,’ said Mum.

‘What?’ he said, clearly shocked.

‘I know, I think it’s rotten too,’ I piped up, delighted that someone else thought it was awful.

‘It was my mother’s name,’ said Mr O’Loughlin, choking up.

21

Siobhan spent the next two weeks at home, sitting on the couch like the Queen of Sheba while endless relations called in to see the baby and shower her with gifts. They ooohed and aaahed and endless discussions ensued: Muireann’s nose was O’Flaherty but her eyes were more O’Loughlin; her forehead was the image of Dad’s but her chin was definitely like Mum’s side of the family; she had a look of someone who’d been here before . . .

‘She’s like a narky, red-faced alien,’ said Finn, who was fed up listening to baby talk. ‘Every time she does a poo we have to celebrate.’

‘I know,’ I agreed, equally sick of hearing about Muireann’s bowel movements. Even Dad was obsessed with them.

‘And I hate it when she feeds her. It’s embarrassing. I don’t want to see my sister’s boobs,’ said Finn, who had nearly passed out the first time Siobhan had breastfed. It was way too much information for a fourteen-year-old boy.

I found it pretty gross myself and would have preferred her to leave the room to feed Muireann. But when I’d said as much, she’d bitten my head off.

'You're so immature. It's the most natural thing in the world for a mother to breastfeed her child. Why should I have to hide away just because you have a problem with it?'

'You look like a cow being milked,' I said. 'It puts me off my food.'

She sighed. 'Some day you'll stop behaving like a child and grow up.'

I couldn't think of a good retort, so I stomped out of the room and slammed the door.

* * *

Then, all of a sudden, overnight, the happy mother and child became the Antichrist and screeching offspring. When Siobhan's elation wore off, her boobs got red and sore, the visitors stopped coming, Muireann stopped sleeping all the time and reality hit her smack in the face. It wasn't pretty.

She snapped at everyone, even Dad, who kept well out of her way. Finn spent all his time playing hurley and Mum seemed able to switch off. She just smiled at Siobhan knowingly when she complained and said, 'Motherhood isn't easy, but it's worth it.'

But the brunt of Siobhan's fury was spent on Liam and me. Since Liam was studying all the time, with his exams only six weeks away, I suffered most.

'Niammmmh,' she'd roar, and I'd have to run in, get pillows for her back, nappies for Muireann, bibs, vests or Babygros. It came to a head one day when she asked me to run down to the chemist and get her nipple cream.

'No,' I said, putting my foot down. There was no way I could ask the cute guy who worked in the chemist for nipple cream. I had limits.

'Muuuuum,' she shrieked. Mum popped her head patiently round the door. 'My nipples are cracked and sore and Niamh won't get me cream for them.'

Mum sighed. 'Niamh, be a pet and run down to the chemist.'

'No!' I snapped. 'I will not. I'm sick of being treated like a slave.'

'Come here,' said Mum, ushering me out of the room. 'Niamh, I know Siobhan's a bit difficult at the moment, but she's in pain. It's not easy for her.'

'What's difficult? All she does is sit around giving orders and making my life miserable. I can't wait to go back to school,' I said, feeling very sorry for myself that my Easter holidays had been ruined by narky Siobhan and her howling baby.

'Niamh,' said Mum, in her serious-chat voice, 'your sister has been through a lot in the last few weeks. While her friends are out having fun, she's stuck in here trying to learn how to be a mother. Breastfeeding can be painful and a lot of new mums get quite down in the dumps in the first few weeks. You'll have to bite your tongue and be nice to her. It's not easy being a mum at seventeen. She'll never have the freedom you will. Every decision she makes from now on—even the most basic ones, like going for a walk—will have to include Muireann. That's a frightening prospect for a young girl. Every action you take has repercussions. Remember that.'

Like I could ever forget! Mum had been saying it to me every day since Siobhan had got pregnant. It was obsessive. I'd come down for breakfast and she'd say, 'Cornflakes or Weetabix? Careful, every decision you make has repercussions.'

She had a point about Siobhan, though. Even when she went for a shower, she had to get one of us to keep an eye on Muireann. It must be really annoying. And she was crying a lot—Siobhan, not Muireann, although the baby did her fair share too. But still and all I wasn't going to get her nipple cream.

'Mum,' I said, using my we're-all-adults-here voice, 'I understand what you're telling me but I still think it's unfair to ask a fifteen-year-old to go to the chemist and ask for nipple cream. It's embarrassing.'

'Niamh,' Mum said, in her I-hear-what-you're-saying-but-I don't-really-care voice, 'Just go and get it. There's no need to be dramatic. Just ask for Lansinoh cream. Now, off you go. Your poor sister's in agony.'

I stormed out of the house and down to the chemist, praying that the good-looking guy wouldn't be working there. But, of course, he was and he was wearing an amazing blue shirt that matched his eyes. I was puce before I'd even reached the counter.

'Can I help you?' he asked.

'I'd like some . . .' Blank. My mind had gone completely numb. I had no idea what the cream was called. My face was on fire and I was sweating.

He smiled patiently.

'It's called Lan-something or Los-something,' I stammered.

'Maybe if you tell me what it's for I can look it up,' he said, being super-efficient as well as gorgeous.

'Well, it's for my sister, she's just had a baby and she's breastfeeding and, uhm, she has, uhm—' I couldn't say it. I just couldn't stand there in front of that handsome twenty-year-old and say 'nipple'. It wasn't fair. I shouldn't have to do this.

'Mastitis?' he suggested.

'Is that when you're afraid to go to mass?' I asked, lamely attempting a joke.

He had the kindness to laugh.

'No, it's when the breast becomes inflamed and tender,' he explained.

It wasn't possible to go any redder than I was now. I wished I was mature enough to stand around shooting the breeze about tender breasts, but I wasn't. It was torture. I took a deep breath. 'No, it's not that, it's her—LANSINOH!' I shouted joyfully, as I finally remembered the name. Thank God I hadn't had to say 'nipple'. I was ecstatic.

He smiled at me—the way you smile at someone who's slightly unstable—and handed over the cream. I paid and hightailed it out of the shop.

When I got home Siobhan was sitting in bed crying, with Muireann howling beside her. I loitered outside while Mum tried to comfort her.

'It's all right, pet. She's just hungry. We might give her a bottle to keep her going.'

'But I really wanted to breastfeed. It's what nature intended,' wailed Siobhan.

'I know you're disappointed, but you need to take a break and give your nipples a chance to heal. You can't breastfeed if you're in this much pain. It's not good for you or Muireann.'

'I don't think I can do it, Mum.'

'It's only a bottle, pet, it won't do her any harm.'

Siobhan shook her head. 'No, I mean I don't think I can be a mother. I don't know what I'm doing. I'm scared. What if I drop her or roll over and crush her in my sleep? I don't like this. I don't want to be a mum—I want it all to go away. I'm too young,' she bawled.

'Listen to me,' said Mum, taking Siobhan's face in her hands. 'Everything you're feeling is normal. All first time mums are scared. I was terrified when I had you. I hadn't a clue what I was doing. You'll get better and better at it and in no time it'll all seem natural. But you need to be patient. I know it's hard on you but you got yourself into this situation and you have to take responsibility for your actions. You have a beautiful healthy baby girl and you need to focus on that. You're good at everything you do so you'll be a wonderful mother. I'm here to help you anytime you need it and so is Niamh. Any time you feel overwhelmed, just tell me. Now, I'm going to let you get some rest and I'll give this little angel a bottle.'

'Thanks, Mum. Could I have a cup of hot chocolate?'

'Of course you can, pet. I'll get Niamh to make you one now. I don't know where she's got to.'

'I'm here. I've got your cream.' I handed it over sulkily.

'Good girl. Now, will you make your sister a hot chocolate?' asked Mum.

'Fine, but when I'm back in school you'll have to find someone else to be your slave,' I said, glaring at them—Siobhan for being the cause of all this unrest and being so demanding, and Mum for telling her I'd help with Muireann any time she needed it. I was a fifteen-year-old schoolgirl, not a fifty-year-old nanny.

22

Thankfully, Siobhan calmed down after a few weeks and seemed a bit happier. She was still hard-going, but at least she didn't cry all the time and Muireann seemed to cheer up too. Sometimes she was even kind of cute. She started smiling, which made a big difference to her face.

I decided that the best way to avoid having to do things for Siobhan was to study, and so, for the first time ever, I actually went into my summer exams and knew the answers. My results were good and I have to say it felt pretty great.

Mum and Dad were thrilled.

'You see? You're as clever as anyone when you apply yourself. I'm so pleased you're taking it seriously now. If you keep this up you'll have no problem getting into college. Well done,' said Dad, patting me on the back as Siobhan simmered in the background.

'Thanks,' I said, basking in the admiration. 'Can I go to the disco in the tennis club on Saturday night to celebrate the fact that I'm not thick?' They had to let me go now. Since Siobhan's pregnancy I hadn't been allowed out past nine. I was fast becoming a supreme nerd.

'Under no circumstances are you going to any disco. The problem with youngsters today is that they have too much freedom. That crowd in the tennis club are a wild bunch.'

'They're not wild, they're perfectly normal teenagers. I never get to go out and I'm sick of it. I studied really hard, I deserve a break,' I whined.

'There's a ceili on in the parish hall. You can go to that. Your uncle Neil is helping organize it so he can keep an eye on you,' said Dad.

'I wouldn't be seen dead at a ceili,' I huffed.

'And what's wrong with it?'

'It's for old people who want to listen to Irish music and talk about green fields and sing songs about the Famine. It's 1986, Dad. I want to go to a disco.'

'Less disco and more respect for your culture is what you need, missy. That's it. My mind's made up. You're going to spend a month back home at Nora's. You need to get back to your roots.'

'No, Dad, please, not Auntie Nora's,' I pleaded, panic-stricken. 'I'll go to the ceili, I'll Irish-dance till my legs fall off, I'll listen to Foster and Allen. I'll do anything you want, but please don't send me there. Mum, help!' I begged.

Seeing my desperation—and not being a big fan of Nora's anyway—Mum stepped in. 'Now, Mick, Niamh's going to spend the summer here with the family. We need her to help Siobhan with the baby.'

'No, we don't,' said Siobhan, smirking at me. 'I'm well able to look after Muireann on my own now.'

'It'll do her good to spend time in Ireland,' said Dad. 'She needs to be reminded of where she comes from. She's too wrapped up in modern mumbo-jumbo. I don't want her to lose her way like her sister,' he added.

Now Siobhan winced.

'Mum!' I pleaded.

'Fine, if you think Niamh really needs to go back to Ireland, she can go and stay with my mother and father. Nora's enough on her plate with that big farm to run. I'll call them now to arrange it. It's the best solution for everyone,' she said firmly.

I wasn't thrilled about being shunted back to Ireland, but at least I'd have a nice time with Granny and Granddad Byrne. I wouldn't be ridiculed for not knowing how to milk a cow and, hopefully, I wouldn't be stoned by the local boys because of my accent.

I followed Mum out to the hall. 'Thanks for saving me from Nora.'

'You're welcome but, Niamh, you have to learn not to wind your father up. You should know at this stage not to belittle Irish dancing and music. It's ignorant. Now, when you go to Dublin you're to be polite about everything. I don't want you giving my parents any problems. Am I making myself clear?'

I nodded. She was crystal clear. I needed to shut up and put up.

Siobhan came out and handed me Muireann.

'You just told Dad you don't need me to help with your baby, so you take her right back,' I said, thrusting my niece back into her mother's arms.

'I can't believe you're getting to go on holidays in Dublin,' Siobhan snapped.

'You've no one to blame but yourself. You said you didn't need me around.'

'Well, I do and I'm going to tell Dad now.'

'No, you're not,' said Mum, stepping in. 'Niamh is going to Dublin. It'll do her good. It hasn't been an easy year for her, with all the goings-on here.'

'Dublin?' said Finn, who appeared from nowhere, hurley stick in hand. 'Can I come?'

'No, pet. Niamh's going to have some time to herself,' said Mum, putting her arm round me for the first time in ages. It felt really nice.

*　　*　　*

Two weeks later I was having breakfast with Granny and Granddad Byrne. I was in heaven. They'd said I could have bacon butties if I wanted and allowed me to slather them in HP sauce.

After breakfast Grandad handed me a sheet of paper. I read it:

Niamh O'Flaherty's Cultural Awakening
Over the next three weeks, you're going to learn all about your culture and heritage from the Famine to the present day. I promise it won't be dull.

Today we're doing a walking tour of Dublin city centre, starting at the GPO. We'll retrace the steps of the heroes of the 1916 Rising and I'll tell you how Pearse, Plunkett, MacDonagh, Connolly, Casement and the others changed the face of our country for ever.

'Granddad!' I groaned. 'I'm on holidays.'

'Your mother asked me to teach you about the history of Ireland and that's what I'm going to do. You're too cynical about it all, so I'm going to show you how proud you should be of the little island we come from,' he said, smiling.

'He's been preparing for days. Humour him,'

said Granny, winking at me.

I shrugged. 'OK, but there'd better not be any homework.'

We set off for the city centre and, to be honest, I thought it was going to be a long day, like a boring history lesson at school, but I was wrong. Granddad Byrne brought history alive. He told the story of the Easter Rising with such passion that I felt as if I was there as it was happening. When he got to the part where James Connolly was so badly injured that he couldn't stand up to be executed, so the English shot him sitting down, I was in tears. How could they have been so cruel? To shoot a cripple! I was incensed. I wanted to know more. I bombarded Granddad with questions, which he answered patiently. I felt ashamed at myself for thinking Ireland was crap.

'Is that what the song "The Foggy Dew" is about?' I sang: '"For those who died that Eastertide/In the springing of the year."'

'Yes, Niamh. That's probably the most famous of the songs about 1916.'

I felt terrible that I'd always laughed when Uncle Donal's eyes misted over as he sang that song. How had I not known about it?

Granddad did a serious number on me. By the time the three weeks were up I was a nationalist through and through. We went to a special Famine exhibition in the National Museum, where I cried at the stories of starvation and coffin ships; he told me about Parnell, explained Home Rule and filled me in on de Valera, Collins and the civil war.

I was enthralled. Ireland was a great country, a brave country, that struggled through years of oppression and cruelty. But it had survived. From

Granddad Byrne I learnt to be proud of my heritage, not ashamed of it. Now I was more confused than ever.

'What am I, Granddad? I was born in England. I live there. I sound English but I use Irish expressions. I like England—it's the only place I know. It's my home. Ireland is a place I go to on holidays. I feel like an outsider here, but now I'm angry with the English for being so mean to poor Ireland. But I am English, aren't I? Oh, I don't know what I am any more. I just want to fit in.'

'You're a mongrel,' he said, laughing. 'You're half English, half Irish, and if you use the best qualities of both cultures and backgrounds, you'll be a very interesting and well-rounded person. Don't deny either heritage. Embrace and accept them. Sure isn't it great to be different? Who wants to be the same as everyone else?'

'I do.' I sighed. 'When you're my age, Granddad, you just want to fit in. Sticking out isn't cool, especially when you're plain, not very popular and never allowed out past nine. I might as well pack it in now and join the Carmelites.'

'You've an Irish sense of humour,' said Granny Byrne. 'You don't realize it yet, but you've a wonderful dry wit. You get it from me,' she added, puffing out her chest. 'That's one of the positive Irish sides to your personality. Nurture it. Boys like girls who make them laugh.'

'That's true,' Granddad agreed. 'I'd a shower of stunners chasing me around Dublin, but none of them made me laugh. So I married the ugly one with the sense of humour.'

Granny Byrne swatted him with a tea-towel. 'The cheek of you.'

'You're a great catch, Niamh, and don't let anyone tell you different. Wait until you meet a boy who appreciates you and doesn't try to change you. That's the key to a successful relationship—that, and a lot of laughter,' said Granny Byrne, hugging me.

'Can I stay with you for ever?' I asked. 'I feel at home here.'

'That's because you get the undivided attention of two doting grandparents. No, pet, you can't stay. You have to go home, back to your life in London, and study very hard so you can go to college and make your mother proud,' said Granddad. 'But in the meantime we have a birthday to organize. What would you like to do?'

The best part of being in Dublin—apart from the fact that I wasn't ashamed of my Irishness any more—was that I'd be celebrating my sixteenth birthday without a big party and a fuss. 'I'd like a picnic by the sea,' I said. The other great thing about Dublin was that there was a lovely beach only ten minutes' drive from Granny and Granddad Byrne's house.

'That's a wonderful idea,' said Granny.

'And Madonna's new album,' I said, knowing they wouldn't have a clue who she was and would therefore allow me to have it; my mother said she was a harlot using the Blessed Virgin's name in vain.

23

When I got home I told Mum and Dad that I was proud to be Irish and that Granddad Byrne was the best history teacher in the world. Dad was beside himself with happiness, and Mum gave him an I-told-you-she-was-better-off-with-my-parents-than-your-sister-Nora look.

I threw myself into my new-found love of Ireland with a gusto that took everyone by surprise. I regaled my family non-stop with Granddad Byrne's history lessons.

Siobhan called me a lick-arse and said I was only pretending to like all the Irish stuff to get Dad on my side. She said he'd soon see through it and I'd be back to being the least favourite again. I told her she was a fat slapper who was jealous because I'd got to spend so much time on my own with our grandparents. She told me I was an ugly loser who'd never have children because no man would go near me. She had a point there, so I left the room before I started to cry because I was going to be an old maid.

Even Finn thought I'd lost the plot. He kept glancing at me and shaking his head. Eventually he asked me if I'd been kidnapped and brainwashed by Irish republican terrorists.

'Of course I haven't,' I said, insulted at the notion that anyone would be able to brainwash me.

'The whole point of being brainwashed is that you don't know you are,' Finn explained. 'Do you remember talking to any strangers or accepting food or drink from anyone you didn't know?'

'No, Finn, I didn't. I was with Granny and Granddad the whole time.'

'Maybe they got to them first,' he mused. 'That would explain it.'

'This isn't an episode of *MacGyver*.' I was exasperated with his conspiracy theories.

'Niamh O'Flaherty, do you know how to make a bomb?' he asked me, looking directly into my eyes.

'Sir, yes, sir! I can assemble an explosive device in under five minutes,' I said, standing up as Finn fell backwards in shock.

'Ah, piss off,' he said, as I giggled.

A few weeks after I'd come home, Mum, Dad, Finn and I were having dinner and I launched into another long-winded monologue about the 1916 Rising. Finn put his fork down noisily and groaned. 'Niamh, would you please shut up? I can't listen to this any more. You're like a record that's got stuck.'

'Don't say shut up. It's rude,' said Mum.

'Fine. Well, please be quiet then,' muttered Finn. 'I can't take any more of your boring history lessons. You sound like a nutter.'

'But I haven't got to the bit about Connolly yet,' I complained.

'He got shot in the chair!' hissed Finn. 'We know. You've told us a million times. It's your favourite bit.'

I noticed no one was jumping to my defence. 'Mum? Dad?'

'Why don't we give the history a rest for this evening?' said Mum. 'I'd like to eat my dinner without listening to the details of Connolly getting shot again.'

'Dad?' I asked my chief ally in all things Irish.

'Well, now, if your mother says that's enough we'll have to respect her wishes,' said Dad.

'Can I sing "The Foggy Dew"?'

'I think we might leave that to Uncle Donal. It's a very grown-up song for a young girl,' said Dad, alarmed at the thought of his sixteen-year-old belting out rebel songs. It was all right for grown men, but not for young ladies.

I sulked for the rest of the meal.

Later, when I was supposed to be in bed, I overheard my parents talking. 'What in God's name did your father do to her?' Dad asked. 'She's like some kind of fanatic.'

'You're the one who insisted on her going to Ireland to learn about her roots. You're the one who's always telling her to be proud of where she's from. All my father did was teach her some history.'

'I only wanted her to understand her heritage. How was I to know she'd take it so much to heart?' exclaimed Dad.

'Well, I know one thing, she can't be going round to people's houses singing "The Foggy Dew"!' said Mum, sounding genuinely worried. 'They'll think we're a bunch of extremists. You'll have to stop your brothers singing their rebel songs till she calms down.'

'They're not rebel songs, they're historical tales,' said Dad, sounding insulted.

'I want no more mention of songs, history or anything Irish for the time being. She's too impressionable and far too passionate. She didn't lick that off a stone,' said Mum, pointedly.

'There's nothing wrong with being passionate about your country and your history. But I have to say I'm a bit concerned at how personally she seems to have taken it all. She gets into an awful state when she talks about Connolly getting shot,' said Dad, sounding perplexed. Clearly my reaction to Granddad Byrne's indoctrination had surprised even him.

'I'm nipping it in the bud now,' said Mum. 'She's sixteen. It's not healthy for her to be going around spouting about the Famine and Home Rule. She should be out having fun with her pals. She's going to the next disco that's on in that tennis club.'

'Hold on, now,' said Dad. 'I don't want her going down the same road her sister did.'

'She's seen what a mess Siobhan made. She won't make the same mistakes. We can't lock her up because of what her sister did. We've been too strict on her, Mick. She needs to have some fun.'

I perked up. This was great. I could feel Dad wavering. Come on, Mum, don't stop now.

'We were going to dances at sixteen, and children need to be allowed to experience life. We can't keep her cooped up. She's a good girl. A bit immature, maybe, but she's no fool. She won't let a boy take advantage of her.'

Immature? Me? I wasn't too thrilled about that. I was way more mature than most kids my age. And if I was so immature, how come I got dumped with Muireann when no one else was around to babysit?

'It's not the same now,' said Dad. 'The boys here are faster than we were back home. All they want is to get into a girl's underpants.'

'I seem to remember a certain young man who was keen to get into mine.' Mum laughed.

'Annie!'

'Well, it's true. All boys are the same. There's nothing different about the young lads over here from you and your pals at that age. It's hormones, pure and simple. Niamh's going to the next disco and that's the end of it.'

'You'll have to tell her about the birds and the bees, then. She needs to understand that boys can be a bit over-anxious physically.'

'For goodness' sake, Mick! Her sister had a baby out of wedlock! She's not blind—she knows what happens if you have sex.'

'No harm in driving the point home all the same. If you want her to go to discos she needs to be fully informed of what can happen.'

'Fine, I'll talk to her,' said Mum, as I cringed. The last thing I wanted was my mother telling me about sex. It was mortifying.

Luckily for me, I only had to wait a few days until the next disco at the tennis club. I asked if I could go and Dad said I could, but only after Mum had had a 'chat' with me.

Mum looked as uncomfortable as I felt when she came into my bedroom and sat down beside me. She cleared her throat. 'Niamh, I need to talk to you about boys. The thing is that boys your age are full of hormones that turn them into octopuses.'

'Octopuses?' I said, confused. I'd thought I was getting the birds-and-bees speech.

'What I mean is that you'll find their hands are everywhere, pulling at your clothes and that. You need to be very careful not to get carried away and let them do things that aren't right.'

'Like what?'

'Like—putting their hands up your shirt or down

your skirt.'

'Do you get pregnant if a boy does that?' I asked.

'Well, no, but it begins with—' Mum stopped as I lay back on the bed and hooted. 'You little brat,' she said, swatting me with a pillow.

'Come on, Mum.' I giggled. 'I'm sixteen, I know how babies are made. And don't worry—Siobhan and Muireann have put me off sex for life.'

'I'm glad to hear it. Now go and have fun. Innocent fun!' she said, and tousled my hair before she walked out of the room.

I rang Sarah, squealing, and told her I was allowed go to the disco. She said she'd call round to pick me up two hours early so we could decide what to wear and analyse what I should say in the unlikely event of a boy asking me to dance. I was in seventh heaven.

* * *

With a couple of inches of Egypt Wonder and half a tube of lipstick on, we headed off to the disco. We ran round the corner where I got changed behind a hedge. Out of sight of my house and Dad's bionic eye, I took off my jeans and squeezed into a denim mini that Sarah lent me.

'Fabulous,' she said kindly.

'Not too tight?' I asked, as I looked down at my protruding stomach.

'No, it's just right,' she said, fixing my top so it covered the spare tyre of white flesh falling over the waistband. 'You've got great legs, you should show them off. Now, come on, have a slug of this.'

She handed me a Soda Stream bottle filled with

yellow liquid. I drank and gagged.

'Yuck! What *is* that?'

'A mixture of different drinks. Vodka, whiskey, gin, sherry and Martini, with some orange juice to make it bearable.'

'It's gross.'

'I couldn't take too much out of any of the bottles or my mum would notice, so I just took a little of all of them,' she said, having a swig and trying not to throw up. 'Come on, one more sip for courage,' she said, as I took it and had another mouthful, which I promptly spat out.

'It's too disgusting,' I said, watching in awe as Sarah knocked back the rest.

When we arrived at the disco, she was a bit unsteady on her feet. By the time her boyfriend, Declan, arrived, she was paralytic. He was not impressed by how drunk she was and when she threw up over him, he walked off in disgust, leaving me to clean up the mess.

I dragged Sarah into the toilet and tried to wipe up the vomit with toilet paper. Then I half carried her to a chair and sat her down while I went to get her a glass of water. One of Declan's friends was at the bar. 'Is Sarah all right?' he asked.

Normally when a boy spoke to me I froze, but because I was so distracted with trying to sort Sarah out, I answered like a normal person. 'Not really,' I said. 'I need to get her some water to sober her up. Her mother will kill her if she arrives home in that state.'

'Do you need a hand?' he asked.

'Actually, that'd be great. I want to get her outside into the fresh air.'

He helped me carry Sarah out and placed her

gently on the grass, propped up against a tree, where she fell asleep.

'Thanks, I'd never have managed it on my own,' I said.

'No problem. I'm Teddy, by the way.'

'Hi, I'm Niamh,' I said, looking at him properly for the first time, now that Sarah was out of vomiting distance. He was cute, if not in an obvious head-turning way. His hair stuck up in a cow's lick at the front and he had a crooked nose, but he had a lovely smile. And he was English. Could I fraternize with an English boy when I'd seen what his ancestors had done to my country? I looked at him again. He was very cute . . . Sod it, I couldn't change history and this was just what we needed: better inter-country relationships.

'How come you're so together and she's in such a state?' he asked.

'Luck,' I admitted. 'The drink she made tasted so awful I spat it out. Otherwise there'd be two of us under the tree.'

He smiled. 'Declan's not too happy with being puked over.'

'Judging by how far his tongue is down that other girl's throat, I'd say he's got over it,' I said.

Teddy laughed. 'You're funny,' he said, as I blushed. 'I haven't seen you here before. Where do you go to school?'

'St Bridget's for holy Catholic girls whose parents want them to become nuns.'

'Do you?'

'Aspiring nuns don't generally wear minis or hang out with drunken pukers.'

'Glad to hear it,' he said, coming closer and taking my hand.

'Nor do they talk to strange men.'

'How about kissing them?' he asked.

'Definitely not in the nuns' handbook,' I said, as he kissed me. And this time it was fantastic, just like in the movies. Not horrible and slimy like my first snog had been.

We were mid-flow when I heard a noise behind me. It was Sarah, sobbing. Part of me really wanted to ignore her and keep kissing Teddy, but she was pretty loud so, reluctantly, I stopped and went over to her.

'I want go *hooooooome*,' she wailed. 'I feel awful. What happened?'

I decided not to tell her about throwing up over her boyfriend and also omitted the fact that he was currently sucking the face off someone else.

'You're all right. The drink just went to your head. Come on, have some water.'

'I don't want water, I want to go home.'

Why couldn't she have stayed asleep a little longer? Now I'd have to take her home and probably never see the gorgeous Teddy again. Typical! The one night things were going my way my friend had to get as drunk as George Best on a bender.

'Where's Declan?' she asked.

'He had to go home early,' said the diplomatic Teddy.

'Did he see how drunk I was?'

'Not really. You fell asleep early on,' I said.

'Thank God. Let's go, Niamh. I need to lie down,' Sarah said, tugging my arm.

'OK,' I reluctantly agreed. 'Well, 'bye, Teddy.'

'Best of luck,' he said. 'Maybe I'll see you here again some time?'

‘Definitely,’ I said, resisting the urge to beg him to call me.

24

The garage door swung open and a red-faced Siobhan glared out. ‘What the hell are you doing?’ she fumed. ‘Are you crazy, waking me up in the middle of the night? This had better be an emergency.’

I decided not to point out that it was only ten thirty-five and most normal people would still be up. ‘It *is* an emergency. I need your help.’

‘What’s wrong?’

‘Sarah’s plastered and I can’t let her go home. I need to sober her up, but I don’t know how to.’

‘Oh, for God’s sake, bring her in. Where is she?’

‘I left her in the hedge, in case Mum and Dad saw her out the window. I’ll go and get her,’ I said, running down the path to extract Sarah from the hedge, where she had fallen asleep again.

‘Look at the state of her,’ said Siobhan, shocked at how bad Sarah was. ‘What did she drink?’

‘A lethal cocktail of everything you can think of with a splash of orange juice.’

‘Did you have it too?’

I shook my head. ‘No, it tasted disgusting. I couldn’t swallow it.’

‘You’re lucky you couldn’t. How come you got lumped with looking after her? I thought she had a boyfriend.’

‘Had,’ I whispered. ‘He found someone else

after she puked on his shoes, but she doesn't know yet.'

'Typical men,' said my sister, as if she'd had vast experience of being dumped and cheated on, instead of having a boyfriend who'd stood by her, married her, then put up with her foul moods and mad crying fits.

Sarah began to slip out of my grasp. I plonked her on the couch where she began to groan.

'She'd better not be sick in here,' said Siobhan, seemingly oblivious to the pungent smell of baby vomit and dirty nappies that permeated her apartment.

'She won't.'

'If she does, you're dead. Now, come on, let's get some coffee into her and see if we can sober her up.'

'What about Mum and Dad?' I asked.

'It's OK, they're watching TV. I'll go and make some coffee for Sarah now. Just keep her quiet so they don't hear you.'

'Siobhan.'

'What?' she snapped.

'Sarah doesn't like coffee.'

She sighed. 'All right, then, I'll make some toast. That should soak up some of the booze. In the meantime, get her to drink as much water as you can. There's a glass in the bathroom.'

'Siobhan.'

'What is it now?' she hissed.

'Thanks.'

My sister came back five minutes later with a big plate of warm buttered toast and a bucket. She helped me prop up the sleeping Sarah. After several futile attempts to wake her by shaking her,

Siobhan slapped her across the face.

'Ouch,' said Sarah, coming out of her semi-coma. 'That hurt.'

'You need to wake up, eat this and drink the water,' ordered Siobhan, shoving the plate into my friend's lap.

Sarah looked at the toast. 'I think I'm going to be sick,' she said, as Siobhan produced the bucket for her to throw up in. She'd thought of everything. I was impressed.

Being sick again seemed to sober Sarah up. Now that most of the alcohol she'd drunk was on the floor of the disco and in the bucket, she was able to speak without slurring. If it wasn't for the smell of vomit, her greenish face and the fact that she kept crying, she might have got away with it.

'Take this into the bathroom and rinse it out,' Siobhan said, and I reluctantly took the stinky bucket from her. My love for Sarah was diminishing by the second.

Siobhan cleaned Sarah's clothes with baby wipes—which I have to say were miraculous. Then she brushed her hair and applied makeup to her pasty face. 'Sarah,' she said sternly, 'you've *got* to stop crying. If you don't want to be grounded for the rest of your life, focus on acting sober and normal. When you get home, try not to talk too much. Just say you had a nice time but you're tired and you want to go to bed. Don't stand close to your parents. You smell of drink. Here, this should help,' she added, drowning Sarah in her favourite perfume, Poison, by Christian Dior. I couldn't believe it. She never let me use it and kept it locked in her jewellery box. 'OK, now stand up straight and smile. You should get away with it,' said my new, sharing, caring sister.

'Thanks, Siobhan,' said Sarah, beginning to cry again. 'I always thought you were a pain. Niamh said you can be a real bitch sometimes, but you've been great tonight.'

I wondered if I wanted to hang around with Sarah any more. She was a liability.

'Come on,' I said, grabbing my ex-best-friend's arm. 'It's getting late.'

I walked her down the road to her front garden. She gushed about how wonderful Siobhan was, not once bothering to mention that *I* had saved her from total humiliation at the disco. Neither did she apologize for ruining my first decent snog. I said nothing until we got to her gate, where I reminded her not to talk or stand too close to her mother. It was vital that she got away with it. If she was caught drunk, I'd be implicated too, and if my father got wind of it, I'd be on the next plane to boarding-school.

I walked home, changed back into my jeans behind the hedge and let myself in the front door.

'What time do you call this?' my father said, tapping his watch.

'Five past eleven,' I answered.

'Exactly, and did I not tell you to be home by eleven on the dot?'

'Ah, Mick, will you leave her alone?' said Mum. 'Well, pet, did you have a nice time?'

'Yes, thanks.'

'Did you get a dance?' asked Dad.

'Yes, I did.' Technically it wasn't exactly true, but a snog was probably the same as a dance in Dad's era, so I didn't feel I was lying.

'Oh, good.' Mum looked relieved. Clearly she'd

been worried that I'd be left in the corner like a big wallflower. It was bad enough knowing your chances were slim—you really didn't need to be faced with your parents' doubts too.

'Well, goodnight, I'm off to bed,' I said, suddenly very tired.

As I was snuggling up in bed, Mum popped her head round the door. 'You didn't sing "The Foggy Dew" tonight, did you?'

I shook my head. 'I'm leaving the history aside for now. It's exhausting feeling passionately about everything. I need to save my energy for discos.'

'I'm glad to hear it,' she said, patting my arm. 'Was he a nice boy?' she asked.

'Who?'

'You know right well who. The boy you danced with.'

'Very.' I grinned, despite myself.

'Good. And you didn't let anything happen that—'

'No,' Mum,' I interrupted, before she could embarrass me. 'No octopus carry-on, I promise.'

'I'm pleased to hear that,' she said, leaning down to turn off the lamp. She kissed my forehead. 'I'm glad you had a nice time, pet. It's wonderful to be young. Enjoy it,' she added wistfully.

'Did you have fun when you were my age?' I asked her.

'Yes, but I got married and had children very early, so I wasn't young for long.'

'Like Siobhan.'

She nodded.

'I think I'll wait until I'm thirty to get married.'

'That's a very sensible idea. Now go to sleep. Sweet dreams.'

I closed my eyes and pictured Teddy . . . mmmm . . .

*   *   *

Sarah phoned the next day to say that when she'd got home her parents were in the middle of a big argument and barely noticed her. She'd been able to stumble upstairs and fall into bed without getting into trouble. I was delighted to hear it as it meant my coast was clear. She apologized for being such a mess and thanked me for being such a loyal, trustworthy, reliable, brilliant friend. Then she asked me to fill in the blanks about the disco and I had to tell her about Declan, which kind of ruined the best-friend love-in. She was devastated. But then I told her about Teddy, and although she was still crying about Declan, she did seem pleased for me.

I decided to keep her as my very best friend. They weren't queuing round the block for the position, and she was a really nice person when she wasn't drinking and falling into bushes, so we made up and spent the afternoon locked in my bedroom discussing Teddy and slating Declan. By the time she left, we'd decided Declan didn't deserve her in the first place and that Teddy was my future husband.

At the crack of dawn the next day—Monday—a very nervous Liam stood at the front door waiting for his exam results. Having spent the summer working on building sites for Dad, he was now hoping to get a place to study law. Since Muireann's birth his relationship with his father had improved. They met up about once a month and Liam wanted to follow in his footsteps.

Liam's mother still hadn't forgiven or spoken to Liam since he'd got Siobhan pregnant. Liam said he didn't mind but you could see he was heartbroken that his witch of a mother hadn't even had the decency to come and see her grandchild.

The postman finally arrived and Liam grabbed the envelope. He ran into the garage to open it alone. We all waited outside the door, listening. We heard a whoop, the door burst open and a very happy Liam hugged Siobhan and Muireann—who began to cry because he was squashing her.

'Straight As!' he shouted. 'I got straight As! I did it! I bloody did it!'

'Well done, son,' said Dad, beaming at him.

'You deserve every one of those As,' said Mum, hugging him. 'I never saw a fella study so hard.'

'Nice one,' said Finn, thumping Liam on the back.

'Congratulations,' I said, and backed away quickly, because Liam had started to cry. It wasn't just a few tears either. It was total shoulder-heaving sobs.

'It's all right, Liam,' Mum said, going over to him. 'Let it out. You've had a very difficult year. You poor old thing. You've been so brave and hard-working. Never a complaint out of you about anything. It's an emotional day. We're very proud of you. I know you wish your parents were here for you, but I'm afraid life can be cruel sometimes. But look at what you've achieved. Muireann will be very proud of her daddy.'

This made him cry even more and Siobhan joined in, followed shortly by Muireann, who grabbed any opportunity to show us her lung capacity. We shuffled about uncomfortably when the doorbell rang.

Finn charged out to see who it was, delighted to have an excuse to get out of the room. It was Liam's father, and we heard Finn showing him into the good room. Mum grabbed a cloth and wiped Liam's face.

'Stand up, son, and hold your head high. You're a credit to yourself and this family,' said Dad.

We marched into the good room where Mr O'Loughlin was nervously pacing the floor. When he saw Liam's blotchy face he looked crestfallen. 'You didn't get enough for law, did you?' he asked.

'Didn't my eye!' snapped Dad. 'This young lad got straight As. He's a genius, so he is. You should be very proud of him. *We* are,' he added pointedly.

Mr O'Loughlin looked at his son. Liam nodded and handed his father the results.

'My God, Liam, this is incredible. I've never known anyone to get straight As. You'll go to King's College, of course, and then you can work for me. Your mother will come round when she sees these results. She might even come to see you.'

'No, thank you,' said Liam, firmly. 'I don't need your help, Dad. I'll be choosing what university I go to and what firm I work for and it won't be yours. If Mum does decide to talk to me again because of my results, please tell her that she will not be welcome. I never want her to darken my door. This is my family. These are the people who stood by me and gave me the freedom to study. They are the only people I care about impressing. I have to go now, I'm late for work.'

Mr O'Loughlin seemed taken aback by his son's steely attitude.

'Don't worry about work today, Liam,' said Dad.

'I'll look after Muireann,' said Mum. 'Take Siobhan out and celebrate.'

'I'd like to take you for lunch at the club,' said Mr O'Loughlin, recovering his composure.

'Sorry, Dad, I've got a date with my beautiful wife,' said Liam, smiling at Siobhan. With that they headed off hand in hand out of the door, looking, for the first time since Muireann's conception, like a carefree young couple.

Irish Daily News

'Shoe shopping'

Niamh O'Flaherty

When Alice goes shoe shopping to find the perfect pair to go with the new dress she's bought for a wedding, she knows it's going to be an experience. She has spent weeks flicking through fashion magazines looking for the right match.

She gets all dressed up, carefully folds her new dress into a big bag and sets off. She is on a high. Shoe shopping is her drug of choice.

She goes into the first shoe shop where, lo and behold, she finds a pair of shoes that matches her dress. With the shoes on, she takes the dress out of the bag and holds it up to herself in the mirror. The shoes are the exact same colour. Perfect.

The sales assistant smiles. 'Shall I pop those in a box for you, madam?'

Alice shakes her head. 'No. I'm not sure they're quite right. I'm going to look around before making my decision.'

Alice then goes into every shoe shop in town trying on shoes—none of which match the dress. After two hours, with sore, swollen feet, she goes back to the first shop to buy the first shoes she tried on. They have been sold. Alice is devastated. She tries not to cry and ends up buying silver shoes that don't match anything.

Mike needs a pair of shoes to go with his new brown suit. He goes shopping in his comfy jeans and sweatshirt. He has ten minutes before Man United v. Arsenal kicks off. He charges into the first shoe shop he sees. It's small, with a limited selection.

He grabs an assistant and says, 'I need a pair of brown shoes, size eleven.'

'Did you have any particular style in mind?' she asks.

Mike laughs. 'Style! No, just brown, size eleven.'

The assistant comes back and says she's really sorry but they don't have any brown shoes in size eleven. They only have brown boots.

'Have you any size eleven shoes?' Mike asks.

'We have these burgundy ones,' she says.

'Grand, yeah, I'll take those.'

'Would you like to try them on?'

'No time, got to catch the game,' says Mike, handing over his credit card.

Mike and Alice go to the wedding. Mike's shoes match Alice's dress perfectly.

25

London, 16 March 1999

The taxi-man peered at me in the mirror. 'Home or holiday?'

I really didn't feel like talking, but I didn't want to be rude. 'Home. Well, I don't live here but I'm back to see my family.'

'Where do you live, then?'

'Ireland—Dublin.'

'That makes a change, English people going to live in Ireland after all the Paddies that have come over here. What made you go there?'

'My parents,' I said. 'They're Irish and always wanted me to go and study there, so I did.'

'Like it, do you?'

'At first I hated it, but now I like it.'

'Oh, yeah? Met a nice local lad, did you?' he said, grinning at me in the mirror.

'Something like that,' I said. 'Actually, I'm engaged.'

'Your dad'll be made up, you ending up with a nice Irish boy.'

'The thing is, he's not Irish,' I said, wishing for the millionth time that Pierre was Irish with bright red hair and freckles. It would have made my life so much easier.

* * *

When I got home, Dad rushed out to pay the taxi for me and help me with my bags. He hugged me, and I sank into his arms, a bit tearful. The stress of having to tell him about Pierre was killing me. I was a nervous wreck. 'What's wrong? Has something happened to you?'

'I'm fine, Dad, just glad to be home,' I said, giving him a watery smile.

'Are you sure? You don't seem fine to me. Did you break up with another boyfriend?'

'No, the opposite, actually. I've met someone.'

'Your mother mentioned something about that. She didn't give much away though. Is he a nice lad?'

I nodded, smiling. 'Yes, Dad, he is.'

'Ah, sure didn't I tell you Irish lads were the best of them all? Annie,' he said, calling my mother who was cooking up a storm in the kitchen, 'Niamh's all emotional about her new boyfriend.'

'Hello, love,' said Mum, kissing me. 'You do look a bit weepy—are you all right?'

'I'm fine, thanks.'

'She's missing the new lad,' said Dad, on cloud nine now that he thought his daughter was paired up with an Irish boy.

'What boyfriend?' asked Siobhan, shoving a large slice of buttery toast into her mouth. 'I thought you were still heartbroken about Sean.'

'I broke up with him a year ago,' I reminded her.

'You kept saying you'd never get over it,' she reminded me, as I winced. I really didn't want to think about the time I'd wasted mourning that tosser.

'Well, I have and I've met someone else now.'

'So it's still going strong, then,' Mum said.

'Yes, very,' I replied.

'Oh dear, she's smitten, all right,' said Mum,

smiling.

'What's his name?' Dad asked.

I took a deep breath. Here we go, I thought. 'His—' Before I had a chance to say, 'Pierre,' my uncle Tadhg came in, said they needed a hand with the float, and Dad rushed out.

'What float?' I asked.

Mum rolled her eyes. 'Your father has decided to build the biggest float in this year's St Patrick's Day parade.'

I glanced out of the kitchen window to see Tadhg and my father trying to lift a giant wooden shamrock on to a cart. Despite myself I began to laugh. 'Oh, God, Mum, it's enormous.'

'I know. They've been at it for weeks.'

'I think it's brilliant,' said my ever-patriotic sister. 'I used to love dancing in the parades.' She sighed, looking down at her fat feet.

'You'll need to lay off the toast if you want to dance again,' said Mum sternly, looking at Siobhan's round frame.

'It's baby weight. I'll lose it soon,' huffed my sister.

'The baby's three, you'd want to get on with it,' Mum muttered.

'TO THE LEFT,' we heard Tadhg roar from outside.

'I'M DOING MY BEST, THIS THING WEIGHS A TON,' shouted Dad.

'JUST A FEW INCHES MORE AND WE HAVE IT,' said Tadhg.

I watched Dad's face turn purple with effort.

'That man's an idiot. He's too old to be lifting that much weight,' tutted Mum, and no sooner were the words out of her mouth than we saw Dad fall sideways. He lay motionless on the grass.

'Mick,' screamed Mum, as we sprinted out of the door, followed by a puffing Siobhan.

Dad was clutching his chest and gasping for breath. While Tadhg ran to call an ambulance, Mum and I lifted Dad's head, loosened his clothes and tried to keep him conscious. Siobhan sat on the grass beside us and sobbed. 'Daddy's dying.'

'Shut up and get him a glass of water,' I snapped.

By the time the ambulance arrived, his breathing had improved slightly, but he was still gripping his chest and unable to speak. Mum and Tadhg went with him in the ambulance and Siobhan and I followed in the car. I rang Finn and Auntie Nuala on the way. But then I had to swap places with Siobhan and do the driving, because she was hysterical and swerving all over the road. I didn't think it was fair to Mum if both her daughters died in a car crash on the same day her husband had a heart-attack.

By the time we got to the hospital, Dad had been rushed into intensive care and was having a variety of tests. Tadhg was pacing up and down the corridor, wailing.

' 'Tis all my fault. I should have been doing the lifting. Mick's that bit older. I'll die if anything happens him.'

'He'll be fine, don't worry yourself. Now, could you do me a favour and get us all a nice cup of tea?' Mum asked. He scurried off, happy to be doing something useful.

'Bloody fool! How could he let poor Mick lift that shamrock?' said Mum, slating Tadhg as soon as he was out of earshot. 'He's eight years younger!

He should have been pushing, not giving instructions. I blame him for this.'

I decided not to mention that I thought the twenty cigarettes a day Dad smoked and his diet of cream and butter probably had a lot more to do with the heart-attack than the float.

'Stupid bloody shamrock. I've always hated St Patrick's Day,' Mum grumbled.

'Mum!' said Siobhan, horrified. 'How can you say that about our patron saint's day?'

'Because I hate wearing a lump of weeds on my coat, I never liked the colour green and, to be totally honest with you, I find the parade an almighty bore.'

'You're just emotionally traumatized,' said Siobhan, refusing to believe that everyone didn't love the parade. 'I'll go and help Tadhg with the teas. I might get some chocolate to keep us going.'

'It'll be OK, Mum,' I said.

'How do you know?' she snapped.

Finn came running in. 'Is he OK?' he asked, as Mum stood up to hug him.

'He's stable. They're running tests on him now,' I answered, as Mum sobbed into Finn's shoulder.

'He'll be fine, Mum. He's a fighter,' said Finn, as Mum gazed adoringly at him. You'd think she'd at least *try* to hide her favouritism.

Nuala rushed over. 'Well? Is he dead?' she asked, cutting straight to the chase.

'Jesus, Nuala, what type of a question is that?' said Tadhg, arriving back with the teas.

'What kind of an eejit are you?' she retorted. 'It isn't tea they need, it's brandy.' She pulled a bottle out of her bag and poured large quantities into the cups.

* * *

After an anxious wait, the doctor came and told us Dad was stable, he was going to be fine but he needed lots of rest, a strict change of diet, regular exercise—not of the heavy lifting variety—and that he was never to smoke again. We were all to make sure he didn't.

'Can we see him?' asked Finn.

'Only immediate family and only for a few minutes. He's very tired and needs rest.'

We left Nuala and Tadhg sitting outside while we went in. Dad was lying in a bed, looking old and forlorn.

'You gave us an awful fright,' said Mum, holding his hand.

'Oh, Dad, we thought you were dead,' said Siobhan, throwing her arms round him as he flinched with pain.

'I'm grand. Now go home and help Tadhg set up the float. I want it ready for the morning.'

'Will you forget about that stupid float? It was nearly the death of you,' snapped Mum.

'I promised Father Hogan I'd have it ready in the morning and I never break a promise. Finn, will you go home and help Tadhg finish the job? Niamh, you can give it a lick of paint. I've a pot in the garage.'

'I'm glad to see you're all right, Dad,' I said, leaning over to kiss his cheek.

'Give it two coats of the paint to make sure it looks good,' he said, as I backed out of the room before he could ask me to push the bloody float through the parade.

* * *

As Siobhan was driving me home, my phone rang. It was Pierre.

'How did it go? Did he take it badly?' he asked.

'I didn't tell him.'

'Niamh,' he said, sounding really fed up, 'you promised you would. I can't believe you chickened out again.'

'I didn't. He had a heart-attack just after I arrived,' I said, beginning to get emotional.

'What? Is he all right?'

'Yes, he's going to be fine. He just needs to rest and change his diet and stuff.'

'How did it happen?'

'He collapsed under a giant shamrock.'

'Is this a wind-up?'

'No, I wish it was. It was for the parade tomorrow.'

'Do you want me to come over and be with you? I can be there in a few hours.'

'No! Not now. It's not a good idea. Look, I'll call you later, I can't really talk at the moment.'

'OK. Well, let me know if you need anything. I love you.'

'Thanks. I love you too.'

'Love!' said Siobhan. 'Wow, it must be serious with this guy.'

'It is. We're engaged.'

'*What?*' She nearly crashed the car. 'Engaged? And none of us have even set eyes on him. How long has this been going on?'

'Six months, two weeks and three days,' I said, smiling.

'Why haven't you mentioned him before? Why haven't we met him?'

'Well, it all happened so quickly, there wasn't really time. Finn met him when he came over last month.'

'Did he? He never said anything about it to me. So, what's he like? What does he do? Where did you meet him? What's his name?'

'He's tall, dark and handsome. He's a professor and we met in a coffee bar. His name's Pierre.'

'What? That doesn't sound very Irish.'

'He's not.'

'Oh, no! Dad's going to freak. He was convinced you'd meet an Irish guy in Dublin. Where's he from?'

'He's kind of French.'

'And he's a professor—is he older?'

'Yes, he's forty-two.'

'Oh, my God, he's practically old enough to be your father. Dad's going to go mad,' she said, staring at me in shock as she swerved all over the road.

'I know,' I said, clinging to the door handle.

'Couldn't you have found an Irish guy your own age? Why did you have to fall for an old French guy? You're looking for trouble.'

'Actually, he's not exactly French.'

'What do you mean?'

'His parents are from Martinique but he was raised in France till he was ten and then they moved to England.'

'Where's that?'

'It's in the Caribbean.'

'He's not—'

'Yes, he is.'

Siobhan stared at me open-mouthed as she crashed into a lamppost.

26

Thankfully the damage to the car wasn't too bad, but I was blamed for the crash and asked to pay for the repairs.

Siobhan kept staring at me and shaking her head. 'You must have a screw loose,' she said. 'Why would you do this to Dad? You know it'll kill him.'

I was sorely tempted to remind her that she had nearly pushed him over the brink with her teenage pregnancy, but decided to bite my tongue. She was wound up enough already. 'I didn't choose to fall for Pierre, it just happened. You don't decide who you're going to love,' I said, pleased with how it sounded. I'd been practising that line for weeks.

'If a black man made a pass at me I'd run a mile,' said my progressive sister. 'You just don't entertain it. You marry your own. With all those Irish boys in Dublin, why the hell did you have to find the only fella from Martinee—or wherever it is?'

'Because he's special.'

'It's so typical of you, Niamh,' hissed Siobhan. 'You can never do things normally, like everyone else. You have to be different, you have to push the boundaries and upset Dad. This is just like when he asked you to do Irish dancing and you had to lie to him and do tap. Why can't you be like everyone else?'

'Have you got amnesia?' I snarled. 'Have you forgotten about your shotgun wedding? Have you chosen to erase the memory of Dad sobbing himself to sleep at night over it?' I said, twisting the knife. I was sick and tired of Siobhan taking the moral high ground.

'Liam is one of our own. Dad's mad about him. He's like a son to him. I don't see him feeling the same way about an old black man.'

'Pierre's not old, and the fact that he's black has nothing to do with anything,' I said.

'That's rubbish and you know it. If you didn't think it was a big deal, you'd have mentioned him before now.'

Sussed.

'OK, I know it's not ideal and I do realize Dad'll go mad, but I was hoping you'd be on my side. I need allies when I tell him. And when you meet Pierre you'll love him. He's amazing.'

'I'm sorry, Niamh, but I don't approve. I think you're mad. Everyone's going to be shocked. No one in the family will support this and Mum and Dad will never accept it, so you'll just have to break it off, find a guy your own age and make sure he's white.'

'Don't approve? Who the hell do you think you are? Do you have any idea how racist you're being?'

'I'm not being racist, I'm being realistic. It won't work.'

'It will work because I've met the perfect person for me. What he looks like is irrelevant. He's my soulmate and I'm going to marry him, regardless of what anyone else thinks. And I can't believe that you, my own sister, won't support me. I presumed you'd be happy for me. I stupidly thought you'd congratulate me and be thrilled that I'd met a great guy, instead of telling me to dump him.'

'I'm being honest. You're living in Fantasy Land if you think this wedding is ever going to happen.'

'I love him,' I said, using my best line of defence.

She looked at me. 'I'm sure you do, but I can't pretend it's OK. The truth is that everyone's going to freak out. You have to be prepared for that. No one is going to consider this a good idea. So you need to think long and hard before you blurt it out to Mum and Dad—particularly Dad in his current condition. He'll probably have another heart-attack. Just wait a few months and see how you feel then. What's the rush anyway?'

'Pierre's been offered a post as professor of linguistics in Vancouver. He's moving to Canada in ten weeks' time. I'm going with him and we want to get married first.'

Siobhan sat back in the crumpled car and groaned. 'Oh, Niamh, I'd hate to be you right now.'

* * *

When we got home, Finn pulled me aside and asked if Dad's heart-attack was really because of the shamrock or was it because I told him about Pierre?

'It was the shamrock, and thanks for implying that my news could kill him.'

'It can and, to be honest, I think it will. Older is bad enough, not Irish is worse, but black . . . Forget about it, Niamh. He's going to flip.'

'You met Pierre, you saw how amazing he is, how can you not be more supportive?' I asked, completely exasperated that everyone was presuming Dad would die when he found out about Pierre.

'He's a good guy and he seems to be mad about you, but none of that will change Dad's reaction.'

'Well, he's just going to have to get over it.'

'You're not planning on telling him now, are you?' asked Finn, looking shocked.

'Of course not. I'm going to wait a week or two until he's feeling better and the doctor says his heart is strong again. Then I'll break the news.'

'When is Pierre off to Canada?'

'Ten weeks.'

'And you still want to get married before then?'

I nodded.

'Why not say you're going to Canada to study and tell Dad about Pierre later?'

'Because Pierre wants to get married now and have kids straight away. He doesn't want to be too old to pick them up and I don't want to have kids unless I'm married. I guess it's the Irish Catholic guilt. Some of it's obviously sunk in. I'm traditional about marriage and kids. Besides, I know Mum and Dad would be even more upset if I did that.'

'I wouldn't describe an inter-race marriage as traditional.'

'You can't help who you fall for. Come on, Finn, I need your help with Mum and Dad. I need you to sing Pierre's praises, tell them how wonderful he is.'

'I'll do my best, but if you get excommunicated, I'm jumping ship,' he said, grinning at me.

'Do you think it'll be that bad?'

'Worse.'

27

Having promised Dad we'd finish the float, Finn and I woke up early on St Patrick's Day and went out to the garden to salvage the shamrock. We somehow managed to lift it on to the cart, while Tadhg—who, having seen his brother's heart give out, wasn't taking any chances himself in case it was hereditary—shouted instructions. Then we painted it three times for good measure. It looked utterly ridiculous and wonderful at the same time.

We wheeled it down to the parish hall where we were met with a startling array of floats, marching bands, baton twirlers and dancing curtains. Siobhan's five daughters—Muireann, eleven, Saibhe, nine, Morag, seven, Blathnaid, five and Ailbhe, three—were all dressed in green Irish-dancing dresses and were leaping about, high as kites with excitement. They were going to be dancing on a float that Liam's law firm was sponsoring. As a former Irish-dancing champion, Liam was keen that his daughters enjoy jigs and reels as much as he and Siobhan had done. Within five years of setting up his own law firm, he had made a name for himself within the Irish community. He was highly respected as a lawyer, although my regard for him stemmed from the fact that he was able to put up with my sister on a daily basis without strangling her.

'Is that it?' Siobhan asked, pointing to the shamrock.

'Yes,' I said, proud of our achievement.

'You didn't do a very good job. The paint's all

streaky.'

'We've been up since seven after four hours' sleep. It's a bloody miracle we managed to get here at all,' growled Finn.

'No need to be so grumpy. I'm just saying Dad wouldn't like to see his hard work displayed like that.'

Finn sighed, pulled out a paint pot and began to smooth the streaky parts, while Siobhan ordered him around.

I went to find Father Hogan amid the chaos to tell him that the shamrock had made it but Dad hadn't. I eventually found him crouched down, trying to persuade a young boy that wearing a green velvet jacket didn't mean he was gay.

'I won't wear it, it's a fag's jacket,' insisted the boy.

'Not at all, Diarmuid, it's a big man's jacket. It's not girly at all.'

'I'm not putting it on.'

'But your poor mother spent weeks making it for you.'

'I'll be slagged in school for looking like a gay leprechaun.'

'But you were specially chosen to portray St Patrick as a youngster.'

'I don't want to be him.'

'But he's our patron saint. It's an honour. Sure didn't he banish all the snakes from Ireland?'

'Fuck Ireland, fuck St Patrick and fuck his stupid snakes,' shouted Diarmuid.

'Don't speak to Father Hogan like that,' I interrupted. 'And if you really think St Patrick's so lame, give the jacket to someone else and let them be a star for the day.'

'Fine, take it,' he said, throwing it at me.

'Are you blind? Haven't you seen how gorgeous the girls are out there? They'll all want to talk to the guy playing St Patrick on the main float. You must be mad not to want to wear the jacket and get loads of attention from girls.'

Diarmuid glanced around at the array of girls dancing, twirling batons and playing musical instruments.

I held out the jacket.

'OK. I suppose a few hours wouldn't kill me,' he said, putting it on and strutting over to a group of girls.

'Well done, Niamh,' said Father Hogan. 'Before you arrived I was definitely losing that battle.'

'No problem. I can't believe he was so rude to you.'

'Ah, sure the young kids today are very aggressive. Not like you lot.'

I thought back to my days of sitting in mass every Sunday, with a face on me that would curdle milk. I might have been a reluctant worshipper but I'd never have dreamt of telling a priest to eff off. Poor Father Hogan, if that was what he was dealing with.

'I wanted to find you to let you know that Dad's float is here. Unfortunately, however, Dad's in hospital. He had a heart-attack trying to get the shamrock on to the cart last night.'

Father Hogan blessed himself. 'Sweet Lord above, is he all right?'

'He's going to be fine, but we all got a bit of a fright.'

'Poor Mick, but sure isn't it typical of him to put so much effort into everything that he does? There are no half-measures with him. He's a great man, so he is. I'll say a prayer for him and pop in to him later on when all this madness is over.'

'Thanks, Father, he'd appreciate that.'

'Are you home for the celebrations? I thought you'd stay in Dublin for the big parade there.'

'No, I wanted to come home to see the family.'

'Ah, sure aren't you great? Your father's always telling me how well you're doing. The apple of his eye, you are.'

Was I? Had I really taken over from Siobhan? I began to realize that maybe I had. After Siobhan's shotgun wedding, things had slowly changed between me and Dad. No longer was I the one he clashed with all the time; the one who was as stubborn as him and determined to do her own thing. I grew up, he mellowed a bit, we argued less and got on. The icing on the cake was definitely when I announced I was going to college in Dublin. Dad thought he'd died and gone to heaven. He wanted Finn to go too, but he'd had no interest. He wanted to go straight into the family business and he was proving to be very good at it.

Sadly, my days of glory were now numbered. Once the secret of Pierre was out, I'd be flung off the pedestal. It had been nice while it lasted.

'Thanks, Father, it's good to be back.'

'I'd better go, but thanks for helping me with young Diarmuid. I owe you one.'

Little did he know that this was music to my ears. Having Father Hogan on-side was something I could really do with.

'Actually, Father, I have a quick question for you.'

'Fire ahead.'

'It's hypothetical.'

'Aren't they all?'

'If a Catholic girl wanted to marry an agnostic would that be really bad?'

'Well, obviously the Church would prefer her to marry a fellow Catholic, but if he was a good man and she loved him, I think that would be fine. Her parents might find it difficult, if they had strong faith, like your parents, for instance.'

'Would the girl be excommunicated if she married this non-Catholic?'

'No. If she keeps her faith then the Church would still welcome her. Would there be any chance of this girl's partner converting?'

'Not a hope in hell,' I said.

'Pity, but sure that's life.'

'Could they get married in a church anyway?'

'They could. However, the Catholic girl would have to declare her intention to continue practising the Catholic faith and do all in her power to share that faith with children born of the marriage by having them baptized and raised as Catholics.'

'So she needs to get him to agree to raise their children Catholic?'

'Yes. I think it would also help ease things over with the girl's family if they knew the grandchildren were going to be raised in the Catholic faith.'

'OK. What if the man was agnostic and black?'

Father Hogan looked shocked, but rallied well. 'We're all God's children.'

'Do you think the girl's family would feel that way?'

'I'm not sure they'd find it easy to accept. It's a

lot to address, but one would hope after time, maybe . . .' His voice trailed off and he avoided eye contact.

'OK. Well, thanks for your time, Father.' I turned to walk off, shoulders slumped. If a priest who spent his whole life saying comforting things to people couldn't help me, I was, in Diarmuid's word—fucked.

'Niamh!' Father Hogan called after me. I turned to face him. 'Does the girl really love this man?'

'Yes, very much.'

'Well, then, I'd be happy to make myself available for advice and so forth when she decides to tell her family. I'm presuming she hasn't already done so.'

'No, Father, she hasn't found the right time yet. But when she does, I'll make sure to get her to call you. I think she's going to need all the help she can get.'

'Wish her good luck from me. She sounds like a lovely girl.'

* * *

I went to find Liam, Siobhan and the girls. Finn was still working on the repaint. Watching my nieces grinning from ear to ear, dancing about, their hair in perfect ringlets, made me smile. They were adorable. Siobhan and Liam were practising a few steps with them and they looked, from a distance, like the perfect family—except for Muireann who seemed a bit sulky. It was nice that, after a difficult start, they had managed to stay together and create a lovely family unit. Liam still didn't speak to his mother. He had never forgiven her for throwing him out and disowning him when she found out Siobhan was pregnant. But his father regularly came to see his granddaughters and catch up with his son.

I wondered would Dad disown me when he found out about Pierre. Surely not. He couldn't be that set against it. Could he? Was I giving up everything to marry Pierre? What was he going to sacrifice to marry me? As if on cue, my phone rang.

'Hello, darling, how's your dad?' asked my fiancé, and my doubts faded away. Just hearing his voice made me smile.

'He's OK thanks. I miss you.' I sighed.

'Good, because I miss you terribly. When are you coming back?'

'I'd like to stay until Dad's out of hospital and spend a few days at home making sure he's OK. I should be back in a week or so.'

'Do you want me to come over?'

'No. When I tell him about you, I'm sure he'll want to meet you, but until then there's no point.'

'When are you thinking of telling him?'

'As soon as he's feeling stronger. He only had the heart-attack yesterday. I can't upset him yet.'

'Fine. Just remember we leave in ten weeks and you've got a wedding to organize.'

'I'm well aware of what I have to do.'

'I don't want to argue, I just want to make sure you're not having second thoughts.'

'Of course I'm not. By the way, how do you feel about bringing our children up as Catholics?'

'Serious?'

'Deadly.'

'I'd rather they were brought up with no specific

religious beliefs and when they're eighteen they can decide for themselves.'

'They have to be Catholic or we can't get married in a church.'

'Since when are we getting married in a church?'

'I've always wanted to get married in a church. I want it all—the big family wedding, the meringue dress, the bridesmaids, the three-tiered cake, confetti, everything.'

Pierre laughed. 'You are funny.'

'I'm not being funny, I'm serious. I've dreamt of this since I was a little girl.'

'I thought we'd do a register office, then go for a nice lunch somewhere with close family.'

Register office? Was he insane? Didn't he know me at all? How come we had never discussed this before? Had I just presumed he knew I wanted a church wedding?

'That's the most depressing thing I've ever heard. It's a sorry excuse for a wedding. How could you not know that I want a big day out?'

'Because you never said so.'

'I've always said I wanted to get married at home.'

'I know, darling, but 'home' is London and it doesn't necessarily imply an over-the-top church wedding for hundreds of people, half of whom we won't know. I'm a bit old for that.'

'Well, I'm not.'

'Let's talk about this later.'

'I won't change my mind.'

'You're upset and emotional about your father. We'll discuss it another time.'

'Pierre, I'm getting married in a big dress in a big church in front of a big crowd. You can either turn up or not.'

'Don't you think they'd notice if the groom didn't arrive?'

'They'll be far too busy being dazzled by my dress.'

'How big?'

'Think Scarlett O'Hara.'

'How many guests?'

'I have eighty-three relations.'

Silence.

'Pierre?'

'Why couldn't I have met a nice quiet girl my own age, who was an only child from a non-religious family?'

'Because you're a lecherous old git who likes young ones in short skirts.'

'Niamh?'

'Yes?'

'I love you.'

'Enough to bring our children up as Catholics?'

'I don't believe in any of it. It's hypocritical.'

'I believe in it.'

'You never go to mass.'

'I did when I was younger and it's good for children to have direction in life. They need rules and principles and guidance.'

'The Catholic Church opposes gay marriage, the social acceptance of homosexuality and same-sex relationships.'

'Yes, but it also says that homosexuals deserve respect.'

'It condemns the use of contraception, even in Africa where Aids is rife.'

'It's the Catholic priests and nuns working in Africa who take care of the victims of Aids. Look, we can argue about this all day. The bottom line is, I was brought up Catholic and you fell in love with me, so obviously it didn't do me any harm, and I want our children to have religion in their life. It'll also help smooth things over with my parents.'

'I'll tell you what, I'll agree to them being brought up as Catholics but they have to be allowed to opt out any time they like.'

'Fine,' I agreed.

'Now, hurry up and tell your parents about us and get your cute ass back over here.'

28

During Dad's short stay in hospital recuperating, Mum decided to spring-clean the house and have it really nice for him when he came home. She was like a whirlwind, taking apart every room and throwing out anything that wasn't 'useful or practical'. Dad had never been sick before and it was strange to see how lost my mother was without him around. She was upset, and the only way she knew how to deal with this was to scrub the house within an inch of its life and cook, then freeze, batches of Dad's favourite food, which I tried to tell her wouldn't be appropriate for a man with a heart condition.

'And why not?' she snapped.

'The doctor said no butter and cream,' I said, pointing to the chicken breast drowning in a sea of creamy sauce.

'It's his favourite.'

'I know, Mum, but he has to keep his cholesterol

down. The doctor said it was vital for his heart.'

'Well, what am I supposed to cook, then?'

'Steamed vegetables and chicken on its own. No sauce.'

'Sure a rabbit wouldn't eat that, not to mind your father.'

'It's for his own good.'

'I'll pour some of the sauce out and only give him a small bit,' she said, spooning half down the sink.

'But it's—'

'I've been cooking for him for thirty years. I don't need advice now. It's the cigarettes and heavy lifting that gave him the heart-attack, not my cooking,' she said, highly insulted. 'A bit of butter never killed anyone. Now, get those gloves on and give the bathroom sink a good scrub.'

'I did it already this morning.'

'Well, do it again.'

'Mum, it's clean. The whole house is spotless. You've done a great job.'

'I want it perfect for him.'

'It is perfect.'

'I need to mow the lawn,' she said, pulling off her apron and heading towards the door.

I grabbed her. 'Mum, sit down. You're going to wear yourself out. Dad needs you to be fresh and rested when he comes home so you can look after him. He doesn't care if the grass is mown or not.'

'I CARE,' she shouted. 'I care! I—' She began to sob. 'I didn't think I'd be so lost without him. This is the first time we've ever been apart. In thirty years we never spent a night away from each other. The bed's awful big without him in it.'

'Oh, Mum,' I said, putting my arm round her.

'Of course you're upset. It must be awful for you.'

I couldn't believe they'd never spent a night apart. It was so romantic. I'd never thought of my parents as romantic. They were always just Mum and Dad, not a man and a woman who had fallen in love and got married. I wondered would Pierre and I be like that. I hoped so.

'Anyway,' said Mum, recovering her composure, 'no time to be sitting around moping. Far too much to do. Pass me that butter.' She scooped half the tub out and proceeded to mash it into the potatoes with a small mountain of salt.

While I was thinking of a new way to approach the need for Dad to have a low-fat, no-salt diet, Nuala came rushing in, flushed with excitement.

'Throw the kettle on there, Niamh,' she said, taking her coat off. 'You're not going to believe this.'

'Go on,' I said.

'Your auntie Sheila's getting married again.'

'No!' said Mum.

'To Brendan Hickey.'

'No!'

'Yes!'

'But I thought he was married?'

'Divorced,' said Nuala.

'When?'

'Last month. He wanted to marry Sheila so he got a quickie divorce.'

' 'Twon't be a church wedding so,' said Mum.

'No,' said Nuala. 'They're getting married in a register office.'

'Ah, well, never mind. I'm glad she met someone.'

'And not just any old person. Brendan Hickey's

loaded. She'll have the life of Riley now.'

'She deserves it,' said Mum, 'after what she went through with Pat. I'm delighted for her. Has he kids?'

'Two sons, grown-up, married.'

'You'd have to feel sorry for his wife,' said Mum.

'Not a bit of it. She's an old witch. He's much better off with Sheila.'

'She looks fantastic lately—I'm not surprised she met someone.'

'The day Pat died was the day her life began. It was the best thing that could have happened. And he's a house in Spain.'

'Brendan?'

'Yes. In Marbella, no less.'

'Lovely,' said Mum.

'That's where he proposed.'

'Has she a ring?'

'A whopper.'

'I wonder what she'll do with her old one.'

'Melt it down.'

'Ah, Nuala, you're very harsh.'

'Sure what would she want that old ring for? It'll only remind her of unhappy times.'

'Where did you get all this information anyway?'

'I met Sally for lunch. She's just popped in to work for a bit and then she's going to call in. I told her Niamh was home, visiting, so she said she'll come and say hello.'

'How is she?' I asked. 'Did she finish her psychology degree?'

'She's doing brilliant,' said Nuala. 'She's fully qualified now and she specializes in helping people with alcoholic parents.'

'She's an amazing girl,' said Mum.

'She said the course was very difficult because you have to go through therapy yourself and she had to deal with her own problems with her father. But she's finished all that now and she's flying.'

'She'll be a real help to people after her experiences,' said Mum.

'As long as she doesn't tell her patients to deal with their fathers the way she did,' said Nuala, winking at me as Mum bristled.

'Nuala!'

'Ah, I'm only joking.' She laughed.

'Does she have a boyfriend?' I asked.

'She does indeed. An American fella, he's a psychiatrist too. His mother's a Kelly from Monaghan.'

Typical! Even bloody Sally had a boyfriend with Irish links. Why couldn't she be going out with a Chinese Buddhist? As if on cue there was a knock on the kitchen door and in she walked.

I got up and went to greet her. It felt a bit awkward. We hadn't seen each other in years and we really didn't know each other. Mum kissed her warmly, then told Nuala she wanted to show her a new coat she'd bought. 'We'll leave you two to catch up,' she said, as they left the room.

I looked at Sally and smiled. 'So, how are things?'

'Really good, thanks. My life is finally coming together. I've faced my demons and dealt with them head on. It was extremely difficult and emotionally draining but I'm in a good place now. I finally feel healed. Helping others with alcoholic parents has been really cathartic too.'

She sounded like that man Dr Phil on *Oprah*. Clearly the therapy had worked. She seemed so happy.

'That's great, Sally. You deserve it.'

She nodded. 'I owe it to myself to be happy. I owe it to that scared, broken little girl to love myself and live a good life helping others to find inner peace.'

It was like talking to a self-help book. Maybe she could give me some advice on my dilemma. Granted, unlike her patients I wasn't the abused child of an alcoholic, but she might have a few tips for me about how to handle my announcement.

'Can I ask you something?'

'Sure, anything.'

'I'm engaged. I've met someone really wonderful and I'm about to tell my parents. But there's a small catch. He's black.'

'I don't see the problem.'

'Come on, you know how conservative my parents are. They're going to freak.'

'They're more open-minded than you think. After everything that happened with my father, your parents were the ones who got me into counselling. Your dad spent years telling me I wasn't to blame and that I deserved to be happy. He said the past didn't matter, it was the future that was important. He was the one who inspired me to do something with my life, to help other people in similar situations. You're very lucky to have a dad like him.'

'Don't get me wrong, I know how great he is, but sending someone to therapy is different from being happy that your daughter's fiancé is black.'

'He'll probably find it a little difficult to accept at first, but I'm sure that when he sees how happy you are and how in love you are, he'll welcome your fiancé with open arms.'

Clearly Sally had done a little too much counselling. She appeared to be delusional. No matter how much I would have liked to believe it, I knew fine well that Dad would not be throwing his arms round Pierre and rolling out the red carpet. Still, maybe she was right about him being more open-minded than I gave him credit for. Maybe he wouldn't go completely mad, just a little bit mad.

I wasn't going to ruin Sally's positive bubble, so I just said, 'Maybe you're right.'

'I know I am. Trust me. Now, I have to get back to work. I have patients to treat and lives to transform.' And with that she gave me a big bear-hug and went off to save the world.

Irish Daily News

'The break-up'

Niamh O'Flaherty

When Mary breaks up with her boyfriend, she calls her best friend and bawls down the phone. Her best friend listens, lets Mary cry, makes lots of sympathetic noises like, 'Oh, no, I see, poor you', etc., but does not interrupt the flow of grief.

When Dave calls his best friend to tell him he's just broken up with his girlfriend, his best friend panics. He doesn't do emotion. They go for pints together, play football on a Wednesday night, go to watch rugby matches, but they don't do emotion. To try to hide his panic, Dave's best friend says, 'Do you fancy a few pints later?' This buys him time to call in the troops and organize a bit of a session where no emotions will be discussed or, worse, displayed.

Mary's best friend calls all her other friends and they arrange to meet in her house that night with supplies of chocolate, Häagen Dazs ice-cream, crisps and tissues.

Dave's best friend organizes for everyone to meet in the local pub for a knees-up.

Mary calls over to her best friend's house where everyone fusses and tells her that she's fantastic, it's his loss, and then they finely dissect what he said when he broke up with her. They say that maybe he just needs some time to himself and he'll come round when he realizes what a big mistake he's made. Maybe when he said, 'It's not you it's me,' he really meant he had to deal with some issues from his past and when they were sorted out he'd come back and reclaim her. Maybe when he said, 'I'll see you around,' he meant, 'I hope I bump into you soon.'

Dave's friends avoid eye contact when he arrives into the pub. No one mentions the break-up. Five pints later, when Dave finally says, 'So did you hear I got dumped?' his friends tell him she wasn't very good-looking anyway and none of them really liked her. They remind him of the freedom he'll now have on the weekends to do what he wants when he wants. Then they ply him with more drink to shut him up and try to force him to go home and shag the East European waitress.

29

London, September–December 1986

After my summer immersed in Irish culture with Granny and Granddad Byrne, autumn came round and I went back to school where life took on its habitual autumn/winter drudgery. I had been to one more tennis-club disco and Teddy was nowhere to be seen, so my plans for us to go steady all year and for me to develop an I-have-a-boyfriend strut came to nothing. I continued my non-boyfriend shuffle and tried to keep out of trouble. I was also studying hard. Having seen what Liam was able to achieve and the fuss that was made when he got his results—not to mention the bonus Dad gave him for it—made me keen to get good results myself. I only had two more years of school before I could go away to university and really experience life—without babysitting on demand and curfews.

December came round and Dad invited Uncle Pat, Auntie Sheila and their kids over for Christmas dinner. Mum didn't look too pleased about it—she got all tight-lipped and silent when he announced they were coming. But it was a done deal and that was that. However, that changed two days before Christmas when someone tried to break down our front door at two in the morning.

I looked out of the window to see my cousin Brian beating on it with his fists. He was in a terrible state. Dad ran down to let him in.

'What's going on?'

'It's my dad! He's had a fall! I think he might be dead,' croaked Brian.

'Jesus Christ. Let me throw on a coat and get my keys,' said Dad, grabbing his anorak and hustling Brian into the car.

The rest of us stood there in shock.

'Do you think Pat fell because he was drunk?' I asked.

'Mind your tongue, young lady,' said Mum, pulling her dressing-gown closer. 'It was obviously a terrible accident. Let's pray he's all right and just concussed.'

She made Finn and me kneel down on the cold kitchen floor and say a decade of the rosary. Siobhan and Liam went to 'check on Muireann' and hopped back into their warm bed.

By the time we got to the last Hail Mary, the phone rang. Mum snatched it up. It was Dad.

'Oh, no, Mick . . . Oh, Lord, that's desperate . . . Poor Pat . . . Was it because he was—you know? What a waste of a life! It was truly the death of him. How's Sheila? . . . Ah, no . . . Hard to take . . . And the kids? . . . Bring them all back here . . . They can't stay there . . . I'll put the kettle on.'

By the time Auntie Sheila and my cousins arrived, Auntie Nuala had already high-tailed it to our house and was ensconced in the kitchen, a coat thrown over her nightie. Mum and she were trying to piece together what had happened. Siobhan, Liam and Muireann were asleep, and when I offered to wake them again, Mum told me to leave them. 'There's nothing they can do. I don't want the baby upset. Let them be.'

Five minutes later the doorbell rang. Mum rushed out to greet Auntie Sheila and the children and brought them into the good room, where Finn had been ordered to light the fire. They looked shell-shocked. We sat around and Mum fussed about them being warm enough and handed them hot tea and cake, which none of them touched. Eventually Auntie Nuala got to the point. 'What happened, Sheila?'

'He fell,' she said, in a strange faraway voice.

'Did he die instantly?' Auntie Nuala asked, as Mum made faces at her to stop interrogating the poor woman.

'Yes. I think he broke his neck,' Auntie Sheila said.

Brian and Sally winced.

'Niamh, take your cousins into the kitchen and give them something to eat and drink,' Mum said.

'But there's tea and cake here,' I said, not wanting to be evicted from the room during Auntie Sheila's cross-examination.

Mum gave me one of her withering looks and I jumped to attention. I led Finn, Brian and Sally into the kitchen and made toast, which Finn and I ended up eating while our cousins sat like two statues.

'Did you call an ambulance?' I asked.

'Yes, but only after Mum tried to resuscitate him,' said Brian.

'Did you see him fall?' asked Finn, wide-eyed.

'No,' said Brian.

'I did,' whispered Sally.

'Did he trip?'

'No. I pushed him.'

Finn gaped at her.

'SHUT UP!' shouted her brother.

'What did you say?' I asked, my voice shaking.

'You heard me,' she said evenly.

'But . . . then . . . you—'

'Killed him? Yes, I did.'

'She doesn't know what she's saying. He was drunk and he tripped,' said Brian. 'She's in shock.'

He could spin it whatever way he wanted but it seemed to me that Sally knew exactly what she was saying.

'Does your mum know?' I asked.

'He was shouting at her and calling her horrible names. I had to help her, so I pushed him.'

'He was drunk and he tripped,' said Brian, sticking to his story.

'It was an accident,' I agreed. 'If he hadn't been drunk he wouldn't have fallen.'

'I had to stop him,' said the cold-hearted murderess.

Beware of the quiet ones! Sally rarely had two words to say and now, suddenly, she was all about the talking. I wished she'd go back to being mute. I wasn't sure how to respond. I didn't know how to handle murderous confessions. Did I have to tell the police? Was it my duty to report that my cousin had killed her father?

As if reading my mind, Brian repeated: 'Sally doesn't know what she's saying. She's traumatized by what she saw. Dad was drunk and he fell down the stairs. That's what happened.'

The door opened and we jumped. It was Auntie Nuala.

'Everything all right in here?' she asked. 'Your mum's asking for you kids,' she said to Brian and Sally. 'She wants you close to her tonight, poor thing. Go on inside to the fire.'

They left the room. Finn and I sat in silence.

I was afraid to speak in case I gave away incriminating evidence. My mind was racing. The best thing to do was say nothing.

'Are you OK? You both look stunned,' Auntie Nuala asked.

We nodded and, thankfully, she left the room.

'Wow!' said Finn, finally finding his voice.

'Look, forget what she said. You heard Brian, she's in shock. She didn't mean it. She didn't push him. He fell. Sure we all saw how drunk he got. He was a basket case. It was an accident waiting to happen.' As the elder sibling I felt I had to protect Finn. He needed to keep his innocence. It was no good for him to think his cousin was a killer.

'Bullshit,' he said. 'She pushed him all right. But I'll say nothing because he deserved it.'

I stared at my little brother. Revenge was obviously a family trait. I'd have to be nicer to him from now on or I'd end up at the bottom of the stairs with a footprint in my back.

Mum came in. 'Nuala said you seemed distressed. Do you want to talk about what happened?'

We shook our heads.

But, as usual, we were ignored. 'Lookit, kids, it's no secret that Uncle Pat had a fondness for the drink.'

No secret! If it wasn't a secret then how come we had to listen to those ridiculous stories about him going on 'holidays'?

'But he was a good man underneath it,' Mum continued.

'That's crap,' said Finn.

'Excuse me?' Mum's head jerked up.

'He wasn't a good man. He was a nasty drunk

and he deserved to die,' said Finn.

Mum was appalled. 'That's a terrible thing to say. Apologize at once.'

'It's the truth and you know it.'

'He's just upset,' I said, jumping in. 'And let's be honest, Mum, Uncle Pat was a mean old drunk. I know it's wrong to speak ill of the dead, but he was no saint.'

'Now, you both listen to me,' said Mum. 'He was your father's brother and he loved him. I won't have a bad word said about him in this house. I won't have you upsetting your father with this kind of talk. Do you understand me?'

We nodded.

'Off to bed with you, Finn, and don't ever let me hear you speaking about your uncle that way again.'

Finn shuffled off to bed, pausing only to roll his eyes at me when Mum wasn't looking.

'What's got into him?' Mum asked, when he had gone.

'He's just upset and shocked, like the rest of us,' I said.

Auntie Nuala came in with a tray of cold tea and uneaten cake. 'I've left them alone for a minute,' she said. 'They're in a bad way. Not a word out of them. Sheila keeps hugging Sally and telling her she's sorry. For what, I ask you? It's a blessing the bastard fell down those stairs.'

'Nuala!'

'He was rotten to the core.'

'He used to be a nice lad,' Mum said. 'Drink is a cruel thing.'

'He was given every chance to get better,' said Auntie Nuala. 'How many times did we pay for him to go and dry out? He was weak. I blame his mother. She spoilt him rotten when he was young. It was always poor Pat this and poor Pat that. While the others were out working themselves to the bone, he was getting drunk in the pub.'

'It's a disease,' said Mum.

'He should have been able to stop with all the help he was given. He was a hopeless case. Poor old Sheila—what she's had to put up with over the years. I wouldn't blame her if she pushed him down the stairs herself.'

'She didn't. Sally did.' It was out before I knew it. Shit! What was I doing? I'd make a really bad spy. I couldn't even hold classified information for ten minutes.

Mum and Auntie Nuala stared at me. I clamped my hands over my mouth, horrified.

'Niamh,' Mum said, coming over to me, 'why would you say something like that?'

'Did she tell you she did it?' asked Auntie Nuala, cutting to the chase.

I remained silent. I wouldn't betray Sally—even though I already had. If she went to prison it'd be my fault. I was a snitch.

Mum and Auntie Nuala looked at each other. 'I'll go and talk to Sally,' said Auntie Nuala.

'No!' I shouted, grabbing her by the arm. 'Don't say anything to anyone. I shouldn't have blurted it out. It's not . . . She didn't . . . He was . . . She had to—' I began to cry. It must have been post-traumatic stress. It's not every day you find out your cousin's a cold-blooded assassin.

'It's all right. Take a deep breath and tell me what happened,' Mum said, guiding me gently back to my chair and holding my shaking hand.

'She said he was shouting at Auntie Sheila and she had to make him stop so she pushed him and he fell.'

'My God,' said Auntie Nuala.

'I'm sure it was an accident. The poor girl's just confused,' said Mum.

'Who else knows?' asked Auntie Nuala.

'Only me, Finn and Brian, and I presume Auntie Sheila does because she was there.'

'OK,' said Auntie Nuala. 'Nobody else can know about this. Do you understand, Niamh? You cannot tell another soul. We have to stop Sally saying things that could get her into serious trouble.'

'She's right, pet,' said Mum, putting her arm round me. 'The rest of the family mustn't find out. Not even your dad and Uncle Tadhg. It'd be too upsetting for them. The fewer people who know, the better it is for Sally.'

'I'll speak to her,' said Auntie Nuala. 'I'll sort it out.'

'No, Nuala, you can't tell her I told you,' I said, panicking. If Sally was capable of murdering her own father, what would she do to a cousin who ratted her out?

'I'll be very careful what I say. I just need to make sure she doesn't repeat the story to anyone else. Your mother's right. It was bound to have been an accident.'

While Auntie Nuala went to do damage control, Mum sat down with me.

'Will Sally be OK?' I asked.

'Don't you worry about her. Nuala and I will look after her. This'll all blow over soon. Once the funeral is done with, they'll be able to get on with their lives. To be honest, they'll be better off now. They won't have to worry about Pat coming home drunk, upsetting and embarrassing them. You know, when I first met him twenty years ago he was good fun.'

'Uncle Pat?' I asked, finding that hard to imagine.

'I know it's hard to believe now, but he was very witty. Back then he drank, but he was good fun with it. He'd have you in stitches with his stories and jokes, but over the years the drink changed him. He couldn't stay away from it. He could never just have a few pints like Tadhg and your dad. He always had to drink till he passed out. It's a terrible disease and he didn't have the strength to fight it.'

'Do you think Sally will end up in a mental institution?'

'No, Niamh, she won't. Nuala and I will make sure she gets the help she needs to deal with what happened.'

'Mum?'

'Yes, pet.'

'When did life get so complicated?'

'I'm afraid it always was.' She sighed.

As I contemplated my mother's cheery answer, Auntie Nuala came back in. 'It's OK,' she said, relieved. 'It was an accident, after all. Sheila, Sally and Pat had a tussle at the top of the stairs and Pat staggered backwards, tripped over his own feet and fell. If he hadn't been drunk he wouldn't have fallen. It's not the poor child's fault at all. She's just confused and traumatized. Now, we need never mention this again. Cup of tea?'

And with that, another family secret was swept firmly under the carpet.

30

The day of the funeral dawned grey and rainy, which suited everyone's sombre mood. For three days the coffin had been laid in our good room. It was open and Uncle Pat was lying inside it in his best suit, looking quite well for Uncle Pat, although he reminded me a bit of the waxwork people in Madame Tussaud's. I found it spooky having him there, but my father insisted that an open coffin was the best way for people to say goodbye. He had no visible bruises from his fall, although they could have been camouflaged with makeup. Finn had told me, 'Undertakers are geniuses at making people look normal, even when they've been in really bad car crashes and their heads have come off and stuff. They have all this equipment they use to make them presentable for their relatives.'

Frankly, the whole thing freaked me out and I couldn't wait for the coffin to be closed and Uncle Pat buried six feet under. Having a dead person in the house was just plain weird. Yet another Irish tradition that I didn't understand or appreciate.

For three days and nights a steady stream of relations, friends and people who just turned up for the free food and drink came through our front door. They cried, sang songs, told stories, recited poems and generally ran the full gamut of emotion on an hourly basis.

Christmas Day had been a mere blur in the middle of crowds of family and strangers coming to pay their respects to Uncle Pat and his loved ones.

People sat around our house day and night telling Pat stories, subtly leaving out the parts where he fell over drunk or passed out. His raving alcoholism was described gently as 'high spirits' and 'his fun-loving side'. His embarrassing antics became his 'little eccentricities' and his failure as a father and husband was brushed aside and he was remembered as 'a family man'. Although there were times when I wanted to shout, 'He was a no-good drunk who terrorized his wife and drove his daughter to push him down the stairs,' I kept my head down and my mouth shut. I was an adult now, privy to family secrets. Mentally I picked up the carpet and brushed my feelings under it.

As we had to wait until 27 December to bury Uncle Pat, he had ended up spending Christmas Day with us after all. Gone was my mother's sumptuous roast-turkey dinner, our presents and the afternoon spent lying by a roaring fire watching Christmas movies. Instead, Finn and I spent ten hours a day boiling the kettle, making sandwiches and washing up. I didn't mind because it took my mind off Sally's crime. Finn never mentioned it to me and I never said a word to him, but every time we were on our own there was an elephant in the room.

Siobhan, loving the drama of a death in the family, became chief mourner. She spent her time sobbing into relatives' shoulders, bemoaning the early demise of a treasured uncle. I could see she was getting on Sally's nerves and I wanted to warn my sister to tone it down. Sally really didn't need to be wound up and, much as Siobhan annoyed me, I didn't want to find her face down in the bath or some such. So I tried to warn her. 'I think you should stop telling everyone how upset you are,' I said. 'He wasn't your dad.'

'He was my beloved uncle and I'm devastated,' she said. 'Just because you're a heartless cow it doesn't mean I am.'

'You didn't even like him,' I hissed. 'All you ever did was give out about him.'

'That's not true. I was very fond of him in my own way.'

'What way is that? Turning your nose up every time you saw him and telling Mum he was an embarrassment to the family?'

'I'm grieving for Dad and Sally and Brian and Sheila.'

'They don't need your grief. They've enough of their own.'

'Why do you care?'

'Because it's annoying for Sally. He was her dad and you're going around wailing like a banshee. She's getting fed up with you.'

'She's a weirdo. She hasn't even shed one tear.'

'People react to death differently. She's probably bottling it all up.'

'Well, she should let it out.'

'If you gave her some air space she probably would,' I said.

'Maybe I should encourage her to talk about it. She needs to get it off her chest.'

'No!' I shouted, as Siobhan glared at me. 'Don't force her to talk. She's a private person. She doesn't want to tell you anything. She's got nothing to say. Leave her alone.'

'She needs to let it out,' said Siobhan, standing up to go to Sally. I grabbed her by the jumper. 'Get off me!'

'What's going on here?' Mum asked. 'What are you squabbling about?'

'Siobhan wants to make Sally talk about what happened and I think it's a bad idea,' I said, staring into Mum's eyes and wriggling my eyebrows so she'd understand my concern.

'Siobhan,' Mum said sharply, 'Sally has been through a terrible trauma. She doesn't want anyone asking her questions. You are to leave her in peace. Is that clear?'

'Fine. God, I was only trying to be nice.'

'I'd like less mourning from you and a lot more sandwich-making. Off you go,' she said, ushering Siobhan out of the room. 'You too,' she said, looking at me.

'That was a close one,' I whispered, as I passed Mum on the way out.

She stared at me blankly. 'I've no idea what you're talking about. Now, get into the kitchen and make yourself useful.'

Mum was a pro. No one, not even MI5 or the KGB, would make her talk.

* * *

After buttering a thousand slices of bread, I felt rigor mortis setting in (stiffer than Uncle Pat's), so I snuck upstairs to my room for a rest. I could hear my mother and father talking in their bedroom.

'. . . had to rule out foul play,' said Dad, sounding upset.

'Don't worry, Mick, it was just a formality. I'm sure the police have to do it with any accident in the home.'

'But they've enough to deal with without the

authorities questioning them. It's not right,' Dad grumbled.

Police! My God, the Old Bill must have been in, sniffing around for possible murder weapons. It's a good thing Sally didn't knife him or something where the weapon might have been found. Thank God they hadn't questioned me. I'd definitely have cracked under police pressure.

'It's over now they've been cleared of any wrong-doing. Forget about it,' said Mum.

'Wrong-doing! As if those young children would hurt a fly, and poor Sheila's a wreck. I know he was my brother and I loved him, but he wasn't much use to his family.'

'Well, he's gone now and it's up to us to support them as much as we can. Actually, I was thinking we might get some counselling for the kids,' Mum said.

'Counselling?'

'Yes, Mick. They've been through a lot, having a drunk for a father, and it'd be good for them to have some professional help getting over this. I've got the name of someone very good and I'd like to set it up.'

'OK, if you think it'll help then go ahead. I'll write you a cheque. I want the best for those kids. They're my responsibility now.'

Responsibility! Oh, no. I prayed they weren't going to come and live with us. It was bad enough knowing Sally was a killer, but having to face it every day over breakfast was too much. I'd need counselling myself.

'You're a good man,' Mum said. 'I definitely got the pick of the O'Flaherty crop.'

'I'm the lucky one,' said Dad, and then I heard

them kiss. I ran to close my door.

*   *   *

Later that day Mum told Finn and me that Sally, Brian and Auntie Sheila were going to be staying the night because the coffin was due to leave our house at ten o'clock the next morning to go to the church for the funeral and they wanted to spend the last night in the same house with him.

'So, Finn, you'll be sharing with Brian and, Niamh, you'll be sharing your room with Sally.'

'Excuse me?' I said, praying I'd misheard her.

'You heard me.'

'Mum, I'm not sharing my room with her.'

'Yes, you are.'

'No, I'm not. I don't want to be strangled in the middle of the night because I snored or made a noise that annoyed her.'

Mum grabbed me by the shoulders and shook me. 'Don't ever let me hear you say anything like that again. Go to your room and make up the spare mattress on the floor this minute.'

I stomped off in a fury. I was fed up with my family—mother, sister, cousins, the whole stinking lot of them. I threw myself down on the bed and stifled a scream in my pillow.

Finn came in and sat on the bed. He was grinning.

'It's not funny,' I moaned.

'Yeah, it is. You get to sleep with the psycho killer,' he said, chuckling. 'You'd better be careful not to piss her off.'

'Go away.'

'Where's your sense of humour?'

'Sense of humour? There is a man lying dead in a coffin in our good room because his daughter shoved him down the stairs in a fit of rage and now I have to share a room with her. Not to mention the fact that Mum is forcing us to pretend nothing happened and I've spent the last three days, including Christmas Day, listening to made-up stories about Uncle Pat being a great guy. What's funny about that?'

Mum walked in. 'You can stop sulking,' she said. 'Sally's going to sleep with Sheila in Siobhan's old room and Brian can sleep in Finn's room and Finn can sleep on the floor in here. Is that better?'

'Yes. Thanks.'

'Look, kids,' she said, and paused to find the right words. 'I know the last few days have been strange and tense and upsetting. But once the funeral's over, we can put all of this behind us. Unfortunately life is complicated sometimes, and we have to muddle through as best we can. The most important thing right now is that you're kind to your cousins. The accident has been very hard on them and we need to be supportive, not judgemental. You've been a great help with the food and drinks and I need you to help out for one more day. Then everything will be back to normal. Will you do that for me?'

Finn and I nodded, then he slunk out of the room. Mum came over to me. I sank back into the pillow in case she decided to shake me again. There seemed to have been an epidemic of violence in our family lately and I wasn't taking any chances.

'Niamh, I'm very sorry for shaking you. You've been really great over the last few days. I don't know what I'd have done without you.'

I sighed. 'It's OK. I know you didn't mean it. I just want our house back. It's been a horrible Christmas.'

'I know, pet,' she said, patting my arm. 'We'll make it up to you all, I promise. We're going to celebrate Christmas late this year, but we'll celebrate none the less. Now, lie back and have a little rest. You deserve it.'

I certainly did. I was exhausted, mentally, physically and emotionally. I lay back in the bed and closed my eyes.

But before I had a chance to relax I heard Siobhan bellowing up the stairs: 'Niamh, we need your help. We've run out of sandwiches.'

'Make them yourself.'

'I can't, I've to feed Muireann. Auntie Nuala wants you down here right away.'

I rolled off the bed and went back to the production line. Children in the sweat-shops in Bangladesh didn't have to work this hard and at least they got paid.

31

The funeral went off without a hitch. Father Hogan skirted around Uncle Pat's drunkenness and talked about his '*joie de vivre*'. Auntie Peggy, my mother's cousin, had offered to do the music and she even brought a tear to my eye when she sang 'Be Not Afraid'. It made the hairs on the back of your neck stand up. At that point everyone started crying and I suddenly realized how sad it was. My anger disappeared and I was left with sorrow for a wasted life and sympathy for a broken family left behind.

Much to everyone's surprise, Brian got up to speak at the end of the mass. His voice was shaky and wobbly but you could hear him. 'My dad was a deeply flawed man,' he said. I began to worry. Was he going to slate his father on the altar in front of all the relations? 'But he was my dad and you only get one of those in your life. Although the last few years have been difficult for us as a family, I do remember good times when he wasn't ruined by alcohol. I remember playing hurley with him in the back garden, going to Brighton to the beach, listening to him singing while he shaved . . . Nice memories. Alcohol destroyed him, and ultimately killed him, but I want to remember him as he was before it completely consumed him, when he behaved like a real dad, when he enjoyed his family and made us proud, not ashamed. I also want to take this opportunity to thank my dad's family for being such a support to us over the years. I don't like singling anyone out, but I must mention Uncle Mick, Dad's oldest brother, who spent so much time and effort trying to get Dad better. He never gave up hope, he never gave up trying, and I'll always be grateful to him for that. I want to thank his family as well, Auntie Annie, Siobhan, Niamh and Finn, who opened up their house and allowed us to say a proper goodbye to Dad. We'll never forget your kindness and generosity. It's made the last few days a little easier to bear. Finally, I'd like to thank you all for coming today and for being friends to us and my dad over the years. I promise to do my best to look after

Mum and Sally now.'

Everybody began to clap and soon the church was thundering with applause. I saw Dad wiping away tears and watched Mum squeeze his hand. I was bawling and even Finn was watery-eyed. Siobhan, needless to say, was howling beside me. I looked at Sally and Auntie Sheila, who were leaning into each other, sobbing. Brian went over to them and they put their arms round each other for comfort.

Dad leant over to us and said, 'I'm proud of all you kids. You've been a credit to me over the last few days,' but then he had to stop because he got emotional again.

I was a bit cheesed off that Siobhan had been credited with being helpful, seeing as all she'd done was be chief mourner and boss me around. Personally I thought I deserved most of the credit, because even Finn had kept sneaking off when no one was looking so I'd been left to butter the lion's share of the sandwiches and do the washing-up.

We left the church and went out to the graveyard. When we got to the plot, we were met with three grave-diggers holding up a placard saying they were on strike because they hadn't received their Christmas bonus. Dad was furious and tried to talk them down, even offered them money, but they said they had their principles to stick to and that was that.

So, on a freezing cold day in December, my father and his brothers took off their good funeral-going coats and dug Uncle Pat's grave in their best suits, while the rest of us looked on, shivering. Everyone gave advice—including the striking grave-diggers who tut-tutted about the way the grave was being dug until Uncle Tadhg told them if they weren't going to dig they could stick their opinions where the sun didn't shine.

Eventually, the hole was declared deep enough by the majority of the mourners, although some felt they should keep digging. Mum was getting into a fury because she could see that Dad and the others were exhausted and on the verge of collapsing, while the rest of us were in danger of hypothermia.

'The hole is big enough and deep enough. Now, can we please lay this poor man to rest?' she said in her don't-mess-with-me voice.

The uncles then lowered the coffin into the not-so-big hole and you could see it didn't fit properly, it was a bit lopsided, but no one dared to complain. They were all afraid of my mother. I was worried that his head would be squashed up against the side of the coffin, but then he was dead anyway so it wouldn't bother him.

Father Hogan said a few prayers, then Auntie Sheila and Sally dropped flowers into the grave and Brian threw in Uncle Pat's favourite cap.

'He'd be better off putting a bottle of whiskey in,' muttered Finn.

'Don't be so disrespectful,' I said, coming over holy now that I knew my help was appreciated and not taken for granted like it normally was. I had a new-found respect for my cousin Brian and his family and I wasn't going to be mean about Uncle Pat any more.

'Killjoy,' said Finn, teeth chattering.

'Shush,' I hissed.

'Amen,' said the mourners, as Dad and his brothers finished putting the soil back over the coffin.

Siobhan was standing on the edge of the grave keening like an old pro.

'Get your sister,' Mum said. 'She's making a show of herself.'

I grabbed her by the arm and yanked her backwards.

'Piss off,' she snapped. 'I'm saying my last farewell to Pat.'

'Mum said you were making a fool of yourself and I was to stop you.'

'She did not.'

'Did too. You're being a drama queen. He wasn't your dad.'

'You're just cold and unemotional. No wonder you don't have a boyfriend,' she snarled.

'Any lad would be lucky to have her,' said Dad, putting down his shovel and placing an arm round me.

Brilliant! For once Siobhan was caught out being mean to me.

'I didn't mean it, Dad, I'm just overcome with it all,' said the actress.

'Lookit, girls. My brother is lying in that grave and I'll never have the chance to talk to him again. Family is the most important thing in life. Don't fall out with each other because when the going gets rough it's only your family you can rely on. So I want you to be nice to each other. No more squabbling. OK?'

'Yes, Dad,' we said.

'Now, let's go home. We've only a few more hours of entertaining and then we'll have the place back to ourselves and we can celebrate Christmas properly.'

Later that afternoon, when everyone was leaving, Sally came over to me. I was, as usual, washing dishes and when I saw her standing beside me I dropped one on the floor. She bent down to help me pick up the broken crockery.

'We're leaving now,' she said, 'and I just wanted to say thanks. I always thought you were a bit self-centred but you've been really nice over the past few days.'

Self-centred! The cheek of her! I was *en route* to being canonized for my selfless acts. I bit my tongue. 'Uhm, you're welcome.'

'You're very lucky,' she said. 'You've got a brilliant father.'

'I know. I'm sorry yours was such a bad one.'

She shrugged. 'Well, he's gone now so we can move on. I guess it's just luck. My Mum's great and so is Brian, so two out of three isn't bad.'

'You got Uncle Pat and we got Siobhan,' I said, as my cousin laughed for the first time—probably—ever.

'Well, I'll see you around.'

'OK. Good luck, Sally,' I said, diving back into my washing-up. I was afraid she might hug me and I was worried her killer instinct might rub off on me via osmosis or something.

She left and I breathed a sigh of relief. Finally, everyone was going and we could get our house and our lives back to normal. I vowed there and then to block the whole murder episode out of my mind for ever.

Finn came in. 'They're nearly all gone,' he said, sitting down on a kitchen chair.

'Where did you disappear to? I've been washing dishes on my own for ages. Grab that tea-towel and help.'

'OK, Bossy Boots,' he said, coming over to dry the dishes. We worked in silence for a while.

'Niamh?'

'Yeah?'

'Did you know the police questioned them?'

I said nothing, determined not to get dragged into a conversation about it. I was trying to erase it from my mind and Finn wasn't helping.

'Well? Did you?' he repeated.

'Yes, but it's all over now, so just forget it.'

'Do you think they'll question us? Ask us if we know anything?'

'No, Finn, they won't. It was just a procedure. They don't suspect anyone and the case is closed. Now forget about it.'

He wiped a dish absentmindedly. 'It's kind of exciting, though, isn't it?' he whispered.

'No, it's sad. Now change the subject.'

Finn, realizing that I wasn't going to entertain his conversation about killer cousins, wandered off, leaving me to tidy up. I was enjoying the peace when Mum came in. 'Thank God that's over,' she said. 'I feel as if we've been mourning him for weeks. Leave those things. Your dad and I'll finish them later. I want you to come inside and sit down.'

Oh, God, not another pep talk. I couldn't take any more heart-to-hearts today. I was worn out. I just wanted to be left alone. Mum took me by the arm and guided me out of the kitchen into the good room, which looked normal again now the coffin was gone.

Dad was standing in the middle holding a big box tied with a pink ribbon. 'Happy Christmas, pet,' he said.

I pulled off the bow, opened the box and inside was a brand new tennis racket, the most gorgeous tennis dress I'd ever seen and Chris Evert runners to match.

'Wow!' I squealed.

'We've got you proper membership to the tennis club, so you can play any time you like. You never know, you might meet that nice boy who asked you to dance again,' said Mum.

I hugged them both. 'This is the best present ever,' I gushed.

'Now, there's not to be too much tennis. I want you to keep studying and be the first O'Flaherty to go to university. But, as your mother told me, a girl needs to have fun and you've been a credit to us lately so we wanted to get you something you'd really enjoy.'

'Thanks, Dad, it's perfect. I'm so glad I got you and not Uncle Pat as a father,' I said, kissing his cheek . . . and if he knew what I knew he'd be thanking his lucky stars he'd got me and not Sally as a daughter.

32

After the drama of Uncle Pat's demise I didn't mind getting back to a normal routine. It was a relief to go back to school and spend all day discussing boys, makeup and how incredible Rob Lowe looked in *About Last Night*. Sarah remained my VBF—very best friend—and had decided to stay away from drink after the last fiasco had cost her a boyfriend and almost a best friend.

Auntie Sheila sold the house and they moved into a new one, south of the river in a non-Irish part of London, away from the rest of the family. She said they needed a fresh start. She wanted Sally and Brian to go to new schools where no one knew that their father had been an alcoholic who fell down the stairs. She wanted the children to be 'normal', to fit in and not be pitied because their father had shown up at the school gates drunk.

Once they'd moved, we didn't see them very often. Dad called in to see them once a month, but they pretty much kept themselves to themselves and got on with rebuilding their lives.

I knew that Dad was sending Auntie Sheila money every month because I'd overheard Mum talking to Auntie Nuala about it.

'How much does he send?' my aunt asked.

'He covers the mortgage and school fees,' said Mum.

'What about the money she got from selling the house?' Auntie Nuala asked.

'Sure she needs that to live on.'

'He's a good man, your Mick,' said Auntie Nuala.

'Well, business is good and family is family. You couldn't see them short.'

'No, that's true.'

'Did you sort that thing out for Sally?' Mum asked.

'I did. She's booked in to see Dr Montgomery next week.'

'Is he Irish?'

'Course he is. The best ones are. Sure we're such a messed-up emotional lot only our own psychiatrists could understand us.'

Mum laughed. 'You're right there.'

* * *

Liam was going to college every day and studying hard, while Siobhan was stuck at home with Muireann. But instead of going back to her books and sitting her A levels, like Mum had told her to, she got pregnant again.

She announced it that spring and Dad thought it was great. She was married now, so as far as he was concerned the more children the better. But Mum was furious. She couldn't even muster a half-smile. When Dad had left the room after congratulating Siobhan, Mum rounded on her. 'How could you be so stupid?' she raged. 'How on earth are you going to raise two babies in the garage?'

'We'll manage,' said Siobhan, clearly put out that Mum wasn't happy for her.

'Where's your brain gone? You can barely cope with Muireann. Why, in God's name, couldn't you wait until Liam had finished his studies, you had your own house and a proper salary coming in?'

'Dad said he'd help us out. It'll be fine. Besides, I don't want my children to be too far apart. I want them to be close in age so that they get on well.'

'Have you conveniently forgotten how difficult you found it after Muireann was born?' Mum asked. 'And, by the way, your father's not made of money. You need to stand on your own two feet and be responsible for your children.'

'Everyone says it's easier the second time because you know what you're doing and it's not so scary,' said the baby factory.

'Easier!' said Mum, laughing. 'How can it be easier when you have a toddler demanding your attention and you're trying to feed a baby? It's twice the work, twice the lack of sleep and twice the worry.'

For a woman with three children, she was being very negative. If this was her reaction to two kids, Finn's arrival must have pushed her over the edge.

'How did you manage with three?' I asked.

'I just got on with it. We didn't have choices in those days. There were no crèches you could drop your child into if you wanted to work. But you do have choices. I told you, Siobhan, that I wanted you to finish your A levels this year. You've no qualifications now, and if you ever want to work you'll find it very difficult to get hired.'

'I do work. I'm a full-time mother,' said Siobhan. 'I choose not to work outside the home.'

'You're only a child,' Mum said, shaking her head. 'You're too young to be tied down with nappies.'

'Why can't you be happy for me?'

'Because I don't like to see you throwing your youth away. You should be out enjoying yourself in college, not tied to the kitchen sink.'

'Look, Mum,' Siobhan said, beginning to cry. 'I know I let you down by getting pregnant and I know you really wanted me to go to university and have the life you didn't have. But I'm trying to make the most of marriage and motherhood and it would be really nice if you could be a bit more supportive and less critical. I know you're ashamed of me, but I'm doing the best I can.'

I actually felt sorry for her. You could see she was really hurt by Mum's disapproval.

Mum went over and hugged her. 'Don't you ever say that again. I'm as proud of you as I've always been. I never meant to make you feel bad. I'm just disappointed that you didn't get more time to be young and carefree. I think you're a fantastic mother to Muireann and I know you'll be wonderful with this baby too. I'll help you as much as I can, and so will Niamh.'

Typical! I knew I'd get dragged into it somehow. I did enough babysitting as it was. Now I'd have to do twice as much. I had to get out of this house and away to college.

Only a year to go . . .

Irish Daily News

'Packing'

Niamh O'Flaherty

When a woman packs to go on holidays she takes out everything she owns and puts it on the floor in the bedroom. She finds things she forgot she had. A pair of jeans she used to love. Do they still fit? She tries them on. They're very tight, but with a lot of effort she can get the zip up. She's thrilled. She finds some old T-shirts and puts those on too. Hours pass as she tries on all her clothes.

Finally, she needs to decide what she absolutely must pack. She has promised her boyfriend she will only bring a small suitcase. After much soul-searching, she packs three pairs of togs and three bikinis. She packs matching wraps, flip-flops and hats for the togs and bikinis. Then she packs seven sundresses, one for each day—they're bound to get dirty with sun cream and she doesn't want to spend her holiday doing laundry—plus a big beach bag, a small casual bag and a dressy going-out bag, one big sun hat, one medium size, and two sun-visors.

Then she packs two pairs of shorts, four T-shirts and three pairs of jeans—travelling jeans, skinny jeans for going out at night and her most flattering suck-my-tummy-in jeans.

She packs three glitzy tops to go with her skinny jeans, three shirts to go with her travelling jeans and two of her favourite T-shirts to go with her flattering jeans. She packs wedge sandals to go with the flattering jeans, two pairs of trainers to go with the travelling jeans and two pairs of high heels to go with the skinny jeans.

She packs three glamorous dresses, in case they end up meeting lots of new people and going out every night—as opposed to last year when they were in a coma every night by eleven. She packs high heels to match each dress and a colour co-ordinated wrap.

She packs her makeup, moisturizer, three sunscreens (factors twenty, twelve and six), special sun-care hair products—shampoo, conditioner, pre-swimming, and post-swimming and anti-frizz serums. She packs her hair-straightener, curler, dryer, plus three adaptor plugs. She packs cotton wool, cleanser, toner, eye-makeup-remover, anti-fatigue masks, moisture-boost masks, anti-ageing masks, hand cream, nail varnish, nail-varnish remover, eyelash-curler, scissors, deodorant (roll-on and spray). Two jumpers in case the weather is cold, a raincoat in case it rains, six books, and two DVD box-sets in case they don't meet anyone and end up staying in and chilling out.

Her boyfriend packs a couple of pairs of boxer shorts and a bumper pack of condoms.

33

London, March 1999

As I watched my strong, confident, mature, healed cousin Sally striding towards her car, I began to think that maybe she was right. Maybe Dad wouldn't react that badly to Pierre being black. Maybe I was underestimating him.

I closed the door and went back in to find Nuala and Mum.

'Isn't Sally great?' Nuala said.

I nodded. 'She's so together. That psychiatrist you sent her to must have been really good.'

'Sheila has to take a lot of credit too. She really turned her life round after Pat died. She never looked back. I should have pushed Tadhg down the stairs years ago and run off with some millionaire.' She giggled as Mum shook her head.

'Sally's a credit to her mother,' said Mum.

'Just like Niamh here,' said my favourite aunt, winking at me. 'So, tell me all your news. How's the newspaper world?' she asked.

'Good thanks. Still working away on my column.'

'Any romance?'

'She's in love,' said Mum. 'She's very secretive about him. None of us have met him yet.'

'Oooh, come on, fill me in,' said Nuala.

'Well, he's tall, dark and handsome,' I said.

'Who is?' asked Finn, coming in.

'Niamh's boyfriend,' said Nuala, as Finn froze.

'Finn met him when he was over,' I said, hoping

my brother would jump in with some high praise of Pierre.

'You never said a word,' said Mum, tutting at Finn. 'What's he like?'

'Well, he's tall, he's definitely dark and he's quite handsome,' said Finn, smirking. 'Sorry to interrupt this little chat but I need a lift to training. Mum?'

'I'll drop you down now on my way to the hospital.'

'I'll stay here with Niamh and hear more about the boyfriend,' said Nuala, as they left. 'I want all the details,' she said, smiling.

I took a deep breath. 'Nuala, when you met Tadhg, did you love him so much it hurt?'

'Not a bit of it. He was grand-looking, honest, hard-working and a bit of *craic*, so I knew he'd make a good husband. On our wedding night, I remember thinking I really didn't know him at all. It was different then. You went out on dates and then you married—none of this sex-before-marriage or living together. Sure we were practically strangers. It was only after a few years together that I really fell in love with him.'

'I think I'd die without Pierre,' I said passionately.

'That'll pass.'

'No, it won't, he's my world.'

'Give him a year or two and he'll be driving you mad.'

'I love everything about him.'

'Ninety per cent of it will drive you round the bend in no time, but as long as you still have ten per cent you like, you'll be grand.'

'Are you determined to ruin my buzz?'

Nuala grinned. 'I'm only being honest, pet. But I'm delighted you're mad about him. It's lovely. Pierre, did you say his name was?'

'Yes, he's French, but he spent most of his life in England.'

'Oh dear, your parents will be disappointed. They were sure you'd find an Irish lad in Dublin.'

'He's a little bit older too.'

'How much?'

'Fourteen years. He's forty-two.'

'They're definitely not going to like that,' said Nuala.

'And there's one other thing.' I paused. 'His parents are from the Caribbean.'

Nuala looked at me blankly.

'He's black.'

Nuala blessed herself. She wasn't religious so this was a really bad sign. 'Sweet Jesus, if he was a one-legged dwarf from Mongolia it couldn't be worse. They're going to hit the roof.'

So much for Sally's theory about our enlightened family . . .

'I know and that's why I need all the help I can get.'

'Are you sure he's the right man for you? Maybe you should take some time to reconsider.'

'I've never felt this way before. I never thought it was possible to be so in love,' I said.

'He's very old. Fourteen years is a big difference. He's only five years younger than me.'

'I like that he's older. All the guys I've gone out with before were my own age and it never worked out. Pierre's taught me so much. I look up to him, I respect him, I adore him,' I gushed.

'If he's so wonderful how come he's still single?'

'He was with a girl for nine years but they broke up last spring. They were living in different countries for the last three years and it fizzled out. And then he met me and knew I was the one.'

'Are you pregnant? Because if you are I can help you. No one needs to know.'

'No! I'm not pregnant but I *am* engaged and I'm going to marry him.'

'Was he engaged to his ex too?'

'No.' I bristled. 'I'm the only person he's ever proposed to.'

'I presume he's not Catholic.'

'No, Pierre doesn't believe in religion. He says it's difficult to credit any one religion as being true when there have been so many throughout history. None appears to have any greater claim to being more credible than any other,' I said, sounding like a brainwashed disciple of the god Pierre. I was doing a really bad job of selling him.

'That'll go down well with your dad,' said Nuala, rolling her eyes. 'What does this Pierre do then?' she asked.

I could tell she hated the sound of him. 'He's a professor of phonetics and he's really wonderful and good fun too.'

'I'm going to be honest with you here, Niamh. He sounds like a dirty old man and a pompous git.'

'No, he's not. He's clever but he's also kind and caring and generous and he really loves me. He makes me feel ten feet tall. I never thought I could feel so good about myself. Until I met Pierre I thought I was ordinary, but he makes me feel really special. I know you'd like him if you met him.'

'Well, that's something, I suppose.'

'Please, Nuala, I'm begging you, give him a

chance. Meet him before you write him off.'

Nuala looked at my flushed face. 'I'll tell you what. I'll agree to meet him and then, if I like him and if I think he's worthy of you, I'll help smooth the way. But if I don't like him and I don't think he's any good for you I'll do everything in my power to stop the marriage.'

I hugged her. 'Thanks, Nuala. This means a lot to me.'

'I hope you really love him, Niamh, because it's going to be an uphill battle.'

'I know.'

'I'm not sure you do, pet. I'm not sure you really understand how difficult this is going to be for your parents to swallow. I'm the most liberal of your relations and I'm shocked. Anyway, lookit, set up a meeting and we'll take it from there. You're like a second daughter to me and I won't have you making the wrong decisions. So, be prepared for honesty.'

I smiled. 'I know you're going to love him, so I'm not worried at all.'

'Ah, the confidence of youth,' said Nuala, shaking her head.

34

A few days later Dad was being discharged and I went in to collect him, while Mum was busy preparing a high-cholesterol welcome-home lunch. Dad was dressed and sitting on the bed, talking to four nurses.

'Ah, here she is,' he said, smiling when he saw

me. 'This is my daughter Niamh, the one I was telling you about. The first O'Flaherty to go to university. We're very proud of her.'

'Your dad's been telling us all about you,' said one of the nurses.

'Poor you!' I said.

'It's lovely to hear a father praising his daughter. You're very lucky. Mine didn't even hang around for my birth,' she said, with a half-laugh.

'I know he's great,' I said, sitting down beside Dad. 'I'm so glad he's better.'

'He's a real charmer,' said one of the other nurses. 'I'd wrap him up and take him home.'

'Go away out of that,' said Dad, thrilled.

'Well, we'd better be off. Mind yourself, Mick,' they said, and one by one they hugged him.

'Good luck with the exams,' Dad said to the first.

'Send your young fella down to me. I'll give him some honest work and we'll keep an eye on him for you. You need to get him away from bad influences,' he said to the second.

'Tell your husband-to-be he's a very lucky man,' he told the third.

'Don't worry about getting pregnant. I'll say a prayer for you,' he said to the fourth.

'Thanks.' She smiled.

'You're all like angels sent from heaven,' added Dad. 'It's because of you that I got better so quickly. Don't mind the doctors. It's you nurses that are the backbone of this hospital.'

They beamed and left the room. I'd forgotten what an impact Dad made on people. He was always so interested in everyone else. He asked questions, and if he could help or give advice, he would. He was a kind and Christian man. He'd made an impression on the nurses and you could see they were fond of him. He had a way of listening that made people want to confide in him, and when they did, he always said something comforting. Maybe I was worrying about nothing. He was as concerned about those four black nurses as he would have been about four white ones. He'd always been nice to people, regardless of their skin colour. He always invited Mr Chow in for a drink when he delivered our Christmas tree and he was very fond of Mrs Singh in the dry cleaner's—he'd hired her son to work for him when he left school. Maybe he'd accept Pierre and not mind about the agnostic and black part.

'Did you see that little nurse there?' he asked me. 'Her son's got into a bad crowd and is doing drugs.'

'Oh, God, poor her.'

'She's sending him off to counsellors. I told her to stop wasting her money and send him down to me. He needs a good kick up the arse and an honest day's work. That'll sort him out,' said the tolerant Christian.

I was delusional—he'd go bananas about Pierre.

I helped him pack a few final things into his bag and then the doctor arrived. 'Now, Mr O'Flaherty, we need to have a little chat before you head home,' he said.

'OK, fire ahead,' said Dad.

'You might like to do it in private.'

'Not at all, I'd prefer Niamh to be here. She'll remember all the bits I don't.'

'OK. Well, first and foremost, you are never to smoke again. It will kill you.'

Dad groaned. 'I've been smoking for thirty years. It's a comfort to me.'

'Sorry, Mr O'Flaherty, that's non-negotiable. I've mentioned a change of diet, and you need to stay away from salt, cream, butter and all high-cholesterol foods. Now, you may find that you feel a bit depressed when you go home, which is normal after having surgery. But you have a very supportive family so I'm sure you'll recover quickly.'

Bloody hell—depressed! I needed him in full health and on top form before I landed my bombshell on him. Now he had a dodgy heart and a bad case of the blues.

'You'll need to rest and try not to do too much. Listen to your body. If you feel tired go and lie down for a while,' the doctor advised.

'Can I get back to work?' Dad asked.

'I'd like you to take a week of complete rest, then ease yourself into it. Now, on the subject of resuming sexual relations with your wife, again, I'd advise that you take it slowly. There's a saying that if you can climb a flight of stairs without feeling out of breath, you're ready for intercourse and—'

I was purple with embarrassment. I couldn't believe I was in the middle of a conversation about my father's sex life. I didn't know where to look.

'That's enough information for one day,' said a horrified Dad, cutting across the surgeon before he could say any more. 'I think we'll go now.'

'Any questions or queries, call me and I'll talk you through it.'

'No, that was all crystal clear,' said Dad. Then, turning to me, he said, 'Come on, let's go.'

We drove most of the way home in awkward

silence until Dad broke the ice by asking me how long I'd be home for.

'I was thinking I'd stay until you're back on your feet,' I answered, hoping he didn't think I was implying I'd stay until he was back having sex with my mother.

'Haven't you deadlines for the paper?'

'Yes, but I can work from here on my laptop.'

'What about your lad? Won't you miss him?'

'Uhm, yes, but it's only a week or two. I'll survive.'

'I suppose he could always come over and see you. I'd like to meet him. You seem very keen.'

'I am.'

'I'm glad for you, pet,' he said, patting my arm.

Thankfully, before he asked any more questions, found out about Pierre, and I had to give him mouth-to-mouth resuscitation, we pulled up outside our house, where Mum was waiting for us. She rushed over to help Dad out of the car.

'Don't fuss,' he grumbled, as she supported his arm.

'I'm only helping. You need to take it easy,' she said.

'I'm grand.'

'No, you're not. You're after having a heart-attack, so just behave yourself.'

They bickered all the way into the kitchen, delighted to be together again.

Mum served up the food and Dad declared it was the best meal he'd ever had. She reminded him that the best meal he'd ever had was their thirtieth wedding anniversary meal that she'd spent four days preparing.

After lunch, Dad went to sit in the good room,

read the papers and rest. But the doorbell rang all day as a steady stream of family and friends trooped in to wish him well and welcome him home. Before long a party was taking place in the front room with everyone smoking and Dad taking the odd, clandestine puff when he thought no one was looking. Food was produced and drinks were poured as the crowd settled in for the night.

But by seven o'clock Dad's head had begun to droop and Mum politely but firmly asked everyone to leave, which they did. After long goodbyes the last guest had gone and Mum sat down with a sigh of relief. 'That's the end of the visitors, Mick. They'll wear you out. No more for a few days. I'm asking them to stay away and let you rest.'

'Ah, sure I'll go mad sitting here with no company,' said Dad.

'You'll manage a few days and don't think I can't smell the cigarette breath off you. Let that be the last of it. The doctor said they'll be the death of you.'

'One puff here and there won't kill me,' muttered Dad.

'What's for dinner, Mum? The girls are hungry,' said Siobhan, who had spent the day plonked on the couch beside Dad, holding court, while I had run around after her children.

Mum, who had spent the afternoon feeding the cast of *Gandhi*, was tired and grumpy. She glared at Siobhan. 'That's it. I've had enough. Out with the lot of you. I want to spend some time alone with your father. I've been working like a slave in that kitchen. Make your own food.'

I hustled my nieces into the playroom and went into the kitchen, followed closely by Siobhan. I made pasta for her children while she sat at the table, polishing off the left-over sandwiches. Finn came in from work—he had started in the family business the year he left school.

'What's going on with Mum?' he asked. 'She's in a right fouler. I just went in to say hi to Dad and she snapped the head off me.'

'She's just fed up cooking for everyone,' I said. 'Pasta?'

'Yeah, great, I'm starving,' said Finn, grabbing the last sandwich before Siobhan ate it. 'So, did you tell him about Pierre yet?' he asked.

I shook my head. 'I'm going wait until next week when he's better. I'm afraid of getting his blood pressure up.'

'It doesn't matter how long you wait, he's going to flip,' said Siobhan. 'The golden girl is not supposed to end up with a black man. You're supposed to have met a nice Irish doctor from a good family, buy a house in Dublin and have sons that play Gaelic football.'

'Yeah, well, he's just going to have to get used to it,' I said, trying to block out the doubt that was creeping in.

'What's Pierre like?' Siobhan asked Finn.

He shrugged. 'Seems like a decent bloke.'

'Is that all you can say?' I wailed.

'Is he good-looking?' Siobhan wondered.

'How would I know? I'm a guy.'

'Does he look like Denzel Washington?'

'No, more like Mike Tyson,' said Finn, finding himself very entertaining.

'He doesn't look like either,' I snapped. 'He looks like himself. If he was white you wouldn't be asking who he looked like.'

'Yes, I would,' said Siobhan. 'You told me your last boyfriend was like Rob Lowe and then I saw a photo of him. He was a lot more like Rob Lowe's ugly cousin with bad skin.'

'He did not. He was the head cut off Rob.'

Siobhan and Finn cracked up.

'Anyway, the point is that Pierre is gorgeous in a unique way.'

'Is he dark black or more milky?' asked Siobhan.

'I can't believe you just asked me that. It's so politically incorrect.'

'Since when has anyone in this family ever been politically correct?' she asked.

'He's kind of got the same skin tone as Denzel.'

'Is he good in bed?' Siobhan asked, as Finn choked on his sandwich.

'Fantastic.'

'Lucky you. Liam and I haven't had sex in months. We're too tired with five kids.'

'Excuse me, ladies, but I really don't want to know about your sex-lives, or lack of them. You're my sisters—way too much information.'

'Speaking of sex, you won't believe what happened in the hospital today,' I said, and proceeded to tell them about the doctor advising Dad to lay off sex until he could climb a flight of stairs.

'I guess it's a good thing we don't live in a bungalow,' said Finn, grinning.

35

The next morning I woke up early to work on my column and tiptoed down to the kitchen to make myself some coffee. I didn't want to wake Mum, Dad or Finn, who was still living at home, but when I went into the kitchen, Dad was standing at the back door, in the new stripy pyjamas Mum had bought him for hospital. He was smoking.

When he heard me, he flung the cigarette on to the ground and pretended to do stretching exercises and deep breathing. 'Ah, it's good to be up early on a lovely day.'

'It's freezing cold. Close the door. You'll get pneumonia.'

'Not at all. Nothing like a good blast of fresh air to start the day.'

'I saw it, Dad.'

'What?'

'The cigarette.'

'What cigarette?'

'The one you were smoking.'

'I don't know what you're talking about.'

I walked over to the door and pointed to the smouldering butt beside his foot. 'That's what I'm talking about.'

'I've no idea how it got there.'

'Come on, Dad, I saw you throw it down. You know you're not allowed smoke any more. It'll kill you.'

'Don't tell your mother.'

'I won't if you promise never to smoke again.'

'I promise to try not to.'

'Dad!'

'It's the one thing I look forward to in the morning. It helps me think straight. It's bad enough that I've to eat tasteless food and walk two miles a day for exercise without a little treat every now and then.'

I decided not to point out that with Mum as his chef his food would still taste pretty good. 'The doctor was very clear. Your heart can't take the smoking. You have to give up. I don't want you to die. I like having you around. Take up yoga or golf or hill-walking.'

He sighed. 'When you get to my age, you want a bit of peace and quiet and a few little comforts—like a cigarette now and then.'

'You can't smoke, Dad. I want you to have a long, healthy life.'

'You're grown-up now, you don't need me. You've a big career and a nice lad.'

'Who's going to give me away at my wedding?'

'Are you getting married?' he asked, excited.

'Well, actually—'

The door swung open. 'I saw you, Mick,' hissed Mum. 'I saw you smoking from the bedroom window. I'll kill you.'

'Apparently the cigarettes will do that for me.'

'What kind of an eejit are you?'

' 'Twas only a little one.'

'Give me the packet,' Mum ordered. Sheepishly Dad handed it over. 'Let that be the end of it,' she said, throwing them into the bin.

'Ah, Annie, what'd you do that for?'

'I don't want to hear another word. Now, would you like a nice fry for breakfast?'

'Mum, he's not allowed fries any more,' I

reminded her gently.

'Nonsense. I'll only use a tiny bit of butter. The man needs to build up his strength.'

I could see it was useless arguing with her so I left them to it and went back upstairs to work.

A little later Finn came into my room. 'How's it going?'

'OK,' I said. 'I'm just working on my column and then I can focus on the wedding.'

'Are you sure you really want to do this?' he asked.

'Yes. Pierre's the one. Didn't you like him?'

Finn nodded. 'He's a nice guy and he seemed mad keen on you.'

'Did he?' I asked, thrilled that he'd noticed.

'Not as keen as you were on him. You were all over him. It was embarrassing.'

'What?'

'I'm only winding you up. Stop fishing for compliments. I'm off to work, I'll catch you later. Let me know when you decide to tell them so I can make myself scarce.'

'I'm relying on you to calm the storm.'

'It'll be more like a tornado.'

* * *

Later that morning my phone rang. It was Siobhan.

'I've been thinking,' she said. 'I want to meet Pierre. Before you cause havoc in the family, I think I should be introduced to him and give you my honest opinion. I'm a very good judge of character, so I'll be able to tell if he's really serious about you or just a dirty old man.'

'Jesus, Siobhan, he's not a dirty old man. He just

happens to be a bit older than me.'

'It's the same age gap as Charles and Diana. Look what happened to that marriage, and they were the same colour and religion, although I don't think those royals are very religious.'

'Well, thanks for that cheery analogy.'

'I'm just being honest. You need someone to be upfront with you about the whole thing. So, when can I meet him?'

'I'll get him to come over next week, but don't say anything to anyone yet.'

'As if I would. By the way, what's his surname? Liam wants to Google him.'

'Siobhan!'

'Of course I told my husband about him. We tell each other everything. That's how successful marriages work, Niamh. You could learn a thing or two from us.'

I bit my tongue.

'Have you met his parents?' she asked. 'What are they like?'

'To be honest with you, they're very posh and intellectual.'

I could hear her bristle. 'And so are we. You come from prime Irish stock and you went to college, for goodness' sake. I was the brightest girl in school and Dad's a successful businessman, Finn's following in his footsteps and Mum reads a lot.'

'I know, you're right, but they're different. They're a bit intimidating.'

'In what way? Did they freak when they met you? Did they mind you being Catholic?'

'They don't think I'm good enough for Pierre. I'm not stylish, bilingual or an expert on history and philosophy, so to them I'm a big fat loser.'

'You are not,' said my sister, jumping to my defence. 'He's lucky to have you. You're very pretty, since you went blonde, and clever. What's so great about them?'

It took me a moment to get over the shock of Siobhan being so complimentary. 'His mother looks like a model and thinks that women who wear tracksuits are lazy, slovenly wenches. She looks like she's going to dinner in Buckingham Palace every day. Head-to-toe Chanel. And Mr Alcee doesn't talk to you, he lectures you. It must be all the years at Oxford, but he can't seem to have a conversation, just goes off on tangents. They're different, very French.'

'But I thought they were from Martinique?'

'They are, but they moved to France when they were eighteen to study there and became more French than the French themselves.'

'Do they speak fluent English?'

'They speak it better than Shakespeare. It puts me to shame.'

'Your French isn't bad. I remember you being quite good at school.'

'Siobhan, I can just about order a sandwich and ask to go to the loo. It's not the same thing.'

'Well, they sound stuck up to me.'

'They're not really, they just have that French superiority complex where everyone else is less cultured than they are.'

'That's rubbish.'

'It's not really. They do have a lot to be proud of.'

'For instance?'

'Food, wine, fashion, literature.'

'And so do we,' said Siobhan, sounding furious.

'Corned beef isn't quite the same as *foie gras*.'

'James Joyce and W. B. Yeats are as good as any writers they have.'

'Good point,' I said, filing that one away for future conversations with my in-laws. 'But Aran jumpers aren't exactly Chanel.'

'Chanel's overrated. A check suit is a check suit. Why don't they do something different for a change? There's nothing original about it. Mrs Alcee should put on a tracksuit and relax.'

I giggled at that vision. Oh, to see Fleur in a saggy-arsed tracksuit!

'Seriously, Niamh, you should be proud of who you are and don't let anyone make you feel second best. I'll tell Pierre myself when I meet him.'

'Hang on, Pierre isn't like that. He's a brilliant mixture of French and English. English sense of humour with French panache.'

'I'm going to hang up now before you start telling me how wonderful he is—again.'

'Siobhan?'

'Yeah?'

'Thanks for the support and the pep talk.'

'Anytime. I have to fly, the girls are dancing in a *fèis* this afternoon. I've to go and curl their hair.'

'Where is it on?'

'Church hall at three.'

'Can I come?'

'Of course. I didn't think you'd want to. You always hated *fèis*,' said Siobhan, plainly shocked that I'd want to attend.

'That's because I had to take part in them. I'd like to see the girls dancing and check out if they've inherited their mother's talent.'

‘Oh, they have, they’re all very talented. Wait till you see them,’ said the proud mother. ‘I actually think Muireann could go on to win a national.’

‘Fantastic! I look forward to seeing her in action,’ I said, hanging up and shuddering at the memory of my mother forcing my unruly hair into ringlets.

* * *

Later that day I arrived at the town hall with Dad—the doting grandfather—to see the girls dance. Mum had said she was busy with something or other; clearly the idea of spending hours in a draughty town hall watching Irish dancing had not grown on her over the years.

When we arrived, the girls were being given last-minute instructions by Siobhan. They looked adorable in their dresses with their perfectly ringleted hair. Siobhan was obviously a lot more talented at doing hair than Mum had been. None of them appeared to have baldy patches where their hair had been pulled out by trapped curlers. It all seemed much more civilized. At only three, Ailbhe was a picture in her little green dress with her big blue eyes wide with excitement.

While Dad shook hands and spoke to everyone there—most of whom he knew from the community—I sat down and watched Muireann practising. She was really good, a natural. She caught my eye and came over to sit beside me. The youngest dancers were going first, so she had plenty of time before it was her turn.

‘Are you nervous?’ I asked my eldest niece.

She shook her head.

'I used to be terrified,' I confessed. 'Then again, I was useless and it was embarrassing having to go on and stumble through my dance. Your mum was really amazing. She used to make it look so easy.'

'Can I tell you a secret?' Muireann asked. She had turned into a beautiful girl, the image of Siobhan at the same age, tall and slim with green eyes and auburn hair.

'Of course.'

'Promise you won't tell anyone?'

'Cross my heart and hope to die.'

'I hate Irish dancing.'

I roared laughing, which was not the reaction she expected.

'Sssh,' she said, glancing round in a panic.

'I'm sorry, pet. It's just that I hated it too. Why don't you like it? Your mum said you're really good.'

'It's geeky.'

'I thought it was cool now, since the whole *Riverdance* explosion.'

She shook her head. 'No, it's not. Being good at tennis is cool. Being good at gymnastics is cool. Irish dancing is for nerds. I hate the stupid dresses and the silly hair.'

'But you look gorgeous.'

'I'm wearing a curtain,' she said, mirroring my exact thoughts at the same age.

'Yes, but you wear it so well. I looked like an idiot in my dresses, but you look like a star.'

'I don't want to do it any more. It's so embarrassing. What I really want is to do ballet. I know I'd be good at it. There's a ballet school in Marylebone that's supposed to be brilliant. I want to go there. They do classes all day Saturday. Make

Mum let me go—please, Niamh.'

I looked down at her pleading face and felt a pang of sympathy. She was just like me when I was younger, desperate to move away from her Irishness and do something more mainstream. But, unlike me, she was talented. 'Don't you want to do something you're good at? You could win competitions.'

She gazed at me scornfully. 'The only competition I want to win is in ballet. I thought you'd understand. I thought you'd be on my side. Mum said you were always causing trouble and fighting with Granddad.'

'I didn't cause that much trouble,' I said, annoyed at Siobhan for slating me to her kids. 'And I am on your side. I just want you to think about what you'd be giving up. You might not be as good at ballet as you are at Irish dancing. It might be a let-down for you. That's all.'

'I want to be a prima ballerina,' she said, getting tearful. 'It's my dream. I'm going to dance at Covent Garden.'

'OK, don't get upset. I'll try and help you, but I'm not sure what I can do.'

'Talk to my mum. Make her see that the ballet school is a good idea. Make her see that I don't want to be a stupid Irish dancer.'

'Has she any idea how you feel?'

'I tried to tell her but she just said I was being silly and went on and on about how great it is to be Irish and how we have to keep our culture alive over here. I don't care about stinky old Ireland. I never want to leave London.'

'You'll change,' I said, smiling at her. She was so like me, fighting to fit in, resisting talk of tradition and heritage. 'When you grow up you'll realize that it's actually quite cool to be Irish and English. You can have the best of both worlds.'

'When I'm eighteen I'm going to change my name. A ballerina can't be called Muireann. It's a stupid name that no one can say. I'm going to change it to Olga.'

I tried to hide a smile. I had predicted that Muireann would be a troublesome name for a girl growing up in London. But the new mature me loved it. 'Olga's a bit Russian, isn't it? Muireann's lovely and it's sentimental too. You were called after your dad's granny.'

She rolled her eyes. 'As if I didn't know that. I hear it every day. Can you imagine a ballerina called Muireann? I don't think so.'

'Olga O'Loughlin's going to sound a bit strange.'

'I won't need a surname. I'll be like Mariah or Shania. No one uses their second names. Everyone just knows who they are.'

She had it all planned out. I just hoped she was good at ballet because it was going to be a big disappointment if she wasn't. She already had her name in lights at Covent Garden. Still, I'd thought I was going to be the next Ginger Rogers. It'd wear off.

'I have to be allowed to do ballet,' she said, gripping my arm. 'I want to wear tutus and ballet slippers, not clumpy black brogues.'

'OK, I'll talk to your mum and try to make her see your point of view, but I can't promise anything. I'll do my best.'

'Thanks,' she said, hugging me. 'I'll never forget this.'

I smiled down at her. In her little eleven-year-old head this was life or death. Just like tap dancing had been to me. We were cut from the same cloth.

It was ironic. Here I was, back in London seeking my sister's help in persuading Dad that marrying a black agnostic was my destiny, and now my niece needed me to persuade Siobhan that ballet was hers. If I could persuade Siobhan to let Muireann do ballet, maybe I could persuade my parents that Pierre was my perfect match.

I waited for the right moment. The six-year-olds were dancing and none of Siobhan's kids was competing. I wandered over to her. 'I was just talking to Muireann,' I said. 'She was saying she's not as keen on Irish dancing as her sisters.'

Siobhan's head snapped round. 'What do you mean? Have you been putting ideas into her head?'

'No! I didn't say a word. She just mentioned she'd like to try ballet. If she's good at Irish dancing she might be good at ballet too.'

'She's not *good* at Irish dancing, she's *brilliant*,' said Siobhan, glaring at me. 'And I'd appreciate it if you kept your nose out of my family's affairs.'

'Jesus, Siobhan, Muireann approached me. All I did was listen to the poor girl. She's really upset. She doesn't want to hurt your feelings. She knows how keen you are for her to continue with the Irish dancing but she wants the opportunity to try ballet. Couldn't you get her a few lessons and see if she's any good? It might satisfy her curiosity. Remember me with tap dancing? It only lasted a few months.'

'You didn't have any talent. If Muireann gives up Irish dancing she's throwing away a God-given gift. It'd be a sin to waste it.'

'Not if she's miserable.'

'Teenagers change their minds every five minutes. She'll get over this ballet thing in a few weeks.'

'What if she doesn't? What if she has a natural ability for ballet too? Surely you don't want to deny her the chance to try.'

Siobhan sighed. 'Muireann saw a film about a ballerina a week ago and since then all she wants to do is ballet. Six months ago she wanted to be Britney Spears. It's a phase, it'll wear off. I know my daughter. She's actually very like you, impulsive and stubborn.'

In the space of a few hours I'd gone from being pretty and clever to impulsive and stubborn. As Siobhan walked off, Muireann came up to me.

'Well? Did you get her to say yes?'

'Not exactly.'

'You mean no,' said my niece, accusingly.

'Sorry.'

'Thanks for nothing,' she said, and stomped off to slate me to her friends.

Judging by my ballet fiasco, I was never going to persuade Mum and Dad that Pierre was the man for me. I was truly, utterly screwed.

36

I went to meet Pierre at the airport. I hadn't seen him in more than a week and I had missed him terribly. I ran over as soon as I saw him and we hugged and kissed like long-lost lovers.

'God, I missed you,' he said.

'Me too.'

'So, have you told them yet?'

'We're going to meet my sister and my auntie Nuala today. After that we'll tackle my parents,' I fudged.

'So you haven't.'

'I told you I wanted Dad to have a week or two to recover first. I'll tell them in the next day or so. By the time you get back from your visit to your parents in Oxford, the deed will be done, I promise.'

'OK, but that's it, Niamh. Friday is the final deadline. We need to get a move on with the wedding plans.'

'I know, I know. Anyway, look, you're getting to meet two members of my family today for lunch. Siobhan, who, although she drives me mad at times, is very important to me, and Nuala, who is like my second mother. If we can get them on-side it'll be a huge help with Mum and Dad.'

'No pressure, then.'

'None.' I grinned.

'Anything I shouldn't say?'

'Don't tell them we live together. Don't mention sex or religion. When they ask you what you do, give them the short version. No offence but the ins and outs of phonetics are a bit heavy for lunch. Don't mention Vancouver and don't mention the wedding.'

'Can I tell them my name?'

'I'm being practical. With my family you feed them information slowly. Siobhan knows about Canada, but Nuala doesn't.'

'Is there anything I can talk about?'

'Me. Tell them how much you love me and how

wonderful I am.'

'I think I can manage that.'

* * *

I had booked Pierre into a hotel in Fulham for the night. He was going to visit his parents the next morning. He checked in and went to drop off his bags. I hurried him along as I didn't want to be late for the lunch. I made him change his shirt twice. Although Pierre was more English than French in his attitude and the way he spoke, his dress sense was a little flamboyant. He was prone to wearing brightly coloured shirts. My family were a blue-shirt kind of bunch. I didn't want Pierre arriving into the lunch in one of his red creations.

'But I like that one,' he complained.

'I know, but trust me, the blue one will go down much better. If you turn up in the red one they'll think you're gay.'

He laughed.

'I'm serious.'

'Come on!'

'Pierre, no man in my family has ever worn a shirt that wasn't blue or white. We had one uncle who turned up in a yellow one and he was slagged so badly he never wore it again. When we're on our own you can wear what you want—although, to be honest, I'm not a big fan of the red shirt, or the bright green one for that matter—but with my family, tone it down.'

'I don't tell you how to dress with my family.'

'No, but your mother does.'

'I wasn't sorry to see the tracksuits go,' he admitted.

'That's all that's going. I like my clothes.'

'I like you out of them,' he said, grabbing my bum.

'Not now, we're late. Come on, put the boring blue one on. Oh, and one other thing. Try not to wave your arms about too much when you're talking.'

Pierre rolled his eyes. 'It was easier to get a degree than meet your family.'

* * *

When we got to the restaurant, Siobhan and Nuala were pretending not to see us, although I could see them staring from behind their menus.

'I presume they're the two ladies sitting in the corner gaping at me open-mouthed,' muttered Pierre.

'Yes, that's them,' I said, as my stomach lurched. I was praying they'd like him.

We walked over and I introduced Pierre. They all shook hands and we sat down. There was silence.

'Harry Belafonte,' exclaimed Nuala.

'I'm sorry?' said Pierre.

'That's who you look like. The image of him.'

'Who's Harry Belafonte?' I asked.

Pierre and Nuala laughed.

'He's one of the most famous singers from the fifties and sixties,' said Nuala. 'He sang "The Banana Boat Song".'

Siobhan and I looked at her blankly.

' "Day-o," ' sang Pierre.

' "Daaaaaay-o," ' sang Nuala.

' "Day-li-light and I wan' go home," ' they sang

in unison, laughing as they finished.

'Oh, I like that song,' I said.

'He was an actor too,' said Nuala.

'And an advocate for civil rights,' said Pierre. 'He was one of Martin Luther King's confidants and helped organize the march on Washington in 'sixty-three.'

'I've never heard of him,' said Siobhan.

'I think he's more our generation than yours,' Pierre said, winking at Nuala—who blushed!

'Oh, now, Pierre, I think I'm a little older than you,' she flirted.

'You certainly don't look it,' said Pierre, using his French charm to win her over.

She beamed at him.

Then, turning to Siobhan, he continued the charm offensive. 'Tell me, Siobhan, how are your daughters? I've seen photos of them, they're cracking-looking girls.'

'Oh, they're very well, thanks. They all won medals at the *fèis* last week. Muireann, my eldest, won best overall dancer. She's very talented.'

'I believe you were a champion dancer yourself. Niamh told me you won every competition you entered.'

Siobhan blushed. Bloody hell, this was incredible!

'I wasn't bad in my day, but sure it's behind me now,' she said, sitting up straighter.

'I don't know about that. Once a dancer always a dancer.'

'Pierre, what is it you do?' asked Nuala, batting her eyelids.

Pierre, despite my warnings, gave them the long version. He was very passionate about phonetics, and although I knew most of what he was saying was going straight over their heads, my sister and aunt hung on his every word like star pupils.

The lunch continued, with Pierre plying Nuala and Siobhan with wine and charming them with stories of moving to Oxford aged ten and trying to fit into his new posh school—French, black and terrified. ‘Can you imagine it? I was an easy target for bullying, but it didn’t last long. I learnt to speak English in record time and lost my French accent as fast as I could. I just wanted to fit in. I was sporty too, which helped.’

‘I can see that. You look very fit,’ said my lush of an aunt.

‘What did you play?’ asked Siobhan.

‘Rugby, and then I did a bit of rowing in college, but it’s a long time ago now.’

‘Once a sportsman, always a sportsman,’ said Siobhan, smiling at him.

I couldn’t believe it. This was so much easier than I’d thought. Maybe Mum and Dad would be fine about it too.

But then Nuala piped up, ‘Niamh tells me you’re not religious.’

‘I’m afraid not,’ said Pierre, as I kicked him under the table to stop him going into a long diatribe on the futility of organized religion.

‘And you’ve no Irish blood in you?’ asked Nuala.

‘None. Sorry.’

‘Do your parents have any Irish friends in Oxford?’ asked Siobhan.

He shook his head.

‘Come on now, Pierre, we need you to help us out here. You’re a lovely lad, very handsome, but Niamh’s parents are not going to be happy about this match. There must be someone Irish in your past,' said Nuala.

Pierre thought for a minute, then said, 'There was an Irish matron at school, Molly. She used to look after us when we were sick.'

'That'll do,' said Nuala. 'We'll focus on Molly. We'll build her up to being a close family friend.'

'I barely knew her, and she's dead now,' said Pierre.

'It doesn't matter,' said Siobhan. 'We can work round it. What was her surname?'

'God, I don't know.'

'Think, Pierre,' I urged him.

'I'm sorry, darling, I have no idea.'

'Hanafin,' said Nuala. 'We'll say it was Hanafin. You can tell Niamh's parents that Molly was a great influence in your life and you'd love them to have met her. But unfortunately she passed away recently.'

'What about religion?' said Siobhan.

'Any chance you'd convert?' asked Nuala.

'None, I'm afraid.'

'But he has agreed to bring up any kids we have as Catholic.'

'Actually, I said I'd think about it.'

'You'll have to give in on that one. That'll be a deal-breaker for Mum and Dad,' said Siobhan.

'If they ask you about faith, just be a bit vague. Say you're open to all religions but haven't fixed on one yet,' said Nuala.

'No, that won't work,' said Siobhan. 'If he gives Dad an inkling that he might be converted, he'll hound him into becoming Catholic.'

'You're right. OK, Pierre, you'll just have to say you're not religious yourself, but you've great respect for the Catholic faith,' said Nuala. 'We're an old-fashioned bunch and we don't like change. Tread softly,' she said, smiling at him. 'Sure it'll be no bother to a charmer like yourself.'

'I presume Niamh told you about Dad's heart-attack?' Siobhan said.

'Yes, I was really sorry to hear of it. She said he's on the mend, though.'

'He is, but he has to keep his blood pressure down and this is going to be a big shock. We need to plan it carefully,' said Siobhan.

'Do you want me to tell him?' asked Nuala.

'No,' I said firmly. 'I'm the one who's going to marry Pierre and I'm the one who'll tell Dad. I'm thinking I'll tell Mum first and, hopefully, she'll help me when it comes to Dad.'

'She will, of course. Once she meets this charmer, she'll forget he's black and older,' said Nuala, never a fan of subtlety.

'How have your parents reacted?' asked Siobhan, winking at me.

'They were a bit surprised at first, but they're coming round to the idea now. They're looking forward to meeting the rest of Niamh's family.'

'One thing at a time,' said Nuala, panic-stricken. 'We can't have you all descending on poor Mick and Annie at once.'

'Don't worry,' I said, laughing at the vision of the entire Alcee family arriving into Mum and Dad's front room—Chanel suits, red shirts and French-history lesson in tow.

'Well, we've a lively few days ahead of us,' said Nuala.

37

Five minutes after leaving the restaurant, I rang Siobhan for feedback. It was pretty obvious that Pierre had been a hit, but I wanted to do a post-mortem anyway.

'So, what did you think?'

'He's OK.'

'Oh.'

'I'm joking. He's great, Niamh, really nice, charming, relaxed and good-looking too. I can see why you fell for him.'

'What did Nuala think?'

'She's here beside me. Hang on,' said Siobhan, passing the phone to our aunt.

'Niamh?' Nuala's voice said.

'Yes?'

'Don't let that fella out of your sight. He's a keeper.'

'Did you really like him?'

'If I was ten years younger, I'd run off with him myself. He's wonderful so he is. No more than you deserve. I think once your mother gets over the shock of him being black, she'll love him.'

'What about Dad?'

'Your father's a whole other issue. I think it'll take him a long time to come round, but I'll be fighting your corner. You've found a good man there. Don't let him go.'

'Thanks, Nuala,' I said, feeling a huge sense of relief. They liked him, and they were going to help win over my parents.

'Niamh, it's me,' said Siobhan, coming back on

the phone. 'When are you going to tell Mum and Dad?'

'I was planning to do it tomorrow while Pierre's in Oxford with his parents. It'll give them twenty-four hours to freak out before he comes back to meet them.'

'OK. I'll keep the day free so I can help you out after you've told them. You'll need it.'

'Thanks, Siobhan. I really appreciate that.'

'To be honest, I didn't expect to like him, but he's a fantastic guy. How did you do it?' she said, as I bristled.

'I didn't *do* anything. He fell for me.'

'There's no need to be defensive. He's just in a different league from your usual loser boyfriends.'

'I know, and that's why I'm going to marry him. Anyway, I'm glad you liked him,' I said. 'It means a lot to have you on my side.'

'Good luck tomorrow. Keep me posted. I'll have my phone with me all day. Call me when you've dropped the bomb. Mum and Dad will listen to me. I'll be able to calm them down.'

'Thanks,' I said, not feeling half as confident of her powers of persuasion as she was.

I hung up and Pierre grinned at me. 'Let me guess, they love me.'

I shook my head. 'Thumbs down, I'm afraid.'

'Bullshit. They were eating out of my hand.'

'OK. You were a big hit.'

'I told you they'd like me.'

'You were right, but don't get too cocky. The real hurdle is yet to come.'

'Piece of cake. Once your parents meet me, they'll come round.'

'Well, we'll find out soon. When you get back on

Friday, I want you to come straight from the station to the house. You should get there at about five. I'll have done the deed and it'll be up to you to launch a serious charm offensive.'

'No problem.'

'Pierre?'

'Yes?'

'You were amazing today.'

'I'm glad they approved. Two down, two to go.'

I spent the night tossing and turning in my childhood bed. I wanted to approach telling my parents in the best way possible. After a sleepless night, I finally decided to tell Mum first. Once she was on-side, I'd tell Dad. If Mum was convinced she could persuade Dad that black was white, she was my most important ally. My plan to drip-feed the information was out of the window. There was no easy or slow way to tell them that Pierre was black and I was moving to Canada. I'd just have to come out with it.

The next morning, while Dad slept in, I got Mum in the kitchen on her own. I kept opening my mouth to tell her, then chickening out.

'What's wrong with you?' she asked. 'You're like a cat on a hot tin roof this morning.'

'Mum, I need you to sit down. I have something I want to talk to you about.'

Her hand flew up to her mouth. 'Please, God, don't tell me you're pregnant.'

'No! Don't worry it's nothing like that.'

'Thank the Lord,' she said, mightily relieved.

'No, Mum, it's something else.'

'Is it your boyfriend? I've been so distracted with your father, I haven't had the chance to ask you about him.'

'Well, yes, it is about him. We're still together and it's got very serious.'

'You want to move in with him? Well, you know I don't approve of living in sin, so you won't get my blessing if that's what you're looking for.'

'Not exactly. The thing is, Mum, Pierre's asked me to marry him and I've said yes.'

'*What?* We haven't even met him! How could you agree to marry someone your father and I've never set eyes on?'

'He only proposed the other day,' I lied. 'It's all new to me too. Besides, you're going to meet him tomorrow.'

'I should think so too,' she huffed.

'I really love him, Mum. He's the most amazing person I've ever met.'

'I'm very glad to hear it, Niamh, but there will be no wedding until we've met him and approved of him. I don't even know his second name!'

'It's Alcee. He's the professor of phonetics at Trinity College, Dublin.'

'Professor,' she said. 'How old is he?'

'Well, he's a bit older than me.'

'How much older?'

'Fourteen years.'

'Lord, Niamh, he's practically old enough to be your father. He's not a divorcé, is he? Please tell me he isn't.'

'No, Mum, he's never been married. I'm the only person he's ever proposed to.'

'Very peculiar, a man of his age not married. He's not queer, is he?'

'Jesus, Mum! No, he isn't. He's a heterosexual man who just didn't find the right person until he met me.'

'It's a very big age gap. When you're forty he'll be fifty-four. You need to think about that.'

'I'm not worried about it, Mum. He's a very young forty-two.'

'My cousin Susan married an older man and it was terrible. He got very sick in his fifties and she ended up being his nurse. She had a dreadful time.'

'Honestly, Mum, when you meet him you'll see how healthy he is. It's not a worry.'

'Maybe not now, not today, but in ten years' time he could have a heart-attack like your father and you'll end up a nursemaid.'

I really needed to get her off the age difference. It wasn't supposed to be the big deal.

'Well, I could marry a guy my own age and the same thing could happen. Look at Charles and Diana. She was the younger one and she died in a car crash. You never know what's ahead of you. But there's no point dwelling on it.'

'Was it a car crash, though? There are many think she was murdered.'

'Don't tell me you actually believe those conspiracy theories?'

She sniffed. 'Anything's possible.'

Rather than get into a long discussion about whether or not Princess Diana's crash was accidental, I brought the conversation back to my fiancé. 'Pierre's been offered a job in Vancouver in Canada and he leaves in a few weeks. We'd like to get married before we go, so I really need your help.'

'Canada? But that's the other side of the world.'

'It's only a plane ride away. You can come and visit.'

'Engagements, older man, moving to Canada . . .

My God, Niamh, are you trying to give me a heart-attack like your father?'

'I know it's a lot to take in and I'm sorry to land it on you, but as I said, Pierre only proposed last week,' I lied again, 'and he only got the job offer a few days ago. I'm still reeling from it all myself. But it's good news, Mum. He's a wonderful person. I can't wait for you to meet him.'

'Well, I can tell you one thing, missy. You're going nowhere with that man until your father and I have had a long talk with him about exactly what his intentions are and find out what kind of morals and principles he has. Is he Catholic?'

'No.'

She put her head into her hands. 'You're not making this easy, Niamh. Your father's going to hit the roof when he hears this man is French, fourteen years older, wants you to move to Canada with him and not even a Catholic.'

'Actually, Mum, there is one other thing that I need to explain about Pierre.'

'What could it possibly be?' She sighed.

'He's not exactly French. His parents are from Martinique in the Caribbean. So he's kind of—'

'What?'

'Not white.'

'Jesus, Mary and St Joseph—BLACK?' she screeched.

I nodded.

Mum fell into the chair beside her and gaped. I stood in front of her, dancing from one foot to the other. She shook her head and tears came into her eyes. She wailed, 'Why? Why do you have to be so difficult? Why can't you be like other girls and bring home a nice local lad? What did I do in a former life to deserve two such daughters? One who has to have a gunshot wedding and another who wants to marry a black man.'

'Shotgun.'

'What?'

'Nothing. Come on, Mum, once you meet Pierre, you'll love him. Honestly, I know you will.'

'No, I will not,' she snapped. 'Do you have any idea what you're getting yourself into? Do you have any idea how hard marriage is? A relationship with someone from your own culture and creed is difficult enough, but with someone from another it's impossible.'

'It's 1999, Mum. People marry outside their comfort zone all the time.'

'Name one couple you know where the husband is black.'

I'd known they'd ask this question so I'd racked my brain for ages and finally come up with Harriet and Jason. They were the only mixed-race couple in our neighbourhood. 'Harriet and Jason.'

'And a fine example they are!' she cried. 'Their poor children didn't know what colour they were supposed to be with a black mother and a white father. They're a mess, drug addicts the lot of them.'

'That's not true. Only Daniel, the youngest, did drugs. The other two are teachers. Besides, Daniel's been clean for ages now.'

'Wild, the whole lot of them,' she muttered, choosing to ignore the facts. 'And what about your children? Have you thought how they're going to feel with a white mother and a black father? It's the children who suffer.'

I willed myself to remain calm. 'They'll have two

parents who love each other.'

'You think you have it figured out, but you really don't have a clue. People haven't changed that much.'

'Yes, Mum, they have. Even Dublin is cosmopolitan now. Times *have* changed and so have attitudes. If you'd just give Pierre a chance, I guarantee he'll win you over. Nuala and Siobhan loved him.'

She jumped up from the chair. 'NUALA!'

'Yes. She met him yesterday and thought he was amazing.'

'How dare you introduce him to Nuala before me? *I* should be the first person to meet him, not your aunt. I'm your mother,' she shouted.

'I'm sorry. I wanted to test the water.'

'Get that man in here immediately. I can't have Nuala telling the whole place about your fiancé and me, your own mother, not even having set eyes on him.'

'He'll be here at five this afternoon.'

'I presume you haven't told your father yet?'

I winced. 'No.'

'If you think I'm angry, he'll hit the roof. I'm not sure his heart can take it. But now that you've gone and introduced him to Nuala we'll have to meet him today. We've no choice or we'll be the laughing-stock of the family. It'll be the talk of the town. No one has ever gone this far. No one has ever done this to their parents. A black man!'

'That's enough,' I snapped. 'Stop judging him by his colour. Meet him and then decide if you like him or not.'

'Don't you raise your voice to me. I'm upset enough as it is.'

'I'm upset too, that you're not giving Pierre a chance.' I sighed. 'Mum, he makes me really happy.'

'It's not all about being in love, Niamh. It's about partnership and having similar interests, goals, respect and compatibility.'

'We have all those things,' I said.

'I sincerely hope you do,' she said.

'Look, Mum, I need you on my side. I need your help with Dad. Remember when you said you could persuade him of anything?'

'I can't perform miracles, Niamh. Besides, I haven't time to talk to him now. I've to go and get my hair done. I can't be meeting your fiancé looking like this.'

38

When Mum rushed out of the house to get her hair done I sat down to gather myself together before telling Dad. Mum's reaction had been worse than I'd thought it would be, so Dad's was going to be horrendous. I took a deep breath and went to find him.

I met him coming down the stairs.

'Where'd your mother run off to in such a hurry?' he asked.

'She went to get her hair done.'

'Oh, right. Well, I'm off to the office to check on things.'

'Actually, Dad, do you have a minute?'

'Sorry, pet, I've to dash. I'm meeting Tadhg there at ten and I'm already late.'

'When will you be back?'

'Around lunch time. Is everything all right? You look a bit tired.'

'Fine, thanks. I just didn't sleep that well. How are you feeling?'

'I'm great today. This is the first day I've woken up and felt back to myself.'

'Does your heart feel strong?' I asked, because it was going to get a big shock.

'As an ox. There's life in the old dog yet,' he said, patting my arm. 'Don't worry about me, pet. Right, I'd best be off.'

'OK, I'll see you later, then. At lunch time?'

'Fine.'

I was almost relieved that he had to rush off. I needed to talk to Mum when she'd calmed down and coax her into helping me with Dad. Hopefully she'd be in a better mood when she came back from the hairdresser.

An hour later, the kitchen door swung open and Mum came in with a very strange hairdo.

'Your hair's nice,' I lied.

'It's a disgrace. I got some young trainee one and I was so distracted I didn't keep an eye on what she was doing and it's lopsided. I was too upset to complain, so I just paid and left.'

'It looks fine to me.'

'Is there anything I can say or do to persuade you to give this man up?' she cut across me.

'No. I love him.'

'If your father and I disapprove of him will you go to Canada anyway?'

'I hope that won't happen.'

'Don't be too sure. Will you go?'

'Yes, Mum, I will.'

'Well, then, I hope for your sake that we do like him.'

'Why can't you be happy for me?' I complained.

'Because I see the hurdles you're going to face and all you can see is love and romance. I want the best life possible for my children.'

'Pierre is the best thing that's ever happened to me.'

The kitchen door opened and Siobhan walked in. Seeing Mum's stormy face she said, 'I can see Niamh's told you her news.'

'Yes, she has. Apparently I'm the last to know.'

'Come on, Mum, it was only Siobhan and Nuala, who's like a surrogate mother,' I said.

'But she's not your mother. *I* am. *I* should have met him first.'

'I agree with Mum,' said Siobhan, as I frowned at her. 'Mum should have met him first. If Muireann introduced her boyfriend to you before me, I'd freak.'

'Were you shocked when you found out he was black?' Mum asked my sister. 'Niamh tells me it's normal nowadays.'

'Normal! Are you mad? I was so shocked I crashed the car.'

'So, I'm not an old fuddy-duddy, then,' Mum said, glaring at me.

'I never said—'

'What's he like?' Mum asked Siobhan.

'He's totally different from what I thought she'd end up with. He's really nice—mature, together and good-looking too,' she said, still sounding surprised.

'Do you think he really loves her?' Mum asked.

'I'm still here, you know,' I reminded them, as

they talked over me.

'He seems to be mad about her and she's gooey-eyed about him. They'd make you sick.'

'Who'd make you sick?' asked Finn, arriving in.

'Niamh and her fiancé,' said Siobhan.

'Fiancé?'

'Yes, we're engaged,' I said.

'I see,' he said, afraid to give anything away.

'It's OK, Mum knows about Pierre. She knows he's from Martinique,' I said.

'No wonder you kept so quiet about meeting him,' Mum said, glaring at Finn now. 'What did you make of him, then?'

'Seems a nice bloke. Just like us, apart from the tan,' said Finn, grinning.

'Is Dad not with you?' I interrupted.

'No, he's stuck in meetings.'

'I told him to take it easy,' said Mum.

'There's a problem with our main supplier, nothing major but Dad has a good relationship with him so he's the best person to smooth it over. He told me to tell you he'd be home by four.'

'What time is your man arriving?' asked Mum.

'He'll be here at five,' I said, panicking. 'I really wanted to tell Dad now, so he'd have a few hours to digest it.'

'You mean hit the roof.' Finn laughed.

'This is no laughing matter,' said Mum. 'Your poor father has a bad heart. I'm not sure he can take it.'

'She has to tell him now. Nuala knows, which means Tadhg knows, and soon enough he'll tell the other uncles and everyone will know,' said Siobhan.

'I'll break it to him gently,' I said. 'I promise to

do it as best I can so he doesn't go off the deep end.'

'And pigs will fly,' said Finn, winking at me. 'Rather you than me, sis.'

* * *

When Dad finally arrived home at half past four, I was pretty sure I was the one who was going to have the heart-attack. I had been pacing the hall for an hour waiting for him, trying to formulate the best way to tell him my news, and failing miserably. I felt sick with nerves.

'Hello, Niamh,' he said. 'On your way out?'

'No, Dad, I was waiting for you, actually. I need to talk to you about something.'

'I'll just make myself a cup of tea and I'll be right with you,' he said, heading towards the kitchen.

'No, I'll make it. Go and sit down and I'll bring one in to you,' I said, hustling him into the good room. I didn't want him to see Mum, who was in the kitchen, with lopsided hair, in her best dress, laying out the good china for Pierre's visit. He'd know something was up. We only ever used this china on Christmas Day, or when Father Hogan came round.

'That looks nice, Mum,' I said, putting the kettle on for Dad's tea.

'I won't have anyone saying we didn't make an effort.'

'Thanks. Pierre will appreciate it.'

'He'd want to,' she snipped. 'Where's your father?'

'In the good room. I'm making him a cup of tea,

then telling him.'

Mum looked at the clock. 'It's twenty to five. You'd want to get a move on.'

'I'm going,' I said, hurrying out of the room with the tea.

I handed the cup to Dad, who was sitting back in the couch, very relaxed.

'How are you feeling?' I asked him.

'Not a bother on me. I'm as good as new,' he said.

'Well, that's great news, Dad.'

'You know, when something like a heart-attack happens to you, it makes you take stock of your life. I've been very lucky, really. I've three lovely children, a wonderful wife and a successful business. What more could a man want?'

'You're right, Dad, there's a lot to be grateful for.'

'When I moved to London thirty-five years ago, I'd never have imagined that things would turn out so well.'

'You worked hard, you deserve it.'

'Your mother deserves credit too, raising you while I was out setting up the business. She's been a tower of strength.'

'Yes, Mum's great. Did you fall in love at first sight?'

'I did. She was the loveliest girl in London. We met at a ceili and I knew the minute I saw her that I'd marry her.'

'Did you ever meet any English girls when you moved over, before Mum?' I asked, hoping he'd had at least one relationship with a non-Irish Catholic girl.

'No. I didn't entertain them. I was only

interested in marrying a nice Irish girl who'd raise a family with me.'

'Would it have been so terrible to marry a non-Irish girl if you'd fallen in love with her?'

'Why would I do that when I knew I'd find a lovely Irish girl, if I searched hard enough? And I did.'

'Dad, when we were born did you worry that we might end up with English husbands?' I asked, trying a different tack.

'I did, of course, but when Siobhan met Liam and you moved to Dublin, I knew we'd be all right. Now, why don't you tell me what this is all about?'

I took a deep breath and sat on my hands to stop them shaking. 'I've met someone I really like.'

'I knew it. It's got serious with this fella in Dublin, hasn't it?'

'Yes, it has. Very serious, actually.'

'Well, isn't that marvellous? I knew you'd find a nice lad over there. Sure you've the pick of the crop.'

'Well, the thing is, Dad, he's not—'

'A brain surgeon? It's all right, I can live with that,' he said, finding himself very amusing.

'No, Dad, it's more than that. He's not Irish.'

Deathly silence.

'Not Irish?' he said. 'I don't understand.'

'He was brought up in England.'

'That's OK. So were you,' he said. 'Don't look so worried.'

'His parents aren't Irish either.'

'What do you mean?'

'They're kind of French.'

'*French!*' he spluttered, standing up. 'I won't have you stepping out with any French man.

They're a slippery lot, surrendering so quickly during the war. I'm sorry, Niamh, but this lad will have to get himself another girl. Go back to Dublin and find yourself a nice Irish lad.'

'But, Dad, I love Pierre and he's asked me to marry him and I said yes.'

'*Marry him!*' he shouted, getting all red in the face. 'You'll do no such thing.'

The doorbell rang. I looked at the clock. Shit! It was five already. Dad looked out of the window.

'I bloody well told them to stay away,' he muttered. Turning to me, he said, 'Stay here, young lady, I'm not finished with you.'

He stormed out of the room and swung open the front door. I followed him. Pierre was standing at the front step, hand outstretched. 'Mr O'Flaherty, it's very nice to meet you.'

'Now look here, young man, I thought I was very clear with your friends who called to the door last week. You're wasting your time here. We're Catholics in this house and we've no interest in becoming Jehovah's Witnesses.'

'Dad,' I said, trying to interrupt him.

'Niamh, go back inside, I'll deal with you in a minute,' he snapped. Turning back to Pierre, he added, 'You're barking up the wrong tree. I don't want you coming round here bothering me and my family again. I know you're only doing your duty, but I don't come knocking on your door telling you to convert to Catholicism, so please respect my privacy and stay away from my house.'

'*Dad!*' I said, grabbing his arm.

'What is it?' he barked.

'This is Pierre. My fiancé.'

39

Dad looked at Pierre, then at me, then back at Pierre, and at me again. He slammed the door in Pierre's face and bellowed, 'OVER MY DEAD BODY.'

Mum came running out of the kitchen. 'Calm down,' she said, rushing to his side.

'Did you know about this?' Dad asked.

'Niamh only told me this morning. I'm as upset as you are.'

I opened the door and Pierre stepped tentatively into the hall.

'Mum, Dad, I'd like you to meet Pierre,' I said, as firmly as I could, trying to salvage some kind of manners. His parents may not have liked me, but they hadn't slammed a door in my face.

'Mr and Mrs O'Flaherty, it's a pleasure to meet you both,' said Pierre, managing to remain calm amid the madness.

Mum shook his hand. 'You'll have to excuse us, Pierre. Niamh only informed us of your existence a short time ago and we're still trying to get used to the idea.'

'I understand completely. I can come back later if you'd like some time alone.'

'If I were you, son, I'd take a very long walk. Maybe the longest walk of your life,' said Dad, 'because there is no way in hell you're going to marry my daughter.'

'Dad!' I snapped. 'Don't be so rude. Pierre's here now and he's not going anywhere.'

Siobhan and Finn appeared. 'Hi, Pierre,' they

said. He looked relieved to see them.

'Come on in and have some tea. Mum has it all prepared,' I said, ushering him into the good room.

'Tea!' said Dad. '*Tea!* Have you all gone mad? Sidney Poitier here is not coming in for tea.'

'Mick,' hissed Mum, 'don't be so rude.'

'Nuala thinks he looks like Harry—what's his name?' said Siobhan.

'Belafonte,' I said.

'He's the head cut off him,' said Mum.

'Can we please stop talking as if Pierre wasn't standing here beside us?' I begged, mortified by my family's rudeness. They were making Pierre's parents seem like the king and queen of decorum.

'I don't care if he looks like Martin Luther bloody King. He's not marrying my daughter and that's the END OF IT,' roared Dad.

'Calm down. Shouting's bad for your heart,' said Mum.

'So is shock,' he snapped.

'Come on in and have a seat, Pierre. We all just need to calm down,' said Mum, showing Pierre to a chair. 'How do you like your tea?'

'Just milk, thanks. You have a lovely home,' said Pierre, somehow managing to block out my father's ranting.

'Thank you. Mick? Will you have some?' Mum asked.

'Is everybody DEAF?' shouted Dad. 'I said, over my dead body will that lad be marrying my daughter!'

'*Dad!* Will you please stop being so bloody ignorant?' I barked. 'Give Pierre a chance.'

'Don't speak to me like that,' he said.

'She's right, Dad, you're way out of line,' said

Finn.

'You're being very unwelcoming and the Irish are known for their hospitality,' added Siobhan.

'I can see I'm not welcome here in my own home, so I'll leave you to your little tea party, but that man had better be gone by the time I get back,' he said, stomping out the door.

'Cake, Pierre?' asked Mum.

* * *

While Dad blew off steam—God knows where—Mum poured tea, cut cake, and tried to excuse Dad's behaviour to Pierre. 'You have to understand that Mick has always believed the girls would end up with nice Irish boys, and, to be perfectly honest with you, so have I. Relationships are difficult enough without dragging differences of culture and creed into them.'

'I agree with you, Mrs O'Flaherty, but you can't help who you fall in love with. Besides, our differences, apart from the obvious one of colour, are actually very minor. Niamh and I want the same things from life: a good education for our children, a stable home environment for them to grow up in with a strong social conscience alongside good family values.'

'Well, that's something, I suppose.'

'I totally understand your reservations and your husband's disappointment. My parents would have preferred Niamh to be French, but in forty-two years I never met anyone I wanted to spend the rest of my life with until I met your daughter. Within minutes of meeting her I knew she was The One. I'm sure you don't need me to tell you how wonderful she is.'

'No, indeed I don't. She's a very special girl and the apple of her father's eye,' said Mum, as Siobhan scowled. 'I have no doubt you both feel very strongly about each other now, but it's down the road, when things get difficult, that your differences will seem a lot more acute than they are now.'

'With Niamh by my side, I believe I can get through anything. Look, Mrs O'Flaherty, I'm not a young teenager. This is not as impulsive as it seems. I simply met the woman I wanted to marry and I acted on it. I realize it may seem sudden, but I feel as if I've known your daughter all my life and I promise to take great care of her. I know what a precious commodity she is.'

As I basked in his praise, I watched Mum beginning to thaw ever so slightly.

'How is it a successful man like you is still single at your age?' Mum asked, as I sank lower into my chair.

'I was in a relationship with a girl for nine years but it didn't work out, and when I met Niamh I understood why Brigitte was not the right woman for me.'

'Nine years and you left her high and dry! The poor girl,' said Mum.

'It fizzled out on both sides,' I added, not wanting Pierre to seem like a cad.

'As Niamh said, the relationship ran its course and we went our separate ways. She has since met someone else and is much happier too.'

'Really? How do you know? When were you in touch with her?' I asked, none too pleased at hearing he'd been in contact with his ex.

'My mother keeps up with her and she told me last night.'

'Oh,' I said, feeling bad for doubting him.

'That's all very well, but how do you know that this relationship isn't a ricochet?' Mum asked.

Pierre looked confused.

'Rebound,' I said.

'Oh, I see. I know it isn't because I dated other women between breaking up with Brigitte and meeting Niamh.'

'I believe you want to take our girl away to Canada,' Mum said, seemingly determined to continue the interrogation until she knew every thought and plan Pierre had ever had.

'I've been offered a very good position in Vancouver, but the decision to move ultimately lies with Niamh. If she doesn't want to go, we won't. I want her to be happy.'

'I want to go, Mum. It's a great opportunity for Pierre and it's supposed to be an amazing city.'

'What about your job? Your column? You love it.'

'I'll find something in Canada. Pierre's already sourcing contacts for me on the local papers over there.'

'And we've been set up in a house close to the campus with plenty of bedrooms to accommodate family and friends,' said Pierre, smiling at Mum.

'You seem to have all the answers,' she said, as the door flew open and Nuala bustled in.

'Hello again, Pierre,' she said, plonking herself down on the couch beside Mum. 'Well, Annie, I've left Mick with Tadhg. Like a bull he is, ranting and raging. I told him to calm down or he'd have another heart-attack.'

'I know, Nuala, I told him so myself,' said Mum, sharply. Nuala hadn't been forgiven for having met Pierre first.

'Well, I told him he was an old fool. That if he made Niamh choose between him and Pierre, he'd lose his daughter. And what good would that do?'

'It's all very well for you to be blasé about it, Nuala, but it's not your daughter who wants to marry a black man,' Mum replied sharply.

'I know, Annie,' said Nuala, patting Mum's hand. 'I was shocked at first, too. But if he was white we'd be popping champagne corks. A professor, handsome, clever and mad about Niamh. It's only his skin colour that has us in a tizzy.' Nuala was a legend. Why hadn't I thought of that line? It was brilliant and so true.

'You can't ignore it,' said Mum.

'No, but you can stop making it the focal point of Pierre's character,' I said, jumping to my fiancé's defence. 'Look, Mum, I never imagined I'd marry a black man either. It just never crossed my mind. But I met Pierre and realized he was the most amazing person I'd ever met, and when he asked me to marry him, I felt like the luckiest girl in the world. Not everyone gets to meet the perfect person for them, but I have and I wish you could get past the colour of his skin and see how happy he makes me and how wonderful he is.'

'OK, I'm out of here,' said Finn. 'This is way too mushy for me. Hang in there, Pierre.'

'I've to go home and get the girls their dinner,' said Siobhan, standing up. 'Goodbye, Pierre, I hope we'll see you again soon.'

'I'll go and see how Mick's doing. I'll ring you to let you know,' Nuala said to Mum. 'Goodbye,

Pierre, it was lovely to meet you again.' Then, turning to hug me, she whispered, 'I'll work on your dad. Don't worry, pet, we'll sort this out. Be strong.'

'Thanks, Nuala. I need all the help I can get.'

They left and it was just Pierre, Mum and me.

'Did you show your mother the ring?' Pierre asked.

I fished it out of my pocket and put it on. Mum turned my hand this way and that. 'It's beautiful,' she said quietly. 'May you wear it well.'

'Thanks, Mum,' I said, beginning to cry.

Pierre came over to put his arm round me. I nestled into his chest, glad to have him by my side. 'Mrs O'Flaherty,' he said, 'I'm sorry for the commotion we've caused. Believe me when I tell you that the last thing I wanted to do was cause problems for you or your family. Please remember that I want the same thing you do—to make Niamh happy.'

Mum sighed and got up. 'I appreciate that, Pierre. And I'd like to apologize for the awful way you've been treated this evening. We were shocked when Niamh told us and I've had longer to digest the news than poor Mick. He only found out a couple of minutes before you arrived, which is why you got the brunt of his anger. You seem like a very nice man and I can see how happy Niamh is with you. Let me talk to Mick tonight, and when he's had time to reflect on the news, the four of us can get together and talk about the wedding.'

'Oh, Mum,' I said, hugging her.

'Thank you, Mrs O'Flaherty,' said Pierre.

'We've a long rocky road ahead of us,' Mum said, drying my tears with her tissue. 'Your father's as stubborn as you are, but we'll get through it. Now that I've met Pierre I can see why you feel the way you do. Now, stop crying and put a smile on your face. You don't want to scare him off,' she said, kissing the top of my head. 'She can be hard work, but she's worth it.' She smiled at Pierre. 'Just like her dad.'

40

'Bloody hell,' said Pierre, sinking back into the couch

'I told you they'd freak,' I said, sitting down beside him.

'I thought you were exaggerating. You're prone to it.'

'It went a lot better than I'd thought. It could have been worse.'

'How exactly?'

'Dad could have physically chucked you out.'

'He slammed the door in my face.'

'He thought you were a Jehovah's Witness,' I said, beginning to laugh.

'I must say that did throw me a bit. I'd no idea what he was talking about.' Pierre grinned. 'I thought he was bonkers.'

'He is a bit.'

'Why did you leave it so late to tell him?'

'He kept evading me. I was chasing him round all day.'

'I thought he was going to have another heart-attack,' said Pierre. 'I'm still reeling. I need a stiff drink.'

'I'll get you one,' I said, rummaging in the drinks cabinet and coming up with a bottle of whiskey.

'Any mixers?'

I shook my head.

'OK, stick it in the tea. I'm desperate. God, I feel like a schoolboy, not a forty-two-year-old professor,' he said, gulping whiskey-laden tea.

'I think the worst is over.'

'Didn't you hear your father shouting, "over my dead body"?' said Pierre.

'He always says that.'

'Really?'

'Doesn't your father ever shout?'

'Never.'

'What?'

'Never.'

'Come on, he must have roared at you when you were younger and did something bold.'

'Nope.'

'So what did he do?'

'He'd sit me down and talk to me about why I'd behaved that way and what the consequences were . . .'

'And he never raised his voice?'

'No. Did yours shout a lot?'

I started to laugh. 'Only about fifty times a day.'

'Really?'

'Yes. He roared when the phone bills arrived, if we were rude to Mum, if we refused to eat while the children in Africa were dying, if we slagged off Ireland . . . He's a very passionate man. He wears his emotions on his sleeve.'

'I noticed. Did he ever hit you?'

'God, yes. We were chased up and down the street with his slipper. If we were bold we got slapped with it on the backs of the legs. Did your dad hit you?'

'Never. He thinks it's the wrong way to raise children. Violence begets violence.'

'A tap on the back of the legs with a slipper isn't violent. We used to laugh about it.'

'I dunno, your family seems like a bunch of nutters. I should reconsider my position.'

'Back out?'

'Maybe.'

'Leave me high and dry at the altar?'

'The madness could be genetic.'

'Do you want to die at the hands of a slipper?'

'You wouldn't dare.'

'Want to bet?'

'Actually, it sounds a bit kinky. Maybe we should give it a try.'

'Pervert.'

'I prefer "randy professor",' he said, kissing me. Suddenly he stopped. 'I'm finding the Pope staring down at me a little disconcerting,' he said, pointing to the large picture of him behind my head.

'He's seen worse.'

'Excuse me?'

'Confession. I have snogged boys in this room before and even gone to second base.'

'You little slut,' he said, laughing.

'Ssh—listen.' I jumped up. 'Dad's back,' I whispered. 'You have to go. I don't think he should see you again tonight. Let Mum talk to him and let him sleep on it. Quick, I'll sneak you out this way,' I said, opening the window.

'You're not seriously suggesting I climb out of that?'

'That's exactly what I'm suggesting. Now go,

before he hears you and starts getting worked up again.'

'This is insane.'

'I know, but I promise you I'm worth it. Things will be better tomorrow.'

'You mean I might actually be able to use the front door?'

'As long as Dad hasn't got a barring order.'

'Hilarious.'

'I try.'

'Goodnight.'

'Goodnight. I love you.'

'I love you too, but I'm not so sure about your family.'

'They'll grow on you, I promise, and if they don't we'll elope to Vegas.'

'Sounds good to me,' he said, leaning through the window to kiss me.

'Isn't this very *Romeo and Juliet*!'

'OVER MY DEAD BODY,' we heard, from the other side of the door.

'Suddenly Vancouver doesn't seem far enough!' said Pierre.

'I wish we were there now.' I sighed. 'I'd better go. I'll call you first thing.'

' 'Bye . . . Ouch—fuck,' he said, tripping.

'Mind the leprechaun gnomes!'

*　*　*

I snuck out of the good room and went down to the kitchen. The door was closed but I could hear Mum and Dad inside, arguing.

'You have to calm down and stop shouting,' Mum said. 'You're getting yourself into a state and the doctor said it's very bad for you to get wound up.'

'Wound up! I've never been more bloody wound up. How can she do this to me? Bringing that man in here and telling me she's getting married. It won't work, Annie, they're too different.'

'He's a very nice man, Mick. You should talk to him before making up your mind. We're not racists in this house. Everyone deserves a fair chance.'

Good on you, Mum, I cheered silently, from my childhood seat on the stairs.

'He didn't even have the decency to ask me for her hand in marriage, like a proper young man should.'

'To be fair, he didn't get the chance. You slammed the door in his face.'

'How was I to know he wasn't one of those bloody Jehovah's fellas again?'

'He really loves her, Mick, and she's as happy as I've ever seen her. You should see them together. They're totally smitten with each other.'

'That won't last. What happens when they run up against trouble, financial or health or children? That's when the rot will set in and that's when they'll realize they're too different to make it work.'

'Maybe the only difference is their skin colour. He has the same principles and morals she does. He wants the same kind of life she does. They're not so different, Mick.'

'What about their children? They'll be half white, half black. Sure they won't know if they're coming or going.'

'Times have changed, Mick. Look around you. Even Dublin is multicultural now. They're not so unusual.'

So, Mum had been listening. She was quoting almost word for word what I had said to her.

'How many mixed couples do we know?'

'Harriet and Jason, and Sammy Davis Junior was engaged to Kim Novak,' said Mum, as I smiled to myself.

'Sammy Davis Junior?' said Dad. 'Is that the best you can come up with?'

'All right, we don't know many mixed couples, but that doesn't mean it can't work.'

'Of all the fellas she could have met! Of all the men in Dublin she has to choose a black one! Why does she always have to be different? Why is she so stubborn? Can she not see what she's doing to me?'

'This isn't about you, Mick. It's about Niamh. She's in love. If we push her away, we'll lose her. Don't make her choose.'

'Is he right for her, Annie? Can he make her happy? Can he look after her and give her a good life?'

'Yes, I think he can. He's a very responsible man. He's older than her and more mature, which is a good thing. And the way she looks at him when he's talking, it's pure adoration. And he's the same with her. You should see them, Mick. It's the real deal.'

'She'll meet someone else. It might take her a few months to get over him, but we can help her meet a nice Irish lad.'

'She could marry an Irish man who treats her badly. Is that better than a black man who loves her?'

'Of course it isn't, but she could have both.

Don't tell me there isn't a decent Irish fella out there that would make her happy.'

'Well, if there is, she hasn't found him. Have you forgotten, Mick? Has it been so long? Have you forgotten what it feels like when you're in love? Nothing matters to them at the moment except each other. They're in their own world.'

'I should never have left Ballyduff. None of this would have happened. Siobhan wouldn't have got herself pregnant and Niamh would never be marrying a black man.'

'Stop your nonsense,' snapped Mum. 'We all left Ireland because there was nothing there for us. We wanted to make a better life for ourselves and to give our children choices. We've raised three wonderful children and had a good life. We're not going to start regretting it now. Besides, it was in Ireland that Niamh met Pierre, not here, in case you forgot.'

'What'll everyone say when they find out? We'll be the laughing-stock.'

'Since when did you care what other people think? The only thing that matters is that Niamh is happy.'

'We don't know anything about this lad. He could be a criminal, he could be married already, he could have a violent streak in him . . . We know nothing about him at all.'

'The only way to get to know him is to talk to him instead of slamming doors in his face and storming out of the house.'

Well said, Mum. Maybe now Dad would agree to meet Pierre and be civil to him.

'I was in shock.'

'I know, Mick. It's not easy to accept, but from

the chat I had with him, he seems a very decent man. I'll get Niamh to bring him over tomorrow and we can sit down and you can ask him all the questions you want. We need to get this sorted out before they go to Canada.'

'Canada?' said Dad. Shit. I'd forgotten he didn't know. I hadn't had time to tell him.

'Yes, Pierre's got a job in Vancouver and they're off in a few weeks.'

'OVER MY DEAD BODY.'

I sighed and climbed the stairs to bed. I'd need as much sleep as I could get, so that I could face the music tomorrow.

41

The next morning when I came down for breakfast, Dad was waiting for me. 'Sit down,' he said.

I sat.

'I've been up all night. Not a wink of sleep did I get with all this nonsense going on. What's this about you going off to Canada with that man?'

'Pierre has been offered a professorship in Vancouver and we're going there after we get married,' I said firmly. He wasn't the only one who hadn't slept all night. At four in the morning, I'd finally decided that Dad needed to understand one thing and one thing only: I was marrying Pierre with or without his approval.

'Are you trying to put me into an early grave?' he asked.

'No, Dad. I fell in love. That's all. I haven't

committed any crime.'

'But he's black, Niamh. You're chalk and cheese. Your children will be—'

'Loved by their parents and, I hope, their grandparents. I never meant to cause you any upset, Dad. I didn't move to Africa and hunt down a black husband. I met Pierre in Dublin and I knew within five minutes that he was The One. Nothing and nobody is going to change that. And I would really appreciate it if you could treat him with a little respect.'

'I'd like some respect too—telling me about him two seconds before he arrives on my doorstep and me with a bad heart! 'Twas an insult to me.'

'I tried to tell you earlier but you were in meetings. Just give Pierre a chance, that's all I'm asking.'

'Your mother's been at me all night. On and on she went about love and happiness and choosing sides and losing a daughter if I refused to accept this lad and so on. So what I've agreed to do is to sit down with both of you and talk to you. If after that I still don't like him and I still think it's the worst decision you could ever make, I'll do everything in my power to stop the wedding.'

'Fine.'

'I want him over here in an hour.'

'I'll call him now.'

'Fine.'

We both stomped back upstairs, equally annoyed with each other for not giving in. Mum was right. We were as stubborn as each other.

* * *

Pierre arrived exactly an hour later, wearing a blue shirt and a smile. I brought him into the lounge and we sat down to wait for my parents to come in for the grilling. Five minutes later they entered the room. Pierre stood up, shook hands with Mum and Dad, then everyone sat down.

Silence.

Pierre cleared his throat. 'Mr O'Flaherty, I'm sorry about the mix-up yesterday. I had presumed you'd been informed of my existence before I arrived on your doorstep to ask for Niamh's hand in marriage.'

Mum poked Dad in the ribs. 'Ah, uhm, yes. Well, thank you, and I suppose I should apologize for my reaction. I was taken very much by surprise.'

'I can imagine, sir,' said Pierre, formal and respectful. 'I realize that I'm not the son-in-law you would have hand-picked for your daughter. I know how important your culture and homeland are to you, but I hope I can convince you that I love your daughter more than any other man possibly could and that I will take great care of her.'

'What does your father make of it?' Dad asked.

'He was a little tentative at first because they had hoped I'd marry a French girl, but once they met Niamh and saw how happy she makes me, he supported my decision.'

'I see,' said Dad, as I silently cheered my fiancé's clever and ever so subtly pointed answers.

'I take it you're not Catholic,' Dad said, as I shuddered.

'No, sir, I'm not.'

The door opened. We looked up. It was Father Hogan. 'Sorry to barge in, but the kitchen door was open, so I popped in that way.'

'Welcome, Father,' said Dad, jumping up. To me he said, 'I asked Father Hogan to call in today to meet your boyfriend and give us some advice.'

'Hello, nice to meet you,' said Father Hogan, shaking Pierre's hand. Then he bent down to kiss my cheek and whispered, 'Don't worry, I'm here to help.'

'We need it,' I whispered back.

'Father Hogan is an old friend of the family,' said Mum to Pierre, by way of explaining why there was suddenly a priest in the room.

'How nice,' said Pierre, looking a little apprehensive.

'He's not Catholic,' said Dad, pointing at Pierre.

'Are you Christian?' Father Hogan asked Pierre.

'Agnostic, I'm afraid.'

'Oh,' said Mum, disappointed.

'But he acts like a Christian,' I piped up. 'He's really kind and always gives money to the homeless people on the street.'

'How do you feel about Niamh being Catholic?' Father Hogan asked.

Pierre shrugged. 'I'm fine with it.'

'If you were blessed with children, would you object to them being raised Catholic?' the priest asked.

Pierre paused, then looked at my pleading eyes and said, 'If Niamh really wanted it, then I'd certainly be open to it.'

'That's good news,' said Father Hogan, beaming.

'Can they get married in the church?' Mum asked.

'They can. As long as Niamh declares her

intention to continue practising her faith and do all in her power to share that faith with children born of the marriage, we can go ahead with the church wedding.'

'Thank God for that,' said Mum, getting emotional. 'I thought we were going to end up in a register office.'

'Over my dead body,' said Dad, as I saw Pierre stifle a smile.

'Where is it you're from?' Father Hogan asked.

'Born in France, raised mostly in Oxford, but my parents are from Martinique.'

'It's in the Caribbean,' said Mum. 'Siobhan looked it up on the Internet for me.'

'Yes, it is,' said Pierre, smiling at Mum.

'And what is it you do?' asked the priest. Dad had obviously told him to do the grilling so Mum couldn't give out to him.

'I'm a professor of phonetics.'

'Well, now, a professor,' said Father Hogan, suitably impressed.

'He's very well thought of,' said Mum. 'Siobhan read me out some articles this morning from the Internet about you. They were very complimentary. He's very highly regarded in his field of expertise,' she added, looking directly at Dad.

'Hellooo, anyone home?' called Nuala, popping her head round the door. 'Oh, sorry, I didn't mean to interrupt, I'll come back later.'

'Not at all. Come in and sit down,' said Mum, who had obviously forgiven her.

'How's everything going?' Nuala murmured, as she sat down beside me.

'Not too bad,' I mumbled.

'Did Niamh tell you Pierre's parents had a great Irish family friend, Molly Hanafin?' asked Nuala, winking at me.

'No,' said Dad, perking up.

'Oh, yes. She was like a second mother to Pierre, apparently,' said Nuala, laying it on thick, as Pierre shifted uncomfortably in his chair.

'What part of Ireland was she from?' Dad asked.

'Uhm, it was—' Pierre fumbled.

'Mayo,' I jumped in.

'I knew a Hanafin from Mayo. Was she one of the Ballina Hanafins?' Dad asked, almost excited.

Pierre looked panic-stricken. He didn't know how to lie.

'No,' said Nuala. 'Didn't you tell me she was from Achill Island?'

Pierre nodded.

'I don't believe it,' said Father Hogan. 'My mother was from Achill. I bet you I know Molly's relatives.'

Bollox. That was the problem with Ireland. Everyone knew everyone else.

'She died a good while ago now,' I said.

'Oh, I'm sorry to hear that. I'd like to have met her,' said Dad.

'How did you come to be such good friends?' Mum asked.

'She was the matron in my school, we got on well and then she became a good friend,' said Pierre, trying to keep as close to the truth as possible.

'Isn't that lovely?' said Mum.

'The Irish have always made the best nurses,' said Dad. 'I'll bet she looked after you well up in the school.'

'Yes, she did,' Pierre agreed.

'And then when poor Molly got sick, Pierre's family took her in and nursed her until she died,' said Nuala.

'Very Christian of you,' said Father Hogan.

'Told you he was,' I said.

'Your mother must be a very kind woman,' said Mum. I grinned at the idea of Florence Nightingale, dressed from head to toe in Chanel, nursing a dying woman.

'Was there a big funeral back in Achill?' Dad asked. 'You must have been impressed with the place. A beautiful part of Ireland it is.'

'No, actually. Molly was buried in Oxford, as she had wished. She didn't have any family back in Ireland and she considered Oxford her home,' said Pierre, who was getting better at bending the truth.

'I must ring my cousin Tommy and ask him does he remember Molly Hanafin. He's lived in Achill all his life,' said Father Hogan.

Jesus, he was like a dog with a bone. I needed to get them off the subject of Molly before they discovered she was, almost, a complete fabrication.

Nuala, obviously thinking the same thing, said, 'So, when's the big day going to be? Have you set a date? It's hard to get good venues, these days. You'd want to think about it.'

'Actually, we were hoping to have the wedding in the church here, if that's all right with you?' I said to Father Hogan.

'Really?' said Pierre.

I glared at him.

'I'd be delighted,' said the priest. 'When were you thinking?'

'In about six weeks,' I said.

'Six weeks?' said Dad. 'Why the big rush? You're not—'

'*No*!' I said, putting his mind at ease. There wouldn't be two shotgun weddings from this house. 'Pierre's new job starts in eight weeks' time now, so Nuala's right, we need to get a move on with our plans.'

'Would you like to book in for a pre-marriage course?' Father Hogan asked. 'They do a very good one down at the community centre.'

'Well, I'm not sure we'll have time,' I said.

'Make time,' snapped Dad.

'OK, book us in,' I said.

'Sorry, Father, what exactly is this course?' Pierre asked.

'Don't worry, son, we won't be trying to convert you.' Father Hogan laughed. 'It's just a day spent in reflection and discussion on the important aspects of a relationship and marriage.'

'I see,' said Pierre, sounding decidedly unenthusiastic. I wondered why he didn't just sprint out the door and leave me behind, with my enormous quantity of family baggage.

'Lord, there's so much to do and so little time,' said Mum. 'Mick, you'll have to call Jerry Maher and see can we get the hotel booked for the reception. Nuala, you'll have to help with the dresses. I'll get the invitations out double quick. Everyone coming over from Ireland will need to book their flights.'

'Mum, we were thinking of a smallish wedding.'

'How small?'

'Seventy?'

Mum and Nuala laughed. 'Don't be ridiculous.'

'It may have escaped everybody's notice but I

haven't given my blessing to this marriage,' Dad put in.

Pierre stood up and took a deep breath. I could see he was getting fed up with it all, but he slapped on a smile and said, 'Mr O'Flaherty, would you please give us your permission and blessing to get married? I promise to do everything possible to ensure Niamh's happiness and well-being.'

Everyone stared at Dad.

'How polite,' said Nuala.

'A gentleman,' said Father Hogan.

'Lovely manners,' said Mum.

'I'm not going to pretend I'm happy about it and I have many reservations, but I'll give you my permission. I know my daughter and I know fine well that this wedding will go ahead with or without my blessing. But before you go off booking venues, I'd like to meet your parents and have a talk with them.'

'Good idea. We'll have an engagement party,' said Mum.

'It's a pity poor Molly's not here to enjoy it,' said Father Hogan.

42

Pierre and I went out for a coffee and a confab.

'Pre-marriage course? Are you kidding me?' He groaned. 'I expected to have to sweat it out with your dad, but not the Catholic Church!'

'I know. I'm sorry. You've been brilliant, so patient and saying all the right things and pushing the right buttons.'

'And why, in God's name, did you and Nuala have to make up that stupid Molly story? Your dad and the priest are obsessed with her. I wouldn't be surprised if they get Interpol to look for any surviving family members and have her body exhumed so she can be reburied in Ireland.'

'I didn't expect them to get so excited about her.'

'What is this course we have to go on?'

'Apparently it only lasts about five hours and you talk about relationships and problems that can come up in a marriage, that kind of thing.'

'Sounds fun.'

'Look, if you want to back out now, I'll understand. I'm sure all this seems ridiculous to you—but I told you my dad was going to be difficult. He's very set in his ways.'

'You can say that again.'

'He'll see sense eventually, but it could take a while. So, if it's too much hassle for you—'

'Don't be silly. I'm not going anywhere. I'm just blowing off steam. I can handle your father. Besides, we'll be on a different continent soon,' he said, grinning at me.

'Vancouver's looking more attractive each day.'

My phone rang. It was Mum. 'Niamh, pet, can you come home soon? We need to organize the engagement party. Will Saturday suit Pierre's parents?'

'I'll check with him. I'll be back in twenty minutes.'

'What's up?' Pierre asked. 'Don't tell me I've to go to Rome for a week to study at the Vatican.'

'No, smartarse. Mum wants to know if your parents are free this Saturday to come to a family engagement party.'

'Now that should be fun,' said Pierre, 'my parents and yours in the same room.'

'Don't. I feel sick just thinking about it. I'll have a word with Dad. I'll make him promise to be on his best behaviour.'

'I'll call them now and see if they're free. Will it be a small family gathering?'

'Yes,' I lied. There was no such thing as a small family gathering. And once word got out that Mick O'Flaherty's daughter was engaged to a black fella they'd come from far and wide to see Pierre. It was going to be a madhouse.

Pierre went back to his hotel to do some work, and I walked home. I found Mum, Nuala, Siobhan and Finn in the kitchen talking about the party.

'I want Pierre's parents to get a real sense of who we are,' said Mum.

'I think the leprechauns in the garden and the shamrock hedge will give them a fair idea,' said Finn, laughing. 'And once they ring the doorbell and hear "Danny Boy", they'll think they're in the heart of Ireland,' he added winking at me.

'I hear Dad gave you permission to marry,' Siobhan said.

'Just about,' I grumbled.

'Well, you can't expect miracles. The poor man's upset,' said my sister.

'Yeah, well, he's not the only one. Is it too much to ask for one member of my family to say, "Congratulations, well done, finding such a great guy"? All I've had is crashed cars, tears and shock,' I said. 'It's supposed to be a celebration.'

'Oh, don't be such a drama queen,' said the biggest drama queen of all. 'Dad wasn't giving me a standing ovation when I got engaged either.'

'You were seventeen and pregnant,' I reminded her.

'I want to say something,' said Mum. 'Now that I've met Pierre properly I can see why you fell for him. He's a lovely man. You can see that he's good, honest, upstanding, and mad about you.'

'Not to mention that he's very easy on the eye,' said Nuala.

'Thanks, Mum,' I said, pleased that she could see how great Pierre was.

'Now, tell me about his parents,' she said. 'Are they as nice as him? What do they like to eat and drink? We're doing a shopping list for the party.'

'Well, they're quite sophisticated.'

Mum looked at Nuala. 'Aren't we all?'

'Absolutely,' agreed Nuala.

'What I mean is that they are used to the finer things in life. His mother dresses in Chanel and his dad wears cashmere.'

Mum pulled her cardigan round her and crossed her arms. 'You father has a cashmere jumper. He wears it on Christmas Day and I wear Chanel No. 5 perfume.'

'I'm not saying they're better than us,' I reassured her. 'To be honest, his mother's a bit of a pain. I'm just warning you that they're kind of highbrow.'

'In what way?' Nuala asked.

'They talk about existentialism and stuff for fun.'

Mum, Nuala and Siobhan looked at each other.

Finn guffawed. 'You must fit right in.'

'What is it?' Siobhan asked.

'It's the philosophical theory that emphasizes

the existence of the individual as a free and self-determining agent,' I spouted.

'Guess who's swallowed a dictionary,' said Finn.

'I still don't understand,' said Nuala.

'Me neither,' I admitted. 'And to be honest I'm not sure Fleur does either, but she plays a good game of pretending. They're very nice people, they're just more bookish and serious than we are.'

'We can be serious,' Mum said. 'Can't we, Nuala?'

'As serious as you like.'

'And we're great readers,' Mum added.

'Eat books, so we do,' Nuala agreed. 'I've just finished the new John Grisham. I can talk to them about that, and your mum's always got her head in a book.'

'I do,' said Mum.

'Mum, I'm not comparing you to them. I'd much rather have my family than his. I'm just trying to prepare you for the meeting. Put it this way, I can't imagine them singing "The Fields of Athenry" at two in the morning.'

'There'll be no one singing at two in the morning,' said Mum, put out. 'It's just a few friends and family in for a quiet drink to meet your fiancé and his family.'

'There's seventy on the list already,' Finn pointed out, 'and I'd like to see you try to stop Tadhg singing after a few whiskeys.'

'Tadhg will be under strict instructions to behave himself,' said Nuala. 'I'll make sure there's no singing.'

'We'll have some wine and finger food, and I'll get your cousin Mairead to play the harp in the corner for some background music. They'll be impressed with her, she's a real talent.'

I'd heard Mairead play the previous Christmas and she had a long way to go before I'd have described her as a talent.

'I'll get my girls to do a welcome jig,' said Siobhan, excited at the prospect. I groaned silently.

'That'd be gorgeous,' said Mum.

'Fantastic,' agreed Nuala.

'I could give them a hurling demonstration out in the garden with the leprechauns,' suggested Finn.

Mum clipped him over the head. 'There's no need to be smart. We're just giving them a nice Irish welcome. Now, where's my list . . .'

* * *

Four days later, I stood in the living room—which had the rug rolled to one side, because my nieces needed to dance on floorboards—surrounded by a hundred people, waiting for Pierre and his parents to arrive.

When the car pulled up outside, everyone surged forward to get a good look. Mum, in her best navy suit, pushed through the crowd to greet them.

Fleur was in an olive green chiffon cocktail dress. Her black hair hung in soft waves round her face and her skin glowed like soft satin. She looked sensational. Jean was in a caramel linen suit with a pale pink shirt and a deeper pink tie that looked fantastic with his colouring. No pasty Irishman could have got away with it, but it was perfect on him. Pierre, to my horror, was wearing his favourite bright red shirt.

'Welcome, *céad míle fáilte*,' said Mum, coming over to greet them.

Fleur glanced at Pierre and muttered, 'I thought you said it was a small drinks party?'

They shook hands with Mum, and then Dad appeared, wearing his one and only green cashmere jumper. He only wore it on Christmas Day because it had big snowflakes all over it. Mum had obviously decided that cashmere was cashmere.

'*Céad míle fáilte*,' he said. 'Welcome to our humble abode. I'm Michael O'Flaherty, Niamh's father.'

'Very nice to meet you,' said Jean, shaking his hand.

'What an interesting garden,' said Fleur.

'Thank you,' said Dad. 'I designed it myself. It reminds me of home.'

'Mind the leprechauns, Maman,' said Pierre, steering her round them.

'What's with the shirt?' I hissed in his ear.

'I like it,' he hissed back.

We moved into the house where Siobhan was waiting for us. No sooner were Jean and Fleur over the threshold than five twirling curly curtains came bouncing towards them clicking, kicking and jigging about, accompanied by two of their friends on the tin whistle. One had an ear for music, the other was clearly there for the *craic* and hadn't a note in her head.

Fleur and Jean stood with smiles plastered on their faces while the dancing went on and on and on, everyone whooping and cheering. When it finally ended they, and Pierre, were ushered into the lounge where everyone lined up to meet them.

One by one they were told how lucky they were to be marrying Mick O'Flaherty's daughter and what a great family this was and how we were the backbone of the whole clan and how Mick had come to London with only the shirt on his back and made such a success of his life. They were told how talented Siobhan was as a dancer when she was young, how I was the first O'Flaherty to go to college, how Finn was a gifted hurley player, how Mum was the best woman a man could marry . . .

While all this was going on, Fleur and Jean were being plied with drink. Every time Fleur said no, she was badgered into drinking more.

'Ah, go on, Flower, get that into you. Sure you'd die of thirst.'

Jean's wine was grabbed from his hand and a whiskey put in its place. 'Have a taste of that, John,' Tadhg said. 'It's Midleton, as rare a whiskey as you can find.'

'She's very glamorous,' Mum said, looking at Fleur.

'I told you.'

'I thought you were exaggerating.'

'For once I wasn't.'

'Do I look all right?' Mum asked. 'Is the suit a bit old-fashioned?'

I looked at my mother's sweet round face and hugged her. 'You're gorgeous, Mum, just perfect.'

'So are you, pet,' she said. 'There's nothing more beautiful than a young girl in love.'

'Do you really like him, Mum?'

She nodded. 'He's a keeper.'

'Nuala's a fan anyway,' I said, laughing, as we watched Nuala lead Pierre around by the hand and introduce him to everyone as 'Niamh's handsome fiancé'.

I could hear Siobhan talking to Fleur. 'The girls were wonderful, weren't they? They get their talent from me. I came second in the UK Irish-dancing championship in 1984.'

'How interesting,' Fleur drawled.

'It was nice of you to wear a green dress for the occasion.'

'I'm sorry?'

'You know, green, our national colour. It was a good choice. We're very proud of our heritage.'

'Yes, I had noticed.'

'Hello, Flower, I'm Johnny Hegerty,' slurred a small man, interrupting them.

Fleur took a step back as he leant in. 'Mick O'Flaherty took me in when I had nothing and gave me a chance. I was sleeping under a bridge and he gave me a job and a reason to live. The man is a saint. Your son is very lucky to be marrying his daughter. Especially with him being black and all.'

Mum and I hurried over to steer Fleur away.

'Don't mind him,' Mum said. 'He's had too much to drink. He means well.'

Fleur said nothing.

'Niamh tells me you're an interior decorator.'

'Designer.'

'Oh, I see. Well, I could probably do with a few tips.'

'The house reflects the person.' Fleur shrugged. 'This is who you are,' she added, waving a bejewelled hand at the photos of the Pope and JFK and the paintings of green fields.

Mum stood up straighter. 'Yes, it is who we are and we're very proud of it. You must be delighted that Pierre met such a wonderful girl. Niamh's a real gem.'

'Mu-uum,' I said, embarrassed.

'You are,' she said. 'He's a very lucky man. Don't you think so, Fleur?'

'Yes, she is a nice girl, but she needs to work on her French and her cooking.'

'You'll have to forgive my mother,' said Pierre, saving Fleur from the wrath of mine. 'Like all French women she is obsessive about food.'

Fleur put her arm round Pierre adoringly. 'I have raised the perfect man.'

'Well, I think so.' I smiled.

'They're well matched, then,' said Mum, putting her arm round me, 'because I raised the perfect girl.'

'I agree with you there,' said Pierre.

'Get that into you,' said Tadhg, filling Fleur's glass to the brim. 'It'll help you relax. You seem a bit uptight. We might do a duet later. I've been practising my "Frère Jacques",' he said, and roared laughing.

I felt a tug on my dress. I looked down. It was the bad tin-whistle player. 'Are you really gonna marry that black fella?'

'Yes, I am.'

'My dad said it was because black fellas have big willies.'

'Well, you can tell your dad he's—'

'Absolutely right,' said Pierre, cutting across me, laughing.

43

By the time midnight came, everyone was very merry. Even Fleur and Jean—who had tried to leave several times, only to be dragged back in by uncles and aunts to have 'one for the road'—were now unsteady on their feet.

I saw Dad make his way over to them. I followed and hid round the corner to listen in. 'Well, then, what do you make of this marriage stuff?' he asked.

'They seem to have made up their minds,' Jean replied. 'Pierre's a fully grown man. He knows what he wants and he seems to be happy with your daughter.'

Good old Jean. At least he could see sense.

'I'm not sure they have much in common but he seems very taken with her sense of humour,' he added, slating me in the nicest possible way.

'She can be funny all right,' said Dad.

'I think it's very hasty,' said Fleur.

'I agree with you,' said Dad.

'They barely know each other.'

'Exactly.'

'But they are determined, so it's a *fait accompli*.' She sighed.

'Unfortunately, Fleur, it seems to be a done deal.'

'That's what I—'

'Niamh's very stubborn,' Dad interrupted. 'Nothing I can do will change her mind.'

'Pierre is the same,' said Jean.

'He's not stubborn,' said Fleur. 'He's tenacious.'

Thankfully, before our characters could be assassinated further, Mum arrived with a plate of cheese squares.

'Can I tempt you?' Mum asked, offering Fleur a chunk of Cheddar cheese on a cocktail stick. She looked at it in horror and shook her head.

'No, thank you.'

'Well, isn't that something? A French woman who doesn't eat cheese,' said Dad, laughing.

I could see from Fleur's snotty face that she thought the cheese squares were awful. Obviously she was only used to the finest French cheeses and Cheddar probably gave her a rash. Mind you, judging by her tiny frame, I'd say she never ate cheese of any description. Absentmindedly Mum popped one into her mouth.

While they tried to think of something to say, Father Hogan saved the day by bounding in the door. 'Hello, everybody. I'm so sorry to be arriving late. I'd a wake to go to before this.'

'Don't worry, Father, the party's only just getting going,' said Dad. Turning to Fleur and Jean, he said, 'This is our parish priest, Father Hogan, a great friend of the family. These are Pierre's parents, Flower and John.'

'Delighted to meet you,' said Father Hogan, shaking hands. 'You've a grand son. A really fine fellow.'

'Thank you. We're very proud of him,' said Fleur.

'Did you say you'd just been to a wake?' asked Jean.

'I did.'

'Was it an open casket?'

'It was, and between ourselves it shouldn't have

been. Mrs Jones was not a good-looking woman when she was alive and in the prime of her youth. At ninety-six she really wasn't a pretty sight. Besides, she'd been lying there for five days waiting for the eldest grandson to get back from Australia. He was off on some desert trek and they couldn't get in touch with him, so she was beginning to go off, if you get my drift.'

'My God!' said Fleur, horrified.

'You need a drink,' said Dad, pouring the priest a large whiskey.

'I hope you're not going to try to convert us,' said Jean, smiling. 'We're diehard agnostics.'

'No, not at all. I'm here as a guest. Ignore the collar. I must say your son's marrying into a wonderful family.'

'So everyone keeps telling us,' slurred Fleur. 'They're a very enthusiastic group of people.'

'Did you know that Mick here came to London with only—'

'The shirt on his back,' said Jean. 'Yes, we've heard all about it. It's similar to my story, actually. I moved from Martinique to France with very little too.'

'You had me!' said Fleur. 'I was with you.'

'Oh, you're in trouble now,' said Tadhg, grinning. 'You forgot about your wife.'

'The wife who worked two jobs while you studied for your degree,' she grumbled.

'Did you?' asked Nuala, looking as shocked as I felt at the idea of Fleur slaving away while Jean studied.

She nodded. 'It was a difficult time, but look at what we achieved.'

'Aren't you a great wife?' said Father Hogan.

'I thought you were born with a silver spoon in your mouth, the way you dress and carry on,' said Nuala.

'You do look very posh,' Tadhg agreed.

Fleur laughed. 'All of this came about over years of trying to fit into Parisian society. We were complete outcasts, so we worked hard, watched and learnt. Eventually we were accepted.'

'Was it worth it?' Mum asked

She shrugged. 'We had no family and no friends, so at least we now had a social life. But we never really felt as though we fitted in.'

'Well, you fit in here,' said Dad. 'We welcome everyone with open arms,' he added, as I choked on my drink. 'Top them up there, Tadhg, and we'll have a sing-song.'

'No, thank you, I really think we've had enough,' said Jean, who had gone a bit green. 'We're not used to such generous hospitality. We must go soon.'

'Don't be ridiculous, it's only half twelve,' said Tadhg, foisting the drinks on to them. '*Sláinte*,' he said, as everyone drank.

'Get that into you, Flower, it'll put hairs on your chest,' said Dad, winking at Fleur.

'Have you got a dress for the wedding yet?' Nuala asked her.

'No. I'll pick something up in Paris a week before so it's not out of season.'

'Paris!' said Nuala. Then to Mum, she said, 'Well, Annie, we'll have to get you something really special for the big day. We can't have you being upstaged by the groom's mother. That wouldn't do at all.'

'I'll wear my good suit. It'll be grand,' said Mum.

'Grand, my arse,' said Nuala. 'Get your cheque book out, Mick. We're going to be doing some serious shopping.'

'Have they set a date?' asked Jean.

I stepped out from behind the door frame. 'Yes, actually, we have. It's May the fifteenth.'

'It's so soon.' Mum sighed.

'I know, but we have to be in Vancouver on June the first and we want to go on honeymoon before then.'

'Don't worry, Annie, we'll all chip in,' said Nuala. 'We did Siobhan's in six days, so six weeks will seem like an eternity.'

Dad went rigid at the mention of Siobhan's shotgun wedding. Wisely Father Hogan stepped in. 'Isn't it an awful pity poor Molly couldn't be here for the celebrations? I'll bet she would have been delighted with Pierre's choice of bride,' he said.

Jean and Fleur gazed at him blankly.

'And I believe you nursed her at home to the very end,' said Dad, as Pierre's parents looked increasingly confused.

'A truly Christian act,' said Father Hogan.

'From Achill Island, I believe?' Dad said.

'A beautiful spot,' said the priest.

'I'm sorry, I'm not sure I—' said Jean.

'Dad, Father Hogan, could I borrow you for a minute?' I interrupted. Then, pulling them aside, I whispered, 'Don't bring up Molly. They're still really upset about it and Pierre said it's best not to ask them about her. It's too raw.'

'OK, not another word,' they agreed.

I hurried over to find Pierre, who was sandwiched between three aunties.

'The head cut off Harry Belafonte. Nuala was

right,' Auntie Pauline said.

'Better-looking,' said Auntie Katie.

'Ladies, please, you're embarrassing me now.' Pierre laughed.

'Do we call you "Professor"?' asked Auntie Teresa, giggling like a schoolgirl. My fiancé had certainly made a strong impression on them.

He saw me. 'There she is, the love of my life. Am I a lucky man or what?'

'You don't need to lay it on quite so thick,' I said, rolling my eyes.

'He's a ticket,' said Auntie Pauline.

'Very easy on the eye,' said Auntie Katie.

'Intelligent too,' said Auntie Teresa.

'You forget he's black after a while,' said Auntie Pauline, as I cringed.

'Pauline!' said the other two aunties. 'You can't say that.'

'It's OK, I'll take it as the compliment it was meant to be,' said Pierre.

'Sorry to interrupt but I need to borrow Pierre,' I said, grabbing his arm.

'Ah, she can't keep her hands off you,' said Auntie Katie.

'Sorry about that,' I said.

'What?'

'The thing my aunt just said.'

'She meant it as a compliment. Their generation says what our generation thinks but is afraid to say. Now, what's up?'

'You've got to get your parents out of here. Dad and Father Hogan are giving them the third degree about Molly.'

'Bloody hell, not that again.'

'They're really confused. They must think Dad

and Father Hogan are bonkers.' I giggled.

'I think they'll be too pissed to notice. I've never seen them so drunk. Come on, let's rescue them.' Pierre and I swooped in, then steered Fleur and Jean to the front door.

While we were waiting for their taxi to arrive, Jean passed out in a chair, and Fleur said, 'You're very lucky to have such a big warm family, Niamh. It makes life easier when you have back-up support like that. If anything happened to Jean I'd be alone in the world.'

'Maman, don't be silly, you'd come and live with me and Niamh,' said Pierre, as I froze.

She might have shown a human side tonight but there was no way in hell she was moving in with us.

'Thank you, darling, you're such a wonderful son. I'm going to miss you so much. I really did a terrific job raising you,' said the self-congratulator.

Thankfully, before Pierre could start booking one-way tickets to Vancouver for his mother, the taxi arrived. While my fiancé helped his father into one side, I helped Fleur into the other. As I was closing the car door she said, 'Grey is really not your colour. You're too pale for it. I suggest you stick to pastels.'

I closed the door firmly on her and breathed a sigh of relief as they were driven away.

'Well, at least the first meeting of the parents is over with,' said Pierre, putting his arm round me. 'I'm exhausted.'

'It's only twenty to one,' I said.

'That's the latest my parents have been out in about ten years,' said Pierre. 'To be honest, darling, I think I might go too. It's been a long few days of interrogation.'

'Pierre, if you leave now, you'll be for ever branded a party-pooper. No matter how hard you throw yourself into parties down the line, you'll always be known as the guy who left his own engagement party early. And that's worse than being agnostic. You have to stick it out. In about five minutes the sing-song will begin and you'll be forced to sing a song.'

'I can't sing.'

'That's irrelevant. No one cares how bad your voice is as long as you take part with enthusiasm.'

'Oh, God,' he moaned. 'It's like an endurance test. By the way, my parents are completely confused about the Molly thing. We're going to have to come up with a solution to it.'

'Sorted. I told everyone that your parents were still grieving and not to ask any questions.'

'Nice work, partner.'

'I aim to please.'

As Pierre leant in to kiss me, Uncle Neil grabbed our shoulders. 'Come on in here for a sing-song,' he said.

And so the singing began. Two hours later Pierre was finally allowed to leave, having been forced to sing every song that was ever written with a mention of Ireland in it. He was hoarse, tired, a little drunk, but happy. 'I think it went quite well,' he croaked.

'They loved you,' I said. 'They only let the keepers sing!'

44

Three weeks later, after sitting through four hours of the pre-marriage course, Pierre flipped when they came to the section about family planning.

'You have got to be joking,' he hissed, as I studiously ignored him. 'Seriously, darling, I can't take any more. I can't sit here and listen to this pair telling me how to procreate. Can we please leave?'

'I think it's really interesting.' I smirked.

'It's torture. Now, come on, I've done my bit. Surely you won't get excommunicated for leaving a bit early?'

'OK, pretend you're feeling sick,' I whispered, as Pierre stood up abruptly, saying he was feeling unwell and needed some fresh air.

'I'll come with you to make sure you're OK,' I said, bustling out.

We ran straight into Father Hogan.

'Is it over already?' he asked, peering at his watch.

'Uhm, not quite. We just had to pop out. Pierre was feeling a bit—'

'Claustrophobic.' The priest laughed.

'Actually, yes,' he admitted.

'It can be a bit intense in a one-day session, but there's no harm in having some time to reflect on the journey ahead.'

'We enjoyed it, Father, it was worth coming to. Thanks for organizing it,' I jumped in, not wanting him to think we were ungrateful heathens.

'It was very enlightening,' said Pierre.

'Excellent. That's all we can hope for,' said the priest. 'Well, I'd best be off. I'll see you both soon to discuss the ceremony.'

As he walked away, Pierre sighed. 'Why didn't we go to Vegas?'

'Because you're a good guy, you want to make me happy, and you didn't want to incur the wrath of my father and his three mad brothers.'

'OK, but that's it. I'm done with the religious side.'

'Fine. Now we just need to run through a few of the wedding details.'

'Can't they wait until later? I'd like to have a non-wedding afternoon, watching sport and drinking a couple of beers.'

'We're getting married in three weeks. We don't have time to lounge around,' I said, dragging him up the driveway of our house.

'I'm happy to leave the flowers and all that up to you.'

'Well, we need to talk about the guest list.'

'I gave you mine last week.'

'Yes, I know. I wondered if you wanted to add a few people to it.'

'I thought we were keeping it small.'

I studied my shoes. 'Yes, we are, but Mum and Dad have invited a few more than expected, so if you or your parents wanted to add some names to the list that would be fine.'

'How many people have your parents invited?' he asked, sitting down in the kitchen as I put the kettle on.

'About eighty,' I said, blushing.

'Lying to your fiancé is not conducive to a good marriage,' Pierre said, wagging a finger at me.

Give me the real figure. I can take it.'

'Two hundred and twenty-three,' I admitted.

'Jesus Christ!'

'One of my cousins mightn't be able to make it.'

'That's a relief. For a minute there I thought it was going to be a circus.'

'They've always wanted a big wedding and Siobhan's was such a rush that they only got to invite a small number. They want everyone this time.'

'Everyone they've ever met,' he grumbled. 'It'll look ridiculous—twenty people on my side of the church and two hundred and twenty-three on yours.'

'I'll lend you some of mine.'

Siobhan came in. 'I've just been to pick up the bridesmaid's dress. It's gorgeous. She'll have the flower girls' ones ready in a few days' time.'

My sister had volunteered herself as my bridesmaid and her five daughters as my flower girls. She had also taken it upon herself to organize the dresses without consulting me. She had asked in passing if I liked pink, and when I said, 'Not really,' she ordered it anyway.

'Let me see,' I said, handing Pierre his coffee.

She pulled the dress out of the bag. It was a big meringue-like creation made of fuchsia pink satin. The underskirts were pale pink netting and the bodice was covered with pale pink lace.

'Oh, my God,' I said.

'Isn't it amazing?' She beamed. 'What do you think, Pierre?'

'I'm speechless,' he said, trying to hide his shock by taking a gulp of coffee.

'Didn't Noleen do a great job? The pink lace

was her idea. She's so creative. She's a friend of Auntie Pauline, and she used to make clothes for Barbara Cartland. Imagine! Princess Diana's step-grandmother!'

'Is this lady making your dress too?' Pierre asked me.

'No, I bought mine ready made, so there'd be no surprises.'

He looked mightily relieved.

'Are the flower girls going to be the same colour?' I asked.

'Don't be ridiculous,' said Siobhan. 'You can't have flower girls in fuchsia. They'll be in lilac.'

My stomach sank. Lilac! I hated lilac. Not as much as I disliked fuchsia, but pretty close. My wedding was turning into a farce. I had no control over it whatsoever. Thank God I'd bought my dress myself, in peace, much to Mum and Siobhan's annoyance. They thought it was far too plain and were furious that I hadn't included them in the choice. But I knew that involving them would have meant ending up in something made by a friend of the family, and while their craftsmanship might be good, they would never have agreed to something so simple and unfussy. In some cultures less is more. In Irish culture, more is more.

Mum came bustling in, carrying a large bouquet of roses. 'Oh, is that the bridesmaid's dress?' she said, somehow spotting the neon meringue. 'It's gorgeous.'

'I know,' said my sister. 'And wait'll you see it on me. I look amazing.'

'Well, I'm glad to see you've lost a bit of weight anyway,' said Mum. 'How did you do it? I've eaten nothing but bread and butter for the last two weeks and I haven't shifted a pound.'

'I'm doing the cabbage-soup diet, but Liam says I'll have to give it up. The house stinks of boiled cabbage.'

'And you're breaking wind like a drunken sailor,' said Finn, who had just come in.

'Finn! We have a guest,' Mum said, as Pierre laughed.

'Sure he's nearly one of the family, God love him,' said Finn.

'That's disgusting,' said Siobhan, blushing.

'It's true, though, isn't it? Your husband told me himself,' said Finn.

'I'll kill him,' said my sister, grabbing her phone and storming out to give her husband a roasting.

'You shouldn't wind her up. She's bad enough as it is,' I scolded.

'Do you like these?' Mum asked, changing the subject and handing me the bouquet.

There were about twenty roses tied in a bunch—ten red, ten pink. 'They're lovely, Mum, but I was going to carry a single flower.'

'What? One flower? Everyone'll think we were trying to save money on the bouquet. You can't have one measly flower on your wedding day.'

'I thought a single white lily would be nice.'

'White? Lily? It's not a funeral, Niamh. I never heard the like. No, you'll have a nice big bunch of roses like this and let that be the end of it.'

'But, Mum, I—'

'I've ordered them now and it's too late to change. It's not easy, you know, trying to organize a proper wedding with only a few weeks' notice. If it wasn't for your aunties I'd be lost altogether.'

Before she began to tell me how ungrateful I was, I jumped in. 'Mum, the bouquet is beautiful—and you're right. One flower would look silly. Let me know what I can do to help.'

'I agree, the roses are lovely,' Pierre added.

'I told you,' Mum said to me. 'Now, I've booked you in for a hair trial with Maggie down the road. She does lovely up-styles. We're going there at three today.'

'I can't, Mum. I'm dropping Pierre to the airport.'

'It's the only appointment she has all week,' said Mum.

Seeing her lip quiver, Pierre said gallantly, 'Don't be silly, darling. I'll grab a taxi. It'll be easier—you won't be stuck in traffic on the way back.'

And so my fiancé, whom I wasn't going to see for a week, was sent back to Dublin for his final week's work in a taxi while I went to the hairdresser's.

'Niamh, this is Maggie Harvey. She's Bill Hegarty's sister's niece.'

I looked blankly at Mum.

'You remember Bill? He's a good friend of your father. They used to go to the races together. He owns the hardware shop, Hegarty's.'

'Ah, yes.' I hadn't the faintest clue who she was talking about, but everyone was related in one form or another so it was much of a muchness, really.

'Well, love, what style were you thinking?' asked Maggie. 'Would you like it all up with curls falling down at the side and a tiara?'

'God, no,' I blurted out. 'To be honest I'm

looking for something really simple. Maybe just a blow-dry and a clip in one side.'

Mum and Maggie laughed.

'Simple? On your wedding day? I don't think so,' said the hairdresser. 'You can't look the same as always on your wedding day. It has to be special—dazzling.'

'Why don't you put it up in a big sweeping bun, then have little flowers all over your head?' Mum suggested.

'Oooh, that sounds nice. And we could curl a few bits at the sides,' said the curl-pusher.

My heart sank. How was I going to persuade them that I didn't want big hair with things stuck into it like a bloody bird's nest? 'Really, Mum, I'd prefer to have it down. Pierre likes it down,' I said, using what leverage I could.

'We could have it down with a few bits up at the side and maybe a few curls,' said Maggie, trying to avoid a fight in her salon.

Mum pursed her lips and crossed her arms. 'Fine,' she said. 'You'll do it your way regardless of what I think anyway.'

'Come on, Mum, that's not true,' I said, wanting to avoid a confrontation with her. It was bad enough that Dad was almost ignoring me, without having Mum annoyed too.

'Arriving home with a fiancé none of us had met. Announcing you're off to live in Canada. Telling us you have to have a wedding organized in a few weeks' time. Getting your poor father into a terrible state.'

When she put it like that I felt ashamed. 'I'm sorry, Mum. I have landed you in it. I didn't mean to pounce it on you like that but I was scared you'd react badly to Pierre being black and that you'd try to stop us getting married, so I waited until the last minute. I was wrong. You've been really great and I appreciate everything. I just wish Dad would come round. Look, if you want me to have my hair up, I'll do it. Whatever you want.'

'What I want,' she said, getting emotional, 'is for you to be here in London, near me, and not off on the other side of the world. I'll miss you.'

'Oh, Mum,' I said, hugging her as Maggie busied herself discreetly at the back of the salon. 'I know it seems really far away, but you can come and visit and it won't be for ever. In a few years' time Pierre can apply for a job back here in England and we'll be together again. I'll come home as much as I can. I'll miss you too,' I said, beginning to cry.

'Come on, now, no tears. This is a happy time,' she said, going into mother mode.

'I know and I am happy, but it's a bit scary too. Overwhelming, really.'

'Of course it is, pet. Getting married is a big enough ordeal without moving country too. But he's a wonderful man. He certainly loves you and you light up in his company. You can't ask for more than that. I think you'll be very happy. I hope so.'

'Thanks, Mum. For everything.'

'OK. Now, that's enough of that. We've hair to sort out. Maggie, you can come back over. We've finished with the tears for now. I need you to make this girl beautiful. Now, I think we'll try that up-style bun I mentioned,' she said, as I sat back and surrendered.

45

The next two weeks were a blur of organizing, being bombarded with questions, aunties running in and out with advice, food, stories, tiaras, shoes, hugs, drinks, dry-cleaning and warm, wonderful support. I'd miss this: the fuss, the camaraderie, the fun, the laughter and the drama. It was home. It was what I was used to. Things would be very quiet in Canada.

As time flew by and my excitement grew, it was tinged with sadness that my father had still not come round. He was civil about the arrangements and he didn't say anything overtly negative about Pierre, but he was still cool towards me, which hurt. But there was nothing I could do. He didn't approve and probably never would. I just had to hope that, one day, he'd realize I had made a really good choice of husband. But not to have his support at such an important time in my life and to feel his disappointment every time he looked at me was devastating.

Finally the wedding day dawned. I woke up early and looked round my childhood bedroom. My posters of Duran Duran were still on the wall. My tap-dancing shoes lay in their box alongside my Irish-dancing shoes. My awful green dancing dresses filled the wardrobe, with my tie-dye jeans, illegal FRANKIE SAYS RELAX T-shirt and luminous leg-warmers. I loved this room, I loved this house. I'd been lucky to grow up in this big, noisy family, with its love of Irish culture and heritage. It was just a pity it had taken me so long to appreciate it all.

My phone rang, bringing me out of my thoughts. 'Hello, beautiful,' said Pierre.

'Hello.'

'Any doubts?'

'None. You?'

'None.'

'Jitters?'

'Only that I don't say the wrong thing in church.' He laughed.

'Just say, "I do". Father Hogan will handle the rest.'

'I can't believe how nervous I am. Maybe it's the speech.'

'Keep it short and simple. Don't try to be funny and no jokes.'

'I thought a few Paddy jokes would go down well.'

'Hilarious.'

'No second thoughts?'

'No, although I do have a confession.'

'It's a bit late for that.'

'I'm bringing Visa bills into this marriage.'

'How bad?'

'Define bad.'

'Oh dear.'

'I'll pay them off when I get a job in Canada.'

'What did you buy?'

'Shoes.'

'They can't have cost that much.'

'You haven't seen them yet.'

'OK, anything else you'd like to confess?'

'I'm not taking your name. Niamh Alcee sounds ridiculous.'

'I can live with that. Is that all?'

'Just that I love you and can't wait to be your wife, except for the name part. You?'

'I'm a little apprehensive about your extended family coming to stay with us in Vancouver. Did you have to invite all your cousins?'

'It's called being welcoming, having an open house.'

'I quite like having my house to myself.'

'You only children,' I sighed, 'never want to share.'

'To be fair, I'm sharing my wedding day with two hundred and twenty-three of your close personal friends and relatives.'

'True.'

'My father just gave me our wedding present.'

'What is it?'

'A very generous cheque to help us get settled in Vancouver.'

'How generous?'

'I'm not telling you, Imelda Marcos. You'll blow it on shoes.'

'*My* father still hasn't spoken to me properly. He can barely look me in the eye.'

'He'll come round.'

'Maybe some day, but in the meantime it looks like I'm going to have to drag him up the aisle.'

There was a knock on my door. 'Can I come in?' asked Dad.

'Shit, it's Dad. I have to go. See you in church,' I whispered, hanging up.

'Come in,' I shouted at the closed door.

Dad shuffled in, looking decidedly uncomfortable. 'I need to speak to you and Pierre before the wedding.'

'I can't see him before the church. It's bad luck,'

I said, determined not to have this meeting. Whatever he had to say, it was bad news and I didn't want to hear it.

'Get that fella over here. I've a few things I want to discuss,' he repeated.

'Like what? You can't start giving us grief now. It's too late—we're getting married in a few hours.' I was panicking. What on earth did he want to say at this late stage? Was he going to try a last-ditch attempt to break us up?

'This is my house and you're still my daughter. Now, get him over here before I cancel the whole day.' He turned on his heels.

I rang Pierre in tears. 'I don't know what's going on but Dad's insisting that you come over now because he wants to talk to us. I think he's going to try to stop the wedding,' I sobbed.

'Calm down, darling. Nothing and no one is going to prevent us getting married. Let him say his piece and then we'll get married anyway. I've had enough of this. Be strong. I'm on my way.'

Half an hour later, Pierre, Mum, Finn, Siobhan, Nuala, Tadhg and I were sitting in the lounge looking at each other nervously.

'What's going on, Mum?' I asked.

'I have no idea, pet. I'm in the dark here too,' she said worriedly.

'He wouldn't say a word to me either, just told me to get over here with Nuala,' said Tadhg.

'It looks bad to me. I'd say he's going to call off the wedding,' said Siobhan, loving the drama.

'He's probably going to give Pierre a lecture on Ireland,' said Finn, trying to calm us down.

Dad walked in and closed the door.

Pierre turned to him. 'Now, look here, Mr

O'Flaherty, I think I've been extremely patient and reasonable, but at this eleventh hour I have to say this to you. I'm going to marry your daughter today, with or without your blessing.'

'Sit down, please, and let me explain why I've asked you here,' said Dad, calmly. Then, turning to address us all, he said, 'Thank you for coming at such short notice. I realize this is bad timing and I apologize for that. But I wanted you all to hear what I have to say.'

'Well, get on with it. I've to fix my hair,' grumbled Mum.

Dad took a deep breath. He looked nervous. 'When Niamh announced that she was marrying Pierre and I saw that he was black and not Irish and not Catholic, I reacted very strongly, some might say badly.'

There was a murmur of agreement with that statement.

'I was shocked to my very core,' he continued. 'I'd never even contemplated something like this happening. All I could see were the problems and complications that they would face as a black and white couple. The evening I met Pierre, I went over to Tadhg and Nuala's house, and while I ranted and raged against the union, Nuala said something to me that struck home.'

'Did I?' said Nuala.

'You said, "I've always respected and looked up to you, Mick, but now I pity you. You're going to lose a daughter over small-mindedness and prejudice." '

'That's right, I did,' said my aunt, clearly pleased with herself.

'And, Pierre, I overheard you saying something

to your father the night of the party that also made sense. You said I saw you as a black man while you saw yourself simply as a man, and I realized you were right. I was stuck in the past, and you and Niamh are the future.'

I squeezed Pierre's hand.

'Annie, my wife, my rock of sense and my voice of reason, told me to stop focusing on the negative and look at how in love they were, at how happy Pierre made Niamh, at how our daughter glowed in his presence. My wife accused me of having forgotten how that kind of love makes you dizzy. How you only have eyes for each other. It's the kind of heady love where nothing matters except being with the other person. She was wrong about that. I haven't forgotten. I remember as if it was yesterday the way I felt about Annie when we first met,' he said, as Mum sniffed into her hankie.

'And when I thought about that, I realized that nothing I did or said would make a blind bit of difference to Niamh or Pierre. Because if they felt as strongly about each other as I did, and still do, about Annie, then they're impenetrable. And as long as that love and commitment to each other holds true, they have nothing to fear.

'It has been a long road to my enlightenment. I've been a blind fool, stuck in the past, in my old ways. All I ever wanted was the best for my children. Niamh has been a source of great pride to me and her mother, and I can honestly say that I've never been prouder of her than I am today. You've found a wonderful man to be your partner through life and I wish you both every happiness. You'll have mountains to climb and crosses to bear, but I'll be right behind you, cheering you on.

I'm only sorry it's taken me so long to see that I was wrong. So I give you both my blessing. And my only advice to you is that you never take each other for granted and never try to change each other. Oh, and let Niamh get her own way. It'll make your life easier,' he said to Pierre, smiling.

We sat in stunned silence for a second or two, until Pierre found his voice. 'Mr O'Flaherty, I cannot tell you how much that means to me and, more importantly, to Niamh.'

'Oh, Dad,' I said, running over to hug him, tears streaming down my face. 'Thank you.'

'I knew he'd come round,' said Nuala, hugging Mum.

'He never said anything like that on my wedding day,' Siobhan complained.

'Jesus, even I feel a bit emotional,' said Finn.

'Well done, Mick,' said Mum, kissing his cheek as he beamed at her.

'Right, well, I could do with a drink,' said Tadhg. 'Anyone?'

'Oh, my God, look at the time!' squealed Nuala.

It was twelve o'clock. We had two hours to get ready and get to the church.

'My parents!' said Pierre. 'They're waiting at the station. I've got to go. See you in church, darling,' he said, kissing me, 'and by the way you look wonderful, even with the curlers.'

'My hair! Mum, quick, help me,' I said, running up the stairs, followed by Mum, Nuala and Siobhan, who was still moaning, 'Dad said much nicer things about Niamh than he did about me, and I married a white Irish Catholic.'

'Oh, belt up. It's not your day,' snapped Nuala.

* * *

Dad and I arrived to the church ten minutes late. It was jammed with every relation and friend that had ever had a cup of tea in our famous kitchen. I looked at my family, my community, my safety-net, my support group. It had been a difficult and emotional journey to get here, but as I gazed at the women and men who had been there for me all my life, I felt blessed.

These were the people who had celebrated my good times and cried with me through the bad. I could see Nuala beaming at me from under her new hat, Tadhg taking pictures of everyone for our wedding album, Finn giving me the thumbs-up, Mum fixing her hair, emotional and proud, and my cousin Mairead plucking away tunelessly on the harp.

On the other side of the church, opposite my mother, Fleur and Jean were impeccably stylish. Fleur looked radiant as she and Jean roared laughing at something Nuala was saying to them, while Tadhg took their photo.

This was my family: my loud, boisterous, talkative, loving, caring, supportive, enthusiastic, loyal, generous and kind family. I was going to miss them terribly.

I turned to Dad. ‘Thanks.’

‘For what?’

‘For coming to England and giving me the best life you could. For giving me all the opportunities I’d never have had if you’d stayed in Ballyduff. For all the personal sacrifices you made in moving to London. I want you to know that I had a great childhood and I’m really proud of everything you've achieved. I love both my Irish and my English cultures and I'm ready now to embrace a whole new one.'

He pretended to cough into his handkerchief, wiping his eyes as he did. Then, looking straight ahead, he took my hand and squeezed it. 'May your children bring you as much joy as you have to me.'

I squeezed back.

We watched as my luminous pink bridesmaid made her way up the aisle followed by her five lilac children. Dad turned to me. 'Ready, pet?'

I looked up at him and nodded.

Holding hands, we stepped forward into my future.

ACKNOWLEDGEMENTS

A book is never a one-man show, so I'd like to thank all those people who helped make it possible with their help and support.

Warmest thanks go to:

My lovely editor Patricia Deevy, who was instrumental in making this book better and for coming up with such a clever title!

Michael McLoughlin, Cliona Lewis, Brian Walker and all the team at Penguin Ireland for making the publishing process so enjoyable.

To all in the Penguin UK office, especially Helen Fraser, Tom Weldon, Naomi Fidler, Catherine Duncan and the fantastic sales, marketing and creative teams. To Hazel Orme, as always, for her incredible copy-editing.

To my agent Gillon Aitken, Kate Shaw, Sally Riley, Ayesha Karim and all at the agency for their hard work.

Thanks to my friends for their unflinching loyalty and enthusiasm, I appreciate it so much. Good friends are invaluable.

To Rachel and Danido for helping with the title.

To my nephews, Mikey, James, Jack and Sam, and my nieces Cathy and Isabel—who shout at the window of bookshops when they see the books!

To my sister Sue, to whom the book is dedicated, for being such a wonderful sister and best friend.

To my brother Mike for being my chief cheer-leader.

To all my in-laws, Jim, Auds, Gary, Bertie,

Shane, DL, Agie, Jackie and Bill for being so supportive and enthusiastic.

To Mum and Dad for always being there and most of all for their unconditional love.

My biggest thanks go to Troy, for absolutely everything. And to Hugo and Geordy the jewels in my crown.